# MODERN

## Glamour. Power. Passion.

**Bound By The Baby**
Nina Singh

**Engaged To The Billionaire**
Cara Colter

## MILLS & BOON

BOUND BY THE BOSS'S BABY
© 2024 by Nilay Nina Singh
Philippine Copyright 2024
Australian Copyright 2024
New Zealand Copyright 2024

First Published 2024
Second Australian Paperback Edition 2025
ISBN 978 1 038 94560 0

ACCIDENTLY ENGAGED TO THE BILLIONAIRE
© 2024 by Cara Colter
Philippine Copyright 2024
Australian Copyright 2024
New Zealand Copyright 2024

First Published 2024
Second Australian Paperback Edition 2025
ISBN 978 1 038 94560 0

MIX
Paper | Supporting
responsible forestry
FSC® C001695
www.fsc.org

Published by
Harlequin Mills & Boon
An imprint of Harlequin Enterprises (Australia) Pty Limited
(ABN 47 001 180 918), a subsidiary of HarperCollins
Publishers Australia Pty Limited
(ABN 36 009 913 517)
Level 19, 201 Elizabeth Street
SYDNEY NSW 2000 AUSTRALIA

Cover art used by arrangement with Harlequin Books S.A.. All rights reserved.

Printed and bound in Australia by McPherson's Printing Group

# Bound By The Baby

## Nina Singh

# MILLS & BOON

**Nina Singh** lives just outside Boston, USA, with her husband, children, and a very rumbustious Yorkie. After several years in the corporate world she finally followed the advice of family and friends to 'give the writing a go, already'. She's oh-so-happy she did. When not at her keyboard she likes to spend time on the tennis court or golf course. Or immersed in a good read.

For the many friends I consider to be my sisters.

# CHAPTER ONE

ENRIQUE MARTINEZ RACKED his brain, trying to think of all his recent transgressions that he might have gotten away with. He'd clearly been mistaken about at least one. Because he was on the phone with the local police station at the moment. An Officer Clark was on the other end of the line, saying they had an important matter to discuss.

Enrique figured the matter couldn't be all that serious, whatever it was. Because they weren't at his door at the moment with an arrest warrant. Or some kind of search warrant, for that matter.

Unless that had more to do with who he was and where he came from. Even in this part of the world, his family name went far to afford him such considerations. Fair or not, just or not. Enrique didn't spend too much time analyzing the advantages his birthright afforded him. It was simply the way things were.

"Maybe we should discuss this face-to-face, Mr. Martinez," Officer Clark said into the phone.

Enrique sighed and pinched the bridge of his nose. He was a busy man; this officer had to know that. His schedule today was particularly chaotic.

"I'm afraid that would be quite difficult to do, Officer."

The other man chuckled lightly before responding. "Yeah, I get it. You must be a busy man," he said, echoing Enrique's exact thoughts. "Being a titan of industry and all."

Enrique pushed his executive chair back from the wide mahogany desk and lifted his feet to the surface, crossing his ankles. Leaning back with his head on the top of the chair, he did his best to summon some much-needed patience. This was obviously going to take a while. He really wished the man would just get to the point already.

"What's this about, Officer?" he asked.

He heard the other man clear his throat. "Well, it's a little awkward. Especially over the phone. But we think we might have something that belongs to you."

Huh. That was rather curious. For the life of him, Enrique couldn't surmise what item they might have of his that would have turned up at a Cape Cod police station.

Had one of his cars been stolen? Highly unlikely. Aside from his state-of-the-art security systems at every one of his residences, his security team on-site would have notified him immediately.

"I'm afraid I have no idea what you might mean."

"Someone dropped off a package at our door sometime in the predawn hours. They were wearing a hoodie and some type of surgical mask. We're still going over security footage, but an ID might be difficult."

"I see. What makes you think it's mine?"

"There was a note saying it needed to be delivered to you ASAP."

Okay.

The man went on. "Believe me, we debated even contacting you. It has to be some sort of scam. So we've already contacted the appropriate agencies."

Enrique swore under his breath. He was more confused now than he'd been at the start of the phone call. This whole conversation was making less and less sense with each consecutive word spoken.

But when the man finally got to the point, Enrique was certain he couldn't have heard him right.

*Infant...*

"I'm sorry. Did you just say that there was a baby left at your station?"

"That's right." The words were followed by a loud clearing of the officer's throat.

Enrique would have laughed if he wasn't so darn confused. "I'm sorry. But what does any of that have to do with me?"

"Well, you see, he was all bundled up and strapped into a basket. With a note attached to his little sweater."

"A note?"

The man cleared his throat again. Clearly a nervous habit. "The note claimed you're the father."

The words echoed in his head before Enrique could fully process them. *Baby. Basket. Father!*

Enrique rubbed his forehead. How was this phone call even happening?

"I know it sounds ridiculous. And I probably shouldn't have bothered you with it, but I figured you should at least know."

That settled it. Someone was almost certainly playing a joke on him. When he figured out who it was, there'd be hell to pay. He didn't have time for such foolishness. But most of the people in his life knew that very well. He couldn't imagine who in his circle might have believed for even a moment that such a prank might be a good idea.

"You're right, Officer," he finally replied when he could get his mouth moving again. "That is ridiculous."

Wasn't it?

A long pause followed from the other end of the line. Enrique wasn't typically at a loss for words. For the first time in his life, Enrique Leon Martinez was completely stumped as to what to say.

The police officer finally broke the silence. "What would you like us to do, sir?"

What did he want them to do? He honestly didn't know. The chance that this infant was actually his had to be slim. But he couldn't claim that it was zero. He frequented the Cape often on business. Even had a residence here.

The last time he was here…

Enrique swore. It had been a little less than a year ago. When he'd purchased the latest resort. He was here now to see about its renovations and rebranding. He'd celebrated his latest acquisition with a fine brandy and gourmet dinner.

And he'd left with the pretty brunette who'd bused his table in between courses. Damn.

Enrique made his mouth work somehow. "About how old does the child appear to be?"

"Well, I have four of my own. If I had to guess, I'd say he's about three months give or take."

Huh. Three months. That would seem to fit the timeline.

Enrique had an urge to ask the man what the child looked like. Or to send a picture. Then he realized how ridiculous a notion that was. There really were only two options here. He could bid this man goodbye and tell him none of this was really any of his business. That it was all clearly some colossal error.

Or he could see for himself personally about this child who was supposedly his.

The officer helped him make the decision a moment later. "The address we have on file for you happens to be on the way to the medical center where he's supposed to be taken for evaluation. It isn't standard procedure at all, but I can stop by on the way," he said. "You know, if you'd like to see him."

Fallon Duvall was trying desperately to stay asleep and ignore the alert sound coming from her phone and echoing off the walls of her tiny room.

What time was it anyway? And who was calling her? No one made phone calls anymore. Served her right for taking her phone off silent in the first place. She'd only done it in case one of the parents she'd been scheduled to meet that evening during parent-teacher interviews might have a need to reach her. She'd forgotten to switch it back.

Her mind still in a fog, she realized that the phone had been ringing for quite a while already. Between her exhaustion and how she'd trained herself to sleep through most noise, Fallon had been able to ignore it. Living right outside the Greater Boston area in a building overlooking the main expressway into the city had necessitated teaching herself how to sleep through almost any sounds. Almost.

Thankfully, the phone went silent. Fallon didn't even have the energy to reach over and fix the setting. She'd spent the day scrubbing and tidying her classroom. Then made sure to give each parent her undivided attention during their one on ones. She was utterly exhausted. Whatever the call was about, it could wait until later this morning.

A mere three seconds passed before her cell rang again.

Okay. Someone was clearly desperate to reach her. Fallon mentally wiped the cobwebs of sleep from her drowsy mind. Reaching for her phone, she switched the bedside lamp on at the same time. And then cursed herself for even thinking about ignoring the call.

The caller was the one person in the world she actually cared to hear from. Sasha.

Fallon nearly dropped the device in her haste to finally answer. "Sasha, hi."

"Hi, sis," came the breathy reply after a lengthy pause.

"Is everything all right?"

"Yeah, yeah. Of course," Sasha said, a little too quickly, and not terribly convincing.

"I haven't heard from you in a while."

"I know, sis. Just wanted to hear your voice, that's all."

A pang of guilt stabbed through Fallon's chest. She'd been so busy these past couple of years, and particularly over the last few months. Sasha had never been the best communicator, but she'd gone particularly silent recently. And Fallon had been too preoccupied with her own life to do anything about it. Finishing up her studies, then becoming certified as a public school teacher, followed by a stressful job search had taken all her time and mental energy. When she'd finally landed her job, she'd been much too busy, between teaching during the day and making up lesson plans in the evenings. Her summers weren't any better with all the waitressing she did just to make ends meet. But none of that was any kind of excuse. None of those accomplishments would even be possible if it wasn't for the woman on the other end of the line. The foster sister who'd taken Fallon under her wing when she'd needed someone the most. Fallon should have never allowed the silence between them to go on as long as it had. Sasha had been struggling for years to get her life in order. The impetus would have been on Fallon to maintain communication.

"It's nice to hear your voice too," Fallon said, lying back flat on her pillow. "Are you sure everything's all right?"

Again, the pause before Sasha's answer had alarm bells ringing in her head.

"Yeah," Sasha answered finally, drawing the word out into three syllables. "I just need to go away for a while. And I wanted to hear your voice before I did," she repeated.

"Go away?"

"Uh-huh. I'm not sure exactly where yet. But I wanted to tell you before leaving that I'm really proud of you."

The guilt in her chest grew by several factors.

Sasha continued. "I'm guessing you're a teacher by now, just like you always planned."

Fallon rubbed a palm down her face. "Uh, yeah. I teach kindergarten in South Boston."

"That's good, sis. Really good. Little kids are cute. They should all be well taken care of."

Okay. Even for Sasha, this conversation was starting to sound a bit too pensive. She was clearly in the depths of some kind of deep melancholy.

"Agreed," Fallon said. It was all she could come up with.

"Remember in that one foster home they sent us to, the mom had just recently had a baby. That kid was real cute."

Not like Fallon could forget. The woman had foisted her kid onto her and Sasha for hours on end. While she went on doing heaven knew what. "He was."

"Remember how she made us look after her baby for hours while she was out and about?"

"I do."

"I was terrible as a caregiver though." Fallon remembered that as well. At one point, Sasha had put the baby's diaper on backward. Then there was the day she had almost dipped his pacifier in a candy syrup and Fallon had luckily seen, or the time she'd turned her back and walked away from the changing table and the baby had almost rolled off before Fallon had rushed over just in the nick of time to catch him.

"I haven't thought about that house in years," Fallon said, though that wasn't quite accurate. She'd made an effort to try and push those days far back to the recesses of her mind. The only good thing about that period in her life had been the increasingly strong bond with the foster sister who'd taken her under her wing and protected her from bullies and leery fellow fosters alike.

The real question now was, why was Sasha bringing all this up?

"I have some news too," Sasha said, rather dramatically.

"Oh?"

Another long empty pause followed. The only sound coming through the tiny speaker was Sasha's quick breathing.

Fallon waited with all the patience she could muster. When Sasha finally spoke, she could hardly believe her ears. "Yeah, so I've had a baby myself, sis."

Fallon bolted upright and bounced off the mattress. She was fully awake now. Had she heard her right?

Sasha confirmed with her next words. "Nearly three months ago."

"Oh, my…"

"His name is Lucas."

"Sasha. What the—" Fallon had no idea what to say. "Are you all right?"

"Yeah, I'm fine. Took a while but I'm all healed up now. I've been staying at a shelter and the ladies there are very caring and helpful."

"And the baby? How is he?"

"I'm guessing he's fine."

The earlier alarm bells in Fallon's head turned to blaring loud sirens. "You're guessing? What does that mean?"

Sasha's large gulp of air could be heard over the small speaker. "See, I just couldn't handle it anymore. The work, the crying in the middle of the night, having another mouth to feed. It was all too much."

Fallon's throat went dry. "What did you do?"

"I left him."

Panic surged through her core. The Sasha she knew would never be careless or cruel. But had she changed so drastically? "What do you mean you left him? Where?"

"Relax, sis. I left him nice and wrapped up in blankets and a carrier outside the Falmouth Police station." Fallon released a deep sigh of relief. The police were sure to have made certain the baby was safe.

"I attached a note instructing them to contact his father," Sasha added.

"Who might that be?"

Sasha actually chuckled. "You might not believe me when I tell you. I can hardly believe it myself. God, it was a fun night."

"Just tell me," Fallon urged, mentally praying to all the deities that it wasn't one of the street criminals Sasha so often befriended.

The name Sasha uttered sounded vaguely familiar. Not a household name, as such, but definitely one she'd heard before.

A quick internet search on the man told her enough to have Fallon reeling in shock. What had Sasha gone and done?

If someone had told him this morning that there would be a police officer standing on his door stoop holding a carrier with a baby, Enrique might have laughed aloud. Added that said baby might actually be his own son made the scenario beyond surreal.

Yet here he was, inviting a uniformed policeman into his foyer and leading him to the sitting room.

"I'm afraid I can't linger here too long," the other man said once he'd stepped inside the room and Enrique had shut the door behind him. He didn't need his staff to see his unusual guest and begin a wave of questions and gossip. "Standard protocol is to take the baby straight to the medical center to be screened and evaluated."

"I appreciate you bending the rules. Not that I'm not thankful, but might I ask why you did so in this case?"

"Well, I hope you take this next comment in the manner it's intended. And that I'm not being terribly forward. But we did some online searches after reading the note. There's quite a few photographs of you on the internet."

"And?"

"And if you don't mind my saying, there appears to be a strong resemblance."

Something fluttered in Enrique's chest. "I see."

The other man's statement landed like a load of bricks over his head. Suddenly, the import of this moment became all too real, no longer a hypothetical.

He'd always prided himself on being fully prepared to tackle any circumstance. To be always ready to deal with any unknown or unexpected curve that might be thrown his way. It was how he'd taken a measly sum of pity money granted to him by his father when he'd turned eighteen and turned it into a vast hospitality empire. But in this moment, Enrique felt at a complete loss. Wholly uncertain as to what to say or how to feel.

Then again, how could he possibly have been prepared

for any of this? He hadn't so much as seen it coming. What in the world would he do if this child indeed was his? How would he even begin the journey of fatherhood? It wasn't as if he had any kind of example to follow. His own father had never been actually present in his life. Enrique wouldn't be able to pick him out of a lineup.

Strong resemblance.

It was time to see for himself. "Do you mind?" he asked, stepping forward and reaching for the carrier.

A wealth of emotion flooded his core the second he peered inside at the tiny bundle wrapped in blankets and wearing a knitted hat. Enrique had zero experience with babies, had no idea what a three-month-old might look like. Were they all this impossibly small?

Then the tiny face scrunched up and made a small whimper of a sound before opening his eyes.

Enrique's whole world shifted. He straightened, trying to get a hold of himself. "If it's all right, Officer, I'd like to accompany you to the medical evaluation."

*One month later*

She'd never been very good at deception. But here she was, about to try and deceive one of the most successful and shrewd men on the planet.

Fallon Duvall inhaled a deep breath and summoned all of her resolve. She could do this. She'd come this far.

She had to believe fate was on her side. Why else would she have overheard the conversation between those two nannies at school drop-off that day? Fallon had hardly believed her ears when she'd heard Enrique's name dropped excitedly and with no small amount of awe. He was apparently on the search for a nanny to care for his son. *Sa-*

*sha's son.* The idea had come to her then and there, and despite how outrageous and far-fetched it sounded to her own ears, Fallon knew she had to try.

After all, Sasha was nowhere to be found and maddeningly silent with no answer to her calls or emails. Fallon had to do something.

She'd enlisted with the nanny service that same afternoon, specifying that she was only interested in one particular opening.

The brief telephone interview with them had gone spectacularly well. Thank the stars above for that, because she didn't know what she'd have done if she couldn't get through that stage. Now, it was time to impress the man's staff.

"You can do this," she repeated, out loud this time. She had no choice but to try.

The door opened before she could so much as knock. A short, rotund woman with a friendly smile wearing a white service uniform greeted her.

"Ms. Duvall?"

Fallon nodded. "Yes, I'm here to interview for the nanny position."

The woman motioned her inside. "Come in, please. We've been expecting you."

Her tone implied that Fallon's arrival wasn't a moment too soon. The woman sounded as if she might be at the end of her rope.

Fallon heard her mumble something under her breath. "Let's hope this time's the charm."

Her heels clicked on the fancy marble tile as she followed the other woman into the grand foyer. Fallon took a moment to observe her surroundings. And what grand surroundings they were. She felt as if she might have stepped into a renowned European museum. Not that she'd know from any kind of personal experience. Traveling to such places had been a dream of hers since she was a child. But she didn't have the resources.

Maybe one day.

Fallon sighed deeply and pushed the thoughts aside. This was so not the time for self-pity. She was here for one purpose only. And there was no plan B. For Sasha's sake, she had to make this work. As well as for the sake of the child she already considered her nephew.

A chill ran over her skin. The house was so very cold, she felt as if she'd stepped into a walk-in freezer like those in the many restaurants she'd worked in as a teen and while putting herself through school. This mansion felt about as welcoming as those freezers too. And just as frigid.

The other woman hadn't so much as looked back over her shoulder as Fallon continued to follow her path through the foyer. A shrill sound suddenly pierced the air. Echoes of it bounced off the walls. The scream of an infant. Fallon's chest tightened. That had to be Sasha's baby. And he clearly wasn't happy.

"I'm Martha Ritter. There are monitors throughout the house," the woman in front of her explained, still without even glancing at her.

She continued. "Both auditory and video."

That explained why she could hear the baby's cries echoing off the walls. Echoes the other woman didn't seem too thrilled with.

Fallon's heart lurched in her chest. If the rest of the staff were anything like this woman, no doubt the baby could sense their resentment. Even small infants could sense when they weren't wanted. And the child screaming at the top of his lungs right now had been born unwanted. Even by his own mother.

Still, Fallon found she could forgive Sasha yet another fault. Her foster sister hadn't had the easiest life. Sasha had probably been confused and scared after having a baby by herself. At least she hadn't abandoned it completely. At least she'd left him in the care of his father.

Who happened to be one of the world's richest and most successful men.

"You'll speak to the head of staff," the other woman was saying as they made their way up a winding spiral staircase. "He'll be interviewing you first."

Another wail pierced the air before the woman got the last word out. Fallon could see her hand tightening on the banister. She whispered something under her breath that sounded less than pleasant.

Fallon didn't think, made a decision before taking the next step. She halted where she was. "If I could," she began.

Martha stopped three steps ahead of her. She turned around to face Fallon, a look of clear frustration on her face at the realization that Fallon had ceased following.

"What is it?" the other woman demanded, her tone rather icy.

"Perhaps I could see the child first?"

Martha's eyes narrowed on her face. Fallon's heart hammered hard in her chest. Great. Now she'd done it. She'd barely stepped into the house and she was about to be thrown out. But she hadn't been able to bear listening to the anguished cries of the baby any longer. He needed soothing. And clearly no one was there to give him any sort of comfort.

"You'd be there to supervise, of course." Fallon pressed

her case. "Perhaps I might be able to see what's distressing the little guy so."

Martha's eyes narrowed even further. "I don't recall that
any of the literature mentioned the baby was a little boy."

Fallon cursed herself silently for the blunder. Frustrated
or not, Martha Ritter was one astute woman.

"Just a lucky guess."

At the next shriek, Martha's features wilted. She
shrugged her shoulders with tight impatience.

"Very well. I'm sure Mr. Watson's busy enough as it is.
A few more minutes won't hurt."

Fallon had to restrain herself from blowing out a breath
in relief.

"This way then," Martha threw over her shoulder and
resumed her ascent up the stairs.

Fallon took a moment to gather herself together and
scrambled after the woman who hadn't bothered waiting
for her to catch up.

A strange tightening squeezed her chest. She was about
to meet Sasha's sweet little boy. A boy she already loved
and cared deeply for despite never having laid eyes on him.

"So, then, Señor Martinez, shall we move forward with
the change in supply order?"

Enrique squeezed his eyes shut and tried to gather his
thoughts. For the life of him, he wasn't sure how to answer. What exactly were the details of this order? It had
been explained to him countless times. But his mind felt
like mush from lack of sleep and sheer exhaustion.

As much as he had come to adore his newborn son, the
child was clearly having trouble adjusting to his new environment. And nothing Enrique did seemed to be helping.

"I'll have to get back to you with the answer," he said

into the phone, knowing yet another delay was costing him precious time and money.

The man on the other end of the phone call remained silent, but his exasperation came through loud and clear.

As did the sudden shift in the air. Enrique's ears perked up at the change in the sounds ringing through his ears. Or lack thereof to state it more accurately. For the first time in what seemed like an eternity, the air was filled with blessed silence.

"I have to go," he said into the phone then clicked off the call, no doubt further frustrating his purchasing agent back in Mexico.

But Enrique couldn't focus on any kind of deal right now. The crying had stopped for more than mere seconds at a time.

What was this magic? Some kind of miracle, no doubt. Whatever it was, he had to figure it out and make sure it never stopped.

Tossing aside the spreadsheets he'd been studying, he strode to the door and out of his study. The golden silence was still there when he reached the nursery. Entering the door, he scanned the room for his son to find him cradled in the arms of a woman he didn't recognize. She certainly wasn't anyone on his regular staff. But she was holding Lucas with an air of what could only be described as familiarity. As if she'd somehow known him since birth.

Ms. Ritter straightened as soon as she saw him while the other woman remained oblivious to his presence. She appeared to be fully focused on the baby she held in her arms.

Enrique motioned toward Ms. Ritter to prevent her from announcing his arrival. In awe, he simply stared at the unexpected miracle he beheld. The woman who held his child cooed softly against Lucas's ear while rubbing his back and rocking him up and down. All the while, she paced slowly along the far wall.

"What's all this fuss about?" she asked softly against the baby's cheek before humming a lullaby of some sort.

Eventually, Lucas began to respond to her gentle voice. Enrique watched in stunned silence as his son began gurgling and cooing happily in answer to her voice.

How hard had he himself tried to elicit such a reaction from his child? To no avail. Enrique had lost count of the number of sleepless nights he'd spent on the rocker or pacing the nursery as he cradled his son. The sheer exhaustion was beginning to catch up to him. Business deals were hanging in the balance waiting for his response. He simply didn't have the time.

Had he ever even heard Lucas's voice except in the form of a screaming wail? Not that he could recall. Enrique could only continue to stare in stunned silence at the scene.

He took a moment to take a good look at her. He'd been right about the miracle. The woman could only be described as angelic. Thick, long curls cascaded down her back, her hair a shade of auburn he'd be hard-pressed to describe. She couldn't have been more than five foot six at most, yet her posture and standing gave an air of height to her. Her eyes were currently so focused on his son that they were slightly scrunched.

Suddenly, without warning, her head snapped up. Those golden hazel eyes zoomed square on his face like a laser beam. A flash of emotion shot behind her pupils that he could only describe as animosity before it was gone just as quickly. Only to be replaced by a questioning stare in his direction. Surely he had to be imagining any kind of negativity in her gaze. The woman didn't even know him, for heaven's sake. Definitely just his imagination. Or perhaps she'd simply been startled. He had been caught staring at her without saying a word, after all. He strode toward where she stood still cradling Lucas close against her bosom.

"I apologize for not announcing myself," he said when he reached their side. "But I didn't want to intrude on the effect you seem to be having on my son."

The baby's eyes were still focused squarely on the woman's face. As if in a trance. Lucas continued to gurgle away.

Angel or witch?

Enrique gave his head a brisk shake to brush off the nonsensical thought. Extending his hand, he waited for her to take it. She merely stared at it before simply offering a small nod of acknowledgment.

It was clearly all he was going to get.

Right. She would have to put the baby down to shake his offered palm. What a silly thing to do. What was wrong with him? With no small amount of awkwardness, he slowly pulled his arm back and jammed his hand into his pocket.

Ms. Ritter appeared at his side. "Sorry if we've disturbed you, Señor Martinez. We were just about to conduct the latest nanny interview. Miss Duvall wanted to meet the child first. I didn't see the harm—"

Enrique waved off the rest of his employee's words with his free hand. "That's fine, Ms. Ritter. I haven't been disturbed."

His employee's shoulders sagged in relief. "We'll just get on with the interview then."

Enrique surprised himself by stopping her again. "Actually, Ms. Ritter. You may go."

The woman blinked up at him. "Go? I don't understand,

sir. The young lady has an appointment scheduled with Mr. Watson."

"Tell him there's been a change of plans."

"There has?"

He nodded. "I've decided I'll conduct the interview myself," he blurted out without any real forethought.

Both women grew wide-eyed in surprise. Well, he'd surprised himself. Of all the items on his to-do list today, interviewing a prospective candidate for the role of nanny wasn't on the list. What would he even ask her? How many diapers she'd changed in her lifetime? Was that even relevant here?

He did know one thing. He wanted to get to know this woman who had such a miraculous effect on his son mere seconds after having laid eyes on Lucas. A nagging voice in the back of his mind taunted that it wasn't the only reason. He shoved it aside before it could grow any louder.

Ms. Ritter looked ready to argue, then must have thought better of it. "I'll leave you to it, then," she said, before giving the nanny a tight smile and turning on her heel to leave the room.

Huh. He'd referred to her as the nanny in his mind. That settled it then. Enrique realized he'd already made his decision. Unless there was some kind of red flag that popped up on her background check that gave him a glaring and obvious reason not to hire this woman, she was clearly well suited for the job.

And he hadn't even asked her a single question yet.

Well, there was one question he could start with. How exactly had she managed to quiet Lucas the way she had?

# CHAPTER TWO

MISTAKE. NOW SHE'D gone and done it. What had she been thinking asking to see the baby first? The impulsive request had only served to draw the attention of the big man himself. Now here he was, staring her down. Demanding he interview her himself.

Stupid. *Stupid.*

She was supposed to stay under the radar, and certainly out of his periphery. Not having one on one's with him for heaven's sake. Fallon gathered a deep breath and willed her pounding heart to still. She needed to land this job. Needed to make sure she was an integral part of Lucas's life, at least until she got assurance that he was being well taken care of.

The moment she'd learned about Sasha's precious boy, she'd vowed that cycle would end with the two of them. Billionaire tycoon or not, she needed to know that Enrique Martinez would be a worthy man where it counted most—as a parent. Fallon had no illusions that he'd be any kind of hands-on parent. Men like him typically left the nitty-gritty day-to-day details of such mundane tasks as parenting to those in their employ, didn't they?

"Can I get you a coffee, Miss Duvall?" His question pulled her out of her thoughts. "I can ring for an espresso or a latte."

Fallon shook her head, the last thing she needed around

this man was any kind of stimulant. His bearing was stimulating enough. The way his employee had scrambled out of the room as soon as he'd dismissed the woman told her at least one person in his employ appeared to be intimidated by him.

Fallon shook her head. "No, I'm fine, thank you."

He nodded, then motioned toward the rocking bassinet in the corner of the room. "Might we risk putting the baby down for a moment while we speak?"

Fallon nodded in agreement and made her way to the bassinet. As gently as she could, she settled little Lucas on the plush, soft pillowy mattress of the small basket. She took a moment to study the piece of furniture. Certainly she was no expert when it came to craftsmanship. Nevertheless it was clear the bassinet was a handcrafted work of art. The mattress and blankets inside were soft as a cloud. At least she could be assured that Lucas's material needs were being met and exceeded.

Fallon stroked a gentle finger down his pudgy soft cheek, then turned around to face his father. She found Enrique standing at a coffee bar, pouring hot coffee out of a shiny silver carafe.

The man was striking.

Dressed in an immaculately tailored steel-gray suit with a magenta tie that brought out the dark highlights of his hair, his charcoal-black eyes must have melted the hearts of females all over the planet. Enrique Martinez was movie star gorgeous. Sasha probably fell hard as soon as she set eyes on the man. But how could she have not seen right away just how far out their league this man was? Though who could blame her? He was tall, imposing, successful. He'd probably flirted with her until all her defenses crumbled. Not that Sasha was exactly known for her restraint or self-discipline.

All the more reason Fallon should have done more to protect the woman from herself as well as from men like Señor Martinez. But she'd been too focused on her own ambitions, her own life. Now, look where they were. In a state of chaos. With an innocent little baby caught in the middle of it all.

Enrique held up a ceramic mug. "Are you sure you don't want a cup as well?" he asked.

Fallon merely shook her head.

He gestured to the sofa between them. "Then please, have a seat."

Slowly, Fallon walked across the room and did as he requested. Enrique didn't follow suit. Instead, he leaned back against the coffee bar behind him, studying her. Fallon immediately felt at a disadvantage. As if the man's natural height wasn't enough to have her feeling inferior, now he was practically towering above her from across the room.

"So," he began, "tell me, Miss Duvall. What brings you here this morning?"

Fallon swallowed. What was he getting at? He knew she was here to interview for the nanny spot. "Please, call me Fallon. And I'm here regarding the position of full-time nanny." *As you very well know*, she added under her breath.

Enrique set his cup down and crossed his arms in front of his chest. "Yes, but why?"

"Why?"

"Why do you want this position in particular?"

Fallon blinked. Could he somehow know her real reasons? How would that even be possible?

For one insane moment, she felt the urge to come clean. To just blurt it all out. To tell him the complete truth.

*That child may as well be my nephew. His mother is practically my sister. We grew up together. I was supposed to take care of her, to keep track of her. I was supposed to make sure she didn't make the kind of mistake that has led me here today.*

What might his reaction be if she simply told him all of that?

No. Bad idea. She had no faith that Enrique Martinez could be trusted to do the right thing with the truth. After all, there was a good chance he harbored resentment toward Sasha for abandoning her child. He might very well resent Fallon by extension if he found out who she really was. Worse, he might accuse her of being here with the intent to spy on him for Sasha.

She couldn't risk telling him the truth just yet.

Instead, she swallowed and took a deep breath. "I'm looking for a change from what I'm doing currently."

That was a lie. One that fell from her lips rather easily, so much so it was disconcerting. Fallon actually loved her job, and it was breaking her heart to have to give it up. Knowing that she wouldn't be returning to her darling students next fall brought a sting of tears to her eyes.

"And what is that exactly?"

"I teach at Latin Elementary in South Boston. Kindergarten. I've been there about two years. I have a bachelor's degree in early education and a graduate degree in child development. My thesis centered around early childhood development and—"

Enrique cut her off with a raise of his hand. "No need to get into all that," he said, surprising her. "I can do it with a simple look at your CV."

"Then what is it exactly that I can tell you, Señor Martinez?" she asked, addressing him the way Ms. Ritter had earlier, figuring that's what he must prefer.

"You've decided to leave your current job. Why is that?"

Fallon shrugged, hoping to sound convincing. "I realized I'd prefer a home setting. And to work with a child or children directly one on one. I believe I'd have more of an impact that way." That was certainly close enough to the truth.

He nodded once. "Well, you've certainly had an impact on my son already," Enrique said, tilting his head in the direction of the bassinet. "I can't recall the last time he's slept so soundly. Why do you think that is?"

Truth be told, Fallon couldn't really explain why she'd been able to soothe Lucas so swiftly and so effortlessly. The only explanation she could come up with was that the baby must have somehow sensed a kindred spirit. He'd instinctively known that Fallon already loved him and cherished him. Or maybe it was much more basic. Perhaps he'd recognized the scent of his mama? She and Sasha grew up sharing the same toiletries and soaps. The same toothpaste. The same lotions. Lucas might just be smelling his mother on Fallon's person. The thought both touched and saddened her.

Enrique cleared his throat across the room. She'd drifted off into her thoughts again and he'd noticed. Fallon gave her head a brisk shake to get her bearings. This was turning out to be much harder than she'd anticipated. But she hadn't counted on even laying eyes on the man himself let alone having him conduct the interview on his own, for heaven's sake.

He was staring at her expectedly. That's right. He'd asked her a question. What was it? Focus!

That was so hard to do with those intense, dark eyes staring down at her with such scrutiny. This was unlike any job interview Fallon had ever been through in the past.

Just as she was about to ask him to repeat his question, he spared her the need. "I see you find it a mystery too. Whatever the reason, my son seems to have taken to you. That's enough for me to have your application move forward. Contingent on a complete background check, of course."

Fallon felt a moment of panic. He was going to do a personal check on her? "I believe the agency has already done a thorough investigation."

He nodded once. "Be that as it may, I prefer to have my own security staff play a role as well. I'm sure you understand. You'll be in my household in charge of my only child. I can't have any questions about your character arise later on."

Fallon did her best to mask the apprehension churning in her gut. She had to relax. It was unlikely even his private security would be able to uncover the fact that she'd grown up with said son's mother.

"Is there a problem?" Enrique asked.

So the mask was less than convincing. She immediately shook her head. "No, no. Just seems like a redundant step, that's all."

"Maybe so. But I'm not a man to take anything for granted. And I always look to see what's below the surface."

Fallon swallowed the lump that formed in her throat at his words. Clearly, the man had trust issues. Someone had to have betrayed him gravely in the past. Well, she could relate.

"You're not a very trusting man, are you?" she blurted before she realized she'd even intended to speak the words out loud.

An expression of weariness washed over his face.

"I'm sorry, I shouldn't have—"

He held a hand up to stop her before she could continue with her apology for being so blunt. "You're correct, Miss Duvall. There are only two people on this planet I trust."

Seemed they might have something in common, after all. Fallon had learned herself at a young age not to easily give her trust away to just anyone. In fact, since the deaths of her parents, Sasha was the only one in her life who hadn't betrayed her in some way or another. "I can appreciate that, Señor Martinez," she answered with sincerity, then just to move on from the rather uncomfortable conversation added, "I look forward to the next steps."

He took another sip of his coffee, not tearing his eyes from her face. "As do I. If you'll just wait here, I'll have Ms. Ritter escort you back out and explain what those next steps will be."

"Then I won't need to meet with Mr. Watson? Or any of the other staff?"

"I don't see any reason to do so. Now that I've spoken to you myself."

Right. That made sense. And she had to get the silly security check out of her mind. Her background was squeaky clean. There was only one secret she didn't want Enrique Martinez uncovering, and it was unlikely to show up on any type of document or computer file.

But as ready as she was to leave this room and Enrique's intense gaze, Fallon's heart lurched in her chest. When would she see little Lucas again?

Try as she might, she couldn't help but turn in the baby's direction to take another look at him before leaving.

"Would you like to say 'goodbye'?" Enrique asked, apparently reading her all too well.

Fallon lied yet again. "Oh, no, that's okay. I wouldn't want to risk waking him."

Or risk appearing even more invested than she did already. Enrique made no move to leave. He continued watching her, his eyes clouded with curiosity. Or suspicion. Probably both.

Finally, he spoke. "Aren't you going to ask?"

Fallon blinked up at him in confusion. "Ask what?"

He put his cup down and wandered over to take the seat across the sofa she sat on. "About my wife."

His what?

Nothing she'd read about Enrique Martinez alluded to him being married. Unless it was a very well-kept secret.

"You're married?"

He slowly shook his head. "No. I am not."

Another flush of relief spread through her chest, though she'd be hard-pressed to explain exactly why.

"Then... I don't understand."

"I just find it curious. That you haven't asked about meeting Lucas's mother. Even though you inquired about other staff."

The man was too sharp by far. Such a simple thing to overlook. It hadn't even occurred to her to pretend to be curious about the child's mother. Because she already knew the truth about her.

Fallon tried hard not to visibly swallow. As nonchalantly as she could, she gave him a small smile, then shrugged slightly. "I just assumed it wasn't any of my business."

To her surprise, Enrique's lips grew into a wide grin and he winked at her. "Discretion is a quality I find important, Miss Duvall," he said. "I think you might fit in very well indeed."

To: sashabird2@ethermail.com
From: Nofall7811@ethermail.com
Subject: Where are you?

I have no idea if these emails are making their way to you, Sasha. But I will continue to send them until you respond. I know I don't have to repeat how worried I am about you, but I'll say it all the same.

Please, if you're receiving these, write back to tell me you're okay. If things work out as I've planned, I hope to have some news for you soon.

Love, your Fallon

P.S. I'm sorry I haven't been there for you.

Fallon closed the laptop lid and pushed away from the coffee table it sat on. The apology was redundant at this point. But she'd felt compelled to sign off with it on each email so far.

Emails that hadn't been returned in weeks now. Wherever Sasha was, she was either ignoring them or not receiving them. Fallon would guess on the former. Sasha had done this sort of thing before, ghosted her because she felt overwhelmed and at odds with life in general.

But never before had the stakes been quite so high.

Speaking of said stakes, why hadn't she heard anything regarding the nanny position? It had already been a week since she'd met with Enrique. Had she imagined his enthusiasm about hiring her? Had someone else come along afterward who'd impressed him more than she had?

Had she turned Enrique off with her bluntness when she'd questioned his trust issues?

That would be the end of the line then. She had no plan B. The best she could hope for if Enrique didn't hire her was to try and keep track of little Lucas from afar through website articles and social media. The thought sent a surge of sadness through her chest.

To think, just a few short weeks ago, she'd had no idea Lucas even existed. She would have been perfectly content sitting in her small, modest apartment with the whole summer ahead of her before the start of classes in September. She'd be wondering which of her creative projects to focus on during the day while earning some pocket cash waitressing in the evenings at the trendy brewery tavern across the river.

Maybe she might have even met someone during one of her shifts. Someone who might have taken her to dinner. Or offered to walk her home after she got off work. Someone who might ask to kiss her after a few dates. Someone with dark hair and dark eyes with tanned olive skin who wore tailored suits.

Fallon bolted upright. That wayward thought had no business skittering through her mind.

She really couldn't go there. Sasha had turned all her summer plans upside down. Now the only project Fallon had occupying her mind and efforts revolved around Sasha's baby. The last thing she needed was to entertain any kind of romantic fantasies about the boy's father.

Rubbing her palm across her forehead, she began to pace the room. Of course, all of that was moot if she didn't even land the job. She would have failed before even starting.

*You're such a failure. Your name should be Failin', not Fallon.*

Her second foster mother had taken immense pleasure in mocking her name for the entire year she'd been with that family. It wasn't long before the other members in the household had followed her lead. Fallon squeezed her eyes shut and shoved the memory from her mind. Though such memories were always just below the surface ready to surge above it at any moment.

The ring of her phone came as a blessed distraction from the hateful recollections of her earlier life. Fallon scrambled to get to the couch where she'd tossed it and answer before it switched to voicemail. The nanny job. Were they finally calling her about it? Would it possibly be Enrique himself on the line? Her heart thudded in her chest at the thought of hearing his voice when she answered. The screen displayed an unknown number, not one in her contacts app. This had to be it.

Fallon quickly clicked the answer button only to be met with disappointment a moment later. The call wasn't about the offer at all. And the caller was definitely not Enrique.

Instead, Mary Harlon's voice greeted her. The vice principal at her school, the woman she directly reported to. Or would have if she were to return. No wonder she didn't recognize the number. Mary must be calling from her personal phone.

"What's this I hear about you not returning?" the other woman asked without bothering with a hello.

Her boss had left for vacation a couple weeks early before Fallon had had a chance to speak to her directly. She was taking a risk, of course. Quitting her job before securing the nanny spot was probably unwise. But she didn't want to make Mary and the others scramble at the start of classes to find her replacement. This way they would have the summer to launch a search. She could always pick up extra shifts at the tavern.

"I thought you liked working at the school," Mary added before she'd had a chance to answer.

"I do, Mary. Truly."

"Then why?"

Fallon bit her lip. This lying thing wasn't getting any easier. "I'm just looking for something a little different this coming year."

"Like what?"

The woman could be persistent. Though Fallon figured it was only fair, she did owe Mary something of an explanation. Not that she could exactly tell her the truth. How in the world would she even begin to explain?

*You see, Mary, I've recently found out there's a child out there I feel a personal responsibility for. And I can't bear the thought that he might be mistreated in any way. I'd like to find out myself for certain. Also, I'd really like to be a part of his life, at least during the early years. Because the thought of Sasha's child experiencing anything remotely like what his mother and I went through growing up is absolutely shattering.*

No, she couldn't say any of that. But she could stick to the truth as much as possible.

"I just find myself needing to do this," she answered simply, then bid the other woman goodbye.

It didn't take long after she'd hung up for her phone to ring again. Fully expecting to have to restate her case to Mary yet again, she was surprised when a male voice sounded from the tiny speaker when she answered.

"Ms. Duvall. This is Lance Watson, Mr. Martinez's personal assistant. I'm calling to offer you the position of full-time caregiver to his young son. I've sent detailed documents to the email address you provided on your application."

Fallon fought the urge to cheer out loud. "Oh. Wow. Uh, thanks."

"You're welcome. Now, how soon can you start?"

# CHAPTER THREE

ENRIQUE'S EYES GREW blurry as he studied the figures on his laptop screen. The baby had cried all night again, and no amount of soothing and rocking had served to calm him until the break of dawn this morning. Thankfully, little Lucas had finally fallen asleep. Leaving his sleep deprived father with a full schedule and loads of work that needed attention that he'd have to attend to now with barely a wink of sleep.

As Lucas's father, it vexed him that he couldn't figure out how to lull his own child to sleep. Shouldn't he have some kind of natural ability to soothe his own baby? Like Fallon Duvall had. He'd wanted to hire her then and there. But of course they'd had to wait for an extensive background check to be completed. Which luckily came back clean. Even with his connections and resources, it had still taken a week. He'd been surprised to hear that Fallon Duvall had grown up in foster care, bouncing from house to house after losing her parents to a terrible accident. Enrique couldn't imagine being uprooted in such a manner. His mother had essentially abandoned him and his brother, but they'd both always had a steady and loving home with his *abuela*. According to the records his security team had dug up on her, Fallon had never known such stability. Rather impressive then just how far she'd come in life despite such loss and lack of resources.

Enrique paused and rubbed a hand down his face. Honestly, he had no business thinking about the woman this much. She was a potential employee, nothing more. It mattered little how impressive she was. His only thoughts should revolve around how she might help him to concentrate on his massive to-do list if she was around to take care of Lucas.

First thing first. He was going to need a gallon of espresso just to get though the morning. How did new mothers do this day in and day out? Particularly ones without the benefit of nannies or close family members nearby to help?

Speaking of nannies, after his espresso, he'd stop by Watson's office to see how negotiations were going with Miss Fallon. The sooner the woman could start, the better for both him and little Lucas.

Much to his surprise, and he had to admit, to his delight, Watson wasn't alone when Enrique made his way to assistant's office twenty minutes later. Very good news. She'd already been hired. At least that part of the process had gone relatively quick, thank the saints above. Maybe he could finally get some work done without constant distractions and actually be able to sleep more than two or three hours a night.

Fallon Duvall sat across the desk, signing paperwork. Neither one noticed him hovering in the doorway. Enrique took the moment to study her profile. A delicate nose above lush, pinkish lips. Her skin slightly darker than olive. A few curls of thick auburn hair appeared to be escaping out of a tight top bun.

She wasn't classically beautiful but he had to admit that she was rather striking. And that figure...

Enrique gave himself a mental thwack. As if this was the time to be entertaining such inappropriate thoughts. The woman was his employee for heaven's sake. Hired to watch his son. He couldn't harbor thoughts of being attracted to her.

Without warning, her hand stilled and she turned her head to look at him over her shoulder. Clearly, she'd sensed his presence. Another point in her favor, she was obviously very aware of her surroundings. His own assistant hadn't even noticed him standing there. And Watson was facing the door.

Watson spoke first. "Enrique. I didn't realize you were there." He gestured to where Fallon sat across the desk as Enrique made his way into the room. "Happy to say that Ms. Duvall has accepted the position. She's ready to start right away."

Fallon turned back around without acknowledging his presence. Why that vexed him, Enrique couldn't begin to explain. The only thing that mattered was what Watson had just confirmed. She'd accepted the job and was ready to start. Enrique resisted the urge to throw a celebratory fist punch in the air.

"Welcome to the staff," he said. She had no idea just how much he meant that.

"Thank you," she replied. This time she swiveled around in her chair to face him fully. The smile on her face was guarded, hesitant. Was it just her personality to be so reserved? Or was there something about him specifically that had her appearing so apprehensive?

No matter. She wasn't there to look after him. Though the thought had a certain appeal.

*Dios!* He really shouldn't be going there. At all.

"We're looking forward to having you to help care for little Lucas, Miss Duvall."

"As am I. But please call me Fallon."

He nodded. "And you must call me Enrique."

"Enrique might finally get a full night's sleep now that you're here," Watson added.

Fallon's eyebrows lifted just enough. "You mean you've been staying up with him yourself?" Surprise laced her voice and words.

"Yes. Of course. He is my son."

"Huh," was all she said in response.

"You sound surprised."

An almost imperceptible shrug of her shoulder. "I guess I am."

Well, she was candid, at least.

She continued. "It's just that, even without the full-time nanny position filled, I imagine you have the staff to take care of such matters."

Enrique walked farther into the room, sat one hip on the desk across from her. "That's true. But as I said, I am the boy's father. I'd like him to begin to recognize me as a source of security and comfort. I know he and I have some time to make up for."

Something shifted behind her eyes at his words. "That's…um…very commendable."

He wasn't sure if that was supposed to be a compliment or not, so he didn't bother to try and thank her for it. Commendable. If she had any idea about how he'd grown up, or any inkling about the man Enrique's own father had been, she'd know just how important it was for Enrique to bond with his child.

But of course she couldn't know. Not many people did, in fact. His father wasn't a topic Enrique liked to talk about. Or a topic he even wanted to revisit in his own head. One day he might have to explore the way finding out about Lucas had brought all the haunting memories of his own childhood rearing to the surface.

But there was no time for that now.

Sasha—
Great news! I managed to get the job. I can keep an eye on Lucas now. They offered me an exorbitant amount of money too. Several times over my current salary at the school.

But of course, this isn't about money. It's about making sure your little boy is safe and cared for. And I have to say, he does appear to be very important to his father. The man was dead on his feet that first morning because he'd stayed up all night with his son. Imagine that. The staff he employs—yet he wanted to stay with his baby himself.

Still, until I know for certain that all is well, I plan on staying close by him. You should see him now, Sasha. He's a bit fussy at times, but such a little sweetheart when he calms and grips my finger or lays his head on my chest. I know you want that too. Don't you?

Please write back and let me know you're okay. I'm so very worried.

Fallon sighed, rereading the message she'd sent weeks ago now that hadn't received a response. Just like all the others. She'd keep trying, though with each passing day she was losing more and more hope that Sasha was ever going to get back to her.

She hadn't been exaggerating in her email about the

hefty salary. She'd make sure to set aside a good portion of the money in a separate account for Sasha to have whenever she resurfaced. That was only fair.

*If she resurfaced.*

Lucas slept soundly in his crib in the corner. She'd already tidied his room of the various toys and books they'd spent the afternoon playing with. His afternoon naps were pretty unpredictable. He could be down for over an hour or barely fifteen minutes. She might not have much time to take a quick break and grab a bite of lunch.

Slipping the baby monitor in her pocket, she quietly opened the door to step into the hallway. Only, she somehow ran into a solid wall instead. A tall, muscled, hard wall that smelled of sandalwood and mint.

It took all her might not to shriek and risk waking the baby. Clasping a hand to her chest against her thumping heart, she looked up to find Enrique watching her with an amused smile.

"Apologies. I didn't mean to startle you."

She gave her head a brisk shake. Even without the element of surprise the man was remarkably startling. Today he wore a casual cream V-neck sweater that contrasted strikingly with his dark features. He'd rolled his sleeves up to the elbows, and it was hard not to stare at the muscled contours of his arms. A pair of tailored black slacks fit him all too well.

"I should have been paying better attention."

He merely stared at her so she felt compelled to break the silence. "Lucas is finally sleeping. I figured this might be a good time to head downstairs for a quick bite before he wakes up."

He nodded once. "Perfect. I'll join you."

Fallon swallowed. She'd hardly seen the man since starting a month ago. Which was a relief as he made her jumpy and anxious for reasons she wanted to kick herself for. "You will?"

"Yes. Lunch is prepared and awaiting me in the dining room. We can eat together."

Right. As if she'd be able to swallow a bite with Enrique sitting at the same table. "I don't want to infringe on your lunch," she protested. "I was just going to make myself a quick sandwich in the kitchen."

He gave a dismissive shake of his head. "You're not infringing. And I'm sure chef's prepared plenty of food. Besides, there's something we need to discuss." He stepped aside and gestured for her to continue.

How in the world could she argue with any of that?

So much for a relaxing breather while Lucas napped. Fallon summoned a calming breath and made her way to the spiral staircase all too aware of the man trailing behind her. What did he have to speak to her about? He couldn't have found out the connection between her and Lucas's mother, could he? The thought of that possibility sent a rush of panic through her chest. She'd never be able to explain herself or justify her motivations in the face of questioning.

But that couldn't be it. For one thing, Enrique appeared much too calm. Surely if he'd found out the truth, he wouldn't be so even-tempered at the moment. He'd probably be demanding answers of her while launching another search with the nanny agency.

By the time they made it to the dining hall on the first floor, she'd managed to get her pulse somewhat under control. Whatever Enrique wanted to discuss, it couldn't have anything to do with her true connection to Lucas. When they reached the table, he stepped behind her to pull her chair out, then took the chair opposite her.

Fallon had to make an effort not to gawk at the surroundings. She hadn't been in this particular room before. It was beyond extravagantly decorated. The table was long and wide, polished to a high shine. She counted twenty-two chairs. Heavy draperies hung over floor-to-ceiling glass windows. A plush Oriental rug covered the floor.

Did the man always dine so formally? Even for a simple midday meal with his nanny?

A middle-aged gentleman in a crisp white shirt and necktie appeared within seconds of them taking their seats. This had to be what dining in a fancy, expensive restaurant must feel like. Except they were the only two people in the room and the man seated across from her happened to own the place. The man addressed Enrique in Spanish. At Enrique's response, he turned to greet her with a friendly smile. "Welcome, miss. Lunch will be served right away."

Less than a minute after he'd walked away, he returned carrying two steaming bowls. The aroma had Fallon's mouth watering. Another employee immediately followed with a tray of assorted rolls and crackers. She willed her stomach not to growl in anticipation when the bowl was placed in front of her. A rich, savory broth with loads of spinach and other colorful vegetables.

"Please, begin." Enrique gestured to the food in front of her.

Fallon draped the cloth napkin on her lap and picked up her spoon. "You said you needed to discuss something with me?"

Enrique picked a plump roll off the tray and nodded. "Yes. I'm afraid our schedule must change. I've had some rather unexpected glitches in a business project that will need my immediate attention."

That's all this was, then? A simple matter of scheduling? Perhaps he was about to travel on business for several days. What a relief that would be. To not be nervous about running into Enrique as she got to know her Sasha's son better.

Fallon released a sigh of relief and dipped her spoon into the steaming hot soup. Only to have his next words stop her midsip.

"We'll be flying into Mexico next week."

Why in the world had she just gone as white as the tablecloth and porcelain dishware? Her pallor was the least of it. Fallon sputtered on the sip of soup she'd just taken, followed by a couple of coughs.

Enrique quickly pushed her glass of water closer within her reach. "Is something wrong? Is the soup not to your liking?"

She actually grunted in answer.

"Is it too hot?"

Fallon shook her head. "Believe me. It's not the soup."

"Then what is it?"

She gingerly took a small sip of water and wiped her mouth with her napkin. Enrique found himself momentarily distracted by the luscious curve of her lips, the way they turned more red as she wiped them with the silk napkin. Kissable lips. Lips that had a man wondering what they might taste like.

And that was enough of that. He still had to figure out why she'd come near to choking on a spoonful of soup she'd barely tasted. Unless…

"You are upset about having to leave the States?"

She hesitated before answering. Her pause was answer enough. Of course, she must have someone she was loath to leave behind. Enrique was pretty certain she wasn't married. A boyfriend or lover then. The thought sent a tightening sensation in his chest that he didn't want to examine.

Her answer was a tight shuttering of her eyes. Enrique knew his next question was borderline over personal. He asked it anyway. "Is there someone here who will be sad to see you go?"

She shook her head. "No. That's not it. I don't really have any family. And I'm not seeing anyone."

The admission sent a lightning bolt of pleasure through his core. Not that he had any right to feel it. "Then I don't understand."

"I guess I'm just a bit surprised."

"But you knew the requirements of the job upon application included a willingness and ability to travel. Why is it a problem?"

She shook her head. "It's not. Really. I just wasn't expecting it to have come up so soon. I've barely been working for you for a month."

"I can have one my personal assistants help you get your affairs in order before you leave."

"That won't be necessary."

"If it's a matter of a passport, we can have it expedited and delivered within a day or so."

"I actually will need to do that."

"Very well." He fished his phone out of his pocket and sent the necessary message to get the process started. "You'll be sent instructions on applying for an expedited one within the hour."

"Thank you."

He studied her. She looked anything but thankful. And she'd clearly lost her appetite. "You're welcome. Yet you remain appearing as if someone has asked you to slay a dragon. Why?"

She ducked her head ever so slightly before answering him. "I've never actually traveled outside the United States before." She looked pained to have had to admit the fact. No excitement about the prospect of heading somewhere new. On the contrary, she looked terrified about the concept.

"Then maybe you can consider it a bit of an adventure." He really didn't want to have to look for a replacement nanny. Plus he'd gotten somewhat used to having Fallon Duvall around. As had his son. No, whatever this issue was on her part, it would have to be addressed and fixed.

For both their sakes.

"Yes, I'll try and do that."

She hardly sounded or looked convincing. Actually, she still looked terrified. He knew some of the more recent news reports from his home country could be a little disconcerting. But that could be said about almost any country. "We'll be traveling to a luxe resort visited by celebrities and other VIPs. You have nothing to be afraid of. As soon as we land in Cancun International Airport, we'll have a car waiting to take us to Tulum."

"I'm sure I'll be fine once we land."

Enrique leaned back in his chair as understanding dawned. "You're nervous about flying."

She ducked her head, averted her gaze. So that was clearly a yes.

"Then, if you don't mind my asking, why did you apply for and accept a job that specifically stated would involve travel?"

She shrugged. "I guess I hadn't really considered it until the very real possibility came up just now."

He reached for his phone again. "That's simple enough to fix," he said, calling up the contact of his personal physician at Boston Medical. "I'll have you see my doctor—he can give you something to calm your nerves before we board."

Something in her expression had him halting before making the call. "You don't like that idea."

She shook her head. "I try to stay away from any kind of mood-altering medications. I never have taken them. And I never will."

Well, that was a rather comforting statement coming from the woman in charge of caring for his son. But her voice was heavy as she said the words. There was a story there. Maybe one day she would confide in him and tell him what it was.

He knew from the background check that she'd lost her parents at a young age. Could her fear of flying have something to do with that loss?

She threw her hands up, palms facing him. "Please don't give it another thought. I'll get over my phobia before we have to begin the trip. I love being Lucas's nanny. Even in this short period of time, I've grown tremendously fond of him. I'll do whatever it takes to get past my fear. I don't want you to even consider finding a replacement for me."

Well, that was good to hear. Neither did he. Still, he had to do something to help her.

# CHAPTER FOUR

IT WAS THE second time in less than forty-eight hours that she nearly ran into Enrique's chest as she was exiting Lucas's room.

"We have to stop meeting like this," he said with a smile and a wink as she did her best to recover her bearings. Why did the man have to smell so good all the time? Why didn't she ever run into him when he was sweaty after a workout or dripping wet from a shower?

Mistake to think that way. Those two images hardly helped her racing heart about having him so near. Why was he again anyway? The last time he'd come to see her, he'd dropped the bombshell on her about leaving for Mexico in a few short days. Was he here to remind her about it? Not that she could have forgotten. She could barely get it out of her head that she'd be thousands of feet up in the air. Just whizzing through the sky in a steel contraption.

"What can I do for you, Enrique?"

"Is the baby sleeping?"

She nodded. "Though, as usual, I have no idea how long he'll be down." She held up the baby monitor in her hand. "It's why I carry this."

He reached for the device and took it from her. "We'll just give this to Ms. Ritter. You'll be coming with me."

She would? "What about Lucas?"

"Martha and Watson can handle him for a bit. We'll only be gone a couple of hours."

He gestured for her to follow him. "Where are we going?" Fallon asked, reluctantly trailing after him.

"You'll see. It's something of a surprise."

Oh, boy. She didn't really like surprises. She hadn't had too many fun ones in her lifetime. Then again, she'd never met a man like Enrique Martinez before.

With no small amount of trepidation, she followed him down the stairs and out the door where a sleek, black sports car sat purring in the circular brick driveway. A young man in a gray sports coat approached them. "I pulled the one you wanted out of the garage, sir."

"Thanks, Mario," Enrique said, passing the baby monitor to him. "Do me a favor and hand this to Ms. Ritter."

"Sure thing," the other man said, giving them both a brief salute before making his way into the house.

Enrique led her to the passenger side of the vehicle and helped her inside.

"Can you give me a clue about our destination, at least?" Fallon asked, her curiosity fully piqued. The warm leathery seats felt like butter against her skin as she pulled the seat belt across her torso and buckled it in place. This piece of art in the form of a car was a far cry from her small hatchback hybrid. It was probably worth more than the entire dealership she'd purchased her own car from.

"I'm afraid not," Enrique answered, retrieving a pair of aviator sunglasses from the console and slipping them on. His sleeves were rolled up again, his collared shirt slightly unbuttoned at the neck.

Dear god above. He looked like something out of a men's magazine spread.

She didn't know what kind of car they were in, just that

it was an Italian model and clearly very expensive. Enrique handled it beautifully. Soon, Fallon felt herself relax
enough to stop fretting about Lucas waking up without
her there and allowed herself to take in some of the beautiful Cape scenery.

If she were the daydreaming sort, she might even indulge in a little pretending. She could make believe that
she was out for a joyride with a date as they toured this
scenic part of Massachusetts. Maybe they were on their
way to the beach to spend some time in the sun. Or perhaps they'd board a boat and spend the day sailing around
the harbor together. In the evening they could share a glass
of wine while they watched the sunset.

It was silly, of course. But a girl could dream. She'd
allow herself this small indulgence.

Until they reached the rotary break in the roadway.
Then her instincts kicked in. Fallon knew enough of the
Cape that she knew this road led to the Hyannis airport.
Already she could see the small prop planes overhead as
they descended toward the runway barely a few miles
away.

Why in the world would he be taking her to the small
island airport? If Enrique thought watching a few small
planes land and takeoff would help her, she wasn't sure
how she felt about that. Nor did she think it might help
her dilemma much.

Then another disquieting thought struck and had her
pulse skyrocketing. "Uh, you're not going to make me get
on one of those things, are you?"

He took a hand off the steering wheel to clasp it to his
chest in dramatic fashion. "You wound me. Do you think
I would do that to you knowing your apprehensions about
flying? Without so much as a warning?"

She would certainly hope not. Fallon felt her shoulders sag in relief. "Phew. For a second there I thought we might be headed to the airport."

"Not exactly."

What kind of answer was that? They were either on their way to the airport or they weren't.

"Trust me," Enrique simply said.

Surprisingly, she did.

Was it foolish of her to trust him? She barely knew the man. Looked like she would find out soon enough. For each passing mile took them closer to the regional airport that mostly serviced small prop planes and other private aircraft.

Another one flew overhead and over the tall steel fence surrounding the runways.

She really didn't want to quit her job, but if Enrique was about to insist she board one of those bucket of bolts, she seriously had to reconsider her recent life choices.

Fallon sighed and leaned back against the seat, closing her eyes. The truth was, she'd do anything for little Lucas. Even get on one of those flying canisters if she had to.

The car seemed to be turning. When she opened her eyes, she saw they'd turned onto a small dirt road just before the gated entrance of the airport. So they hadn't actually turned toward the runways. Probably too early to breathe a sigh of relief though. She wasn't going to do that until they were far enough away that no more planes were flying overhead. Soon, they approached a long hangar-type building with no windows, just a tall steel door in the center of the side wall.

"Is there a plane in there?" she asked, a heaviness settling into her stomach.

Enrique flashed her a smile. "Probably, but that doesn't concern us."

Okay. So far so good, she supposed.

Enrique was at her side and opening her door an instant later. Stepping out of the car, she adjusted her eyes, squinting against the bright sunlight.

"Although," he began, shutting the car door behind her, "if you were to change your mind, it does seem to be a beautiful day to take a quick spin in the air above the Cape."

She immediately shook her head. "The chances of me changing my mind are slim to none. Closer to none."

The steel door opened as they approached, and a man around Enrique's age strode over to them wearing scrubbed jeans and a pea green military-style puffed jacket. His smile was both familiar and friendly. The two men executed one of those combo handshake slash shoulder claps as they greeted each other.

When they were done, Enrique gestured to where she stood. "Fallon, I'd like you to meet Manuel Esposo. He's an expert pilot who has flown everything from cargo planes to commercial jumbo jets. Trained via the United States Navy. Semiretired. Does some teaching but still spends most of his time in the sky. Manuel, this is Fallon Duvall. She takes care of my son."

Two things struck Fallon as Enrique spoke. One, he hadn't referred to her as any kind of help or nanny. She couldn't help but feel touched by that.

Second, now she understood what they were doing here. Enrique had brought her for some sort of encouraging pep talk from an experienced pilot. Go figure. Who knew if it would even work or not. But a tingling sensation crawled up her spine at the thought that he'd made an attempt at finding a solution for her rather than telling her to just get over her fear. Or, heaven forbid, telling her she was relieved of her duties and that he'd just find someone else. Instead, Enrique had gone out of his way to have her talk to an expert who probably experienced daily what she was so apprehensive about trying even once.

That theory flew out the window when Manuel spoke. "Nice to meet you, Fallon. So, tell me, are you ready to learn how to fly a plane?"

Turned out, Manuel hadn't been referring to an actual plane. Thank heavens. Much to Fallon's relief, he'd led the two of them to a darkened room in the back of the hangar. Against the wall was a bevy of instruments, panels and screens. And two tall leather chairs.

"It's a flight simulator," Enrique announced.

A very convincing one at that. If Fallon had awakened in here facing this wall, she wouldn't guess that she was in an isolated room within a hangar and not the cockpit of an actual aircraft.

Enrique continued. "This is how Manuel starts teaching his students."

"That's right," the other man added. "They spend hours and hours in here before even stepping foot in an actual plane."

Enrique thrust his hands into his pockets. "I figured if you saw how the controls worked, how experienced pilots handled them, it might make you feel better about flying in a few days."

So it wasn't just a pep talk he'd brought her here for. It was to be much more hands-on apparently.

Fallon wasn't sure exactly what to say, or even what to think. No one had ever tried this hard to make her feel comfortable before. She knew Enrique's primary motivation was driven by his son. Fallon wasn't naive enough to think this gesture might have something to do with her personally. Still, Enrique could have very easily left her to her own devices to figure out her hang-ups about flying to Mexico.

"Have a seat." Manuel gestured to the seat on the left and waited until she sat down before adding, "You too, copilot."

Enrique sat down next to her.

With a flick of a switch on one of the panels, the green screen in front of them came on and Fallon's breath hitched at the result. The screen turned into a landscape that looked so real, Fallon might have sworn he'd lifted a blind to reveal a large window. Or that some magic had opened a portal into the outside. But it was completely virtual. The most realistic looking runway with greenery along the path and city buildings in the distance. A glance in Enrique's direction told her he was equally impressed. He was smiling from ear to ear.

That was something. At least he was enjoying this. He had to be a busy man. Not only had he planned all this, he'd taken time out of his day to be here.

"First thing first," Manuel began. "Before anyone touches any of the buttons, experienced pilots always take a moment to study the environment in front of them. Check out all angles around the aircraft. Make a note of anything that might seem out of place, any kind of obstruction or hazard. Your eyes and ears are your most relevant instruments, above all these knobs and buttons."

With that, he handed them each an earpiece. "This is what you'll use to communicate with your crew and with ground air traffic control."

For the next hour and a half, Manuel meticulously went over the functions of the various knobs and buttons. He demonstrated the best way to adjust the steering apparatus and explained the communications and safety devices in detail.

By the time they left and made their way back outside, Fallon's trepidation about flying had lowered by several degrees.

"Wow," was all she could think of to say.

"Wow good?"

She nodded. "Definitely 'wow good.'"

She couldn't even begin to figure out how she might thank him for being so thoughtful. And to think, she'd been afraid at one point that he might insist she get on a small propellor aircraft, that it might have been some sort of test to see if she was scared enough to back out of the actual trip.

It was as if Enrique read her thoughts. "Did you think, even for a moment, that I might make you do something against your will?"

The answer to that question surprised her. Deep down, she really hadn't believed that he might. Or she wouldn't have even stepped out of the car when they'd first arrived. Sometime within the last few weeks, since she'd started working for him, Fallon had realized she could indeed trust him.

She'd learned to trust her instincts over the years, in both good situations and bad. So far, all her instincts told her Enrique was a man of character. One who not only loved his son, despite the way he'd discovered the child's existence, but a man who'd gone out of his way to make his newly hired nanny feel comfortable.

Definitely not what she'd been expecting when she'd first walked through his door.

"To be honest, I wasn't sure what to think."

"And what about now?" he asked. "Did Manuel's lesson help to ease your anxiety at all?"

She couldn't help the smile that formed on her lips. "You know what? I think it did. Some of the mystery and uncertainty has been alleviated. And the way he explained how everything is controlled and monitored was more helpful than I might have guessed."

Enrique let out a whoop and said something in Spanish that definitely sounded congratulatory. He reached for her then and for an insane moment, Fallon thought he might embrace her. But he lifted his hand in the air instead, palm open. She high-fived him with an unwelcome sense of disappointment. Of course her employer wasn't going to hug her, for god's sake. There was no reason for her to want him to.

"This calls for a celebration," he announced. "It's Friday afternoon. There's a beachside clambake on Sterling beach. I say we celebrate with steamed clams, some lobster and corn on the cob."

As wonderful as that all sounded, she was beginning to think about Lucas and how he might have reacted upon awakening and not having her there to greet him.

He held a hand up before she could mention her concern. "I know what you're going to say. And he's fine. I've been checking throughout the afternoon. Ms. Ritter says he was a bit fussy when he first woke but calmed right down after she handed him the little bunny you always use when you play with him.

"I'm famished and this will be our last chance for a good beachside meal around a bonfire for at least the next few months. You don't want to deny me one last clambake, do you?"

Fallon couldn't come up with any argument to counter that. Especially since he'd assured her that Lucas was fine. In fact, she felt rather guilty that it hadn't occurred to her to check on him during the ninety minutes they were in the simulation. She'd just been so preoccupied. But Enrique had thought to do so.

"Come on," he said now, nudging her to answer yes. He dramatically cupped his hand to his ear. "Do you hear that?"

"I don't hear anything but the airplanes above."

"Well, then, their noise is covering up the sound of my grumbling stomach."

Fallon had to laugh at his exaggerated pained expression. She didn't have it in her to argue. Besides, she felt a bit hungry herself. She couldn't recall the last time she'd had lobster. And she'd certainly never had it at a beachside clambake. And wasn't it good for Lucas to spend some time bonding with other people in the household?

"What do you say?" Enrique pressed her.

She didn't have the heart to say no. And she didn't want to.

# CHAPTER FIVE

THAT WENT A lot better than he'd hoped it might.

Enrique removed his shoes and socks and tossed them in the trunk of the car. Hard to believe he'd found parking along the quaint town street during one of the most popular times of the week to be here. He motioned for Fallon to do the same, but for some reason, she just stood there staring at him. Did she not like being barefoot?

"Is something wrong?" he asked.

She inhaled and released a quick sigh before answering. "No. Nothing's wrong. You're just not what I expected."

What a curious thing to say. "How do you mean?"

"You don't really fit the picture I might have had in my head."

Huh. Did that mean she'd been thinking about him? Exactly when?

"Go on," he prodded, interested to learn more about what specifically she meant about him that didn't fit the mold she'd somehow preconceived.

"It's hard to explain, really. But then again, I don't have much experience with men like you."

"Men like me?"

"You know, megamillionaires who take time out of their day to put their newly hired nanny at ease about a trip. Who drives what has to be a million-dollar car and parks it on a busy town street to attend a clambake. A serious businessman with a mountain of responsibilities who stays up all night with his son himself despite having plenty of staff."

The fact that she'd made note of all those things about him sent a hit of dopamine through his system.

She continued. "You take off what I'm guessing has to be an expensive pair of Italian leather shoes and cuff tailored pants so that you can walk on a sandy beach. It's quite remarkable really. You're definitely not what you appear to be on the surface."

Did that mean she found *him* remarkable?

If she only knew how humble his early life had been, how hard he'd had to work to get to where he was today.

She'd underestimated the extent of his wealth and the price of the car. Not that he was about to point those things out. As far as the rest went, he wasn't quite sure whether he should be thanking her for all she'd just said. How did one respond to such a thing?

It wasn't often a woman, or anyone else for that matter, rendered him uncertain about what to say.

"I know what you're going to say," Fallon said.

Well, that was good. Because he really had no idea. "What's that?"

"That I'm old enough to know not to judge a book by its cover."

Enrique chuckled. "I wasn't sure what to say, honestly. But most of that sounded complimentary. So, thanks? I guess."

She sent him a smile that caused a flipping sensation in the middle of his chest. "You're welcome."

To curtail the onset of an awkward silence, Enrique figured he should move things along. "You know what else I might have said? That we should go get some lunch finally."

She nodded once. "Right. Your grumbling stomach and all."

"Yes, and all this fresh sea air is only making me hungrier. Let's go."

The line for food was several feet deep when they made their way onto the beach. "Mind securing us a picnic table while I wait in line?" Enrique asked.

"Sure thing."

She had a way of walking that Enrique couldn't help but appreciate. A slight sway of her hips that brought attention to the contours of her waist and bottom. And what a delectable bottom it was.

Enrique squeezed his eyes shut and pushed the thought out of his head. He really couldn't be appreciating his nanny's body parts. Wholly inappropriate. He wasn't some hormonal teenager who couldn't control his thoughts. He had to do better.

Tearing his gaze away, he turned back to face forward to realize the line had moved on and he hadn't even noticed. The couple behind him gave an impatient huff and he strode along to close the gap. He'd actually been gawking at his son's nanny long enough that he hadn't noticed the line moving. How mortifying.

When it was finally his turn, he ordered two steaming buckets of clams and lobster with all the trimmings. He added a big basket of greasy fries and two bottles of water. Fallon waved him over from one of the tables when they handed him the food on a tray almost the size of a card table.

Between the deep sand and the size of the tray, it took a good half minute to get to where she sat.

"I'm sorry. I didn't realize we'd have company," she said when he finally reached her and sat across from her on the bench seat of the picnic table. "We're clearly meeting several other couples as all this food can't possibly be for just the two of us."

Couple. Enrique knew her statement was innocuous and she certainly wasn't implying anything. But to anyone else here on the beach with them, they must have indeed looked like some kind of couple out on an afternoon date. The idea held more appeal than he wanted it to.

"Are you kidding?" he asked, starting in on the clams first. "I believe I mentioned I was starving. I'll eat any part of your share you leave behind."

Now he was speaking as if they were a couple, offering to polish off her share if she didn't eat it all.

Fallon didn't seem to notice. "Something tells me you might have to do that. There's no way I can finish all this." She gingerly took the lobster out of the basket and set it on the paper plate in front of her. "It's been a while since I've had one of these."

"Would you like me to crack open the claw for you?" Another thing part of a couple would say. Why couldn't he revert to being the formal-sounding boss he was, already?

"I think I have it," she responded, then promptly dropped the lobster. "Ow, it's really hot."

She stuck the pad of her thumb in her mouth and gave it a small suck. A kaleidoscope of wholly inappropriate images traveled through his mind's eye. Enrique completely lost focus on anything around him except what Fallon was doing with her injured thumb.

*Just. Stop.*

Without asking for permission again, he reached for her lobster and made quick work of removing the claw, then breaking it open with the silver seafood cracker. He did the same with the other claw before handing her back her dish.

"Thanks."

"Sure thing," he answered, anything to get her to stop sucking on her thumb in front of him and giving him all sorts of untoward ideas. Though watching her take a bite of buttery lobster meat before slowly chewing wasn't all that much better. He really had to get a grip. What a cliché he was turning into. Having the hots for his son's nanny.

Well, he didn't have the hots for her. He was overwhelmed after finding himself in a whole other reality with a son he'd only recently found out about. No wonder his brain was looking for a distraction. This just happened to be a very inappropriate one.

Well, he couldn't very well sit here and watch her eat. He had to redirect his attention somehow.

He was scrambling for a way to make conversation and get his mind off her lips when she beat him to it.

"So, we'll be heading to Mexico soon."

There was still a hint of trepidation in her voice at the prospect, but he also sensed maybe a smidge of excitement in her tone as well.

Enrique took a swig of his water before answering. "That's right. And I might have fibbed a little earlier when I was trying to convince you to come to lunch."

Both perfectly arched eyebrows rose with curiosity. "You did?"

He nodded. "Yep, had to. A starving man makes desperate decisions. It wasn't a very big fib though."

Fallon reached for her own bottle and twisted off the cap and took a small sip. Her eyes remained focused on him. "What did you lie about?"

He wagged his finger at her. "Fib. That's different than a lie. Lies are less forgivable than harmless fibs."

Something shifted behind her eyes, and she quickly averted her gaze back to her food. "I suppose that's true."

"It is. And I fibbed about not being able to eat beach-side anymore once we get there. We'll be staying at my private villa on the resort. There are nightly fiesta meals for the guests right by the water."

"That sounds lovely."

Was he imagining a hitch in her voice? Perhaps her anxieties about flying were arising again. His gut told him that wasn't the case. Something about this conversation had suddenly made her uneasy.

He was less curious than he was disappointed. He wanted to return to the easy camaraderie they'd been enjoying just moments ago.

"Tell me about the resort," she said, wiping her mouth with the paper napkin after taking another bite of lobster.

That he could do easily and with a great deal of enjoyment. The Martinez Tulum resort had been his very first major business venture after scraping by for years and investing what he'd earned.

"It's in Tulum. In a prime location on the coast. The first resort I built and started. Nothing but a couple of cottages at first. Now I can brag that it can host two hundred families and is one of the most successful vacation spots this side of the world."

Her eyes had grown wide. "I had no idea. How many do you own?"

He popped a greasy french fry into his mouth. Why did such tasty, fat-laden food have to be so bad for one's health?

"There are a dozen Martinez resorts scattered across the world, including the one just opened on the Cape."

"That's why you were in Massachusetts about a y—" She cut off whatever it was she was about to say and cleared her throat. "That's why you've been in this part of the United States, I mean."

"Correct. I was here to broker the deal with the investors. Now that we've broken ground in Falmouth and construction has begun, I can refocus my attentions on the expansion on the flagship property in Tulum."

"Is the expansion not going well?"

He shook his head. "I'm afraid not. Everything from bad weather to labor disputes with the construction workers to corrupt suppliers. I had hoped to stay here a while longer while building on the Cape is set to begin. But I'm afraid I can't afford to ignore Tulum any longer."

"That's why we're rushing there so suddenly."

It occurred to him just how unfair he'd been. He'd simply announced that they'd be leaving without explaining any of his reasons. No wonder Fallon had been hesitant and uncertain.

"I'm sorry for not having laid all this out much sooner. You should have known the reasons earlier."

"You don't have to apologize to me, Enrique. Trust me on that."

It was a rather odd thing to say. And Fallon had barely made eye contact in the last several moments. Maybe it was time to address the proverbial elephant in the room. "As you can imagine, such moves were logistically much easier before I discovered that I was a father."

Another fact of his life she deserved to know about as Lucas's primary caregiver.

"You sound as if it came as a shock."

"It did. See, I had a very uncharacteristic one-night stand during my initial trip out here. Not something I'd ever done before or since. One of my investors is Greek. He had a particularly potent brand of ouzo that he poured generously and often. I'm embarrassed to say that I didn't handle my consumption as well as the other men. And I came across an attractive woman who made it clear that she was interested in a very quick, no-strings-attached encounter. I never heard from her again after that night."

"Enrique, you don't need to explain any of it to me."

Maybe he did and maybe he didn't. But the more he talked to her about it all, the lighter he was beginning to feel.

Sasha

I wish I could explain to you the character of the man you share a child with. You would be so pleased. I have to admit to being quite frustrated that you'd just abandoned your baby with instructions to have him delivered to his father. It could have gone so horribly wrong. That's why I had to do everything I could think of to make sure.

Only, it didn't go badly. He's a caring father and a thoughtful man. If you only knew. I'm having a lot of conflicting emotions about my duplicity. My sense of guilt at not being truthful is growing by the day. Maybe I should just tell him the truth. But how would I even begin?

How I wish you would tell me what you think!

But enough about all that. You wouldn't believe what's happened. I'll be heading to Mexico in two days to care for Lucas there for the next several weeks. Definitely an unexpected turn. I'm both nervous and excited.

But I'll keep trying to contact you. As always, with the fervent hope that you will respond.

Fallon's hope of having that happen anytime soon was growing dimmer and dimmer. In the meantime, her life was on a fast track she could have never seen coming.

If someone had told her a few short weeks ago that she'd be traveling via private jet to Tulum, Mexico, in the employ of one of the wealthiest men in this hemisphere, Fallon would have laughed until her belly ached.

The fact that said man was the father of Sasha's baby only added another layer of surrealism to the whole scenario.

Another thing she found hard to believe—her anxiety about flying was almost near zero once the jet had taken off. Enrique's plan to have her learn about piloting a plane had most certainly helped. Plus she hadn't really had much time to focus on her own comfort as Lucas had become quite irritable and cried nonstop for the first hour or so. Poor thing seemed to be trying to tug at his ears, no doubt bothered by the changes in air pressure. It took a great deal of effort to coax him into taking his pacifier, which seemed to help. By the time Fallon had settled him and gotten him to sleep, they were well on their way.

Also, it didn't hurt that they were on board what could aptly be described as a flying hotel suite, complete with a wet bar, two queen-size beds on either side of the cabin and a full-size shower Enrique had had told her she was more than welcome to use during the fifteen-hour flight. A crib for Lucas had been set up beside the bed she'd be using.

He was working at a large wooden table when she drew the curtain around Lucas's bed and entered the main cabin. His laptop and a slew of paperwork consumed his attention.

Or so she thought.

"You should have something to eat while he's down finally," he told her, without looking up from his screen. "I can have Sandy prepare you a sandwich. Or she makes a mouthwatering pasta verde."

A small tingle traveled up her spine. She hadn't announced herself or made so much as a sound. Enrique seemed to be in tune to her entrances and very aware of her in general. A notion that both excited her and made her nervous.

"Maybe I'll have a bite later. I'm not very hungry right now."

"Then why don't you go lie down and get some rest."

"Thanks. I don't really feel like resting, either."

He looked up at her then. "Is something wrong? You seemed comfortable on the plane."

She shook her head. "It's not that. Between Manuel's lesson that day and the luxury of this plane, I feel perfectly at ease in the air."

"Then what seems to be bothering you?"

If he only knew. There was no way to explain. Their conversation on the beach last week, about how he'd discovered he was a father, the way he'd felt the need to explain to her how it came about, the guilt felt like an anvil on her shoulder, growing heavier and heavier.

"I guess I'm just a bit in awe, that's all." That was true enough.

"In awe?"

She motioned around her. "This is all quite something. I mean, I've seen pictures of private jets in magazines and online and such. But I couldn't have imagined the true splendor of such an aircraft. I feel like I'm in an entirely different world than what I'm used to."

The corners of his mouth lifted ever so slightly and he leaned forward, his eyes sparkling with what appeared to be amusement. As if she might have told a funny joke or punch line.

"What if I told you that it's all relatively new to me as well?"

For one thing, she would have a hard time believing it. Enrique seemed to fully fit his environment. She'd done enough background research to know he wasn't born into such wealth. But he'd clearly grown acclimated to it. "How do you mean?"

He shrugged, pushing the laptop away and leaning back against his chair. "I barely had enough to eat when I was a child. I never had any contact with the man who fathered me. My single mother worked a few odd jobs here and there until she gave up altogether, foisted me onto my grandmother and went back to my father."

How unexpected. Maybe the two of them had more in common than she might have thought.

He continued. "Didn't hear her from aside from a phone call around Christmas. Not even my birthday. As if she only thought to call because the holiday itself reminded her of my existence."

Fallon remained silent, a man like Enrique wouldn't appreciate even a hint of anything resembling pity. "Then she showed up a few years later to hand another child over to her mother and leave once more. Luis, my younger brother."

Luis. Fallon had wondered how Sasha had decided on the name Lucas for her baby. Enrique must have mentioned his younger brother and she'd chosen something similar.

"You and your brother are close?"

"He's a major pain in my backside." Despite the harsh words, there was clear affection in his tone. "He's six years younger than me, and we're as different as the stars and the ocean. You'll meet him when we get there. As well as my *abuela*."

His grandmother. His voice had grown even more tender as he'd said the last word. She knew it was none of her concern but her curiosity got the best of her. "And what of your mom?"

He shrugged again. "You're more likely to see a Mayan goddess. She gets a hefty amount of funds deposited into her account regularly and occasionally sends a postcard. Neither Luis nor I have so much as heard her voice for over three years now."

Fallon couldn't help but feel moved for him. And for the little boy he'd been. She'd lost her own parents to tragedy and the loss had both shattered her and upended her life. To be deserted by the people who were supposed to love you more than anyone else was such a betrayal. At least Lucas was too young to be aware that his mother had left him. Plus he had the benefit of one parent to love him and make sure he was cared for. It was no wonder Enrique was such a devoted father already despite the circumstances. He wanted more parental love in his child's life than he'd been given.

Many men might have taken the exact opposite approach. To want as little to do with their unintended offspring as possible. But not Enrique.

# CHAPTER SIX

WHY IN THE world was he getting into all this? And why now, with this particular woman? Enrique couldn't remember the last time he'd discussed his mother with anyone. Let alone someone who worked for him. The simple answer was that he was drawn to Fallon in a way he couldn't explain. And in a way he hadn't experienced with anyone else.

"Is there anyone else I should be prepared to meet once we arrive?"

"Such as?"

Her cheeks reddened to a soft pink and he instantly realized what she was asking. She wanted to know if he was involved with anyone romantically. A shiver of pleasure ran up his spine that she was interested in such a detail. It had to be more than curiosity.

Her face was tight when she spoke again. "I mean, I would imagine a man such as yourself doesn't often lack for female companionship."

She would be surprised. "As a matter of fact, I haven't had time for much of a social life these past few years." Hence, part of the reason for such an indiscretion back in Massachusetts over a year ago. Not that it was any kind of excuse. "The encounter with Lucas's mother was the last time."

Heavens. Her cheeks were growing redder by the second.

"It's really none of my business. I just wondered if Lucas would have to adjust to someone else in the household who wasn't a relation."

Of course. She was only asking out of concern for Lucas. Which confirmed that she was a good nanny who cared about his son. So why did he feel a frisson of disappointment in his chest that her questioning hadn't been for a more personal reason? "No. There is no such concern," he admitted.

So now she knew about the lack of a partner in his life. And she also knew how he'd grown up. About being abandoned by both his mother and father. He supposed that was fair. After all, he'd done an extensive background check on her.

"You grew up in foster care."

She swallowed before speaking. "That's right. I lost my parents in a boating accident on the Charles. I've always been hesitant to board any kind of boat since. I hadn't realized the fear extended to aircraft until…" She trailed off.

"I'm so sorry, Fallon," Enrique said, imaging the hurt and lost little girl she must have been and vowing to never ask her to board any kind of maritime craft unless she was absolutely ready and willing.

Her eyes glistened slightly. "Thank you. After they were gone, there was no one else. My grandparents had all passed when I was a toddler." Her eyes gained a faraway look and she turned her head to the side. "I had to go into the system."

"You have an aunt. Your mother's sister. She's married to a very successful investment banker. Were you not able to go live with them?"

She chuckled in a way that held no mirth. "I wasn't invited. They wanted nothing to do with a child who wasn't theirs."

Enrique knew he couldn't hide his distaste. How utterly inexcusable for a couple with such wealth. "Despite their resources?"

Another small laugh. "If I had to guess, I'd say it was because of their money. They didn't want an outsider sharing any of theirs."

"You are her niece. A blood relative."

She did a small eye roll. "That didn't seem to mean much to them. I don't think my mother and my aunt were close. She didn't even bother to come to the funeral service, just sent a large bouquet of flowers."

Enrique felt an overwhelming sense of revulsion for a woman he'd never met. Fallon's wealthy relatives had everything at their disposal to bring her into a loving home. Instead, they'd turned their backs on her and let her go into the system.

"That is unforgivable of them. As much as a pain as my brother can be, I can't imagine turning my back on him under any circumstances. Or any child he may eventually have."

She tilted her head, studying him. "That's very admirable. Not everyone is as honorable as you clearly are, Enrique. As I personally know from experience."

Honorable. Admirable. The way she described him sent vibes of pleasure deep within him. He wanted her to see him in the best possible light. For some reason, it was important to him that she do so. "I'm sorry you were put through that. You deserved better." He meant every word.

"I have to admit, the sting of rejection after such a tragic loss was a bit hard to take. Not to mention…"

"Tell me," he prodded.

"I shouldn't be unloading on you in such a manner. You hired me for a job, not to use you as a sympathetic ear."

"And yet I have two I'd like to lend to you right now."

She clasped her hands in her lap. "It's just…not every family I was placed with was exactly pleasant."

An icy sensation speared his chest. "Do you mean to tell me you were abused?"

"Never physically. Though the danger of it happening was certainly there."

How many moments had she lived through where she felt the eyes of her foster father inappropriately ogling her. Or the threatening taunts of the school bullies who mistook her quietness as weakness to be exploited.

She added, "I learned ways to protect myself, to stay out of the way. Taught by a foster sister much more savvy than I was."

Enrique sucked in a breath with relief. "Thank heavens for that foster sister. I'm glad you had at least one person on your side."

If he ever came across this sister, Enrique would make sure to find a way to thank the woman.

She was floating on clouds. The sky was crystal blue. She felt peaceful and calm. But what was that noise? Fallon could hear a sound. A sound she should pay attention to. But she felt so relaxed. So at peace. Couldn't she just ignore the sound a little while longer?

Fallon's eyes flew open as her fogged mind realized she'd fallen asleep on the reclining leather bucket seat chair in the cabin. The lights of the aircraft were dimmed, and someone had settled a thick, plush throw over her. The noise she was hearing was the baby. With a silent curse at herself, she flung the blanket off and jumped up.

How long had Lucas been fussing? "I'm coming, dear one," she said, rushing to the crib. Only the baby wasn't in it. In fact, he didn't appear to be crying anymore. A deep voice reached her from behind.

"We have it covered here—you can go back to sleep."

She turned to find Enrique standing a few feet away, Lucas cradled in his arms, the baby's cheek against his chest. His bare chest.

The sight had her breath hitching. Enrique had changed into gray sweatpants and not bothered with anything on top. It was so very hard not to gawk at the chiseled muscles along his torso, chest and arms. Dear heavens, please let it be too dark for him to notice just how much gawking she was doing. But she'd been taken by surprise.

What would his skin feel like if she were to touch it?

Hard and smooth, no doubt. And darned if her mind didn't perfectly conjure up exactly how that would feel against her own. Her fingers tingled and she crossed her arms tightly across her chest. Somehow, finally, she averted her gaze.

Then the horror of what had just happened hit her. She'd slept through the baby awakening. Enrique had had to come himself to soothe him.

"I'm so sorry," she began, moving to take Lucas. "I don't know how I fell asleep so soundly. You can go back to bed."

But Enrique stepped aside, shifted the baby higher against him. "He's fine. We both are. I've got a bottle warming up to give him."

"You shouldn't have had to do that! That's my job."

"Your job does not require you to be beyond human. You clearly needed the rest. You should be the one to go back to sleep."

Right. As if she could drift off again now, between the chagrin of having slept through the baby's crying and the picture of Enrique standing in front of her without a shirt on. In fact, she was going to have trouble getting that picture out of her head for the foreseeable future.

"I'll just go get his bottle, and then I'll take him."

"No, you won't, Fallon," he said in a firm tone that left no room for argument. "I'm going to get his bottle and stay with him while he drinks it and eventually falls asleep. You are going back to bed."

She opened her mouth to counter, but his expression left no ambiguity. "I guess if you insist."

He nodded once. "I do. Go get some rest. We have up to a two-hour drive ahead of us when we land. And then it will be one thing after another." He rested his chin on top of his son's head. "Besides, us boys are spending some quality time together."

That settled it. Far be it from her to further interrupt a tender moment. She began to turn around but indulged in one last look at the two of them. Lucas was nestled tight against his father, his palms resting on Enrique's chest by his rosy cheeks. Enrique was swaying gently back and forth. The two of them made such a touching picture, something shifted in the vicinity of her heart.

If she thought the man was attractive dressed in a business suit and holding a laptop, the way he looked with his son cradled against him had her heart hammering against her ribs. A heaviness settled deep within her core.

This was bad. She was falling deep. Between her love and affection for Lucas and her growing attraction to Enrique, she wasn't sure what she'd managed to get herself into. Or how in the world she would get out again when the time came. And it would come. This wasn't going to last forever. Someday, maybe sooner than she could guess, Enrique would meet someone who would happily play stepmother to his son. Where would that leave her? As much as she loved Lucas, would her heart be able to handle seeing Enrique belong to another woman day in and day out? Would she feel out of place and in the way?

Would the future wife see her that way? Worse, might Enrique also come to see her like that?

She'd do anything for little Lucas. Would love to watch him grow up. But she would be sticking by him for her own selfish reasons.

That she wouldn't be able to live with.

Then there was the fact that she'd installed herself in their lives under dishonest pretenses. How would she ever be able to explain that if it came to light before she figured out a way to tell Enrique?

Settling back in the chair, she pulled the throw over her face in case Enrique walked out and saw how miserable she was. It had to be written clearly on her face. As it was, she was barely keeping the stinging in her eyes from turning into falling tears.

Enrique had told her to go back to sleep. But there was no chance of that happening now.

Her heart felt too heavy to allow it.

When she saw Enrique again in the morning, the sweatpants had been replaced by pressed black slacks and he had a shirt on. A deep, rich blue shirt that brought out the dark depths of his eyes. Dear lord, there she went again. She'd sworn last night that she'd fight her ever growing attraction to him as hard as she could. So far, that pledge wasn't exactly going so great.

So try harder.

It didn't help that he was smiling at her with that charming smile of his, having freshly showered and dressed while she was still in her crumpled clothes that she'd fallen asleep in.

"Lucas is still asleep. You have time for a shower and some coffee before we land," he told her. "In any order you wish."

That was a tough choice. She was in desperate need of both. She mentally flipped a coin and pointed to the steaming hot carafe sitting on the tray in front of him next to a large round plate laden with various pastries.

"I'll start with the coffee, thanks."

He poured her a generous cup and handed it to her. "So how much time do we have exactly?"

He glanced at his watch. "Approximately twenty-five minutes. Give or take."

They dropped wheels on the runway at Cancun International Airport exactly twenty-seven minutes later. A car and driver awaited them on the busy roadway outside.

Enrique addressed the driver in Spanish and helped Fallon inside the back seat where a baby's car seat was already tightly secured. Fallon settled the baby, then buckled herself in next to him. For his part, Lucas appeared to be fully aware that something different than his regular routine was happening. He seemed to be studying his surroundings and trying to figure it all out.

Fallon could relate to the little fella. This was all quite new to her too. She'd never been on a plane before and she'd just taken a shower on one, for Pete's sake.

"What's so funny?" Enrique asked.

She hadn't even realized she'd actually chuckled out loud. "Nothing. I just wish there was a way that we could explain to Lucas what's happening. I wonder if he's confused about where we are."

Enrique's features tightened. "Yes, he's had quite a bit of disruption in his young life already so far. I'm going to do everything I can to ensure that he experiences a routine now, for as long as possible."

He really was a devoted father. Considering how little time he'd had to get used to the title and the responsibility, Enrique was wholly embracing his role. Look at the way he'd stayed with the baby last night when Lucas had awakened.

"What?" he asked. "Why are you looking at me like that?"

Oh, lord. How was she looking at him exactly? Was her attraction and admiration written clearly on her face? She really had to snap out of it. She had to stop focusing on all the good traits the man had and remind herself he was simply her employer. One she was keeping a rather heavy secret from.

"I guess I'm just nervous about being here. It's all so new. And about meeting your grandmother and brother."

He flashed her another heart-tripping smile. "That's the last thing you need to be nervous about. Abuela will love you. And Luis will try to charm you with such sweetness, your teeth might actually begin forming cavities."

"He sounds like quite a character," she laughed.

"He is. Believe me." Again, his tone held pure affection for his sibling. Luis was lucky to have Enrique as a big brother. And Lucas was lucky to have him as a father.

*Just stop.*

There she went again. Focusing solely on the man's virtues. The problem was, she had yet to see anything but admirable qualities in the man. There had to be at least a few flaws, didn't there? But damned if she'd seen any yet. Maybe she just had to look harder.

He leaned over suddenly, reaching over the baby and pointing to the scenery outside. "The ruins lay over that way. Tulum was one of the last cities built by the Mayans. You can see part of the wall that surrounded the city borders. So much history and culture here. The city is an intriguing blend of Mexico and Caribbean influences. But to me, it's just home."

"It's lovely so far," she said, taking in the view outside her window. A crystal blue sea could be seen in the distance. Lush greenery surrounded the road. The water appeared calm and smooth. Very different than the choppy waves of the Cape Cod beaches she was more familiar with.

"I think you'll like it," he declared, returning to his side of the car. But the scent of his now familiar aftershave still tickled her nose.

To distract herself, she dug one of Lucas's toys out of the diaper bag and dangled it in front of him. The baby gave her a wide-eyed look before trying to grasp the plastic toy key ring that also served as a teether.

"You won't have to keep him distracted too much longer," Enrique told her.

They then passed much of the rest of the journey in a tense silence until Enrique said, "We're approaching the resort. The villa is just a couple minutes after that. Abuela is already waiting with bated breath to dote on her great-grandson. And she's looking forward to meeting you."

That gave her pause. "She is?"

"Of course. I've told her all about you. And what a godsend you were when Lucas and I most needed help."

His words sent a bolt of pleasure through her center.

That was something, wasn't it? She may be here under less than truthful circumstances, but she was needed. Lucas appeared to be thriving now, his fussiness vastly reduced. Overall, he was a happy baby who appeared to perk up when he saw her or Enrique.

She liked to think she'd played a part in that improvement.

Still, the feeling of guilt gnawing at her was only continuing to grow.

# CHAPTER SEVEN

"WE'RE HERE," Enrique announced after about ninety minutes in the car. Lucas had drifted off to sleep, lulled by the ride.

The car turned onto a winding paved road that led them to a large, wrought-iron double gate. Fallon watched as a uniformed man stood up in a narrow booth behind the gate stand and gave them a small wave. Slowly, the two panels opened and the driver proceeded forward.

She wasn't sure what she'd been expecting but, just from what she could see from the car, the poshness of Enrique's flagship resort was breathtaking. Luxurious cabanas, marble bridges connecting blue water pools, dining areas and trendy-looking shops—all set against the backdrop of a sandy beach and sparkling ocean. The resort was like its own little town within a city. A paradise of a town at that.

And it was clearly a popular destination. People clad in everything from swimsuits to casual shorts to formal attire milled about. A group of about half a dozen children were kicking around a soccer ball on a patch of green grass.

"Wow." It was the best her brain could come up with.

"What do you think so far?" Enrique asked.

"I think this is as close to paradise on earth as is possible."

Enrique returned her words with that dazzling smile

of his. "Perfect. That's exactly the mood we're trying to accomplish."

"It's clearly working. The resort seems very popular, packed with visitors."

"It is. We have trouble keeping up with the booking requests. Hence my need to fly down here so suddenly. I'm trying to expand the accommodations with a new high-rise hotel as well as individual cabana cabins. But as I mentioned before, the expansion has not gone smoothly."

"I'm sorry about that."

He shrugged. "The nature of the business. But first thing first. Let's get to the villa and introduce this little one to his *gran abuela*."

That's right. Enrique didn't just live in a house next to his private resort, he owned a villa. How could she have forgotten? She really had somehow entered an entirely different universe than the one she knew.

The shops, cabanas and swimming pools soon gave way to a singular, narrow road. They traveled up a hill until the car finally came to a stop in front of a sprawling structure straight out of a storybook. The red brick hacienda-style building might have featured in one of the telenovelas Fallon occasionally came across while surfing channels, complete with a circular fountain in front and bendy palm trees along either side.

"Home sweet home," Enrique said, once the car had come to a complete stop. He unclicked the belt on Lucas's car seat and gently lifted his son out. What he called his home would be considered a palace by most of the world's population. Including her.

Did Sasha have any idea what her son was born into? What would her reaction be once she found out? There was no way to know anything about Sasha as long as she kept ghosting her. Fallon badly wanted to tell her about her son, about all of this. But her emails still went unanswered, no doubt going out into the nothingness of the cyber universe without Sasha so much as receiving them. Wherever she was.

"You seem to be a million miles away," Enrique said, pulling her out of her thoughts.

"Just taking it all in," she answered, resisting the urge to pull her smartphone out and check for any messages that might have come in. Not that she had any real hope there would be any.

"I'll give you a grand tour once we get this little one settled. After he meets his great-*abuela* and his *tio*."

"That would be lovely."

What would be really lovely was if the woman who'd actually given birth to Lucas was here to see this, to truly comprehend who her son was and the family he'd been born into.

But that would have meant Fallon herself would not be here. She might not have even met Enrique let alone started working for him.

And maybe that's how things should be.

*You don't belong here. You don't belong with us. I'm sorry, that's just how things are.*

Wow. Her aunt's voice hadn't surfaced in her mind for a good while now. Yet here it was again. Reminding her of all the ways she was out of place once more.

"Are you okay? You seem to have gone rather pale."

Fallon forced a relaxed smile on her lips. "I'm fine. Just a little jet-lagged, I think."

"Then I think I know how you should spend your afternoon once we've seen my grandmother and this little guy goes to sleep."

"How's that?"

"There is a world class spa at the resort. With master masseuses and skincare experts. I think you need a spa day."

That sounded like a luxurious indulgence she'd normally never be able to afford. She was more tempted than she wanted to admit. "That sounds like it would take longer than a five-and-a-half-month-old's afternoon nap. What about Lucas?"

"Between my grandmother and me, I think we can handle him. Besides, something tells me Abuela isn't going to want to part with him until they're both good and tired. He might actually sleep well into the night. They both might, for that matter."

There was that smile again. And the charming sparkle in his eyes. His aftershave subtly filled the car interior, invoking yearnings within her she had no business feeling.

"In fact, I insist you take me up on the spa day offer." He pulled out his phone and fired off a message before she could guess what he was doing. "I've notified them that they should expect you and to schedule you for the full treatment."

She didn't deserve this. Didn't deserve his kindness or his thoughtfulness. Once he learned the truth about who she was and why she was here, would he gift her with that dashing smile ever again?

The answer wasn't hard to guess.

*"Ay, mi bambino!"*

His grandmother's booming voice greeted them as soon as they exited the car. Enrique was relieved to see she was as sprightly as ever, despite her advancing age. Each time he went overseas, his concern for her grew that he might be away if she happened to need him. The woman had not only raised her own child, but she'd reared her daughter's two unwanted sons as well. She deserved to live out her later years in comfort and peace. And Enrique would do everything in his power to ensure she did just that.

His businesses took him away from home so often, he couldn't help but feel guilty about leaving her behind. Granted, there was a full regular staff of fifteen here at the hacienda as well as seasonal employees who returned yearly. A few whose job was to ensure Abuela was safe and taken care of. But he was blood. At least Luis was often home.

Of course, today there was a particular reason for the bounce in her step. She was about to meet her first great-grandchild. She barely acknowledged him and made a beeline straight for the baby he held in his arms. Cradling his small head in her wrinkled hands, she whispered to Lucas in Spanish. The baby was smart enough to recognize a loving soul and offered a toothless smile at her. Enrique could practically sense his grandmother's heart melting in her chest.

"May I take him?" she asked, her hands outstretched.

Remarkably, Lucas answered for him. He shifted himself toward Abuela as if he wanted to go to her. Beyond pleased, Enrique handed him over. The last time he'd seen his son react that way had been with Fallon that first day.

Fallon stood off to the side, watching the three of them. Her stance gave every indication that she was unsure what to do. For such a smart, accomplished woman, she could act quite uncertain at times.

Enrique waited a few moments while Abuela snuggled with her great-grandchild. Then he took Fallon by the shoulders and pulled her forward with him.

"Abuela, this is Fallon Duvall. She's the one who came to our rescue when we needed someone to help care for Lucas."

Fallon hesitantly stepped forward, her hand extended. Abuela ignored it, instead shifting the baby and using her free arm to pull Fallon into a three person embrace. *"Gracias, gracias. Tu eres una angel."*

Fallon recovered quickly from the clearly unexpected embrace. Then she surprised him by answering his grandmother in Spanish. *"De nada. Es un placer."*

Huh. He'd had no idea she was even trying to learn any Spanish. She gave him a small shrug when he shot an inquisitive glance in her direction.

"You are trying to learn Spanish?" Abuela asked her.

"Yes, I'd like to very much. I'm afraid I'm not very far with it yet," she added.

She hadn't shared that with him. The discovery sent a jolt of pleasure through his chest. She was already so ingrained in his life, the fact that she was trying to learn his mother tongue touched him deep within.

He studied her now, as she spoke to his grandmother while they both doted on his son. They were discussing the benefits of raising a child bilingual if possible. How it enriched their communication skills and opened up a world of opportunities.

Whatever had caused her shyness and hesitation earlier, Fallon had clearly gotten over it. Enrique was happy to see she'd relaxed. But Abuela had that effect on most people with her natural warmth and graciousness.

He didn't often bring women to the hacienda. And Fallon certainly wasn't any kind of date. For an insane moment, Enrique couldn't help where his mind wandered. Couldn't help wishing that things might have been different between them. It was pure fantasy, but how much more fitting it would be if Fallon was Lucas's mother. If they were embarking on parenting together.

If maybe they would be up to exploring what else might develop between them.

She looked right here, in his home. Like she belonged.

Like she belonged by his side. As more than just an employee.

What would be so wrong with that? Sure, it was risky. But so was any kind of personal involvement with another person. Would it be so wrong to try and get to know her?

Maybe it was wishful thinking. Maybe he was growing tired of not being in a meaningful relationship at his age. He was a father now. He had more than his own future to think about.

Lucas deserved to be brought up in a stable home with two loving parents. And by some inexplicable stroke of luck, Fallon seemed to love the baby deeply.

"Luis is away for several days on a university outing," his grandmother said, pulling him out of the rather surprising and probably ridiculous thoughts skittering through his head. The notion of he and Fallon becoming more personal was just that; ridiculous. Wasn't it?

She turned to Fallon. "He's a postgraduate student at Universidad de Cancun. Studying archaeology. They're always on some expedition or other," she explained in perfect English with a slight charming accent.

She turned to Enrique. "Speaking of which, his department is holding another one of their extravagant parties in two weeks to raise money. Of course, he expects you to be in attendance."

Enrique chuckled. "No doubt he also expects a generous donation and has probably already committed to one in my name."

"I'm almost positive he has. But he was absolutely insistent that you attend when he heard you'd be back in Mexico."

He nodded once. "I'll clear my calendar." Enrique worked to keep the begrudging groan out of his voice. He despised attending such events in general. At Luis's department galas, he often stood around munching on dry food and making small talk with people whose names he couldn't remember. While Luis spent the evening with friends, Enrique pretty much spent the evening by himself surrounded by strangers.

He glanced over to where Fallon stood. Maybe this time he didn't have to.

She'd forgotten what it was like to enter into a loving home. What it was like to be a part of a family unit where you felt you belonged, knowing the people within those walls loved you and always would. She'd only met Enrique's grandmother seconds ago, but she knew instantly and without a doubt that that's how Enrique had grown up in the care of this woman.

Perhaps she herself would never have that again.

But it warmed her soul to know that Lucas would grow up that way, just as his father had. No matter what Sasha ultimately ended up deciding about her part in Lucas's life, the boy would always have what Fallon was witnessing right now.

"What a lovely child," the older woman was saying now, dropping a light peck on Lucas's cheek. "You have done such a good job taking care of him, Señorita Duvall."

"I had a little something to do with it too, Abuela," Enrique said.

"Hmm," was his grandmother's only response.

Fallon chuckled at the exchange. "Please call me Fallon."

"Very well, then you must call me Rosa. Agreed?"

Fallon had the strong sense that she might agree with anything this woman said. She had such warmth and such an inviting spirit. It was easy to see where Enrique got his charm from. "Agreed, Rosa."

"*Bueno.* Now, you two must be so tired after such a long journey. Let's go inside and get some refreshments. I've had some chalupa prepared and a corn salad. Also, some refreshing *ponche.* Enrique's favorite." She bounced Lucas on her hip. "And maybe this little one can have a siesta, *sí?*"

She and Enrique followed Rosa inside, and Fallon did another double take once they entered the foyer. There was almost as much greenery inside the house as there was out. A red tiled floor and stucco walls topped by a high arched ceiling overhead. Across the doorway, a V-shaped stairway led to opposite sides of the house. Despite the grandeur and highly polished floor, the house lent an air of welcome and warmth.

"Let's eat on the terrace, shall we?" Rosa suggested. "It's such a beautiful day."

"I'm afraid I can't join you," Enrique announced, with a tight expression at his phone. "Word is out that I've arrived and I've already been called to a scheduled meeting with our workmen and suppliers."

Rosa reached over and patted his cheek with affection. "You work so hard. At least take a chalupa to go. We can wrap one up for you."

"Wouldn't turn that down, Abuela."

"I can do it, Señora Rosa." A petite brunette with blond streaks wearing a white uniform darted from around the corner as they entered the patio. The young woman's eyes were planted squarely on Enrique, loaded with adulation. She may as well have worn a neon sign on her chest that declared she had a major crush on him.

Fallon sighed at her eagerness to tend to him. She could certainly relate. She and this young employee had a lot in common. After all, that's pretty much what she was also— an employee who had the hots for her boss.

"*Gracias*, Maria," Rosa said.

Fallon thrust her hand out in Maria's direction to introduce herself. "Hi, I'm Fallon. I'll be working here too. I'm the baby's nanny."

Maria shook her hand with a smile, then got to work wrapping food for Enrique to take. Much to the young woman's clear disappointment, Enrique was still rather distracted by his phone and only offered a quick thanks before bidding them all goodbye then leaving.

Rosa had a cushy playpen set up for the baby with a slew of plush toys. She set him down gently and cradled a fluffy faux fur toy monkey against his side.

Fallon waited for Rosa to sit before taking a chair across from her at the wooden table. The other woman had referred to this as a patio, but the word didn't do the area justice. It was more a courtyard that overlooked a lush, green garden dotted with colorful plants and flowers and palm trees surrounding it all. Fallon could hear and smell the fresh air of the ocean in the distance.

"This is so beautiful out here."

Rosa began pouring from a frosty glass pitcher into two tall glasses. A bright red beverage with chunks of fruit and a cinnamon stick floating on top. It tasted like ambrosia when she took a sip.

Rosa gestured toward the garden. "It's how I spend most of my time now, tending to these flowers and plants. A fitting hobby for an old woman without the energy for much else."

Rosa appeared plenty energetic from what Fallon could see. And the beauty of this garden was more than the result of just a hobby. "I imagine it's a lot of work."

"Enrique does hire landscapers to help me, I must confess. The rest is a labor of love on my part."

"It's lovely," Fallon said, taking another sip of her drink.

"It occupies my time," she said, then glanced in the direction of the crib. "And now I have this precious *bambino* to occupy it as well."

"He is indeed precious," Fallon agreed.

"He looks so much like Enrique as a little boy."

A gentle warmth spread through Fallon as she thought of a younger Enrique, playing with the types of toys his son held.

Rosa's affectionate smile turned downward. "I do often wonder about the mother though. Enrique says he hasn't heard from her and wants to respect her obvious wish to remain anonymous. I do hope she's all right and safe wherever she is."

There it was. An opening. A segue of sorts. A confession suddenly materialized on the tip of her tongue. She could take this opportunity right here and right now to admit who she was and exactly who Lucas was to her. Rosa seemed so kind and genuine. Surely she'd be the understanding type, wouldn't she? Maybe Fallon should finally take the opportunity to get the truth off her chest and soften the blow from Enrique discovering it later.

No. Of course she couldn't do such a thing. How horribly unfair it would be of her to burden Rosa in that way. Fallon's cheeks reddened with shame that she'd even considered it for a moment.

Suddenly, the tasty food and fruity punch no longer held much appeal. She'd lost her appetite.

"I hope she's okay, too," she said through a dry mouth. Rosa had no idea just how much she meant it.

# CHAPTER EIGHT

THE BLASTED MEETING had gone much longer than he might have guessed. Enrique rubbed a palm down his face and strode through the patio and into the hacienda, making a mental note to go over the details he might have missed when his mind had wandered. As it often had. It didn't help that he was so distracted throughout that several points had to be repeated to him. His mind had kept wandering to Lucas and the way he was settling into his new surroundings. Luckily, the others in attendance had attributed his uncharacteristic attention deficit to jet lag.

*Right*, a voice in his head mocked. Lucas hadn't been the reason he'd been distracted. No, it had been the auburn-haired, doe-eyed nanny who was taking care of him who'd kept steering his focus away from business.

Enrique knew Lucas was being well taken care of. But how was she settling in? She seemed to be getting along very well with Abuela when he'd left earlier. He wasn't surprised. Fallon was charming and warm, characteristics his grandmother would have picked up on immediately. She often complained about the perils of getting older, but the woman was as sharp as she'd ever been.

He found Abuela exactly where'd he'd expected to find her. Puttering around in her garden.

"You're back, *hijo*," she said when she saw him.

"Finally." He glanced around. She was alone.

"Your son is down for his afternoon nap," she informed him.

"Great. That's great." He wanted to ask where Fallon was but didn't want to appear too anxious.

"I take everyone has been settling in okay, then?"

His grandmother tilted her head and gave him a knowing smile. He had no intention of asking exactly what she might think she knew. "Yes, they have."

He simply nodded.

"There's something I need to ask Fallon about."

Was it his imagination or did Abuela's eyes just brighten with merriment? "She is upstairs. I showed her to her suite after she fed the baby and he fell asleep."

"Great," he repeated like a stuttering fool. Why was she studying him like that? "Thank you for doing that. I guess I'll go find her, then see about settling in myself."

Another wide, knowing smile. "You do that, *hijo*."

Sometimes, he had to wonder if his grandmother was too sharp for his own good. He turned to leave then pivoted back around. She was still studying him, the smile still firmly in place.

"I promised her some time at the resort spa. I just want to see that she intends to take me up on it. She's been working really hard since coming on as Lucas's nanny," he said, not sure why he was trying to explain any of it. Of course, there was something else he wanted to ask Fallon about, but his grandmother didn't need to know that. In case she said no.

That thought had his chest tightening.

"Then you should absolutely see that she does," Abuela said.

"Right. I will."

When he made it upstairs, he checked in on Lucas in the nursery first. His son was sound asleep, clutching what appeared to be a fluffy dragon about the same size as he was.

Fallon's suite was the one adjacent. He knocked on her door and waited. No answer. Maybe she'd indulged in a nap herself. She could probably use it.

A wave of disappointment washed over him. He'd been looking forward to seeing her. To ask how she was adjusting to her new home. That was all. What kind of employer would he be if he didn't check on her the first afternoon?

He was about to give up and turn away when her door swung open. She clasped a hand to her chest at the sight of him. "Oh! I thought I heard a knock. I was listening to some instructional videos and wasn't sure."

"Instructional videos?"

She nodded. "Yes, about bringing children up in bilingual households. The best ways to go about it."

So even during her downtime she was still technically working. He wagged a finger at her. "You should be resting. You've had a lot thrown at you in the past week."

She gave a small shrug. "I want to be sure I know what I'm doing when it comes to Lucas. I'm learning a lot already." She paused to take a breath. "What can I do for you, Enrique?"

Now that was a loaded question. She'd changed into a pair of red shorts and sleeveless collared shirt a shade darker. Her feet were bare, revealing brightly painted toes. He was finding it difficult not to stare at those shapely legs so he kept his gaze firmly on her face.

"First of all, I'm here to make sure you take me up on the spa package. The technicians are waiting for you."

"Oh, I see." She glanced back over her shoulder in the

direction of the desk and the laptop sitting on it. Her expression clearly said she was torn.

"Lucas is sound asleep. I just checked on him. And if that changes, my grandmother has the baby monitor in her skirt pocket."

Fallon bit her bottom lip. "The massage cot is being heated to the ideal temperature as we speak," he said, a little verbal nudge.

A sigh escaped her lips. "A heated massage does sound rather lovely."

He stepped aside, motioned with his hand. "Then let's get going. I'll show you where the salon is. And you can see part of the resort as we walk."

He could sense her weakening resolve but still held his breath until she finally let out a breath and nodded. "Okay. You're on. Let me just get my shoes."

He'd managed not to gawk at her bare legs but couldn't help himself from admiring her shapely behind once her back was turned. Barefoot, she walked with the slightest sway to her hips.

Enrique cursed under his breath. He had to keep his thoughts about her platonic and tame if he was going to ask her what he wanted to as they walked to the spa. He couldn't be thinking about the shape of her bottom, or her golden tanned legs, or her pretty pink toes...

*Ay, Dio.* Enrique rubbed a palm down his face in frustration. Telling himself not to think about those things only had him doing just that.

They made small talk as they walked along the property to reach the resort border. Enrique pointed out the new double pool with the connecting bridge and told her how he was modeling the Cape Cod property along the same lines as this one. And then he could think of nothing else to say. Except to do what he planned and ask her about attending the university gala ball with him.

For the life of him, he couldn't seem to just come out and say it. Beyond frustrating. He'd asked countless women out before. There was one big difference here, though; he didn't have the same confidence that Fallon would actually accept.

It hit him all at once.

*Que sorpresa.* He was actually nervous! To ask a woman out on a date. And it wouldn't even be a real date! Her accompanying him was simply a matter of practicality. He just had to explain that to her and that would be that.

"Is there something on your mind, Enrique?" Fallon asked. Clearly the silence had gone on long enough that she'd noticed it.

He stopped strolling to face her. "In fact there is. I want to run something by you."

She lifted an eyebrow. "Oh? What is it?"

"You were there when Rosa mentioned that Luis attended the University of Cancun."

She nodded. "Yes. He's studying archaeology. This must be a particularly rich part of the world for that field."

"Right," he answered, hoping he didn't sound dismissive. But now that he'd begun, he wanted to plow forward and just get this over with. "You also heard that his department throws a fundraiser every year. A fancy ball where they serve dry appetizers and convince past benefactors to write bigger checks than they did last year. There's also music, speeches. All quite dull." Probably shouldn't have said that. He was about to try and convince her to go, after all. Hardly a good way to sell it.

"Sounds fancy," she said, a smile lifting the corners of

her mouth. "I can't wait to hear all about. I haven't been to many such parties. The ones I attend run more along the lines of pizza and cake."

"That's just it."

"What is?"

"You."

She gave her head a shake in confusion. Man, he was really making a mess of this. Why was he acting like some awkward teenager about to ask out his school crush?

"Me? What does any of that have to do with me?" Fallon asked.

"I'd like you to come with me." There, he'd said it. Or he'd blurted it out, would probably be more accurate. Judging from Fallon's expression, maybe that hadn't been the best approach.

She tilted her head, her eyebrows drawn together in confusion. "Me?" she repeated. "Why me?"

Enrique rubbed his fingertips along his forehead. He really was botching this. First of all, he probably should have asked her back at the hacienda rather than in front of a loud, crowded pool.

"These events are rather tedious. And I often find myself alone fending off unwanted conversations about the next big business deal I should be looking into." Or fending off the advances of the women in attendance when they thought their significant others weren't paying attention.

"But I don't understand. Why are you asking me? Instead of going through what I'm sure is an extensive contact list of women."

He wasn't sure what might have given her the impression that he kept such a list. He decided to let it go.

"This would simply be a platonic event. Just to have

a companion by my side to make it a bit more bearable. That's all."

Her lips tightened before she spoke. "Surely there must be other women who would jump at the chance to attend a fancy gala with you, Enrique. If a simple companion is all you're after."

Did that mean she wouldn't be one of such women?

He pinched the bridge of his nose, trying to come up with a way to answer that wasn't going to sound arrogant or muleheaded. "In the past, when I've asked acquaintances to events like these, there's been some misunderstandings." He cringed as he recalled the up-and-coming telenovela star who posted pictures of them all over her social media accounts throughout the entire night. The posts released a flood of gossip about "their budding relationship."

"Oh," Fallon said on a small chuckle. "I get it. It's simply easier to ask me then. No expectations or ambiguity."

He nodded with relief. She was indeed getting it then. "Exactly. Just an evening out so that I'm not bored to tears and/or swatting away unwanted conversations."

"I just don't think I'll fit in. What if I say or do something wrong? I don't want to embarrass you in any way."

"I have zero concerns that might happen."

She shook her head. "That makes one of us. I don't tend to mingle much with the type of people who donate to universities."

"I'll be there with you."

Her head tilted as she studied him. "What does that mean?"

"It means you'll fit in because you'll be my plus-one."

She crossed her arms in front of her chest, tapped her

toe. Enrique wasn't quite sure what to make of the action. "What about Lucas?"

Of course, he should have led with that particular concern. "This will be fairly late at night. I can't imagine he'd still be awake. If so, Abuela is there, and Maria is scheduled to work Saturday evenings."

She looked off to the side.

He pressed. "Who knows, you might even enjoy yourself."

She looked quite skeptical on that score.

"Yours are the tensest shoulders I have ever worked on."

The accented feminine voice lamenting about her muscles belonged to the masseuse currently kneading her skin like a mound of dough. Ilga, who was here on a work visa from Sweden. Somehow, she was strong yet gentle at the same time.

"Sorry, I've just come off a rather vexing conversation."

Given just how luxuriously she was being pampered, Fallon was having an incredibly hard time relaxing. Enrique wanted her to attend some fancy party with him.

"Ack!" Ilga hmphed above her. "You've somehow gone even tighter just now."

Fallon closed her eyes and inhaled deeply the lavender infused air. Ilga squeezed some more heated lotion on her back and she tried to loosen the muscles she rubbed. Easier said than done. It would be a much easier task if she could just get Enrique's voice out of her head.

Of all the ways she'd been asked out by men in the past, she could hardly think of a time when she'd felt less flattered. But that was just it. He wasn't actually asking her out. He just wanted someone to be there with him. A body. Nothing more.

And why in the world did she find that disappointing in any way? On the surface, everything he'd said was logical and sensible. He didn't want to attend the party alone. And he didn't want to ask a woman who might entertain any romantic thoughts about his invite. Clearly, he expected her to do no such thing.

So why was she doing just that? Why was she imagining how it might have felt to have him really ask her out? If he'd wanted to walk into that ballroom with Fallon on his arm simply because she was the only one he wanted to be there with.

"Do you want to talk about this conversation that has you tense as a brick wall?" Ilga asked, sounding exasperated.

"I don't think that will help, honestly."

"Then you should try and forget about it. At least for now."

Ha! As if she could do that. She still owed Enrique an answer, telling him she'd think about it. As if she'd be able to think about anything else.

"Maybe we'll try some music," Ilga said, walking to the other side of the room. A moment later, a slow, soft melody began to play. Fallon took another deep breath and tried to focus on the soothing song.

"That's a little better," Ilga said, resuming her kneading of Fallon's shoulders. "Let's try to keep it this way, can we?"

"I'll try."

"I have to admit," Ilga said, "I find myself very curious about what has you so…out of sorts during what should be a relaxing massage."

Fallon puffed out a breath of air. "I just have a decision to make and I'm having difficulty deciding."

"I see. The best approach would be to weigh the benefits and cons, then. Look at the question from all angles. Yes?"

Right. She could do that. Were all massage therapists this wise?

On the one hand, it was only one evening. He really wasn't asking for all that much. But there were so many other hands, so to speak. For one, she really was concerned about how she might come across to such a group of people. Unlike Enrique who seemed to think she'd fit in fine, she wasn't nearly as secure. What if she said or did something inappropriate? Like use the wrong fork?

What if someone asked her about her background or family?

People at this kind of event could never understand how awkward and uncomfortable it felt to talk about having grown up in foster care. They couldn't relate to wearing secondhand clothes or going days eating nothing but crackers because there never seemed to be enough food to go around.

The dry appetizers Enrique complained about being served would have probably felt like a feast for her and her foster siblings all those years ago.

Then there were the practical issues. She was absolutely certain she didn't have anything remotely appropriate in her closet for such an event. What would she even wear?

She must have mumbled the question out loud because Ilga actually answered her. "I think, with your coloring, you should wear something red. Burgundy or a rich wine color."

Huh. That was actually helpful.

"There's three specialty boutiques on the resort," Ilga added.

Too bad there wasn't a thrift store. Because she definitely couldn't afford any kind of boutique. Let alone a specialty one on a world class resort.

"Thanks, Ilga," she said.

Another errant thought hit her. What if there was dancing at this party? She had no idea how to dance. Unless it was in a downtown Boston club. She didn't know any kind of a waltz or a foxtrot or…she couldn't even name any other dances. There was no way she was going to dance.

"Are you sure?" Ilga asked. "Dancing is fun," she declared, digging her elbow under Fallon's shoulder blade.

She must have been more relaxed than she realized, considering how she kept speaking her thoughts out loud.

"Sure, if you know how," she said through a labored breath, given the sharp elbow digging into her back.

"I bet you could learn."

Fallon was really starting to like Ilga. And not just because the woman seemed to have magic hands. Her muscles really were beginning to feel rubbery and loose in a very pleasant way. She'd had no idea just how tense and stiff her whole body had become caring for a baby every day.

She didn't plan on admitting it to him, but Enrique had been right. The spa visit was doing her a world of good. Once again, just like back on the Cape with the aerial simulation visit, he'd been considerate enough to arrange something special for her.

She could at least seriously consider granting his ask about attending the fundraiser.

# CHAPTER NINE

FALLON HAD TO be back by now.

Enrique knew he shouldn't go seek her out. But trying to get any work done was proving futile. He wanted to hear how her spa treatments went. Also, what she thought about what she'd seen of the resort so far.

And he wanted to know if she'd given any more consideration to attending Luis's fundraiser with him.

Funny, really, he couldn't ever recall being this distracted before. Working was typically his refuge. Hours would often go by without him even noticing the passage of time when he was at his desk. He might have blamed fatherhood. But knew that wasn't an excuse.

He just couldn't seem to get Fallon out of his mind.

Another glance at the laptop screen in front of him told him it was no use. He stood up and closed the cover in frustration. He just couldn't bring himself to stare at the spreadsheet any longer.

He needed a stroll.

And if he happened to come upon a pretty nanny along his wandering, well then so be it.

He walked out of his study and strolled along the hall. Both Fallon's suite and the nursery doors were wide open with no one inside. Enrique made his way down the stairs and to the kitchen first. Empty. Grabbing an apple from the large fruit bowl in the center of the table, he tossed it in the air before taking a bite. He'd try the sitting area next.

He could hear Abuela's voice as he got closer, followed by several other gushing and cooing female voices. Sounded like his grandmother had some friends over and was showing off the baby. He pivoted away before they were aware he was nearby and could try and snag him for what could be an hour of dull conversation.

Fresh air. That's what he needed. The sun was just about ready to set, his favorite time of day. He'd grown tired of the apple by the time he made it to the patio door and tossed in a nearby bin before he strode outside to the patio.

And there she was.

Fallon sat reclined on a cushioned wicker chair in the corner, facing the house with her back to the garden, a paperback propped open in her hands. The title told him it was a book on infant development.

She looked up when she saw him, and the smile she sent him had a fluttering sensation gliding within his chest.

He walked over to the matching seat next to her, and she closed the book and set it down on the glass table between the chairs. "I see you found your way back okay."

"Yes, the walk back to the hacienda from the resort was almost as therapeutic as the spa treatments."

Good to hear. She'd enjoyed the massage and other services he'd had set up for her. Enrique studied her from the side. Her skin had taken on a golden glow; her cheeks were slightly red. He imagined that's how she might look after an amorous night spent with a man.

*Do not go there.*

He shoved the thought away before it could take further root in his mind. Dangerous territory. The images alone might have him tempted to take her by the hand and ask her to follow him upstairs.

"So you enjoyed the massage and the rest then?"

She nodded emphatically. "Ilga was lovely. A real magician with her hands."

He could make some magic happen with his hands too if she was so inclined.

*Just stop!*

"A girl could get used to such treatments," she said.

"Then plan on having them regularly." She was clearly much more relaxed. A regular massage was the least she deserved given how hard she worked.

"Oh, no," she immediately replied. "I couldn't do that."

"Why not? You can consider it part of your benefit package as an employee." Enrique had to pause on the last word. Calling her that no longer felt right. She was so much more now. Exactly what, he couldn't quite define just yet. "As you can see, Abuela is happy to spend time with the baby if you want to head to the spa for a few hours each week."

"The baby is with your grandmother now," Fallon said, effectively changing the subject. Why was the woman so hesitant to indulge herself? It was as if she wanted to deny herself any pleasure. "She has some friends over and wanted them to meet Lucas," she added.

"I heard. We'll have to bathe him a bit longer this evening."

She tilted her head in question. "Why is that?"

"My son is going to smell like four different varieties of women's perfume by the time the visit is over."

She chuckled. "He's also going to be rather exhausted. They're taking turns holding him and playing with him."

"I'm guessing the ladies are going to be rather tired as

well. There was quite a commotion of laughter and cooing when I walked by."

Fallon laughed again. "Maybe they'll all need naps after."

He returned her laughter. "They just might."

"I don't know how to dance," she blurted out suddenly.
Enrique felt completely thrown off by the rather random
change in conversation. Had he heard her right?

"I beg your pardon?"

Fallon leaned her head against the back of the chair,
blew out a deep breath as she stared at the sky.

"If I go to this fundraiser with you, if there's any kind
of formal dancing involved, I'm afraid I don't know how."

Enrique couldn't help the laughter that rumbled from
his chest. The woman really was something else, unlike
anyone he'd ever met. She was actually nervous about how
she might dance at a benefit gala.

"You're laughing, but it's the truth."

Enrique turned in his seat to look at her. She was bit-
ing her bottom lip, her fingers tight around the binding
of the book she held.

"Well, there is typically an orchestra and a dance floor,
but you absolutely need not dance if you do not want to."

Her shoulders actually sagged in relief. "Phew. That's
good. Really good."

Enrique resisted the urge to do a fist bump in the air.
She hadn't exactly come out and said yes to accompanying him to the fundraiser.

But it certainly seemed implied.


Well, that was at least one less thing to stress about. If she
were to accept Enrique's invite, at least he knew not to expect her on the dance floor.

"I think you'd be good at it, though," Enrique said.

Leaning back in his chair with his ankle propped on the opposite knee, he looked relaxed and fully at ease. He'd undone the top three buttons of his shirt, revealing a triangle of hard chest muscle. The man was such a specimen of good looks and allure. To think, she'd be spending the evening with him as his date.

Well, not really. He'd made sure to tell her it wasn't to be a real date at all. He'd made that abundantly clear.

And when exactly had she actually decided?

"If you gave it a try," he added.

What was he referring to? It was so hard to focus with him sitting across from her with his shirt partially undone, smelling the way he did, looking at her so intensely.

"Good at what?" she asked.

His lips twitched with mirth. "Dancing, of course. The topic at hand."

Right! How could she be so out of it? "Maybe. I'm not sure a fundraiser would be the best time to find out."

"Let's find out now, then," he said. To her consternation, he then stood and extended his arm out to her.

He couldn't be serious. "What, here?"

He nodded once. "Why not?" He pulled his phone out of his pocket and clicked on the screen. Soon the notes of classical music sounded from the small speaker.

Fallon hesitated, staring at him.

He wagged the fingers of his outstretched hand in an inviting gesture and flashed her a mischievous smile. "Come on, just give it a try. What do you have to lose?"

What a loaded question. She couldn't remember the last time she'd danced with a man. Or when she'd been held by one for that matter.

"You're overthinking this," he told her with a tilt of his head.

He was right. He was only asking to show her how to dance. A completely innocent gesture. At the least, it would give her a chance to prove that any such effort would be futile.

Fallon took his outstretched hand and stood. "All right. But I have to emphasize that I'm clumsy and have two left feet."

He merely chuckled at that.

"Now," he began, "I'll lead so all you really have to do is follow me. Just in the opposite direction."

"Got it," she answered, stepping into his embrace. His free arm went around her waist and her breath hitched in her throat. Would that distinctive scent of his ever cease to make her dizzy?

Enrique took two steps forward and then a few backward. Fallon did her best to follow without stepping over his toes. But it was so hard to focus on what her feet were doing with Enrique up against her length. The warmth of his body sent waves of heat along her skin, his breath hot on her cheek, the scent of him filling her senses.

She didn't dare risk a glance up at him. No doubt he'd be able to read her tumultuous emotions all over her face.

"You're doing great," he assured her.

"If you say so," she managed to answer through lips that had suddenly gone dry.

He continued to lead her, staying in step with the music coming from his phone while Fallon continued to stare steadfastly at her own feet, willing the song to end already.

Enrique had been so very wrong earlier. She hadn't been overthinking this at all. If anything, she should have thought long enough to realize what a bad idea it was. Did she honestly think she wouldn't be affected after stepping into his arms and having him hold her?

She missed a step and managed to recover with Enrique's gentle nudge against the small of her back. One...
two...three...

Had he chosen the extended version of the melody? This
was turning into an exercise in sweet torture.

It was only a matter of time before she stumbled again.
Fallon's mind barely registered that her toe had caught
on one of the brick tiles of the patio floor when she went
tumbling forward, straight into Enrique's chest. Her urgency to pull away only made things worse, and she further lost her balance.

A pair of strong arms instantly gripped her like a vise
around her center, managing to keep her upright. The problem was, Enrique was the only thing keeping her up.

Fallon knew she should try to pull away again, but
couldn't seem to do it. She felt so right to be in his arms,
with his warmth surrounding her as he held her tight.

He'd kept her from falling. But she was falling in another, much more dangerous way.

She was only stumbling because she was clearly so tense.
Why? She couldn't be that concerned about her dancing
skills.

"I'm so sorry," she said abjectly against his chest. "I
tried to tell you I'm rather clumsy with two left feet."

He'd never noticed any hint of clumsiness in her. Well,
not until now. So why had she made such an admission
so emphatically? Someone must have done a number on
her somewhere in her past. Given her the impression that
she was a klutz. A wave of anger washed over him. That
anyone would have put her down so carelessly, hampered
her self-confidence.

"Nonsense," he replied. "You just need to relax. Think

of how you felt after the massage earlier. How loose your muscles were. Try and regain that sensation. You'll be less prone to missteps the more at ease you are."

"I'll try," she answered, hesitant and uncertain. He began the count again.

They managed a few more strides than the last time when she took a step that was too big and her foot landed on his and he had to catch her again. Her cheek collided with his chest, her head under his chin.

Enrique wasn't even sure what happened next. One moment she started looking up at him with yet another apology on her lips, the next their mouths were less than a centimeter apart. The rush of desire hit him like a punch in the gut. The scent of her under his nose, the heat lighting up her eyes, her breathless pants. He could take no more. It was all too tempting. He had to taste her.

"Fallon?" Her name left his lips on a whisper.

"Yes," was her soft reply.

And then he gave in. With an urgency that shocked him, he pressed his lips against hers, relishing the feel of her mouth on his. The gentlest of a nudge and then she was opening to him, welcoming his kiss to deepen. He didn't hesitate to take her up on the invitation. The taste of her was like an ambrosia he'd never get enough of. The feel of her against his length sent pulse waves of desire throughout his core and moved lower.

Nothing else existed in the moment but his desire for her. And her reaction told him her longing for him was just as strong.

He'd known, hadn't he? On some level he'd always anticipated this exact scenario would happen. Deep in his gut he'd acknowledged that at some point they'd be in this very position. With Fallon in his arms and his lips against hers. Maybe he'd known it the very first day he'd laid eyes on her.

So one would think he'd be better prepared for the reactions coursing through his body. He had half a mind to lift her up and carry her upstairs to his suite of rooms. The way she was kissing him back right now, he knew without a doubt that Fallon would be willing. They could worry about the consequences later.

His assumption was confirmed when she ran her hands up along his arms to his shoulders and moaned against his mouth. Enrique lost the ability to breathe at her roaming touch. Instinctively, he pulled her tighter against him, showing her the vast strength of his desire.

At this rate, if he wanted to act on his desires, they might not even make it upstairs. Her hand moved along his shoulders until she reached the nape of his neck and she thrust her hands through his curls.

That was it. He had to know. He had to ask her if she was ready to find a more private spot to take things further. To finally give in to what they both so clearly wanted.

He was about to do just that when a commotion of voices echoed from down the hallway. His mind barely registered enough to identify the sound.

Abuela. Along with the friends she had visiting. They were making their way to the patio and drawing perilously close to walking in on him and Fallon. And what a scene they would encounter if that happened.

With a reluctance that was almost painful, Enrique made himself pull away from Fallon with a gentle nudge so that they might both take a step back. The confusion and desire behind her eyes and the way she rubbed her lips nearly had him reaching for her again, damn the consequences if they were to be seen.

"Oh...my..." she whispered before her eyes grew wide as she noticed the approaching intruders as well. Her cheeks, already blushed pink, turned crimson. Clasping her hand to her mouth, she whirled to face away from him.

Abuela and her friends entered the patio a moment later. The babyish sound of his son's cooing could be heard among the noise. He and Fallon had been mere seconds away from being discovered in each other's embrace.

How careless. How utterly impulsive of him. Fallon was new here in his home. She'd only just met his grandmother. She certainly didn't know Abuela's friends. She didn't need the kind of talk that would be triggered if she were to be caught being thoroughly and passionately kissed by her boss. The fuel that would throw on the all too ready gossip mill was immeasurable.

And what was he thinking anyway? He couldn't be giving in to his whims like some hormonal teenager, no matter how strong they were. Fallon was here as a professional to care for his son. He couldn't do anything to jeopardize the stability and affection she provided as Lucas's nanny. He couldn't risk losing her. Neither could Lucas.

As much as he wanted her, and as much as Fallon seemed to reciprocate that desire, he had to keep his hands to himself.

Fallon still had her back turned to him as the ladies strode over to where they stood. When she finally turned, she stepped right past him and over to where Abuela stood with Lucas in her arms. The baby immediately began squirming and leaning toward Fallon when he saw her, a toothless smile on his face.

His choices were clear. His wants and desires would have to take a back seat to his son's well-being.

# CHAPTER TEN

"SO, WHEN I move forward, you would move back," Fallon said to the baby as she gently twirled slowly in a circle, holding Lucas against her chest. "Well, you would if your legs reached the ground, that is."

Lucas's response was to stick his tongue out and gurgle. As far as partners to practice dancing with over the last few days, she figured she could do worse. Though, Lucas was no match for his father.

Enrique. Fallon's lips tingled as they did every time she thought of him since. She'd had to keep averting her eyes from the spot where he'd held her and kissed her whenever she'd made her way out to the garden with Lucas. As if any amount of avoidance was going to get that kiss out of her head anytime soon.

Still, the fresh air and sunshine and being surrounded by lush greenery served to help to clear her head and unjumble her thoughts. The kiss was a momentary lapse in judgment. It could never happen again. She would make sure of it.

It should have never happened in the first place. Fallon should have never succumbed to her desire and returned his kiss the way she had. As for Enrique, she was aware that he regretted losing control as he had. It had been written all over his face when his *abuela* had come upon them with her friends, and she'd hardly seen him since.

Heat rushed to her face as she thought about how close they'd come to being discovered in such a state. Fallon would have been horrified. So the small twinge of hurt in her chest at the way Enrique had swiftly broken their kiss and nudged her away was absolutely ridiculous. If anything, she should be thankful for his quick reflexes when she herself hadn't even heard the others approaching.

He was her employer. She had no business being attracted to him. This wasn't some type of Valentine's romantic movie of the week. Or her own version of *The Sound of Music*.

Giving her head a brisk shake to push away the images, she continued moving through the garden, holding Lucas and mimicking the dance steps Enrique had shown her.

She'd racked her brain each night, trying to figure out if she should find some way to back out of going to the fundraiser with him. The evening was sure to be tense, with the specter of their kiss hanging awkwardly between them. But she'd already committed to being Enrique's "date." It would be untoward of her to back out now.

"I think I can guess which one of you is leading." The masculine voice came from behind her and startled Fallon out of her thoughts. She panicked for an instant before realizing that, although similar, the voice didn't belong to Enrique.

She turned to find a lean, dark-haired young man striding toward her, a wide and charming smile on his face. He had the same sharp, dark features Enrique did. But his were less angular somehow, with a softness to his mouth and eyes that Enrique lacked. Still, the family resemblance was as clear as the morning sky.

"You must be Fallon," he said when he reached her side, his smile growing wider.

She nodded. "And you must be Luis."

*"Sí, es mi,"* he said, his gaze falling to Lucas. "And this must be my handsome nephew," he added, running an affectionate finger along the baby's cheek. Lucas's response was a messy sneeze in his uncle's face.

Luis chuckled as he wiped his cheek with the back of his hand. "Is that any way to greet your uncle upon our first meeting?" He gave the baby a gentle tickle on his tummy. Lucas let out a giggle and pumped his legs.

"May I?" Luis asked, and held his hands out toward the baby.

Fallon handed him over and watched as the baby placed his little hands on his uncle's cheek and continued giggling at him. Warmth spread over her chest at the sight. Yet another image to show just how loved Lucas would be throughout his life. Another blood relative who would care about him and look out for him. She couldn't have asked for more for the baby.

"You're starting him with the dance lessons early, huh?" Luis asked, his affection for the nephew he'd just met clear in his eyes.

She ducked her head in embarrassment. What a sight she must have made, dancing around Rosa's garden to imaginary music with her charge. At least it hadn't been Enrique who'd walked in on it. "That was more for my benefit. In case there's any dancing that I can't avoid at your university's event next Saturday."

"Ah, yes. I'd heard you were the saint kind enough to accompany my brother this year. Maybe he'll be less surly this time having you with him." He bowed, ever so slightly, lowering the baby before straightening again. "My deepest, sincerest thanks."

Well, that settled it then, didn't it? If she backed out of attending now, she'd be disappointing not just one but two Martinez men.

"Uh, you're welcome? I guess?"

"I'm hoping he won't behave the way he normally does when he's there if you're with him."

"And how is that?" Fallon asked.

"The man checks his watch about a hundred times during the evening, looking miserable and completely put-upon. Which, of course, in reality he is."

"I heard that." The three words came from a booming masculine voice sounding from the direction of the patio. This time, there was no mistaking the source. Enrique.

Fallon's heart did a giant leap in her chest as he approached the three of them.

Luis didn't bother to turn Enrique's way when he answered. "You heard the truth, *mi hermano*." He shot Fallon a playful wink before finally turning to his brother.

"I see you met your nephew," Enrique announced when he reached their side. "And Fallon." He gave her the slightest nod in acknowledgment, without a hint of anything out of the ordinary. As if his lips hadn't been plastered against hers only a few days ago.

*"Sí,"* Luis answered. "And I was just about to remark to Fallon how lucky this little man is."

Enrique reached for his son and cupped his palm around his small head. "Yeah? How's that?"

"Well, he doesn't appear to look like you very much. Thank heavens."

"You need to work on your insults, little brother. That was a rather lame one."

The teasing banter brought a smile to Fallon's lips, despite the rapid pounding of her heart at seeing Enrique.

Enrique hadn't missed the flirtatious wink his brother had sent Fallon upon his approach. Not that surprising. It was second nature for Luis to flirt. His brother had never been one to hold back the charm. Particularly when it came to an attractive woman like Fallon. So why was it bothering Enrique more than usual. Why did he have the sudden urge to wrestle his brother to the ground and give him a good throttle the way he had wanted to when they were kids?

It also wasn't surprising that Luis had been slighting him to Fallon when he'd walked out to the garden. Enrique didn't often miss an opportunity to taunt his brother. Luis gave as good as he received. But did he have to make Enrique sound like such a curmudgeon too? He didn't behave that badly at those blasted fundraisers, did he?

When had Luis returned home anyway?

Enrique had spent most of the morning trying to figure out what exactly he would say to Fallon so that they could get past that ill-conceived kiss. He couldn't just keep avoiding her. When he'd finally summoned to courage to seek her out and do so, Luis was there with her, thwarting his plans.

Not that he'd had the slightest idea exactly what he would say to her. Maybe Luis had done him a favor. His appearing back home at this particular moment might prove to be a welcome distraction. Then he and Fallon wouldn't even have to discuss what had happened between them. They could both simply let it go as…well, as one of those things. The less made of it, the better.

Plus he had to acknowledge, it was good to see his sibling again after so many weeks in the States. They spoke on the phone whenever they had the chance to. But long-distance conversations didn't prevent Enrique from missing his only sibling. Not that he would ever admit any of that to Luis.

Fallon hadn't said a word since he'd arrived.

He glanced at her now. She seemed to be directing her smiles to him and Luis in turn. Though she wasn't quite meeting his eyes. Luis seemed oblivious to any tension that may be in the air. So clearly they were both hiding it well. As well they should. They were both mature adults who'd just gotten carried away.

"So, what does this little man have planned for today?" Enrique asked by way of conversation.

Fallon pointed to Luis and the baby. "Well, I figure I'll let these two get acquainted for a bit. They seem to really be enjoying each other's company."

Luis gave his nephew a bounce resulting in a squeal of delight. "I'd like that," he said. "Lucas seems to be a cool little dude. I wouldn't mind spending some time with him. But only until he looks like he might begin to cry," he said in a solemn tone, his features growing serious.

Fallon gave him a mock salute. "Understood. I will stay close by to intervene ASAP at the first sign of fussiness."

"On whose part?" Enrique asked dryly. "From Luis or the baby?"

"Either or," came Fallon's quick reply.

"Very funny, bro," Luis said with a grin. "I think I'll go hang with my nephew one on one for a while," Luis said before reaching for Fallon's hand with his free one then bringing it to his lips for a small kiss. "Pleasure to make your acquaintance," he said, fluttering his eyes in such a dramatic way, it had to be intentionally comical. "I look forward to seeing you in a fancy ball gown. I'm sure you will wear it well," he added before walking to the patio and settling into the wooden swing with the baby. He bounced Lucas on his knee while swinging him back and forth.

Enrique felt his midsection tighten. It was one thing to flirt but kissing Fallon's hand followed by the comment about what she might wear was a bit much. He would have to speak to him about conducting himself better around his son's nanny.

The hypocrisy of that thought wasn't lost on him.

"Why do I get the feeling Luis is going to be the type of uncle who spoils his nephew rotten every chance he gets?" Fallon asked, her gaze fixated on where Luis and the baby sat.

"Leaving us to deal with the aftereffects."

Fallon's smile faltered slightly. The "us" hung heavily in the air. "You've read my brother well," Enrique added, to move the conversation forward past the awkwardness.

Easier said than done. Fallon still hadn't quite met his eyes.

"Uh, speaking of the dress," she began after several heavy moments of silence. Her voice sounded tight, troubled. "I'm not quite sure exactly how I'm supposed to be attired at this thing. And I fear I haven't packed anything that may be appropriate."

Enrique wanted to kick himself. He'd been totally remiss about making sure she felt ready for the fundraiser.

"Think nothing more of it," he told her. "I will have a stylist from our premier boutique bring over an array of choices. You may pick whichever one you like."

Her hands and lips grew tighter. "I don't think I can afford that, Enrique. As well as you pay me, I still have school loans I'm responsible for and other debts that take a good chunk of my earnings each month."

The woman was quite remarkable. She actually thought he would make her pay for a dress she needed for an event she was only attending as a favor to him.

He knew better than to try to persuade her to accept the dress as a gift from him. He may have only met her recently, but he knew Fallon well enough that she would steadfastly refuse any such giveaway.

"The merchandise in all the resort shops are my assets. Consider it a loan that you will be returning."

She looked ready to argue but Enrique held up a hand to stop her. "I insist."

He didn't give her a chance to say any more, knowing she was sure to try and turn down his offer.

He had no intention of letting her.

Dearest Sasha
It's been several weeks now. I'm worried about you still.

Fallon's fingers stalled over the keyboard, unsure what to say next. Or even if what she'd already written was worth sending. What was the use, really? The emails were clearly not being read. For all she knew, Sasha was holed up in some shelter or some kind of medical center without access to any kind of technology.

Or she was in an even worse predicament. That thought had tears stinging her eyes and she shut the laptop cover without trying to write any more.

As difficult as it was, she had to remain positive. Sasha was a fighter who knew how to take care of herself. Her friend had to be fine. She had a little boy to see again someday.

A faint knock sounded on her door, pulling her out of her erratic thoughts. Fallon rose from the desk and took a deep breath before getting up to answer it. A petite blonde woman stood on the other side. Her hair was done up in a complicated bun at the top of her head, and she wore a simple beige wraparound dress that showcased her hourglass figure.

Such a simple outfit. But this woman looked like the most stylish person Fallon had ever laid eyes on.

"I'm Tiffany," she announced, reaching out a slender glossy manicured hand. "I'm the new stylist from the Debutante Boutique. We have an appointment?"

Well, that made sense. If anyone fit the image of a fashionable stylist, it was this woman. Though she'd be equally fitting on a walkway modeling haute couture.

"Yes, please come in," Fallon said, opening the door wider and stepping to the side.

Tiffany wasn't alone. Two men also entered the room, each pulling two long clothing racks behind them. Yet a third wheeled in a large wooden chest. Depositing it all in the center of the room, they gave both ladies a friendly nod before leaving.

Tiffany pulled the chest over and opened it, turning it into accordion-style shelves with shoes and accessories. Fallon's room had become a fashionable women's store in the blink of an eye.

"Where would you like to start?" Tiffany asked.

Fallon had no idea. Most of her clothes were purchased from local thrift stores, and she'd certainly never had the need to buy anything more than slacks and tops for work, with the occasional overcoat for the harsh New England winters. She owned all of three dresses for the occasional school function.

"You have a lovely neckline," Tiffany declared, stepping closer. "May I?" she asked.

May she what? Fallon didn't know but nodded anyway. The woman cupped her chin and lifted her head, studying her.

"I'm thinking a low plunging high waisted number. In red. Yes, I think that's your color."

Huh. That's what Ilga the massage therapist had said too. Fallon had no idea she'd even had a color.

Tiffany pulled a bright crimson red dress off one of the racks. "Let's start with this one." She laid the garment on the bed and made a motion with her hands in Fallon's direction, signaling her to disrobe.

Growing up in various foster homes, this wouldn't be the first time she'd been in the company of another female in only her bra and panties. She'd had to share a room with at least one other girl at all times. Making fast work of changing, she turned to look in the mirror. And her breath caught in her throat. She hardly recognized herself. Even without her hair and makeup done and nothing but sandals on her feet, the dress made her feel like Cinderella.

"*Oui*, it is quite breathtaking," Tiffany said. "I believe your husband will thinks so too."

Fallon clasped a hand to her mouth. "Oh! He's not— I mean, I'm not—" She took a deep breath before continuing. "I'm just the nanny," she explained. "I need a dress for something of a work function."

"Dresses like these? For a work function, huh?"

"Yes, I'll just be there to fill a seat, really."

Tiffany shrugged one elegant shoulder. "So terribly sorry, then," she said, though she hardly looked bothered. Fallon got the impression that not much bothered this woman. She exuded self-confidence in waves. Fallon couldn't help but feel envious. She couldn't recall a time she'd ever been that sure of herself.

"I just started at the boutique. I'm new in Tulum," Tiffany informed her. "Still getting to know everyone."

"Me too." Sadly, that was probably the only thing she had in common with this stylish, secure woman who, judging by her accent, must have spent some time in Paris. Someone like Tiffany was much more likely to be married to a man like Enrique.

She may feel like Cinderella at the moment, but the notion that Enrique might be her husband was indeed a genuine fairy tale.

He felt like a teenager on the day of the prom. Enrique glanced at his watch again, barely listening to his project manager on the other end of the line. He'd actually been counting the hours all day. How ironic; he usually dreaded this event. But now he was incredulously waiting with bated breath for it to start.

But his anticipation had nothing to do with the fundraiser itself. It had everything to do with Fallon.

And wasn't that a sorry state of affairs?

He seemed to feel more and more drawn to her with each passing day. He could no longer deny it. Did he even want to?

Two hours later, he was showered and shaved. When the time finally came to get Fallon and be on their way, he practically bounded up the stairs to knock on her door.

The world stopped short once she opened it. His mouth went dry at the sight of her. She was a vision out of a storybook or some kind of movie. Enrique liked to think of himself as a worldly man. He'd had his share of romantic encounters and might have even considered himself falling for a woman once or twice. It took a lot to take Enrique's breath away. But the Fallon before him indeed left him breathless.

*"Ay, mi Dio..."* The words escaped his lips before he could help himself.

Fallon's eyes grew wide and she rubbed a hand down her midsection. "Is that good? Will this work? I can quickly change, if not."

She had no idea just how well it was all working. Her hair fell in luxurious waves over her shoulders. The dress fit her like a glove, hugging her curves in all the right places. And the color. He wondered if there was any way to mandate that she wear that shade of fiery red at all times.

"It's good," he answered when he finally found his voice, thinking what an understatement that was.

# CHAPTER ELEVEN

ALL THE NOTABLES were here.

Enrique scanned the ballroom to find the usual impressive crowd. Some of the continent's most influential and successful entrepreneurs and businesspeople. A few politicians. Fallon stood rod stiff next to him, her grip on his forearm vise tight. He wished he could get her to relax. Though part of him understood. She was in a new environment for her. Both foreign and unfamiliar. It wasn't all that long ago that he himself would have felt out of place at such a soiree. Not long enough that he'd completely forgotten.

Fallon was breathtaking. And those around them were starting to notice. More than a few heads turned in their direction as they walked in. Appreciative male glances landed on Fallon and lingered before catching Enrique's glare.

Not that he could really blame the gentlemen, as well as several ladies, who seemed to be staring. Fallon was the most striking woman here. Though perhaps he was a bit biased about his date.

He'd had to fight the urge during the drive over to redirect the chauffeur. The temptation to instruct the man to drive right past the venue and instead take them somewhere private where they could enjoy a real dinner and each other's company was nearly overwhelming. Then they would have been able to see where the evening might lead, and damn the consequences.

Common sense had prevailed and he'd resisted. But it had been close.

He stole a glance at her now as they moved farther into the ballroom. Despite the fact that she was clearly nervous, she appeared to be glowing. The auburn streaks in her hair shone under the yellow-hued mini chandeliers hanging from the ceiling. She wore nothing but simple gold earrings in the way of jewelry, yet her neck bare was magnificently showcased over the low neckline of her dress. A slit in her skirt showed off just enough shapely leg to have his pulse humming with each step she took.

He wouldn't be surprised if by the end of the evening, he'd have to beat the men off her. Starting with his own brother, who was making a beeline for them. Luis's gaze was fixated squarely on Fallon, with barely a glance in Enrique's direction.

"Oh, my," his brother said, reaching for Fallon's free hand. *"Muy, muy, bonita,"* he added, dropping a small kiss on Fallon's knuckles, just as he had the other day when he'd first met her in the garden.

"Lovely to see you again, Luis," she said with a dazzling smile in his brother's direction before addressing both of them. "Do you both mind if I go freshen up quickly?"

"Of course," they said in unison.

"Your nanny seems to be attracting all sorts of attention this evening," Luis said, watching Fallon's back as she walked away.

"So it appears."

"And what about you?" his brother asked knowingly.

"What about me?"

"I'm guessing you're pretty distracted by her as well. She's a knockout, you have to admit. Maybe you should tell her so."

Enrique swiped a flute of champagne off the tray of a passing waiter and took a small sip. "I've made sure to mention how nice she looks."

Luis grunted a laugh. "Nice. Is that what you said to her? That she looked nice?"

Little did Luis know. He'd barely found any words to say to her at all, as gobsmacked as he'd been at the first sight of her this evening.

"Well, if you won't tell her how much more than *nice* she looks, maybe I will."

Enrique knew his brother was simply indulging in his favorite pastime of taunting him. And he knew he shouldn't take the bait. He made himself silently count to ten before answering.

Luis let out a burst of laughter.

"What's so funny?" Enrique demanded, draining the last of his champagne.

"You're practically snarling at me, bro. Simply because I mentioned wanting to compliment your date. That's what's so funny."

This night was going to be a memory she would cherish forever. Fallon knew that as soon as Enrique had arrived to fetch her at her door. Her pulse jumped under skin, her senses on overload. She just needed a moment to compose herself.

It hadn't helped that dozens of sets of eyes had landed on them as soon as she and Enrique had entered the ballroom. Nor had the close proximity to Enrique in the limousine on the way over. In a well-fitting tux with his hair combed back, the man looked like walking temptation.

After splashing some cold water on her face, making sure not to mess her makeup, she made her way back to the ballroom. Enrique and Luis were in the same spot she'd left them.

Fallon paused at the image the two of them presented. The Martinez brothers seemed to command the room, though she would bet neither of them knew it.

By far the most handsome men in here, with Enrique a distant first. Luis was drop-dead good-looking, no denying it. But his was a boyish, mischievous handsome, while Enrique's features were striking in a much more mature way. She supposed enough women found Luis more attractive, the young boyish type.

Not so herself.

No, she much preferred the quiet maturity behind Enrique's allure. The man was successful, considerate, and he'd taken to fatherhood like a charm.

Someone accidentally brushed past her, bringing her back to the moment. What was she doing? How long had she just been standing here gawking at the two of them? At Enrique in particular. It would be horrifying if he were to look up and catch her staring at him like a besotted schoolgirl. Gathering herself, she made her way back to his side. Just as another woman approached the two men from the opposite direction.

Fallon watched as without any hesitation or preamble, the woman leaned into Enrique and gave him a kiss square on the mouth then patted his cheek, her moves full of familiarity and affection.

The next moment, she was tugging Enrique onto the dance floor. He didn't hesitate to follow her.

\* \* \*

Luis gave Fallon an exaggerated bow as she approached. It took some effort but she managed to pull her gaze from Enrique and the mystery woman long enough to return his smile.

He extended his hand out to her, palm up. "May I have the pleasure of this dance?"

Surprisingly, the rush of apprehension she'd been expecting at having been asked to dance didn't appear. Rather, it was replaced with a crushing dose of disappointment that Luis was the one asking her.

"I don't think you know what you're getting yourself into. It's probably not a good idea. You risk crushed toes and banged shins." She glanced in Enrique's direction once more. Unlike his dance partner, with her smooth and graceful movements, Fallon was likely to appear stiff and she was certain to miss at least one or two steps.

Luis gave a solemn shake of his head. "Tsk, tsk. That's nonsense. I've seen you practicing in the garden, remember?"

"Hardly the same thing."

"Close enough." He waved his fingers at her. "Come on, one song."

Despite her misgivings, she took the hand he offered and followed him onto the dance floor.

"Something tells me you don't get told no very often, do you?"

"Ah, but it pays to be persistent."

"So it seems."

They moved in silence for several beats. So far, so good. She was managing to keep up with him and no stumbles. Yet.

"I know you're dying to know, so go ahead and ask me already."

"Ask you what?"

"Who Enrique is dancing with."

Was it that obvious? She'd been trying so hard not to look over at them. Clearly, she'd failed.

Luis didn't wait for her to respond. "Esmerelda Pina. Highly popular influencer with over three million followers."

Great. An accomplished, beautiful woman, leagues above her. Not that she was competing with anyone.

"I'll tell you a secret," Luis began, then leaned closer to whisper in her ear. "Enrique's not terribly fond of her."

The rush of pleasure at those words was actually a tad embarrassing. "Oh?"

"He's probably cursing silently and willing the song to end already. I'm sure he didn't want to embarrass her by turning down the dance, though he wanted to."

"Why's that?"

"Every move Esmerelda makes is so she can post it on her social media pages. Enrique's not a big fan."

"Huh."

"The last time he went out with her, he found himself plastered all over her feed."

Did that mean that if Esmerelda promised not to display him on her pages anymore, he might ask her out again? Was she doing so even now? Apologizing and swearing it wouldn't happen again? After all, she hadn't hesitated to approach him mere minutes after their arrival.

"So, you don't have to worry about her," Luis added.

Fallon felt a rush of heat to her face at his assumption. "I'm not. At all," she said, stuttering. "It's really none of my business, is it?"

Luis narrowed his eyes on her. "I don't know. Is it?"

"No," she said with an emphatic shake of her head. "Absolutely not. And for all you know, Enrique's forgiven her and they're rekindling their relationship."

He threw back his head and laughed before answering. "Highly unlikely."

"You don't know that for sure," Fallon argued.

"Ah, but I do. My brother finds it hard to trust others— and he is certainly not the forgiving type."

That statement ran a shiver down her spine. Chances were high she was going to need Enrique's forgiveness herself in the near future. Once he found out the truth. Luis's statement did not bode well for how that might go.

Fallon was desperate to change the subject. "So this is all to raise funds for your department, then?"

Luis flashed her an amused smile that said he knew exactly what she was doing. *"Sí,"* he answered, indicating he would play along. "Those archaeological digs get pricey between the equipment and all it takes to make sure the discoveries are handled well and preserved."

"It sounds fascinating."

"It is. Tulum is an ancient city with vast numbers of undiscovered sites still. And what had been uncovered is majestic. The city is rich with ancient history."

"I hope to see more of it."

"You have to see the ruins first. They're breathtaking. In fact, I'll take you myself. We'll strap the baby in his stroller and head out late tomorrow morning."

"My very own archaeology expert as a tour guide. I'm beyond excited."

"Excited about what?" The question came from a deep baritone voice behind her. A voice she would now recognize anywhere. Enrique.

Without waiting for an answer, he addressed his brother

in Spanish. Fallon didn't need to be fluent to gather that he was asking to cut in.

"Of course," Luis answered, then gave her a friendly nod before stepping away.

Fallon's heart fluttered in her chest as she stepped into Enrique's arms. Her breath felt labored. Why did this man have such an effect on her? He was paying her to take care of his child. That's all there was between them. Why did her traitorous body forget there could never be anything more between them? For a moment she wanted to heed all those physical reactions. Pretend there was a chance for something more. What would it feel like if she really were here as his date? What if she were his wife? The thought had her mentally gasping. It was hard not to remember the last time they'd danced together and how it had ended in a deep, passionate kiss that had her knees buckling.

"Your breathing is heavy," Enrique commented, leading her on the dance floor. "You really must be excited about something."

Huh?

Enrique answered her unspoken question. "That's what you were saying to Luis when I walked over."

Right! The ruins. The distraction that was Enrique Martinez had zapped the conversation right out of her mind. "Oh, that. Your brother has kindly offered to take me and Lucas to the Tulum Ruins tomorrow and act as our expert tour guide. I'm quite looking forward to it."

Enrique's lips tightened. "He did, did he?"

"Yes, it was quite nice of him, offering to take time out of his day."

"Hmm. My brother is so very selfless," he said, his voice tight and strained.

Enrique's tone nowhere near matched his words.

* * *

"I think I could use some fresh air."

Fallon forced herself to step out of Enrique's arms as soon as the current song ended. Otherwise, it was just too tempting to linger in his embrace, to ease into the next song and the next and let him continue holding her, as she'd been doing for the last hour or more.

She didn't think her senses would be able to take it. She needed to keep her wits about her if she was to have any hope of getting through the rest of the evening without her heart turning into a mush of goo in her chest.

"As you wish."

She knew she didn't imagine his hesitation in releasing his grip before he led her off the dance floor and toward the back of the ballroom. They reached a set of double doors that led to the rear of the building.

Enrique held the door open for her and she stepped outside to a sprawling garden with a tall fountain a few feet away. The full moon above cast a silver glow across the surface of the gushing water. The breeze tickled her cheeks. Fallon felt as if she might have stepped into a scene from a storybook. Complete with a dashing, handsome hero beside her.

A chill ran over her skin.

Enrique shrugged out of his jacket and draped it over her shoulders apparently misinterpreting her reaction to him as her being cold. The scent of him off the jacket immediately engulfed her senses, further magnifying the effect he was having on her. Heaven help her, he was now rolling up his sleeves to reveal tanned, muscular arms. The man was much too handsome in a tux as it was. Partially out of one, he was downright scorching.

"Warm enough?" he asked.

If he only knew. She was a river of molten lava inside. "Yes. Thanks," she answered abruptly.

Maybe it hadn't been such a good idea to want to come outside, after all. At least inside they'd had the buffer of other people. Out here they were completely alone. Together.

"So, this takes place every year?" she asked, grasping for a subject of conversation. Any subject would do to try and take her mind off her out-of-control attraction to him.

"Unfortunately," Enrique answered. "Although it's much more bearable this time."

They'd reached the fountain. Enrique planted one foot on the rim and leaned his forearm over his knee.

"Luis is lucky to have you," Fallon said, determined to keep the focus of the conversation on relatively benign matters.

A smile of affection spread over his features. "I make sure to tell him that as often as I can."

Fallon chuckled. "It's the truth. Not every big brother would go out of his way to show such unwavering support. I mean, you could easily write a check and essentially be done with the fundraiser. Yet, you attend the gala every year."

And she was guessing Enrique was the one paying for Luis's education.

Enrique released a long sigh, the smile faltering ever so slightly. "I'm the closest thing to a father he's ever had. I figure at least one of us should have a father figure in their lives."

The man was too good to be true. Did he have any flaws whatsoever? Luis had told her in the ballroom that it was hard for Enrique to put his trust in people easily. But that could hardly be considered a flaw. Especially considering the current circumstances. It galled her that she might turn out to be one of the people who proved him right to be so mistrustful of others.

"Our own father never wanted anything to do with either me or Luis."

Fallon wrapped the jacket tighter around herself, her heart tugging at the bitterness and hurt in his voice. "He was married into a very powerful and wealthy family in South America. After my mother dumped me on Abuela, she was his mistress for years until he decided he needed a younger model. She was eventually tossed aside just like the two of us were."

"Do you think she regrets her choices?"

He scoffed out loud. "No. The exact opposite in fact. She views that relationship as the highlight of her life. It afforded her exactly the kind of lifestyle she wanted. And the small trust fund she convinced her lover to set up for me, her oldest son, enabled me to make other profitable investments and eventually led to my line of luxurious resorts. All of which allows her to maintain said lifestyle. I think she believes she was quite shrewd actually."

Tension seemed to be rising off him in waves. It was beyond apparent that this wasn't a topic he spoke of often. Yet, here he was, opening up to her so completely. The ever-present guilt sitting like a boulder in her rib cage grew heavier. What a coward she was. How could she not have found a way to come clean already?

"I hope you realize what an extraordinary man you are, Enrique. The way you've built so much from so little, the way you take care of your little brother and your grandmother, it's all so impressive. Not to mention, how much of a devoted and loving father you are to Lucas."

Fallon wanted to clamp her hand to her mouth. She hadn't meant to say any of that out loud. She'd just bared her feelings about him, which hovered much too close to the surface.

Even in the dark she could see the full impact of her words. Enrique's eyes narrowed on her, a muscle twitched along his jaw. "Careful there, sweetheart. I might begin to think you find me appealing or something."

He leaned closer, trailed a finger along her cheek. "Do you?"

Her mind seemed to shut down, and she moved closer too. There was only a hair's breadth between them now. The next moment, she felt his lips on hers. There was no telling even which one of them had moved first. The kiss was the barest brushing of his lips against hers, gentle as a light feather. Yet she felt the effect in every cell in her body.

"Fallon." He whispered her name against her mouth. It was a question. Heaven help her, she knew exactly what he was asking, wanted desperately to say yes.

"There you two are," came a masculine voice from the direction of the building. Luis.

Though it felt like ripping a scab off a wound, Fallon made herself pull away. Luis was far enough away and the evening dark enough that she didn't think he could have seen much except for their silhouettes.

Thanks heavens.

She'd barely recovered her breath by the time he reached their side.

"I'm going to head out with my friends now," Luis informed them. "Just came to say good night."

Fallon couldn't decide if she was grateful or not for his appearance.

She was wreaking havoc on his senses.

Enrique escorted Fallon out of the ballroom to the limousine waiting outside the venue. A surprising whisper of sadness echoed through his head that the night was over. What a turn of the screw that was. If someone had told him at the last gala he'd attended that he'd be disappointed to see the evening end, he would have laughed until he was out of breath.

But the truth was that he wanted this night to continue. He wanted to watch Fallon sipping champagne through those luscious ruby-red lips of hers, holding the narrow crystal flute in her elegant fingers. He wanted to feel her against him in his arms as they moved on the dance floor.

The dress she had on complimented her perfectly. Whoever the boutique had sent had done a commendable job of dressing her. The rich red color brought out the golden specks of her mesmerizing eyes. The material hugged all her curves in the most enticing ways. The neckline just low enough to have his imagination running wild.

The driver saw them approach and immediately opened the door. Enrique helped her into the car then sat in the seat opposite. What he wanted to do was sit next to her, hug her shoulders and pull her up against him. He wanted to take up where they'd left off before Luis had so maddeningly interrupted.

Heaven help him, then he wanted to kiss her again. Like he had back by the fountain this evening and that day in the garden the other week. He'd lost control with her twice already. He couldn't seem to get enough of her.

Fallon released a melodic chuckle, luckily pulling him away from his wayward thoughts. But what sweet, enticing thoughts they were.

"I'm so relieved that went well," she said in a breathless tone. "I didn't even make a fool of myself on the dance floor."

She really was rather self-deprecating. For the life of him, he couldn't understand why. How did she not realize how magnificent she was?

"On the contrary, you moved beautifully. You had nothing to worry about," he assured her.

Her lashes fluttered downward. "Well, to tell you the truth, I've been practicing a bit. With a very motivating partner."

Enrique felt his fists tighten. Who would have been practicing with her? The only logical conclusion was his brother. He wasn't foolish enough to suspect there was anything between Luis and Fallon, but it still riled his blood pressure that his brother had been spending time with her, twirling her in his arms.

"He's a little on the young side and I have to be the one to lead," she added.

Who in the world...?

"And he almost always falls asleep immediately after," she added.

What she was getting at finally registered and Enrique had to chuckle. "I hope my son was the perfect gentleman during your practice sessions."

"Of course he was. A total angel, as always."

How imbecilic of him. Was he that far gone on her that he was so ready to bristle with jealousy at the thought of another man—his younger brother—dancing with her? Clearly so. The ramifications of that acknowledgment were almost too much to weigh right now.

They arrived at the hacienda twenty minutes later. Enrique spent most of that time debating how and if he should find a way to invite her to spend more of the night with him. He shouldn't even be entertaining the idea, let alone acting on it in any way. After tonight, they would have to go back to their initial working relationship. He was nothing more than her employer. Starting any kind of relationship with his son's nanny was asking the universe for trouble. He couldn't forget the truth of that.

Easier said than done.

Not to mention, he hadn't missed how often Fallon had yawned during the ride back home, her eyes slowly drifting closed until she realized it and blinked them open again. The woman was clearly tired, no doubt a combination of excitement and the hour growing late.

She turned to him after her helped her out of the car. "Thank you, Enrique. I genuinely enjoyed myself this evening. I honestly wasn't expecting that."

Ouch. Enrique decided to let that comment go for the sake of his masculine ego. "I'm the one who should be thanking you. You did me quite the favor this evening."

She immediately shook her head. "No, that's not how it felt at all."

Enrique paused on the veranda, knowing he shouldn't ask what he was about to ask. He should just walk her to her room and bid her good-night. But here he was, stalling. Fishing for some kind of acknowledgment that she'd enjoyed the evening because he'd been with her. "Oh? What did it feel like?"

She ducked her head. "Well, for one thing, once I finally managed to relax a bit, I actually started to have fun," she said.

"Surprisingly, I had fun too." *With you.*

She laughed. "Glad to hear it. We both expected the worst and look how it turned out."

*It doesn't have to end.* The words were on the tip of his tongue. He resisted uttering them out loud when all he wanted to do was lean over and whisper them softly in her ear.

Several moments of awkward silence hung in the air before Fallon finally broke it. "I think all the excitement has caught up with me. I should head on up to bed."

*Invite me to come up there with you.* Enrique willed her to say the words he so desperately wanted to hear.

Instead, she handed back his jacket, then cupped her palm over her mouth on another soft yawn.

If he didn't feel so pathetic, he might have actually laughed at himself. The woman could barely stay awake in his company. While here he was entertaining romantic thoughts about her he had no business thinking.

Pathetic indeed.

# CHAPTER TWELVE

FALLON SHUT HER door behind her and leaned her back up against the cool wood, willing her racing pulse to slow.

Highly unlikely anytime soon.

Enrique had just walked her to her suite and bid her good-night. All the while, looking devilishly handsome. His sleeves rolled up to his elbows, the top buttons of his crisp white shirt undone. He looked like a man out of every red-blooded woman's fantasy.

A fantasy she had to get out of her head once and for all.

All that yawning had been more due to her nervousness, coupled with fighting the urges she'd had all night. Like the urge to lean tighter up against Enrique's length when they'd been dancing. Or the urge to trail her hand along his upper thighs during the ride back to the hacienda. What about the urge to ask him to kiss her again to see where it might lead?

He hadn't even asked her to share a nightcap with him.

And why would he?

Only one of them here had wholly inappropriate feelings they had to fight against. Sure, he'd gotten carried away back there by the fountain, they both had. But she couldn't look too deeply into the how and the why when it came to that kiss. The romantic setting, the fake date, the novelty of a gala ball—it had simply led to a tender moment, that was all.

It was just as well he hadn't asked to extend the evening. She would have had no excuse but to come clean about her identity after the evening they'd spent together. And she simply didn't feel prepared.

A voice in her head mocked her immediately. The truth was, she didn't want anything to mar this magical night in any way. Better to have it end than have it end badly.

Fallon kicked her stilettos off and slipped out of the dress, then hung it carefully on the suede covered hanger. The chances of her wearing such a fancy garment ever again were highly doubtful.

As was any chance of her attending another gala event on the arm of a successful, handsome, billionaire.

*Womp-womp.*

She was skating perilously close to self-pity here. She wouldn't allow it.

The evening had been one of the best times she'd spent. She should be happy it had ever happened. Not woeful that it had come to an end.

Her heart had other plans.

With a sigh, she made her way to the bathroom to wash her face and clean up, certain that a sleepless night awaited her.

Despite all the yawning, her adrenaline was too high. Her mind too focused on the man under the same roof. So close and yet so far out of her league.

Oh, and then there was that whole other complication about who exactly she was to his son.

Fallon sighed and stared at herself in the mirror, the realization washing over her. She had to tell him. The deception had gone on long enough.

Somehow, someway, she had to sit Enrique down and explain exactly who she was.

And if he sent her packing?

It was chance she had to take. And hope he understood and considered her motivations and how much she loved little Lucas.

She would just have to convince him to let her stay.

But first she had to get through tonight and try and get some rest. Or she'd be useless tomorrow to Lucas.

As far as Luis's invitation to see the ruins, as much as she wanted to, it would have to wait. She simply couldn't imagine summoning that much energy. Not to mention, how preoccupied she'd be with the nerve-racking task that awaited her.

Or the uncertainly about the aftermath of her confession. A sob tore out of her throat at the thought that this time tomorrow, she might well be on her way back to the States and never see little Lucas again.

Nor his father, the man she was so headily falling for.

By the time the morning sun rose in the distant horizon, Fallon was convinced she'd barely managed to sleep more than a few extended winks.

Coffee. She desperately needed coffee. The soft sounds of Lucas gurgling echoed from the monitor telling her the coffee would have to wait. Dressing quickly, she made her way to the nursery.

Lucas lay on his back in his crib, wide-eyed with his fist partially in his mouth. "Hey there, little man." Fallon lowered the side panel of the bed and reached for him. "I missed you last night. Did you behave for your great-*abuela*?"

Fallon lifted him into her arms and gave him a gentle hug. He'd grown so big since that first day she'd interviewed for the position as his nanny. And her heart had grown with more love for him. Enrique wouldn't be cruel enough to overlook that love once he found out the truth, would he?

She shuddered to even think about it.

"I'll bet you were a really good boy last night, huh?" she asked, lifting him up off the changing table once he'd been cleaned up.

"Abuela says as much," came an answer behind her. Her heart did a somersault in her chest, the voice unmistakably Enrique's.

Even if he hadn't spoken, the now familiar, masculine scent of him reached her nose the moment he entered the room and had her pulse racing.

"She says he was an absolute angel all night," he added.

"I'm glad to hear it but not surprised," she managed to say, doing her best to focus on the conversation and not the way Enrique's mere presence affected her.

"So different than the first few weeks after he arrived at my door," he said, before his gaze found her. "I have you to thank for that."

How she wished he hadn't said such a thing given what she would be divulging to him soon.

He was at her side a moment later, and Fallon had to remind herself to breathe. The effect this man had on her was turning her to mush inside.

And she had no idea what to do about it.

He stepped closer and cupped his hand around Lucas's cheek. Fallon had to resist the urge to lean closer into him against his chest and inhale deeply of that tempting, alluring scent of his.

"So, a big outing planned for today for this little fella. He's sure to nap well himself after all the fresh air and excitement." He reached out and took his son into his arms. "He can stay with me while you go get ready."

Right. The ruins.

She was about to tell him about her plans to ask Luis for a rain check when his next words stopped her.

"Oh, and you won't be going with Luis, after all."

That gave her pause. What had changed since last night? He answered her next question before she could ask it. "I'll be accompanying you myself."

She certainly hadn't seen that coming.

Fallon was totally unprepared for Enrique's announcement that he'd be taking them out today instead of Luis. In her surprise at the unexpected announcement, she'd totally forgotten about wanting to postpone the outing.

*Right,* a little voice inside her mind mocked. *As if that's the reason.*

She sighed as she gathered Lucas's bag with the essentials he would need for a day away. If she were to admit the truth to herself, she would have to acknowledge that she'd changed her mind about not going. And that change of heart had everything to do with Enrique.

As much as she enjoyed Luis's company, spending the day with Enrique held an entirely different appeal. Her heart had done a little leap of excitement when he'd told her the change in plans.

Oh, man, she had it bad, didn't she?

What if he wanted to kiss her again? Heaven help her, Fallon didn't think she could resist him a third time.

The car was waiting for them when she went back downstairs with the bag and her own items. Enrique had instructed her to bring a bathing suit for both herself and the baby. Just in case it was needed.

So they might be spending some time at the beach. The thought of seeing Enrique bare chested again gave her heart a thud. She would have to make sure not to ogle the man. Her imagination was already running wild with all sorts of images.

She took care of feeding the baby during the ride. So that by the time they arrived at the ruins, he was fed, dry and seemed content. He didn't even make a fuss when Enrique strapped him into the stroller like he usually did when placed in it.

"Welcome to one of the most visited sites in Tulum," Enrique announced, pushing Lucas toward the structures. Fallon's mouth fell open in awe. She could clearly see in her mind's eye the grandeur this place must have held all those centuries ago despite their crumbling status now.

"This is amazing."

"I figured I can show you around them just as well as Luis. And you won't have to put up his nerdy overexplanations. Besides, I think I should be with my son the first time he lays eyes on such a historical sight in his ancestral home."

So the swapping places with his brother had nothing to do with her at all. How silly of her to have entertained such a notion for even a brief moment.

He let go of the stroller to point into the distance. "The Mayans built this before the thirteenth century. A self-contained city bordered on one side by the sea and a wall for protection on the other."

"I've never seen anything like it."

Enrique's smile at that response had her skin tingling. He seemed pleased at her reaction. But how could anyone not be awed by this place?

"That building over there is the Temple of the Frescoes.

They used it to track the movement of the sun. Tracking the sky like that was way ahead of the time for that era."

A sudden movement near her foot stopped her midstep. She looked down to find what could only be described as a shrunken dragon, mere inches from her foot. Black with sharp spines running down its back and along its tail, the creature looked like something out of a nightmare.

Fallon couldn't help the shriek that tore from her throat. Nor could she help the way she pushed the stroller away from it. All the while she hurled herself at Enrique, then jumped at him so that he had no choice but to catch her.

"What is that monster?"

Enrique's response was a hearty chuckle. "What's so funny?" she demanded to know, calculating if she'd pushed Lucas far enough away from whatever it was.

"Relax," he told her through a grin. "It's just a basilisk lizard."

"A what?"

"A type of iguana. They make their home here among the ruins. It's here to say hello."

"Well, I don't want to make its acquaintance, thank you very much."

"Aw, that's too bad. They're so used to the tourists they actually greet them. Look, it's bobbing its head at us."

"I half expected it to start breathing fire."

Enrique laughed again, his chest vibrating against her. That bewitching scent of his surrounding her, his closeness sending pulsing waves over her skin. She almost forgot about the lizard, which had by now skittered away. Then common sense finally kicked in. She had to get down.

With no small amount of reluctance, Fallon lowered her feet back to the ground and stepped away.

"Sorry about that then."

His eyes darkened and his lids lowered, the smile faded from his mouth as his expression grew serious. "No need to apologize."

Several beats passed in silence. What exactly was happening between them at this moment?

She didn't get a chance to examine it any further as Lucas let out an impatient cry. He'd been dormant too long.

Fallon gave herself a quick moment for her heart rate to settle. She couldn't even be sure what had spiked it more, the lizard or the way Enrique had caught her in his arms. Or the way he was looking at her now.

"What's that other tower," she finally managed to ask after several beats, to try and refocus. It worked. The ad hoc history lesson fascinated her more than she would have guessed.

"That's the Temple of the Descending God. It's got some impressive carvings. The devout often used it as a place for confessionals. Let's go take a look."

Confessionals. Fallon paused. It was as if Enrique had given her a perfect segue. Once they got to the tower, she could take the opportunity to announce that she had something to confess herself. An ancient tower for confessions was an apt place for such a revelation, was it not? Her heart started pounding in her chest. She had to take the opportunity to finally come clean.

They hadn't gotten far when an older couple approached them, smiles wide. They'd clearly witnessed her little jump scare at the lizard and seemed amused.

*"Hola,"* they said in unison. *"Buenas tardes."*

Fallon and Enrique both returned the greeting.

Their eyes focused on Lucas in his stroller.

Fallon could make out just enough of the Spanish to get the gist. *Hermoso bebe… Que angel…encandora familia.*

Fallon felt a tug at the last word. That one was easy to guess. Family.

The couple could be forgiven for their mistaken assumption. To any observer, they must look the perfect image of a happy couple out with their new baby. They had no idea what a fantasy it all was. On her side anyway. With a lengthy sigh, she waited for Enrique to correct them.

But his reply surprised her. *"Gracias,"* was all he said.

The interaction was enough to dissolve her earlier resolve. She couldn't do it here. Not in front of all these strangers at such a sacred place.

*Yet another excuse*, whispered a nagging voice in her head.

She ignored it.

Enrique figured he'd done a pretty good job introducing Fallon to Tulum's history. Sure, Luis would have had much more detailed information at the top of his head, given his field of study. But Fallon could hear about all that at some future time. He'd gone to bed last night with his decision made. As a native son, Enrique knew enough about his ancestral lands to make today an informative visit for her. Besides, he wasn't going to sit around in his study all day staring at a spreadsheet or a computer screen while the three of them were out playing tourist.

Now, on the beach as he waited for Fallon to change into her bathing suit in the nearby cabana, he knew the decision had been the right one. Though he hadn't appreciated the knowing look on his brother's face when he'd informed Luis of the change.

He couldn't remember the last time he'd skipped out on a day of work to hang out at the Tulum Ruins and then the beach. Nor could he remember the last time he'd enjoyed himself quite so thoroughly.

Lucas seemed to be enjoying himself too. The baby was clear-eyed and alert, and appeared to be studying his new surroundings with a look of fascination on his cherubic face.

How new and full of wonder the world must seem to the little guy. Enrique was looking forward to watching his son discover his world as he grew up, though he had no illusions about all the hard work and challenges that would come with being a single father.

Only, he didn't feel quite so alone on his fatherhood journey. He had Fallon to partner with him in raising his son.

The realization had come to him gradually but it was clear. She was so much more than a nanny.

That was why he hadn't bothered to correct the older couple at the ruins earlier when they'd assumed her to be his wife and Lucas's mother. They were already something of a family. She was a large part of their lives now.

And if things between the two of them continued to develop, who knew where it might lead? For as much as he'd fought it in the beginning, there was no longer any denying that there was a pull between them that could no longer be ignored.

And he no longer wanted to ignore it, in fact.

The jolt of desire he felt when she reappeared after changing confirmed his thoughts. Her suit was modest by any means. A tankini that covered her midriff with matching boy shorts. But the way the fabric clung to her enticing curves and the way the shorts accentuated her shapely legs made it hard not to stare.

He wasn't sure how he'd cope if she asked him to rub sunscreen lotion on her back.

Not that he'd imagined doing that very thing upon seeing her.

She lowered herself onto the beach blanket next to him, rubbing Lucas's cheek. "So, is it safe here?"

"Safe?"

"No lizards lurking about, I hope?"

The comical shudder that shook her shoulders as she said the last word made him laugh.

"It's not impossible but highly unlikely. They prefer the shaded stones at the ruins."

"Glad to hear it."

Although, if the appearance of a basilisk had her jumping into his arms again, he wouldn't exactly complain about it. It had taken all of his will not to lean down and drop a gentle kiss along her lips as she clung to him. Dancing with her last night and feeling her against him again today, he was starting to get used to touching Fallon and holding her. She felt right in his arms.

He couldn't recall having that thought about any other woman.

He wanted to touch her now. To run his fingers along those shapely curves then trail them higher up her body. Then...

Enrique gave himself a mental shake, grateful for the loose fit of the swim shorts he'd changed into earlier. He had to cool down here.

He reached for the baby. "What do you say we introduce this little guy to the ocean?"

Fallon jumped up with an excited clap. "Yes! I can't wait to see his reaction."

He was pretty excited about his son's first ocean swim himself.

When they reached the edge of the water, Fallon waded in without hesitation. Enrique followed, then gingerly set his son's feet in. Lucas gave a gasp, then looked up at his father in question.

"He doesn't look as if he's too sure about this," Fallon said above their heads.

"No, he certainly doesn't."

Just when he thought he might have to pull the baby out and try again some other time, Lucas gave a kick of his little legs. Then he did it again.

Fallon squealed with delight. "He likes it!" She dropped to her knees next to them. Lucas was kicking with both feet now, splashing the water and clearly enjoying himself.

Fallon gave him a little tickle on his tummy. What happened next had Enrique's heart flooding with emotion.

His son gave his first proper belly laugh.

Fallon cupped a hand to her mouth, her eyes wide. She'd made note of it too.

One of many of his son's firsts Enrique had no doubt they'd witness together.


"I'm starving," Enrique announced about three hours later as the day slowly drew to a close. The sun had just begun its descent, washing the sky in bright color with streaks of lavender and bright orange over the water. If she ever took up painting, this would be the view Fallon would strive to capture on canvas.

"If we rush back, I can help Abuela prepare dinner," she said. "I think this little one will be out cold by the time we make it to the front veranda."

It struck her then what she'd just said. She'd actually

referred to Rosa as Abuela, a note of familiarity she had no claim to. If Enrique noticed, he didn't acknowledge it.

"Abuela isn't home," Enrique responded, gathering the baby's things. "It's her monthly game of conquian. We'll be lucky to see her before midnight. Those ladies take their card games seriously."

"I suppose I can throw something together. Though obviously it won't stand up to Rosa's usual fare." She'd made sure to use the elder's real name this time.

Enrique stood, hoisting Lucas up with him in his arms. "I have another idea. There's an outdoor cantina about a quarter mile down the beach. It's always booked weeks in advance."

"Do we have reservations?" If they did, why hadn't he thought to mention it?

"No," Enrique answered. "But I think they'll fit us in."

"Because you're the owner of the town's most renowned resort?"

He smiled at her. "Something like that."

About fifteen minutes later, they were walking up a wooden pathway to a straw-roofed open-air eatery. The place looked packed, every table full. The bar area appeared to be standing room only.

Regardless of Enrique's prominence in town, Fallon didn't see how they could possibly find a spot. Before they'd made it to the entrance, a middle-aged woman wearing a smock and a tight bun appeared out of nowhere and made a beeline for Enrique. Fallon watched as she patted his cheek and then clasped her hands to her chest as her gaze fell on the drowsy baby in his arms.

*"Ay, hermoso bebe,"* she said, followed by rapid Spanish Fallon had no hope of interpreting. Luckily, she switched to English right after. "What took you so long to get here,

*hijo*?" she asked Enrique. "We've been dying to finally meet this little one."

*"Lo siento,"* Enrique answered, handing the baby to her outstretched arms. "We are here now, Tia."

"Blessedly so."

Enrique turned to Fallon. "Fallon, this is Anna. I call her Tia Anna. She owns and runs this place with her husband, Tio Ramon. And the two of them gave me my first job busing tables when I desperately needed one."

Well, the connection explained why he'd been so confident about getting a table at such a popular spot.

"So nice to meet you," Anna said, giving Fallon a one-armed hug while she cradled the baby with the other, her voice full of warmth and joy.

Fallon's heart flooded with happiness at the affectionate way the older woman held Luis against her bosom and nuzzled his chubby cheek. Yet another person who seemed to adore him.

"Come, come," Anna said, motioning them forward. "I'll take you to the table in the back."

They followed her past the crowded bar and through the dining area until they reached a sliding screen door. Anna opened it and ushered them through to a patio outside with a long wooden table. Tea lights were strung from wooden poles and trees. Bouncy salsa music sounded from floor speakers on opposite sides.

*"Siéntate,"* Anna instructed, motioning to the chairs. Enrique pulled one out for her and waited for her to sit before taking his seat outside.

Lucas was staring in awe at the tiny light bulbs scattered around the patio.

Before Fallon had even had a chance to settle into her seat, a trio of people arrived through the screen door, each carrying a tray of food. Two others arrived on their heels, one holding a pitcher full of golden icy liquid, the other two long-stemmed bowl glasses.

How had Anna summoned them so fast and when exactly had she even done it?

Fallon felt like a VIP being catered to with designated staff. Which she supposed was exactly what Enrique was.

The food smelled mouthwateringly good. Fajitas sizzling in cast iron pans, a variety of tacos, a large plate of cheesy tortillas and thick rolled chimichangas. Her stomach began to grumble.

*"Comer,"* Anna said, bouncing the baby on her hip and motioning to the food.

Just as Fallon was about to ask where she could heat up little Lucas's baby food, Anna added, "I'm going to go puree some vegetables and fruit for this little one."

That was so much better than the prepared packaged food she would have had to give him. And rather selfishly, Fallon figured it would also give her a chance to dig into this amazing spread.

"Your *tia* was so nice to have all this ready for us," Fallon said, unable to decide where to start. "I'm glad I got a chance to meet her."

Enrique reached for a tortilla and popped it in his mouth. "You haven't seen anything yet," he told her, his voice dripping with amusement.

"What do you mean?"

"You're about to meet a slew of other people. This meal could take a while."

Before she could ask him to clarify, two tall men strode through the doors greeting Enrique with smiles and claps on the back. One wore a chef's apron and the other had a bar towel draped over his shoulder.

Enrique introduced them as two servers who'd started working here around the same time he had. Following on their heels was an older gentleman about Anna's age. Fallon guessed that would be Tio Ramon. She was right. She'd barely gotten a chance to be introduced to him when two teenagers dashed in and each gave Enrique a hug. Anna came back still carrying the baby, with a middle-aged woman behind her pushing a high chair for Lucas. She sat him down and began feeding him.

Fallon's head was spinning. This was more than a meal at a family-owned restaurant. It was more like a celebratory party. Before she even knew what was happening, there were close to a dozen others around the table, laughing and joking and clearly enjoying each other's company. And they seemed to be taking turns doting on Lucas who was having a grand time and basking in all the attention.

It was chaos. In the best possible way. And so different than any meal Fallon had ever been a part of before. The bond this group of people had with each other was palpable.

More than once, Enrique flashed her a dazzling smile from across the table. At one point, he actually winked at her and she felt pleasure flush through her core. As much as she was enjoying herself, a trickle of apprehension nestled at the base of her spine. What she wouldn't give to enjoy a meal like this again sometime soon, to be part of this group of people and be included in such gatherings as a matter of course.

Could this possibly be the kind of future she might be able to look forward to? Could there be more days and evenings like this in her future?

The answer depended on how understanding Enrique would be when she finally told him the truth.

# CHAPTER THIRTEEN

SEVERAL DAYS AFTER visiting the ruins and the beach followed by the boisterous dinner, Fallon still couldn't stop thinking how magical that day had been. This morning was no different. To her delight, Enrique had offered to show her more of the city this weekend. Just the two of them. Rosa confirmed she'd watch the baby so that they could stay out later and see more of the nightlife.

She'd hardly slept the night before in her anticipation and excitement. To spend all that time alone with Enrique.

Maybe he'd even kiss her again.

A nagging voice surfaced in her mind that this was her chance. The outing today would finally give her the perfect opportunity to tell Enrique the truth about who she was to Lucas and his mother.

No more excuses; she had to get it done. Enrique would understand her motivations, he had to. She would find a way to make him.

Her excitement faded at the thought of finally making her confession.

She had to do it today. Somehow. Some way. She couldn't let another day go by with her secret between them. How angry could he possibly get? After all the time they'd spent together since she'd been hired, and the way their relationship had grown, surely he'd understand that she'd only had the best intentions. That she'd only been looking out for Lucas in her own way.

First thing first, she had to make her way downstairs and get some coffee if she had any hope of functioning this morning given how elusive sleep had been last night.

Luckily, the baby monitor remained silent as she slipped it into her robe pocket. Hopefully Lucas would even stay asleep long enough to let her enjoy the cup with some amount of leisure.

She found a pot already brewing when she made it to the kitchen. Luis was already at the counter taking a large mug out of the cabinet.

"One for me too, *por favor,*" she said, grateful when he nodded then began pouring coffee for both of them. He turned to her with a smile, offering the precious, very much needed brew in his hand then pulling out a chair for her.

"I'm not sure how long I can sit." She extracted the monitor out of her pocket and set it on the table between them.

Luis sat down across from her. "I'm sure my nephew will be cooperative enough to let you have your hit of caffeine before you're summoned."

"Let's hope so," she answered, taking a long sip of the rich, hot coffee and savoring every drop.

"I hear your day visiting the ruins went well," he said.

"You were so right, Luis. The ruins were magnificent. Thank you so much for offering to take me, even though it didn't work out that way."

Luis's eyebrows lifted about an inch as he took a sip of his coffee. He looked like a toddler who'd swiped a cookie from the cookie jar and had gotten away with it.

"What is it?"

"Why, I have no idea what you mean." The fluttering of his eyes said otherwise.

"I think you do. Now, fess up," she urged, amusement and curiosity twisting in her stomach.

"Let's just say I know my brother well."

The implication wasn't lost on her. Of course. She should have guessed all along. "You knew he'd want to come with Lucas and me instead, didn't you?"

Luis responded with a mischievous smile and a sly wink.

Before Fallon could process his motives let alone come up with anything else to say, Lucas's long wail sounded from the monitor. He didn't sound happy.

"I should get up there," she said, standing up. "I think the poor little fellow might be on the verge of teething. He's been quite ornery in the mornings recently."

"Yet another way he takes after his father," Luis quipped. "And Enrique doesn't even have an excuse like teething."

Fallon couldn't help but chuckle as she made her way upstairs, gripping the hot mug firmly in both hands and drinking as much of it as she could before she'd have to set it down and tend to the baby. All the while contemplating the ramifications of Luis's setup.

Well, she'd just have to focus on it later. Lucas needed her. He looked miserable when she went to his crib and lifted him. After giving him a quick change and retrieving his bottle from the warmer, she sat down with him in her lap and began to rock while feeding him.

He definitely wasn't as enthusiastic about feeding as usual. Poor thing was clearly uncomfortable. To comfort him, she began humming a familiar melody that absent-mindedly came to her head before she recognized it.

"You know, this was your mother's favorite song," she told the baby, talking more to herself. Not like Lucas understood a word she was saying. "She used to sing it all the time. I told her often that I was tired of hearing it. But I wasn't serious. She actually had a good voice and could carry a tune. I just said that to tease her because she knew it wasn't true."

She rubbed her cheek against the top of the baby's head. "I really miss her, did I ever tell you that?" she went on. "Still no replies to any of the emails I've been sending her. She'd be so emotional to see what a sweet and adorable child her baby is. If she would only return my messages. I'd be so happy to finally be able to talk to her about you."

Fallon couldn't explain the sense of unease that settled over her in that moment. It was more than her usual concern for Sasha. An alert had set off in her mind and her gut subconsciously.

The heavy footfalls on the stairs in the next instant surged the unease into alarm. Enrique swung open the door a moment later, his eyes wide and accusing. His fist in a tight grip on whatever he was holding.

She didn't need to identify the object he held to guess what it was. His expression said it all. The baby monitor. In her tiredness and haste to get to Lucas, she'd left it behind on the table.

Enrique had heard her every word.


"Who are you?"

Enrique searched Fallon's face for an answer, any answer that might make some kind of sense. Because she clearly wasn't who she'd said she was. And he'd been a fool to take her at face value.

She stood, still cradling the baby against her chest. "I can explain."

He strode into the room, holding up the incriminating

monitor in case she had any doubts about all that he'd just heard and how he'd heard it. A maddening mixture of disappointment, hurt and anger was whirling like a storm in his center. "Please start."

Fallon swallowed, her face pale. She looked panicked. Just how bad were her answers going to be? "How much of what you've told me is a lie?"

She visibly cringed, her face tightening. "Not a lie. Not exactly."

Semantics? She was talking semantics with him at a moment like this?

"Then what?" he demanded.

"More of an omission. I'm exactly who I said I was. Just like your background check proved."

"You know what I'm asking. Who are you really? To Lucas? To his mother?"

"You know I grew up in the fos—" Before she could get the words out, Lucas started wailing in her arms. The poor little guy no doubt could sense the tension in the air.

He had to calm down. Enrique took a deep breath, released it slowly. It didn't do much to scale down his red ire. "I'm sending Abuela up to take the baby. Meet me in my study downstairs as soon as she gets here." It wasn't a request.

When he tracked his grandmother down in the garden, Abuela looked startled at his expression and curious about his request to have her rush upstairs. Luckily, she was astute enough not to ask any questions and simply nodded in agreement.

Good thing. How in the world would he begin to explain any of this? He couldn't wait to hear Fallon's explanation himself.

All this time, she'd been lying to him. She'd tried to

call it something else. But Enrique wasn't buying it. A lie by omission was still deceit. And he intended to get to the bottom of why she would have done such a thing.

She didn't bother knocking when she appeared in his doorway moments after he'd gotten to the study.

Still pale, her hands tight against her sides, she appeared to be shaking. For one insane moment, Enrique longed to go to her. To tell her not to fret. He wanted to ease the anguish visibly rushing over her. Apologize for not approaching her better earlier. Then his common sense prevailed. If there were any apologies owed right now, he wasn't the one in debt. She also owed him an explanation still.

"Tell me," he said simply.

He didn't bother to take a seat. Nor did he offer her one.

She took a hesitant step farther into the room. "You know I grew up in foster care."

"Yes. My security firm did a thorough background check that verified your history. What does this have to do with my son and his mother?"

She squeezed her eyes shut. "Sasha and I were foster sisters for about five years before we aged out around the same time. She was the closest thing I've ever had to family after I lost my parents."

Enrique stood silent, absorbing the information. He nodded for her to continue.

"She took care of me. Made sure I was safe. From the over friendly father in the home we were assigned to. And from the bullying antics of other siblings or classmates who saw my shyness as a weakness. She often did so at great cost to herself."

He still wasn't hearing the piece of the puzzle that he needed to understand.

"Once we left the home, our lives took very different

paths. I knew she was hanging with the wrong kind of people. She was in trouble with the law often. I only heard from her sporadically. Usually via email. She'd sign on in a café or the library."

Enrique knew something about Sasha's troubles with the law. Fallon wasn't the only one he'd done an investigation into, but not much else had turned up.

She continued. "Over three months ago now, I got a phone call from her after not hearing from her for several months. She told me that she'd given birth due to a night of 'fun,' as she called it."

It was Enrique's turn to cringe. The uncharacteristic loosening of his restraint after too much ouzo had had such dramatic consequences. But he wouldn't regret the ensuing result—his son.

"She told me that she couldn't take care of the baby," Fallon said. "She told me she intended to make sure the infant, who'd she'd named Lucas, would make his way safely to his father. You."

Well, that certainly gave him a hearty dose of information. But nothing she'd said so far explained why she was here in his home under false pretenses. "Why did you do it? Why did you deceive me and my family?"

She physically winced as if he'd struck her. When she spoke, her words were closer to a sob than conversation. "I owed Sasha. And I was concerned for her child. I wanted to make sure he was being taken care of and not neglected. The way I'd seen happen all too often."

And the way she'd experienced for herself, no doubt. Which was legitimate, he wouldn't deny. But it didn't give her license to lie to him nor was it an excuse for what she'd done.

"I began to look into you and who you really were. I

was just trying to get some more information. But then I heard that you wanted to hire a nanny..." She trailed off.

"And you had the inspired idea to apply yourself."

She nodded. "It didn't seem like a good idea to tell you my connection to your baby when I first interviewed. And then there just didn't seem to be an ideal time to finally come clean."

She took another step in his direction. "You have to believe that I wanted to, that I eventually would have."

But she hadn't. Instead, she'd let him get to know her better, to begin growing fonder and fonder of having her around.

To slowly start to fall in lo—

Enrique stopped the train of thought in its tracks and bit out a vicious curse.

Served him right. For the first time in his life, he'd let his guard down. Had taken a chance on someone who clearly didn't warrant such trust. What a fool he'd been.

Turning his back to her, he willed the burning fury in his core to cool. Something told him that wasn't going to happen anytime soon.

A boulder sat in the pit of her chest, crushing her from the inside. As bad as she'd imagined this moment might have been, this was so much worse than she ever would have believed. Enrique's face was tight with fury; his expression held nothing but hostility. For her.

She couldn't blame him. She had no one to blame but herself.

"Why?" he demanded, cramming his hand through his hair. "Why wouldn't you just tell me the truth from the very beginning?"

Fallon stepped forward, then immediately regretted it

when Enrique flashed her a fiery glare. "I wanted to. There were so many times it was on the tip of my tongue."

He actually scoffed. "But you just couldn't bring yourself to do it."

"I was trying and failing to come up with a way to explain it." Fallon heard the pleading in her tone, had no way to stop it. Wasn't sure she even wanted to. "I didn't know how to make someone like you understand."

"Someone like me? What's that supposed to mean?"

Fallon squeezed her eyes shut, grasping for the right words. "I know how much you've had to overcome in your life. How you were betrayed by those who should have loved you."

His darkening glare immediately told her she was on the wrong track, but there was no going back now. "But you still had Rosa. And Luis. Not to mention all those people at the cantina who clearly love you."

"What does that have to do with any of this?"

"I've never had anyone but Sasha ever since my parents died. She took me under her wing when I needed someone the most. I owed it her to make sure her son was okay."

"So you decided to lie. And to spy on me for her, is that it?"

"No!" Fallon longed to reach for him, to somehow make him see. But she was making a mess of this. It was just so hard to find the right words. "That's not what I was doing."

Enrique looked beyond skeptical.

"You have no idea how lucky you are to have your family." Tears stung her eyes, the words scratched her throat as she said them. "Like I said, I've only ever had Sasha. And now she's gone too. I haven't heard from her in months. Was it so wrong of me to want to take care of her baby?"

But Enrique either didn't hear her or he didn't care

to answer. Several moments passed in agonizing silence. Nothing but anger and accusation between them. "Please go back upstairs," he finally said, his voice full of steel and ice. "See if Abuela needs help with the baby."

Fallon began to argue then deflated like a pinned balloon. The stiffness in his shoulders made it clear there was no use.

Enrique's stance was beyond clear. As far as he was concerned, there was nothing more to say for either of them.

# CHAPTER FOURTEEN

HE WAS AVOIDING HER.

A full three days had gone by since Enrique had confronted her after her horrid fiasco with the baby monitor. He was gone in the morning when she awoke, and arrived late at night after everyone had retired for the night.

It served to add another layer of guilt to her already crushing load. Because of her, Enrique was spending less time at home and hence less time with his son. No one to blame for it but herself.

For all she knew, he was spending some of that time away in search of her replacement. He might be calling agencies and having his staff screening potential candidates and was getting ready to show her the door.

Which meant she would have to leave the hacienda and leave Lucas. She might never see him again if she was fired.

Nor would she see Enrique.

It didn't bear thinking about, as it was crushing her heart. Fallon released the sob she couldn't hold at bay and turned over onto her back in bed. The clock read eleven thirty. She had no hope of falling asleep anytime soon.

Was he back home yet?

Was he really planning on firing her and shipping her back to the States? Had he ever felt a smidgeon of affection for her? Because she could no longer deny that she'd fallen head over heels for him. The look of betrayal on his face had nearly shattered her. That's when she'd known just how far she'd fallen in love with him. Because his disappointment in her had devastated her.

Would he ever be able to forgive her?

So many questions scrambled around in her brain. Suddenly, it was all too much. She had to know, had to search for some answers.

Tossing the covers aside, she rose out of bed and strode to the door. If Enrique was home, she was going to find him and ask him once and for all what her fate was to be. Rushing out of the room before she lost her nerve, she didn't bother with a robe or slippers.

She almost lost her nerve midway down the staircase.

The house was eerily quiet when she made it downstairs. The kitchen and hallway dark. The only light she could see was the dim one spilling in from the outside window.

The veranda.

With a deep breath and a silent prayer, she made her way to the front door and stepped outside.

Enrique didn't seem surprised to see her.

Reclined in the wicker chair, he gave her a perfunctory look, as if he'd been expecting her.

Fallon's heart lurched in her chest at the sight of him. The top three buttons of his shirt were undone revealing a triangle of olive skin, his sleeves rolled to his elbows. One ankle resting on his opposite knee.

A surge of longing so strong rushed over her it nearly had her knees buckling.

How could she have not acknowledged sooner that she'd fallen in love with the man? The way her entire body reacted at the mere sight of him left zero doubt of it. She just hadn't been ready to face the inconvenient truth.

And now she may never get a chance to.

"Is there something I can do for you?" he asked, his voice so devoid of any emotion, her eyes stung.

"I just wanted to see if you were home."

"I am. As you can very well see."

Every instinct told her to turn tail and run. He was clearly still angry with her. Somehow, she held her ground, kept her gaze steadily on his. Several awkward beats of silence pulsed between them rubbing her nerves raw.

Surprisingly, he gave in first. "How is my son?"

A slow breath of relief left her lungs. At least he hadn't sent her away. Yet.

She took a cautionary step closer. "Good. I believe he's about to pop a tooth through any minute now."

One eyebrow rose at her announcement. "Oh?"

She nodded. "Won't be long now. He's practically worn out his favorite teething ring."

"Hmm," was his only response.

"Will you be sending me away then?" she blurted out, the question rushing out of her before she'd even known she'd intended to say the words. "I wouldn't blame you if that's what you intend. But I implore you to reconsider."

His eyes narrowed on her before he turned away and stared into the dark, starry sky. "So you'd like another chance, is that it?"

"Yes," she answered plainly. "I would. My intention was never to mislead. I thought I was looking out for a child I care for and trying to be a good friend to someone who means a great deal to me. In the process, I deceived you and your brother and grandmother. I will always regret that decision."

There, she'd finally said it all. Finally got off her chest all that she hadn't been able to put into words that day in his study when she'd been too stunned to string any kind of sensible sentence together.

The ball was fully in Enrique's court now.

He took an agonizingly long time to answer, still hadn't bothered to look back at her, his gaze focused on the stars in the distant sky.

Finally, when she thought she couldn't stand the silence any longer, he rose out of the chair and turned to face her.

"You should know I've begun the search for another nanny," he said, without any preamble or emotion. So matter-of-fact, each word landing with an icy spike into the pit of her stomach.

So she had the answer to her question then, didn't she?

How ironic that she felt the loss so deeply. Of something she'd never even actually had. But she did feel it. She felt hollow and raw. And she felt the loss each day of what might have been developing between her and Enrique.

It was painfully clear he had no intention of even entertaining the possibility of forgiving her. Not ever.

She thought back to the night of the fundraiser when Luis had told her that Enrique wasn't the forgiving type. She should have paid more attention.

The warm and genuine man who'd taken her to a flight simulator to ease her fears, the one who had insisted she needed a day at the spa and had set it up for her was no more. That Enrique was gone.

How unfortunate for her that she'd fallen head over heels in love with that Enrique. This new one she didn't recognize. Which was just as well. Because he wanted nothing to do with her.

He was polite if not curt when they happened to run into each at the hacienda. But he was completely cool and distant with her at all times. His attitude was no less than what she deserved, so she would take it without complaint.

Still, the change in his demeanor toward her was chipping away at her heart, bit by bit.

As much as she tried not to let his coldness affect her mood, it was hard not to give in to melancholy at times. The weather these past few days certainly hadn't helped. It had rained and been overcast in Tulum for close to a full week.

So this morning when she'd seen the sun finally peek out from behind a thick, fluffy cloud, she hadn't hesitated to pack the baby up and make their way outside. She was convinced Lucas felt as stifled by being indoors as she did. The resort sported a top-line playground for the little ones who visited. The baby was too young to enjoy much more than the toddler swings. So off they went right after his midday lunch.

She used the time walking from the hacienda to the resort grounds to clear her head. In hindsight, she would have done it all so differently. First of all, she would have been up-front that first day about who she was and why she wanted to be hired to watch Lucas. But that cliché about hindsight existed for a reason, it being clear in the rearview and all that.

The playground was relatively empty when they arrived. The guests no doubt waiting for things to dry out before venturing out to play. She for one couldn't wait. Using one of Lucas's diapers to dry off one of the toddler swings, she strapped him in and began gently rocking him back and forth. His little burble of giggles told her he was enjoying himself.

From what she could ascertain, Enrique hadn't shared what had transpired that afternoon with Rosa or Luis. She didn't even know what to feel about that fact. Maybe they ought to know who she was too. Would they think less of her for not telling them sooner? The way Enrique clearly did?

Maybe Enrique was being gracious enough to leave the decision to her. Or perhaps it was a test of her character, one she was failing badly just as she had from the beginning.

*You'll always be a failure. You can't do anything right.*

Fallon shook the harsh memories away and gave Lucas another gentle nudge in the swing, her thoughts a mishmash of questions scrambling around in her brain.

It didn't take long before he started to loll his head and his eyelids grew droopy. He needed to be put down for his nap. It was time to go back.

Fallon did her best to focus on the baby and the routine she'd established to get through the day. She'd spent a lot of her life alone. She was used to loneliness. But this time, the sensation cut deeper. She'd come so close to having so much fulfillment in her life. And her own stupidity and cowardice had been the reason it had all been snatched away.

What she wouldn't give to talk to someone right now. To talk to Sasha in particular. Her foster sister had always known what to say. But Sasha was being as silent as ever. There was no way to know if Fallon's emails were even being read.

Fallon had to accept reality. She was on her own. Sasha wasn't going to ever answer her messages—Fallon could only hope she was okay. Enrique barely tolerated her presence, and that was only because he was avoiding her at all times.

Fallon had no one.

They made it back to the nursery just in time to get Lucas changed and fed before his eyes fluttered closed and she laid him down in the crib.

One thing was certain, she couldn't go on this way. Even the baby could sense that she was off. He was fussier than usual. Less willing to take his naps and quicker to cry at the slightest discomfort.

She couldn't risk having her mood affect Lucas in any way. It appeared she had a decision to make.

Enrique had told her he had already begun his search for her replacement. With his resources, the process was certain not to take long. Between Enrique, his brother and grandmother, Lucas was sure to be well taken care of until another nanny was hired. Just the other day, she'd seen a woman she recognized from the resort's childcare program enter Enrique's study. It didn't take a sleuth to surmise her reason for meeting with him.

The writing was on the wall. Fallon's days at the hacienda were clearly numbered anyway.

Her choice was clear, wasn't it? She would spare Enrique the effort of sending her away.

It was the very least she could do.

# CHAPTER FIFTEEN

"Ms. Duvall? Is that right?"

Fallon gave her head a brisk shake and pulled her focus back to the whiteboard. The figures were a blur, and she couldn't tell what Missy had written down as the final answer to the calculus problem they'd been working on.

No wonder. She'd been on the verge of crying again.

Blinking away the moisture, she brought her attention back to the present, to the small study room in the Boston Public Library where she was spending her days tutoring high school students until her shift at the riverside tavern began in the early evening.

As nice as the metro Boston library was, it was a far cry from the paradise she'd left two weeks ago.

"Yes, Missy, that looks right," she said when she could clearly see the figures. "Good work."

She glanced at the simple office clock hanging on the wall. "That should do it for the day."

The teen didn't need to be told twice. She immediately started packing up her things and bounded out the room.

Her tutoring students were much older than the kindergarteners she'd been teaching before. But until she found another teaching job, she had to make do with whatever helped to pay her bills.

Again, a far cry from just a few short weeks ago when

she'd been living in a grand mansion and being paid handsomely to take care of a child she loved.

Thoughts of Lucas brought the all too familiar burn of tears back to her eyes.

How she missed him. She missed his little palms against her cheek, the way he smelled after his baths, his toothless smile. Had that one tooth finally made its way out?

Lucas wasn't the only one she badly missed.

Fallon squeezed her eyes shut to push away the wayward thoughts that did nothing but make her want to weep. Tulum was behind her now. She had to accept it and move on.

Packing up, she hurried out of the room and made her way to the first floor to catch a ride share. There wasn't much time for her to get home and grab a bite of a snack bar, then change. Her shift at the tavern started in under an hour.

Fallon released a deep breath as she ran to the sidewalk. How her life had changed. At least she had a routine. In the mornings she worked on applying for teaching jobs, did her tutoring in the afternoons, then served tables until last call at night. Then the pattern repeated the next day. And the next day. And the next day.

So different from Tulum. She'd looked forward to waking up in the mornings. Now, she had nothing to look forward to. Her only hope to keep from weeping all day was to stay busy.

But the pang of longing caught up to her every once in a while. When she least expected it, it would all come rushing back. The way Enrique smiled at her, the charming winks he would occasionally send her way, making her heart melt. The scent of him.

*Just stop.*

The memories did nothing but tug at her heart. There was no point in rehashing them. Enrique probably hadn't given her another thought after she'd left Mexico. He hadn't so much as contacted her to make sure she'd arrived back in Boston all right, or to give her any kind of update on Lucas.

A myriad of emotions roiled in her center as she located her waiting ride and climbed in. Everything from sadness and despair to anger. She'd messed up. Of course she had. She should have never kept her secret for so long. But Enrique hadn't even considered her motives. Hadn't bothered to listen when she'd tried to explain. He'd simply wiped his hands of her. She shouldn't have expected anything more.

You'd think she would have learned her lesson as a teen when she'd expected her one remaining family member to take her in and instead her aunt had happily sent her away into the foster system.

Her aunt had wiped her hands of her too. Fallon had thought that particular rejection would be the worst one she'd ever have to face. Little had she known.

"Are you all right, miss?" the driver asked, extending a box of tissues over the seat to her.

Damn it. She hadn't even realized she'd actually sobbed out loud. She had to get ahold of herself. She had to forget she'd ever come across Enrique Martinez.

By the time she made it to her shift an hour later, she'd almost convinced herself that was possible.

Enrique knew his brother was back home the moment he arrived. Commotion and noise seemed to follow Luis, and it was no different today. Good. Enrique could use the break. He'd been poring over supply sheets and construction plans all day. He wanted the distraction of hearing about the excavation in Peru his brother was returning from.

Luis didn't bother to knock when he showed up in his

office moments after Enrique had heard him enter the hacienda and greet Abuela.

"I'm ho-ome," Luis declared, striding inside the room and plopping down into the chair across from Enrique's desk. "Did you miss me?"

Enrique couldn't help the smile that tugged at his lips. The truth was, he had missed his little brother. The last two weeks at the hacienda had been dark and depressing. The halls had felt empty. The rooms and gardens too quiet.

Maybe having his brother back would finally alleviate some of the bleakness.

Right. As if that was possible.

The truth was, the emptiness Enrique felt in his hollow core had nothing to do with Luis and everything to do with Fallon.

"How's my little nephew?" Luis wanted to know. "I missed him more than I would have guessed. Is he up in the nursery or does Fallon have him out in the gardens?"

So Abuela hadn't told him yet. Made sense. She finally figured, correctly, that it was Enrique's responsibility to break the news to Luis about Fallon.

This wasn't going to be easy. He just had to rip the proverbial bandage off and let Luis know what had gone down during his absence.

"He's in the nursery. But he's not with Fallon."

"Oh, does she have the day off? I hope she's out shopping at the resort. Maybe I'll try to catch her later. I wouldn't mind running into that new stylist from Paris."

Enrique dropped the pen he'd been jotting notes with and leaned back in his chair. "Fallon's not on the resort. In fact, she's not here in Tulum. She's gone."

Luis lifted one eyebrow. "Gone? What do you mean gone?"

"Would you prefer I say it in Spanish? She isn't at the hacienda. She's left Mexico."

"But why? She loved that *bambino*. Why would she leave him?"

"She's no longer in my employ as a nanny." There, it was out. He'd said it. Now, he just had to explain it. Somehow.

Luis narrowed his eyes on him. "What did you do, *hermano*?"

Enrique pinched the bridge of his nose and tried to ignore the irritation his brother was calling to the surface. Little did Luis know, he was already perilously close to losing all sense of balance here.

"I didn't do anything. Fallon Duvall was not who she presented herself to be. She lied to me."

"What in the world are you talking about? What did she lie about?"

The question somehow opened the proverbial floodgates. Before Enrique knew he'd intended to do so, he found himself spilling the whole story. Every detail, some he hadn't even realized he'd been thinking of, poured out of him like water through a sieve. He actually had to catch his breath when he was done.

Luis sat staring at him, open-mouthed.

"It's shocking. I know," Enrique said. Luis merely shook his head slowly from side to side. Once, then again. "What's shocking is that you let her go."

Whoa. Not the reaction Enrique was expecting. Why wasn't Luis outraged? He'd been duped. They all had.

*"Por que?"*

"You let that woman walk out of your life when she was the sole reason that I'd ever seen you happy, actually happy. And her only crime was to personally ensure your son was being well taken care of. That's all she cared about. And you punished her for it."

Well, when he put it that way.

But... Fallon's deception couldn't be ignored. "Don't you get it?" he demanded, pushing back the chair and standing. "She lied to me."

Luis tilted his head, crossed his arms in front of his chest. "Oh, I get it. Loud and clear."

"Huh?"

"I don't think I've ever seen you scared before, bro. No wonder I didn't recognize it. But she did it. She scared you."

Enrique scoffed but the effect fell flatter than he'd intended. "Scared of what? Do tell."

"Scared that you'd fallen for her," he declared, shaking his head again. His expression could only be described as one of pity. "So you saw an excuse to send her away and you took it. You took the easy way out."

Enrique did his best not to react to that statement. "That's not what happened. She lied to me," he repeated, sounding like a petulant child even to his own ears. "After leading me to trust her."

Luis narrowed his eyes on him. "Really? Are we really going to go there? Any fool could see it, the way you looked at each other when you thought no one was watching. And it frightened you."

Huh. Had he been that obvious?

"Yes, it was that obvious," Luis said, somehow reading his unspoken question. "And it spooked you in case she rejected you like our dear parents did. So you let her walk away."

What in the devil was he talking about? Luis didn't know the details. He had no idea what had happened between him and Fallon. Sure, he'd thought he might be developing feelings for her, but that had taken a major hit when he'd overheard her on the monitor. Unless...

Had he used the incident as an excuse to push her away? Could his pesky, annoying brother possibly be right that he'd done so out of some kind of fear of ultimately being rejected himself?

"Do you know exactly where she is?" Luis wanted to know.

Enrique nodded, his heart pounding. "She's back in Boston. I'm assuming she went back to her apartment. The same address listed in her employment papers from the agency."

Luis clapped, frustration etched in his features. "You're a fool if you don't go get her right now. You and I both know it."

"There's a gentleman who insisted on being seated in your section."

Fallon had barely managed to get her apron on after clocking in for her shift when the bartender let her know. "He was adamant. You want me to tell him to scram?" he asked.

She could guess who it was. Mr. Ramos. He came in every Friday around the same time. She'd happened to wait on him once, and they'd gotten to talking about her time in Tulum. He was from Cozumel and had recently lost his wife. The man just wanted an ear to listen. He was lonely.

Fallon could certainly relate. "No, it's okay. I'll wait on him."

She didn't even need to check his order; he asked for the same thing every time. A bottle of beer, which he called *cerveza*, and a plate of the tower-high nachos. He always got the key lime pie for dessert. Fallon went to put the order in and then walked over to the booth to say hello.

Then stopped cold in her tracks. The man sitting there was most definitely not Señor Ramos.

She made herself blink to ensure she was seeing straight. Once, then again. Yet the image didn't change.

"Enrique?"

"Hi, Fallon."

She had to be imagining this. Maybe she'd fallen asleep after her tutoring session and she wasn't even here at the tavern. She was still back at library study room, pressing snooze on her phone alarm and falling back asleep on the table.

"Is that really you?"

He stood, did a slow turn. *"Sí, es mi."*

Certainly sounded like him. And the accent seemed authentic. She pinched herself on the arm just to be sure.

Heaven help her, she felt the pinch. It *was* him. He was really here.

"What are you doing here?" A curl of hope sprung in her chest before she squashed it down. She couldn't make any assumptions. There had to be a logical explanation why he was here that had nothing to do with her. He was angry with her. He hadn't so much as sent her a text since she'd left.

He was in Boston on business. That had to be it. It was the only explanation that made sense. A flush of disappointment washed through her. She tried to paste a casual smile on her face.

"Uh, it's nice to see you. Is… Lucas with you?"

He shook his head. "No, but he's one of the reasons I'm here."

Alarm bells rang in her head. Why had Enrique felt the need to travel all the way to the States on Lucas's behalf?

"Is he all right?" she asked, feeling the color drain from her face.

Enrique held up his hand, palm up. "Yes, he's totally fine. It's just his last nanny didn't work out. I'm looking to make other arrangements for him."

Huh. So that was it then. He was here to visit the agency he'd used before. How silly of her that for even one moment she'd thought he might be here for her.

"I see. I hope the search goes well. How is he? He must be getting so big. Do you have any pictures?"

She didn't want to sound too anxious, but she couldn't help herself. She'd missed the baby terribly. And having Enrique here was wreaking havoc on her senses. It was hard to think straight.

"I can do better than show you a picture. Come back with me to see him."

She recalled hearing he had a town house in Boston. Excitement speared through her chest. To be able to see Lucas again, to hold him in her arms!

How kind of Enrique to do this, given how irate he must still be with her. She whipped her apron off. "I'll see if someone can cover for me for a couple of hours."

He tilted his head. "A couple of hours? It's going to take longer than that."

What did that mean? Was Lucas at the Cape instead? Crushing disappointment shot through her. There was no way she'd be able to get coverage for that long. She couldn't just take off for several hours, she needed this job.

But if Lucas was at the Cape? Why was Enrique here?

"Where is he?" she asked.

"At home. In Mexico."

Was he being cruel? Had he come here just to punish her? Maybe she'd underestimated just how cross he was with her.

He reached for her then, trailed a finger along her cheek. "Come with me to see him," he repeated. "He misses you. I miss you."

But that would mean…

She couldn't dare hope, could she?

"Enrique. I think you have to be really clear now about exactly what you're doing here."

"Fair enough," he said, dipping his hand into his pocket. "I'm here for you, sweetheart. Because nothing has been the same since you left. The hacienda feels empty. My life without you feels empty." When he pulled his hand out, he held a small box in his palm.

Fallon's breath caught when he flipped it open. Inside sat a sparkling solitaire cut diamond set on a thin gold band. "It was Abuela's," Enrique said. "She insisted I give it to you when I told her I was going to propose."

A loud ringing sound echoed through Fallon's ears. Her knees nearly gave out. "Propose?"

*"Sí,"* he said, taking her by the hand and pulling her toward him. "Marry me, Fallon. You're the best wife I know I don't deserve and the best mother my son could hope to have. You've been the only mother he's ever known, and I was selfish to forget that for even a moment because of my pride. I've been a stubborn fool who didn't know how to accept happiness when it found me. Please forgive all that and do me the honor of saying yes."

It took several moments for Fallon's mouth to work in tandem with her mind. When she finally found her voice, the whole tavern heard, if not the entire street.

"Yes, my love! A million times yes!"

# EPILOGUE

*One year later*

Dear Fallon

I know this message has been a long time coming. Please forgive me for how long it's taken. Know that I've read every single word of every note you've ever sent me.

My dear sister, please understand that I kept quiet because I wasn't sure what to say. I was lost and confused and didn't know where the next roof over my head might be. But I've come a long way since then.

Somehow I ended up at a counseling center on a ranch in Western Colorado. And now I can't imagine being anywhere else. I don't know if it's the air or the vastness of the land or the clear skies. My head feels clear for the first time in as long as I can remember. I look forward to waking up in the morning. That's never happened before. I even help the counselors with other patients now. I've found my calling, sis. For the first time ever. And unfortunately that calling doesn't seem to include motherhood.

You've always been the more nurturing one. I don't have what it takes to be a good mom to little Lucas.

You do.

Thank you for taking care of him for me. I can rest easy knowing he's in your very good hands. I'm not sure when I'll write again, sis. The past seems so distant behind me now and I'd like to keep it that way. All of it.
Love always
Sasha

FALLON READ THE email and then read it again, tears filling her eyes and streaming down her face. Sasha was alive. And she was fine. She was more than fine. Even through the electronic screen, Fallon could sense a peace from her sister she'd never witnessed in her before. As much as she missed her, Fallon could understand why Sasha had felt the need to go quiet all this time. And her need to keep her distance going forward.

All that mattered was that Sasha was in a better place now. And that Lucas was thriving with two parents and an extended family who loved and cherished him. A family that was about to grow by one.

Her dear, dear sister was responsible for so much good that had happened in Fallon's life. Fallon would always be there for her when and if Sasha ever wanted her.

"Almost ready, *carina*?" Enrique's voice sounded behind her. Fallon wiped the tear away from her cheek and clicked off the message before turning to her husband.

"*Sí*, I'm ready," she answered.

A mischievous smile spread over his lips before he managed to hide it. He still thought she didn't know. The ruse was that he was taking her to a late lunch at the seaside tavern they'd visited that day after they'd visited the ruins. But she'd figured it out. Various clues dropped here and there along with Luis's inability to keep any kind of secret and she'd put two and two together. They weren't heading to a simple meal.

She would make sure to act surprised when she walked into the baby shower they'd all planned for her.

Just a small fib.

* * * * *

# Engaged To The Billionaire
Cara Colter

# MILLS & BOON

**Cara Colter** shares her home in beautiful British Columbia, Canada, with her husband of more than thirty years, an ancient crabby cat and several horses. She has three grown children and two grandsons.

This book is dedicated to all those who
still find enchantment in the written word.

# CHAPTER ONE

*DISASTER HAD STRUCK.*

Jolie Cavaletti had been back in Canada for three whole hours, and her sense of impending doom had proved entirely correct.

She stared down into the white elegant rectangular box. It appeared to be entirely filled with pale peach-colored ruffles.

"Isn't it, literally, so beautiful?" her sister, Sabrina, breathed.

Jolie was fairly certain she heard a stifled laugh from at least two of the other members of the small gathering of the bridal party. She shot a look at Sabrina's old friends from high school, Jacqui and Gillian, or Jack and Jill as Jolie liked to refer to them.

*It's only a dress,* Jolie told herself. *In the course of human history, a dress can hardly rate as a disaster.*

Holding out faint hope that the bridesmaid dress her sister had chosen for her might look better out of the box, she buried her hands deep into the fluffy fabric and yanked.

The dress unfolded in all its ghastly glory. It was frilly and huge, like a peach-colored tent. The ruffles were attached to a silky under sheath, with a faint pattern on it. Snakes? Who chose a bridesmaid dress with snakes on it?

Oh, wait, on closer inspection, they weren't snakes. Vines. No sense of relief accompanied that discovery.

Jolie did feel relieved, however, when she contemplated

the fact her sister might be playing a joke on her. The feeling was short-lived. When she cast her sister a look, Sabrina was beaming at the dress with all the pride of a mother who had chosen the best outfit ever for her firstborn child entering kindergarten.

Jolie glanced again at Jack and Jill, who were choking back laughter. She shot them a warning glance, and they both straightened and regarded the dress solemnly.

Inwardly, she closed her eyes and sighed at how quickly one could be transported back to a place they thought they had left behind.

Her sister, by design, or by the simple human desire to form a community based on similarities, had always surrounded herself with friends who were astonishingly like her. Sabrina took after their mother, tiny, willowy, blonde, blue-eyed, bubbly.

Beth, Jack and Jill, all of them with their blond locks scraped back into identical ponytails, seemed barely changed in the ten years that had passed since Jolie had last seen them. They were like variations on a theme: Beth shorter, Jill blonder, Jack's eyes a different shade of blue, but any of them could have passed for Sabrina's sister.

The odd man out, the one who could not have passed for Sabrina's sister, was Jolie. She took after her Italian father and was tall and curvy, had dark brown eyes, an olive complexion and masses of unruly, dark curls.

Maybe it explained, at least in part, her and her sister's lifelong prickliness with one another, a sense of being on different teams.

"Do you like it?" Sabrina asked.

"It looks, er, a little too big."

Jolie would, in that dress, walk down the aisle and stand at the altar with the rest of the bridal party, looking like Gulliver in the land of Lilliputians.

"Well," Sabrina said, accusingly, "that's what you get for being in Italy both when I chose the dresses, and when we had the fittings."

This was said as if Jolie had opted for a frivolous vacation at an inconvenient time, when in fact she lived in Italy, going there directly after high school, attending university, earning her doctorate in anthropology and never leaving.

"It will look better on," Beth, Jolie's favorite of all Sabrina's friends, said kindly. "I didn't like mine at first, either."

"You didn't?" Sabrina said, a bit of an edge to her voice. Jolie looked at her sister more closely, and saw that premarital nerves, right below the surface, were raw.

Well, why wouldn't they be? Sabrina and Troy had been married before. A wedding that Jolie had not been invited to, not that she planned to dwell on that.

It had, according to Sabrina in way of excuse for not inviting her own sister to her nuptials, been a spur-of-the-moment thing, basically held on the front steps of city hall.

Jolie, more careful in nature than her sister, did not think a spur-of-the-moment wedding was the best idea.

Though she had not felt the least bit vindicated when things did not go well. Jolie had lived far enough away from the newly married couple that she had been spared most of the details, but her mother had reported on a year of spectacular fights before the divorce. The fights, according to Mom, who spoke of them in hushed tones that did not hide her relish in the drama, had continued, unabated, after the split.

"It reminds me of your father and me," she had confided in Jolie.

A psychiatrist could have a heyday with her sister choosing the same kind of dysfunctional relationship Jolie and Sabrina had endured throughout their childhood. Her father and mother had a volatile and unpredictable relationship, punctuated with her father's finding someone new, and her mother begging him to come back.

All that ongoing angst had made Jolie try to become invisible, hiding in books and her schoolwork, which she'd excelled at. Somehow, she had hoped she could be "good enough" to repair it all, but she never had been.

She shook off these most unwelcome thoughts. She had hoped she'd spent long enough—and been far enough—away not to be dragged back into the kind of turmoil her childhood had been immersed in.

But here Sabrina was, determined to try the marriage thing all over again, convinced that if she did the wedding entirely differently this time, the result would also be different.

A part of Jolie, which she didn't even want to acknowledge existed, might have been ever so slightly put out that her sister was having a second wedding when Jolie had not even had a first.

She had come oh-so close! If things had gone according to plan, she would be married right now. Sabrina would have been *her* bridesmaid. She could have tortured her sister with unsuitable dresses. Not that she would have. She would have picked a beautiful dress for her sister. No, better, she would have let her sister pick her own dress.

Thankfully, they had not gotten as far as the selection of wedding party dresses.

Though no one knew this, not her mother or her sister, Jolie had purchased her own wedding gown, purposely not involving her family.

Because they somehow thought she was *this* horrible peach confection.

Her wedding dress, in fact, had been the opposite of the peach-colored extravaganza she now held. It had been simplicity itself. Beautifully cut floor-length white silk, sleeveless, with a deep V at the neck that had hugged all her curves—celebrated them—before flaring out just below the knee

Even though Jolie was thousands of miles—and a few months—from Anthony's betrayal, the pain suddenly felt like a fresh cut, probably brought on by exhaustive traveling, and now being thrust into bridal activities without being the bride.

How she had loved him! In hindsight she could see that she had been like a homeless puppy, delirious with joy at finally being picked, finally having a place where she would belong. Riding high on the wave of love, she had missed every sign that Anthony might not be quite as enthused, that her outpouring of devotion was not being reciprocated.

Her breakup was three months ago, her wedding would have been in early June, if Anthony—the man she had loved so thoroughly and unconditionally, who she had planned to have children with and build a life with—had not betrayed her.

With another woman.

Something else a psychiatrist would no doubt have a heyday with given the fact she had grown up with her father's indiscretions.

And so Jolie found herself single and determined not to be sad about it. To see it as not a near miss, but an opportunity.

To refocus on her career.

To celebrate independence.

To *never* be one of those women who begged to come first. Jolie's name on her birth certificate was Jolie, not Jolene, but she had not a single doubt her mother had named her after that song.

And also she never wanted to be, again, one of those women who *yearned*, not so much for a fairy-tale ending, as for a companion to deeply share the simple moments in life with.

Coffee in the morning.

A private joke. Maybe even a laugh over a dress like this one.

A look across the table.

Someday, children, running joyous and barefoot through a mountain meadow on holiday in the Italian Alps.

Jolie tried to shake off her sudden sensation of acute distress. She made herself take a deep breath and focus on the here and now at her sister's destination wedding.

The bridal party—Jolie, Sabrina and Sabrina's other three bridesmaids—were currently having a little pre–big day preview of the facilities, which had led to this tête-à-tête in the extremely posh ballroom of a mind-blowingly upscale winery in Naramata, deep in the heart of British Columbia's Okanagan Valley.

Jolie was all too aware she was in possession of the world's ugliest dress, and that it was somehow woven into the fabric of her sister's hopes and dreams.

Unlike Jolie, sworn off love forever, Sabrina was braver. Her sister still had hopes and dreams! She was going to give love another chance.

Which kind of added up for Jolie to *Suck it up, buttercup.*

She calculated in her head. It was Wednesday already in Italy, which made it Tuesday evening here. The wedding was Saturday. She only had to get through a few days.

Anybody could do anything for a couple of days. In the course of human history, it was nothing.

"I think I'll go try it on," Jolie announced.

"Yes, immediately!" Sabrina ordered, flushed with excitement that Jolie could see the unfortunate potential for hysteria in. "You're the only one who hasn't tried on your dress."

Reluctant to actually wear the dress, but eager to get away from her sister and the bridal party, Jolie gathered up the box.

She went into a nearby washroom—as posh as the ballroom—and entered one of the oversize stalls. She stripped down to her underwear, dropped her clothes onto the floor and pulled the dress over her head. It settled around her with a whoosh and a rustle.

She opened the door of the stall and stepped out, resigned to look at it in the full-length mirror that she was quite sorry had been provided.

It was as every bit as horrible as she had thought it would be, a fairy-tale dress gone terribly wrong, with too much volume, too many ruffles and way too many snakes. *Vines.*

A lesson in fairy tales, really.

The bridesmaid dress made Jolie feel like a paper-flower-festooned float in a parade welcoming the *carnevale* season to Italy.

Her sensible bra, chosen for comfort while traveling, did not go with the off-the-shoulder design of the dress, and in one last attempt to save something, she slipped it off and let it fall to the polished marble floor.

No improvement.

She fought the urge to burst into tears. She told herself the sudden desire to cry was not related to her own broken dreams.

It was because she had been home less than a few hours, and already she was *that* person all over again. Too big. Too awkward. Too *everything* to ever fit in here.

*The exact kind of person a beloved fiancé—the man she would have trusted with her very life—had stepped out on.*

A tear did escape then, and she brushed it away impatiently with her fist. She was just experiencing jet lag and it wasn't exactly home, she told herself firmly. Even though she was back in Canada for the first time since she had graduated from high school, Jolie was about a million miles from the Toronto neighborhood where she had grown up.

Her scholarly side insisted on pointing out it was two thousand eight hundred and seventy-nine miles, not a million.

It was that kind of thinking that had branded her a geek in all those painful growing up years. She had skipped ahead grades, and so she had always been the youngest—and most left out—in her school days. Her senior year—shared with her sister, Sabrina, two years her senior—had been the worst.

In fact, it may have been the most painful year of all.

*Not counting this one.*

See? Jolie could feel all the old insecurities brewing briskly right below the surface. Who wouldn't have their insecurities bubble to the surface in a dress this unflattering?

Privately, Jolie thought maybe since it was a second marriage—albeit to the same man—Sabrina could have toned it down a bit. But toned down was not Sabrina under any circumstances, which was probably why she was so eager to have a redo of the vows spoken on the city hall steps.

And really, all Jolie wanted was her sister's love of Troy to end in happiness. One of them should have a love like that!

And a more perfect location than this one would be hard to imagine, and that was from someone who had spent plenty of time in the wine country of Tuscany.

Taking a deep breath, reminding herself of her devotion to someone in the family getting their happy ending, Jolie picked as much of the dress as she could off the floor and headed back to the bridal party and braced herself for Jack and Jill's snickers, Beth's kindly pity, and her sister's enthusiasm.

But even her sister was not able to delude herself about the dress.

As she watched Jolie make her way across the ballroom to

the little cluster of the bridal party at one end of it, her mouth opened. And then her forehead crinkled. And then she burst into tears, and wailed. "It looks as if it has snakes on it!"

# CHAPTER TWO

JOLIE WAS UNCOMFORTABLY aware of the sudden silence that followed her sister's observation, and of the four sets of blue eyes regarding her critically.

"No, no," Beth finally said soothingly, "they don't look at all like snakes. Definitely vines."

"Even Chantelle can't fix that," Jack decided to weigh in.

"Chantelle?" Jolie asked baffled, noticing how the mention of the name deepened her sister's distress.

Jill rolled her eyes. "Only the most well-known photographer in the fashion world."

Jolie recalled it—vaguely—now. Sabrina had gushed in an email that her soon-to-be husband had some kind of connection to the famous Chantelle—one name was enough, apparently—and that she had agreed to do the wedding photography. When she *never* did weddings.

"You are literally going to ruin everything," Sabrina said to Jolie.

"I didn't pick the dress!"

"You didn't leave me time to fix it, either. Why couldn't you have come a week earlier, like I asked?"

After traveling halfway around the world to be here for her sister, it would be so easy to be offended, but Jolie recognized, again, that hysteria just below the surface.

"Sabrina, I have a job," Jolie said, striving for a reasonable tone. "I can't just put everything on hold because—"

"Oh! The all-important doctor!"

Jolie flinched that her accomplishment—a doctorate in anthropology—was being seen in this light, as if she was a big shot, flaunting her successes.

"And why would you put everything on hold," Sabrina continued, "for your sister who is marrying the same man again? You probably think it's doomed to failure. You're probably still mad that I didn't invite you the first time."

Jolie was aware vehement denials were only going to feed the fire Sabrina was stoking, and that there was a tiny kernel of truth in each of those accusations. They might hardly ever—make that never—see eye to eye, but sisters still knew things about each other.

"I can fix the dress," Beth said gently, as if any of this had anything to do with the dress. "Look!"

She got behind Jolie and pulled in several inches of excess fabric. Jolie felt the dress tightening around her.

Sabrina regarded her hopefully for a moment, then her whole face crumpled, and she wailed and ran from the room.

Jack and Jill scurried after her, sending Jolie accusing looks over their shoulders.

Beth let go of the dress. "She's just tired," she said, trailing out after her friends.

This to the woman who had left Rome over twenty-four hours ago, and been traveling ever since.

A waiter, very formal in a white shirt and black pants, came in with a tray of wineglasses. He looked around at the empty room, but did not allow the smallest flicker of surprise to cross his deliberately bland face.

"Wine?" he asked her smoothly. "I have our award-winning Hidden Valley prosecco or I have one glass of bubbly juice here, if you'd prefer?"

Bubbly juice? Jolie could not imagine any of those women

choosing juice. Was it a dig at her? That drunken prom night?

Of course it wasn't. That was ten years ago. She was being overly sensitive.

"Yes, to the prosecco."

He slid a look at the dress. "Take two," he suggested.

"Thank you. I will."

The waiter glanced around the empty room, "The deck is lovely at this time of the evening."

She took his suggestion, and let the dress trail along the floor since her hands were full. She moved outside. Indeed, the deck was lovely.

*Relax*, Jolie ordered herself. She had to look at the events that had just unfolded lightly, through the lens of human history, even.

The dress and her sister's snippiness were hardly disasters. Didn't family frictions always surface when a little stress was added to the mix?

She settled in a lounge chair, the dress surging up and around her as though it intended to swallow her. She set down one of the glasses on a table beside the chair, took a deep breath, moved a wayward ruffle away from her face and then enjoyed a long greedy drink of the prosecco.

*Ahh.*

From her place on the deck, she made herself focus on the good things. Her mother was not here yet to weigh in on the dress, or anything else for that matter.

And her father was not here yet, either, bringing the more inevitable friction.

Weddings, rather than being fairy-tale events, came with plenty of tension. Strain on broken vessels—which her family could certainly be considered—was usually not a good thing.

"Here's to not having a wedding of my own," Jolie said,

raising her wineglass to the glory of the evening light. She lifted her face to the last of the sun. The heat of the scorching July day was waning.

Jolie took another deep breath, and another sip of the prosecco. Well, maybe more like a gulp. She made herself focus on her surroundings rather than the troubling intricacies of her family.

The view was panoramic with lush hills, grape vines, copses of conifers and deciduous trees, a verdant green lawn stretching all the way down to the sparkling waters of a lake. Canoes bobbed gently, tied to the dock. The air had a faintly golden, sparkly quality, and a luscious sun-on-pine scent to it.

The patio was located off the ballroom and just to the side of the main entrance of the lodge. She imagined the beautiful doors thrown open for big events, people flowing seamlessly between the outside and the inside, laughter and music riding on the night air.

The main building of the Hidden Valley Winery was a sweeping, single-story log structure, at least a hundred years old and lovingly preserved. The manicured grounds only hinted at an interior that was posh beyond belief, the Swarovski crystal chandeliers and Turkish rugs inside the lobby in sharp and delightful contrast to the more rustic elements.

Jolie, to her everlasting gratitude, especially now, had found on her arrival that she had been assigned her own cabin.

*I hope you don't mind*, Sabrina had said. *Most of us are staying in the main lodge, but there aren't enough rooms.*

Even though Jolie was aware of already being cast on the outside of her sister's circle, she found she didn't mind at all. Especially now that she was pretty sure the tone for the wedding had been set.

Seeing her sister, with all that crowd of high school girls in the background, Jolie realized how invested she was in giving a different impression, showing them she was not that same geeky, gauche girl they might remember from their senior year.

If they remembered her at all.

A sound drifted on the summer air. Laughter. It would be unkind to think of it as cackling. Jolie recognized her sister's girlish shriek. So, Sabrina had returned to good spirits after she had dumped Jolie.

It made Jolie even more annoyed that her reintroduction to her sister's clique had gone so off the rails.

She'd barely finished exploring her little cabin when she'd been summoned. The cabin was one of a dozen or so structures scattered through the woods that surrounded the lodge. It was completely self-contained and an absolute delight, the same mix of posh and rustic that made the lodge so charming.

But the dress reveal had been called practically before she set down her bag. Her makeup had long since given out, and her hair had gone wild. Her outfit—that she had spent way too much on in anticipation of that very moment—was travel rumpled and stained from holding her exhausted seat partner's baby for half the journey.

So, even though it meant keeping the others waiting, Jolie showered and clipped her wild abundance of dark curls, holding them back to the nape of her neck. Taming the hair was something she was much better at now than she had been in high school. She had put on a dash of makeup, pleased she didn't need much as her work, which was mostly outdoors, gave her a healthy glow. Then she had carefully chosen a skirt that showed off the length of her sun-browned legs, and a crisp white top that was casual in the way only truly expensive designer clothing could be.

She had been annoyed at herself for being nervous when she stepped out of the cabin toward the people she had not seen for ten years.

*Cavaletti*, she had told herself sternly, *you are not a gladiator going into the games.*

The thought filled her with longing for the research her team was doing at the Colosseum.

And that helped her with perspective. In the course of human history, the encounter she had just survived was *not* a disaster. Not even close. And four days? Gladiators had lived below the Colosseum for years, trapped by their fates.

So the dress, technically, didn't qualify, either.

There. That was settled. In the course of human history, several days trapped at a family wedding was not even a blip on the radar. She vowed she would focus on all the good things, such as the incredible quality of the glasses of prosecco she had been given.

The first glass had disappeared rather quickly, but she *was* relaxed. Philosophical, even. She took a slower sip of the second one and worked on convincing herself that she no longer cared about being part of the *in* crowd. At twenty-six, she had lived abroad for ten years. She had a doctorate in anthropology. She was working on what she considered to be one of the most exciting projects in all of Italy, a project at the ruins of the Colosseum.

She could handle this reunion with aplomb.

Aplomb!

She wasn't the same girl in the high school annual with a *Most Likely To*...title put under their picture.

Some of them had been ordinary: most likely to marry Mike Mitchell; most likely to run a pet store; most likely to become a doctor.

And some had been surprisingly cute and original: most

likely to run away with gypsies; most likely to win the Iditarod; most likely to be a lifeguard on Bondi Beach.

And then there had been hers.

*Most likely to enter religious life.*

Her family had been Catholic, but not exactly what anyone would call practicing, with her parents divorced. She and Sabrina had not been inside a church since their first communion.

What had earned her that awful descriptor was that fact that Jolie had been a full two years younger than the rest of the grads. The suggestion she would join a convent and become a nun was a dig at her relative innocence. She was fairly certain it was meant without malice—someone's idea of being funny and original—and yet she could still feel the sting of it, even now, ten years later.

Which explained why she had splurged on a wardrobe that did not have one single item in it that would have been chosen by someone likely to enter religious life.

As she soaked up the serenity of the evening, she watched as a convertible sports car, top up, a deep and sleek gray, slid into the driveway and nosed expertly into a tight parking stall.

So there it was, just a little bit behind schedule.

Jolie was pretty sure this would qualify as a one hundred percent bona fide disaster.

Because look who was getting out of that car.

As soon as she saw him, Jolie knew she should have known better than to let her guard down, to think she could outrun the embarrassing decisions that high school annual judgment on her had caused her to make.

She should have known better than to think her maturity and successes were going to make this wedding/high school reunion a breeze.

Because that man who had just gotten out of the car was the man she least wanted to see in the entire world.

Jay Fletcher.

And that was before she factored what she was wearing into the equation!

Despite the fact she had been bracing herself to spend a week with the high school crowd she had only been reluctantly accepted into because of her popular sister, at no point had Jolie prepared herself for Jay. You would think Sabrina could have mentioned he would be here.

But no, there had not been a single mention of his name.

In high school, Jay Fletcher had been the antithesis of everything Jolie Cavaletti had been.

Popular. Athletic. Sophisticated. The high school hero.

Under his picture in the high school annual? *Most likely to succeed.* And while everyone else in the grad class had only had one *most likely* under their yearbook picture, an extra accolade had been heaped on Jay. *Most likely to take the world by storm.*

If the car—sleek, rare, expensive—was any indication, he had done just that.

And Jay looked every ounce the successful man as he paused and took in his surroundings. He stretched, hands locked briefly behind his neck, and Jolie noted he still appeared to be the athlete he had once been, long-legged, broad across the shoulders, narrow at the waist and hip, some extraordinarily appealing masculine hardness in the lines of his body.

He radiated confidence, which he had never had any shortage of. But now there was a subtle masculine power about him as well. A man who had come fully into himself.

Was he beautifully dressed, or could he have made sackcloth look worthy of a *GQ* cover shoot? Really, his clothing was ordinary, just pressed khaki shorts ending in the middle of a tanned and muscled thigh, a solid-colored navy blue golf-style shirt that didn't mold his perfect build but hinted at it, which was, oddly, even more enticing. When he stretched like that, the muscles in his arms leaped appealingly.

The evening light danced in his short neatly trimmed hair, threading the light brown through with gold. It also flattered features that needed no flattery. If anything ten years had made him even more perfect.

Jay Fletcher was simply and stunningly handsome: wide brow, high cheekbones, straight, strong nose, firm, full lips, a faint cleft in a square chin.

As Jolie watched, he lifted his sunglasses. Even though she could not see the color of his eyes from here—of course she couldn't—memory conjured up the deep, cool green of them that had always made her young heart flutter.

The gaze, she reminded herself, a little desperately, that had cut her to ribbons the last time she had seen him.

Besides, she was not the young girl she had been. Not even close. In fact, she was bitter and heartbroken enough to be immune to any man.

Up to and including Jay Fletcher.

# CHAPTER THREE

As JOLIE WATCHED, Jay lowered the sunglasses back over his eyes, moved to the back of his sleek, expensive vehicle, popped the trunk and threw a bag over his shoulder.

Jolie would like to claim she had barely spared him a thought over the past ten years, but that was not true. She *had* wondered if he had aged well. She *had* wondered if he was happy. She *had* wondered if he had ever spared her a thought after that last embarrassing moment together.

And yet, even as she had wondered, she had avoided asking her sister, knowing Sabrina might have guessed her pathetic interest and been cruelly amused by it.

And Jolie had certainly avoided looking Jay up online, because that would have felt as if she was indulging a secret longing for the impossible.

When she had heard his father died, her second year at university in Italy, she sent a card, but she had *wanted* so much more. To call him. To hear his voice. To be the one who soothed his pain, as if she knew things about him that others did not.

Which was silly! They had worked on a science project together and, having come to know him a little, she had deeply embarrassed herself at senior prom.

When she'd become engaged, all *that*—secret crushes and childish illusions—was left, finally, behind her. Her old life was in the rearview mirror.

But watching Jay Fletcher move toward her, his stride long and easy, Jolie knew she had been lying to herself. You didn't leave some things behind you.

And maybe it was because she was not engaged anymore that seeing Jay made her feel as if she was sixteen all over again.

Awkward.

Hopelessly out of her depth.

Like she wanted things she could not have.

She realized she had to get out of here. The jet lag. The sparkling wine. The dress. The old gang. Now Jay. It was all too much.

But then she realized, with a hint of panic, there would be no slipping away, not in this dress! She'd look like a barge heading off into the setting sun. It was too late to compose herself for the reunion she had not expected. At all.

The man Jolie Cavaletti least wanted to see in the entire world was already halfway up the walkway. Jay came up the wide stairs that led to the entrance of the Hidden Valley Lodge.

She held her breath.

Maybe she'd be lucky and he'd just go in those wide front doors, with barely a glance toward that side deck, dismissing the woman sipping wine alone as some kind of crazy eccentric in her peach explosion.

For a moment, as impossible as it seemed with the dress screaming, *Look at me*, it actually seemed that might be how it would play out.

He glanced her way, but didn't even change his stride. Just when she thought she could breathe again, he stopped abruptly, took a half step back and stared at her. And then he lifted his sunglasses.

She'd remembered his eyes with one hundred percent accuracy, unfortunately. They were absolutely, gorgeously mesmerizing, as luminescent and as multilayered as green jade.

A smile tickled across the unfairly sensuous wideness of his lips.

It was a good thing she was well armed with cynicism, otherwise she might find his attractiveness tempting.

She'd allowed herself to give in to that particular temptation once before, she reminded herself tartly. The memory of how well that had gone should have kept her in check.

"Jolie?" he asked. "Jolie Cavaletti?"

That voice, damn him! Who had a voice like that? A movie star voice, a bit raspy, a bit tinged with laughter, a bit like fingertips touching the back of her neck.

Now what? Did she get up from her lounge chair and go over to him. Offer her hand? Say in dulcet, husky tones, *Nice to see you again, Jay. It's been a long time.*

Pretend she wasn't wearing the dress?

Instead of getting up, Jolie hunkered down deeper into the folds of her fashion catastrophe, took a fortifying gulp of prosecco—good grief, where had that second glass gone— and lifted a hand. She hoped the gesture was casual—maybe even faintly dismissive—but she feared she had only managed to look like a fainting Southern belle.

"Jay," she said.

He didn't appear to notice lack of invitation in either her tone or her feeble hand gesture. He strode right over, and looked down at her.

His scent—soap and, more subtly, mountain-air-scented aftershave—whispered across the space between them.

*Don't look at his eyes*, she ordered herself. *You'll turn into stone.*

But, of course, that wasn't really her worry at all. The opposite. That the light in those eyes could melt the stone she had placed around her bruised heart.

She looked at his eyes.

They were the color of a cool pond on a hot day, sparking with light like sun dancing across a calm surface.

"How are you?" he asked.

*I've had better moments.*

"Peachy," she said.

It was unfair how the amused upward quirk of that sexy mouth created a dimple in his cheek and made him even more breathtaking. It was unfair to notice that his hair was the exact color of a pot of melted chocolate, and that the faintest shadow darkened his cheeks and chin.

She had a completely renegade thought: she wondered what those whiskers might feel like scraping against tender skin.

Those kinds of thoughts were not permitted in a woman newly dedicated to being independent, to creating her own happiness.

She gave the prosecco an accusing look, then couldn't decide whether to take another fortifying sip or set it down. So, she did the logical thing. She did both.

Apparently oblivious to his effect on the jet-lagged, deeply embarrassed woman in front of him, he tilted his head and looked at her more deeply.

"A peach. Picked fresh off the tree."

"Well, not picked by me," she said. She hoped for an airy tone. She sounded defensive.

The upward quirk at the corner of his lip deepened, and so did the dimple. "Of course you didn't choose that dress. So not you."

Did she have to be reminded, right out of the gate, why she had had such a crush on him? He had always seemed to see in her something that everyone else missed. Jolie was engulfed with a sense of being starstruck and tongue-tied and sixteen all over again.

*Cavaletti*, she told herself firmly, *stop it.*

"I've seen a lot of ugly bridesmaid dresses over the years," he decided, leaning toward her and regarding her intently, "but that one might win. Are those, er, worms?"

"I thought snakes."

"Hmm. I'm pretty sure that involved an apple, not a peach."

Really? Being with a man like this made the temptations of the garden seem all the more understandable.

"And maybe a fig leaf," she replied, "which would be a considerable improvement over this dress."

She intended the remark lightly, but for a moment something scorching hot flashed in his eyes, as if he imagined her unclothed in the garden.

Jolie could feel a blush heating her cheeks. She had intended the comment to be funny and sophisticated, to wipe memories of her sixteen-year-old self from his memory.

However, it had come across as risqué. She hoped the gathering darkness hid the blush from Jay. He would think she was still the innocent woman-child who once had a crush on him.

Less than two minutes with him, and she could feel an old flame leaping back to life. This was what he had always done. Made her aware of some age-old and primal longing inside of herself to explore every single thing it meant to be a woman.

Still, she admitted to herself that she enjoyed the heat in his eyes and the fact that, finally, she had managed to tempt him.

The last time they'd been together, he'd been convinced she needed his protection.

Protection from herself, her crush on him and the embarrassing proposition he had rejected that night.

Her worst memory of all time.

\* \* \*

Jay was tired. It had been a long drive. He'd had a sense, though, of it being worth it as he had finally arrived at Hidden Valley Winery. The sun was setting and it drenched the land in light, almost mystical in its beauty.

His sense of being caught in something otherworldly had only deepened as he had gone toward the entrance of the winery.

At first, in the fading light, he hadn't seen the woman there.

But then he had caught a glimpse of her, peripherally, and though he was not a man given to enchantments, that had been his thought. Enchantment.

He'd been shocked that it was Jolie Cavaletti. Of course, he'd known she would be here. She was the bride's sister.

But somehow he'd been unprepared for her, and especially unprepared for her turning that hideous dress into something else altogether. A fairy, sitting in gossamer folds, bathed in the golden hues of a sun already gone down.

A fairy, but as always with Jolie, there was the tantalizing contradiction, because as he'd gotten closer he'd been aware of seeing, not fairylike innocence, but a certain understated sensuality that made him aware of her as one hundred percent fully adult woman.

This had always been her contradiction. In high school, she'd been so much younger than everyone else, and trying so hard to overcome that, to be accepted. And yet, at the same time, she had remained the earnest little scientist, with big round glasses and owl eyes. He remembered her in white lab jackets, usually with some kind of stain or burn on them. The absent-minded scholar.

But then there was the contradiction: the woman's full curves, the corkscrews of curls she was never able to tame, the delicious plumpness of her bottom lip, the cinnamon scent of her.

He found himself leaning in.

Yes, it was still there, exotic and spicy, a hint of something Mediterranean.

Her remark about the fig leaf had intensified his awareness. She wasn't an off-limits kid anymore, and that felt wildly dangerous. Maybe because the drive had left him tired, he gave in to the desire to play with the danger a tiny bit.

"Why don't you surprise Sabrina?" he suggested, deadpan. "Can you imagine her face if you came down the aisle in a fig leaf?"

He saw that look in her eyes that he'd had to fight until the very last moment he had seen her, Jolie going in the door to her house, shoulders slumped, after the senior prom.

She'd turned around that night, and touched her lips with her tongue. If it had been sensual as she intended, instead of uncertain as it had presented, they might have ended up in a different place that night.

Instead, he'd had to be haunted for years, by her despondent, small voice.

*Is that your final answer?*

Of course, she'd been trying to be funny. It had been a question posed by a game show that had been popular at the time. Only smart people need apply. If Jolie Cavaletti had gone on it, she would have been a billionaire long before he was. But somehow, it had not come across as funny.

If she licked her lips right now, he'd be helpless.

But she didn't.

She snickered.

In some ways it was worse than the lip-lick because it reminded him of how she had been. Shy and earnest, but with something wilder and bolder brewing right beneath the surface, that dry sense of humor that he, as an adult, now associated with keen intelligence.

Which, even then, she'd had in spades, an intellectual giant who towered over kids much older than her.

"Fig leaf down the aisle," she mused, considering. And then she said, "I will, if you will."

Just like that they were laughing together. The shared laughter did the very same thing to him that it had done ten years ago.

Made every other care in the world become nothing more than motes of dust, dissolved by the light that sparked in Jolie Cavaletti's doe dark eyes.

A waiter appeared, with two flutes of what appeared to be a sparkling wine, which would never be his first choice.

"I can't have one more drop," Jolie said. "I've got jet lag so bad it's wiping me out. I mean fig leaves really aren't something I would normally bring up."

"You don't say," he teased her.

And then she was blushing.

*Blushing.*

And it was as if not one day had passed since prom night and a slightly drunk sixteen-year-old Jolie Cavaletti—who had not looked sixteen in a gorgeous gown, with makeup on, and her hair, for once tamed, piled on top of her head—had leaned into him and whispered a dangerously tempting proposition in his eighteen-year-old ear.

To this day he was not sure how he had managed to put her needs ahead of his own, resist her invitation and hustle her back to her house before she found somebody who would not be able to resist her considerable temptation, who would not have given her the correct final answer.

Which was no.

The waiter had two flutes and he offered one to Jay. "Sir?"

"Oh, why not?" Jay took the proffered glass, let his bag

slide off his shoulder and settled easily into the lounge chair beside her.

In the last of the day's light, with a chilled glass in his hand and night closing in around him, with Jolie's cinnamon scent tickling her nose, and the dress making her look like a fairy in a flower, he felt...not just enchantment.

Something far, far more dangerous.

A sensation of coming home.

# CHAPTER FOUR

OUT OF THE corner of his eye, Jay watched Jolie fight with the temptation of the wine for a second or two.

And then with a resigned sigh, she picked it up, twirled the stem between her fingers and took a sip.

"Don't even think about the last time I was drunk with you," she warned him.

"I wouldn't," he promised, ridiculously, since he already had. "Not that you were exactly drunk. Tipsy."

*Uninhibited.*

"I probably should have thanked you for that night. For you know…"

She was blushing again.

He did know. Saying no. Not taking advantage of her. He was sorry she was still embarrassed about it.

"I don't know what got into me."

"I do."

"Pardon me?"

"Some of us spiked the punch."

She glared at him as if suddenly it had happened yesterday and not ten years ago. Was she going to slap him?

"And I thought it was just your good looks and charisma that were intoxicating me!"

"I thought we weren't going to think about it," he reminded her hastily.

"If it was never mentioned again, I'd be okay with that," she said.

"Deal." He paused. "Even if you are in a dress that makes one think of a peach, ripe for the picking."

She did hit him, then. A light slug on his shoulder. He liked it. He laughed. So did she, and that awkward moment—this one, and the one that had happened ten years ago—were both gone.

For now.

With a woman like her—innately sensual, both then and now, without an awareness of that—those moments would never really be gone.

And she was no longer a child. He felt the danger of her again.

"How's your family, Jay? I'm sorry about your dad."

She had sent a card. Strange that he would remember that at all through the haze of pain. There had been a hundred cards. More, maybe. It must have been the Italian postmark, or maybe it had been her words. She had shared a memory of seeing his mom and dad walking hand in hand in their Toronto neighborhood, and said she had felt the love they had.

That she had felt it and that everyone who had ever been around them had felt it.

There was no better question than *how is your family?* to diffuse his dangerous awareness of her.

Because his perfect family had become a mess that day, and they still hadn't recovered. His mother and father had had one of the greatest loves he'd ever seen.

He'd been in university when his father had been diagnosed with cancer.

He had died with stunning swiftness. Jay's mother had never recovered. Her hero was gone. It was as if his illness had betrayed her in a way she could never get over. She was simply unprepared to deal with life alone, without her soulmate.

And so Jay had been left with the terrible lesson, that love, the thing he'd grown up believing was the strongest and greatest of all forces, was also a destroyer.

His mom, to this day, lived in the family home, but she had let the flower beds go, and watched too much television, and couldn't seem to muster any interest in life.

After the death of his father, there had been no choice. He had left college and gone home to look after the family his mother, swamped by grief for his father, abandoned. One minute, he'd been involved in football and frat parties, the next he'd been trying to cook dinners and check homework, and tell his sister, Kelly, that no, she could not wear that to school.

Out of all the people who had surrounded him during those sparkling days of high school and college, only Troy, his neighbor and best friend since he was four, had remained when Jay's world had been shattered.

Always there. Showing up with pizza for the whole Fletcher crowd. Dropping by with movies and popcorn, taking the kids to the amusement park so Jay could have a break from the sudden dump of responsibility.

Of course, Jay would accept the invitation to be best man—for the second time—for the man who had been there for him, always, even as his own mother had not.

She had been like a ghost during that time, which caused a confusion of feelings: sympathy, worry, anger, resentment, powerlessness.

*Mom, snap out of it. The kids need you. I need you.*

But nothing he had said could snap her out of it. Love had destroyed her, and she would not allow love—not even the love of her children—to repair her.

His two brothers, Jim and Mike, thankfully, were on their

career paths, and Kelly, the youngest—the one who accused him of being commitment phobic—was just out of university. She had a newly minted degree in clinical psychology and a certain frightening enthusiasm for saving the world's damaged people.

Of which she considered Jay to be one.

Was it so hard to see all that responsibility had exhausted him?

He returned to Jolie's question. How was his family? It was a complicated question. He answered it as he always did.

"Fine. Everybody's doing fine." He turned the question away from himself before she probed any further, because she was gazing at him with eyes that threatened to see things others did not. "I heard you're a doctor. Should I call you that? Dr. Cavaletti?"

"Good grief, no. As soon as people hear that, they feel compelled to unburden not so interesting medical stories and conditions on me."

"Actually, I have this lump—"

He was rewarded with another thump on his shoulder. For someone who had become so wary of all the things associated with home, he wondered why it felt kind of good to feel at home with Jolie.

Jolie was way too aware of the nearness of Jay, of the wideness of his shoulders, the hard muscle of his thigh beneath the fabric of his shorts, the long length of his legs as he stretched out comfortably on the lounge chair. His scent, mountain fresh and masculine, as intoxicating as the wine, danced on the air in the space between them.

Jolie knew she absolutely did not need another glass of prosecco, but the waiter had set it down on the table beside her and whisked away the empty glasses.

*Not even one more sip*, she had told herself.

But, somehow, she picked up that glass, twirled it between her fingers and lifted it to her lips almost as if she had no control over herself.

And that was the only thing she needed to remember about Jay Fletcher.

That when a woman most needed control, around a man like him, it might be as impossible to achieve as resisting one more sip of wine.

"You haven't changed a bit," Jay decided.

"Well, except, hopefully, for the dress."

"We've already established you would never pick a dress like that."

She wondered if feeling like kissing a man could simply be interpreted as gratitude for being *seen*?

"Thank you," she said simply.

"Not then, not now. The absent-minded genius. Inside-out shirts. Chemical stains on your lab jacket."

If she'd been absent-minded around him, it hadn't been because she was a scholar. She was not at all surprised by his memory of the inside-out shirt. That reflected, exactly, how he had made her feel. Inside-out. She hadn't been able to think straight around him, her normally logical brain completely scattered.

"You would have set a dress like that on fire on the Bunsen burner."

"On purpose."

They were laughing again.

"Do you love Italy?" he asked her, after a moment.

"Love. I finally found a place where I fit."

She hadn't meant to blurt *that* out. Of course, how much of fitting in had to do with being welcomed into the folds of Anthony's large and boisterous family, the kind of family she had always dreamed of?

She thought of his *nonna* always cooking, always laughing, always bouncing babies and shooing children, and giving her the one thing she'd never had, a sense of belonging.

*Like this*, Nonna had said, then watched Jolie approvingly as she stretched the pizza dough. That pinch on the cheek.

If she was honest, she missed all that much more than she missed Anthony.

He regarded her thoughtfully. "You didn't really fit."

"And still don't," she said with a sigh.

"It's what I liked best about you."

That took her by surprise. Until that embarrassing night of the grad prom, she was pretty sure, that she had barely been a blip on Jay's radar.

He'd liked something about her?

His lips quirked upward. "Remember that science project?"

She pretended to be thinking about it, scanning the banks of her memory for something elusive.

"We extracted DNA from a strawberry?"

He remembered that stupid experiment. What she remembered was her stomach jumping at his closeness, the scent of him filling her nose, liking his laughter, the excuses to brush against him, touch his hand with hers...

"Did we?" she asked.

"When the teacher first assigned you as my partner, I was so disappointed."

"Don't hold back," she said.

"Not because of *you*. I wanted Mitch Ryerson. I thought he was the smartest person in the class and that he could drag my sorry ass through it. And then I found out you were the smartest person in the class. Possibly in the whole world."

"That's an exaggeration," she said.

He cocked his head at her. "How many grades had you skipped by then?"

"Two," she said, "And I don't remember you having a sorry ass."

Though she remembered his ass—and coveting it—with embarrassing clarity.

*Do not blush*, she ordered herself. "So, what's your connection to the wedding party?" she asked, which was so much more cosmopolitan than *what are you doing here?*

"I'm the best man."

Of course he was. Most likely to be the best man.

"I was the best man at their first wedding, too," he said, and something flitted through his eyes. "Troy and I were next-door neighbors since we were four."

"Oh, really? I don't even remember Troy in high school. I thought Sabrina said she met him at one of the neighborhood pubs."

If she had known they were such good friends she might have been better prepared for this meeting.

"He never went to our school. He went to private school. We're kind of like family, always there for each other."

Family. Always there for each other. Maybe he could send a memo to Sabrina.

"I wasn't able to get back in time," she said, which allowed her a little more dignity than *I wasn't invited. To my own sister's wedding.*

"Yeah, it seemed very, er, spontaneous. Just four of us, at city hall at high noon."

"I think Sabrina always regretted that. That she didn't have the traditional wedding. I think she wants everything to be different this time."

*Everything.* Especially the result.

He didn't say anything, and she felt compelled to rush into the conversational lull.

"So, what have you been doing with yourself?" she asked. And then wished she hadn't. The whole wedding party was going to be here until next Sunday morning. There would be lots of time to find out what he was doing with himself.

Or maybe not.

Maybe this would be her only opportunity to be alone with him.

*Please, God.*

But she was aware of the ambiguity of the prayer. *Please, God, no more opportunities to be alone with Jay Fletcher*, or *please, God, lots more opportunities to be alone with Jay Fletcher?*

"I started a little sporting goods company. It's done okay."

She couldn't resist glancing over at the car. That was a pretty expensive bag draped over his shoulder, too. She suspected he had done quite a bit better than okay.

She frowned. Another sports car was pulling in, way too fast. The sudden screeching of tires was incongruous to the deep evening quiet settling over wine country. They both focused toward the parking lot.

This car was also a convertible, candy apple red, with the top down, spraying gravel in a show of the vehicle's great power. It flew into a parking spot, nearly careening into the car beside it. The driver did not correct the awkward angle, but shut off the car.

Jolie actually felt terror as she glimpsed, over the back headrest, the bright blond hair shining like an orb against the pitch black of the completely fallen night.

*Please don't be him*, she thought.

Jay Fletcher moved down one notch in the list of people she least wanted to see in the entire world as she watched the vehicle, her heart thudding in her throat.

She stared, with disbelief, as disaster struck, this time for real. Not the least debatable on the disaster scale.

She wasn't aware she had made a sound, until Jay touched her arm. "Are you okay?"

"Only if you have an invisibility cloak," she managed to say, and then wished she hadn't, because despite her distress over Anthony's appearance, that was a particularly nerdy thing to say.

What could her ex-fiancé possibly be doing here, in a popular tourist region in Canada that was nonetheless hard to reach. It was *not* a coincidence.

She got up out of the chair, looking for an escape route. There was none. Still, she felt everything in her try to shrink, to disappear—as if that would ever be possible in this dress—as her former fiancé, Anthony Carmichael, got out of the vehicle. He didn't open the car door. He leaped over it.

In the range of chance, what were the possibilities that she would have to face the two men she wanted to see the least in the entire world in the very same instant?

And here came Anthony, charging up the steps, all that energy snapping in the very air around him.

He was stunningly handsome, but in a totally different way than Jay Fletcher was handsome. He looked like a man in those old paintings, posing, one hand tucked inside a brocade waistcoat, a certain arrogance stamped across perfect, fine features.

Stunned, Jolie realized Anthony did not look anything like his boisterous Italian relatives. He looked something like her mother. And her sister. And every other member of the wedding party.

Considering how Italy had made her feel like she fit in for practically the first time in her life, how was it she had gravitated toward him?

Another heyday for a psychiatrist!

# CHAPTER FIVE

FOR A HOPEFUL moment Jolie thought that, just like the other man she had least wanted to see, Anthony's endless energy would propel him right on by her.

Of course, she was not that lucky. He stopped in his tracks when he saw her. He took her in, changed course, bearing down on her with frightening singleness of focus. Finally, he stopped. Too close. In her space.

Good grief. It looked as if he intended to take her hand, kiss it and bow. She tucked her hands behind her.

"Jo," he said. "You are like something out of my dreams. That dress!"

Having been deprived of her hand, he kissed his own fingers then flicked the kiss to the wind.

Had he always been so affected?

Of course he had. She had been so in the throes of love she had been blind to every flaw. Except the last one.

She was suddenly aware of Jay getting up from his lounge chair and coming to stand beside her. She glanced at him, and he slid her a questioning look out of the corner of his eye. Something changed in his stance. He inserted himself, ever so subtly, between her and Anthony.

"Anthony, what are you doing here?" she stammered to her former fiancé.

Anthony, ever jealous, shot Jay an appraising look. She could sense Jay grow in stature, a quiet intake of breath, a subtle broadening of already broad shoulders. When she glanced at him again, he was returning Anthony's look with a flinty steadiness. Anthony looked away first, focusing on her with that familiar intensity.

"Your sister invited me," he said. "She knows the truth!"

Jolie registered Sabrina's betrayal like a blow. "The truth?"

"We belong together," Anthony exclaimed, switching to Italian. Anthony was an expat, like her. He'd grown up in Detroit, Michigan. He'd gone to Italy in search of roots almost forgotten by his family. He had found them, on his mother's side, and been instantly welcomed into the fold. As had she, when she started dating him.

Still, Anthony's Italian wasn't perfect, but it served him to switch languages in order to lock Jay out of the conversation.

Jay shot her a look. She felt as if her pathetic love for this man who had betrayed her was an open book. Jay inserted himself more firmly between her and her ex-fiancé.

Jolie could probably count the impulsive things she had done in her life on one hand. The most regrettable involved the man, not in front of her, but beside her.

Maybe what happened next could have been Jay's fault, just like him spiking the punch on that long-ago night. Maybe he coaxed out her impulsiveness. Or maybe her need for self-protection trumped common sense at the moment.

More likely, it was way too much prosecco, an empty stomach and jet lag. And maybe the dress could even be thrown in for good measure.

But, whatever the reason, she stepped more closely into him, and then firmly took Jay's hand in her own.

She wasn't expecting the fit to be quite so comfortable. She wasn't expecting to feel his strength surging into her.

She wasn't expecting—given the awkward discomfort of the circumstances—to be so *aware*.

"You and I don't belong together, Anthony," she said. Her voice reflected the strength she was gaining, through osmosis, from Jay.

"We do!" Anthony insisted, still in Italian.

"We don't." She spoke English, her voice clear and certain. "This is my fiancé, Jay Fletcher."

Jolie felt Jay's shock ripple through him. She braced herself in case he dropped her hand. But instead, his grip tightened on hers. She glanced, once again, quickly, at his face. He did not look stunned at all. In fact, he smiled at her with just the right touch of possessiveness.

On the other hand, Anthony looked, unsurprisingly, completely stunned. For a blissful moment, she almost believed he would accept defeat.

But then Anthony's brow furrowed. He looked between the two of them suspiciously.

"This isn't even possible," he declared, as if he was in charge of all the possibilities in the world. "You are just trying to discourage me. It happened too fast."

He spoke English this time, to make sure they both understood him.

It had been three months since her breakup with Anthony.

"It's not fast," Jay said firmly. "Jolie and I have known each other forever. Haven't we, honey?"

*Honey.* Under other circumstances she would have certainly savored that sweetly old-fashioned endearment coming off his lips.

"Forever," she agreed.

For a moment, Anthony looked uncharacteristically flummoxed. But that look lasted only a moment before his customary confidence returned.

Only with Jay standing beside her, she felt as if she was redefining confidence. Anthony's posture had something faintly off-putting about it, the posture of a man who swaggered.

Why hadn't she seen it before?

Blinded by love, that's why! A good reminder of what love did to people, especially with her hand nestled so comfortably in Jay's, as if it belonged there, as if it had always belonged there.

"You don't have a ring!" Anthony pointed out, triumphant.

"We decided we didn't want to take away from Sabrina and Troy's big event," Jolie said smoothly, shocked at how easily the lie slid off her lips. "We're going to announce our engagement after the wedding."

Anthony glared at her. He gave Jay a distinctly pugnacious look, as if he might be planning on inviting him to a duel.

In Italian, she said to him, "Please, just go. You are going to make things awkward. You'll ruin the wedding."

*If the dress doesn't do it first.*

"Your sister invited me," he reminded her.

She would be having a talk with Sabrina about *that.*

"She doesn't know about Jay and me As I said before, we didn't want to take away from her big day."

"I'm not leaving," he answered in Italian. "I'm winning you back."

"You can't win me back. As you can see, I've moved on. You cheated on me." She was glad that humiliating detail was revealed in Italian.

He lifted a shoulder. "I've apologized. I have promised to change. For you."

As if he was willing to put himself out, *for her.*

"It's too late," she said firmly. How could she have ever fallen for him? The thing was, despite what Jay had said about her being the smartest person in the world, she was not.

In some areas, she was downright dumb.

Needy.

Naive, even.

Look at the way she felt about the hand in hers, despite her near-miss with Anthony!

Her former fiancé looked narrowly at her, and then at Jay.

"He's not for you," he proclaimed, still in Italian. "What's he got that I haven't?"

Since they were speaking in Italian, and since Anthony was determined not to get the message, she felt as if she had no choice but to be a tiny little bit cruel.

"He's got quite a bit that you don't have," she said with a coy smile.

Anthony's mouth fell open. His whole face reddened. And then he said huffily, "It doesn't matter what you have. It matters how you use it."

Jolie felt increasingly desperate to get her message across. That she had moved on. That it was well and truly over and that Anthony had absolutely no chance of winning her back. Ever.

Words, obviously, were not enough.

She turned into Jay.

He'd been a good sport so far.

*Please don't step back*, she pleaded silently as she stepped right into him.

Full contact. She could feel his heat radiating out from under his shirt. She could feel the strength of him. She could feel the hard, steady beat of his heart.

She looked up at him, looked deeply into the amazing green of his eyes, touched her lips, tentatively, with her tongue.

Then, she committed. Jolie wrapped her hands around his neck, and she drew his lips down to her own.

She kissed him.

And she kissed him hard.

As soon as her lips met his it felt as if she had been waiting for this very moment since she was sixteen.

And that it was worth a ten-year wait.

Everything else, including Anthony, faded away.

If Jay Fletcher was going to pick his top ten most unexpected moments, Jolie Cavaletti claiming his mouth with her own would certainly be up there.

Her lips were soft, and he found the invitation of them irresistible. She tasted of wine and night and the stars.

The kiss quickly moved into the number one position of his life's unexpected moments, just nudging out his other surprising encounter with Jolie, which had held the number one position for ten years.

He remembered this study in contrasts. How could someone be sweet and on fire at the very same time?

How could a kiss that was staged—a pretense—feel like the most real thing that had ever happened to him?

"He's gone," he said against her mouth, looking over her shoulder.

She broke away from him abruptly. Her lips looked puffy, and her cheeks had spots of color in them. Her eyes sparked with the fire he had tasted.

"Wow," he said softly, "you look like a princess in a fairy tale."

"It's the dress," she said, sharply. "Don't let it fool you. I don't believe in fairy tales, and I certainly don't need a prince to wake me up."

It was a rather shocking lack of gratitude given how gamely he had played along with her ruse when her spurned lover had showed up.

Maybe she was just covering her embarrassment, or maybe she didn't want him to know that she had found that as delightfully unexpected as he had.

But she was definitely trying to cover something, looking avidly and hopefully toward the parking lot, as if she was totally focused on the *goal* of that kiss and not the unexpected treasure discovered.

"He went the other way. To check in, I assume."

She swore in Italian.

They both came from the same heavily Italian neighborhood in Toronto, but Jay was Italian on his mother's side, and she had been blue-eyed and fair, as were many of the people from Cremona where his maternal grandparents hailed from.

It seemed duplicitous not to tell Jolie, right now, that he spoke Italian. In fact he spoke it far better than her ex-friend. On the other hand, he was feeling a bit annoyed with her.

"That was kind of a déjà vu moment," he said, unkindly.

"I thought we agreed not to talk about that."

"Not talking about it doesn't make it go away. There are some things a man doesn't forget. Strawberry DNA, a pretty girl offering her lips."

She'd actually offered quite a bit more than her lips, but her blush was already deepening, so he was pretty sure she did not have to be reminded of the details.

"I was young and stupid."

Ouch. Why did that sting?

"That's the difference, all right," he said softly. "You're all grown-up."

In fact, her lips on his had let him know just how grown-up.

*That night, years ago, it had been so evident that she was the farthest thing from all grown-up.*

She cast a glance at the doors of the lodge. "He went in there? Really? Like he's staying?"

"I think you've got yourself a determined fan there," he said.

"More like a stalker. How could my sister do this to me? Her and my mother met him in Italy. They couldn't stop gushing about how he was the perfect man. He's here because they don't feel I can do any better. And that's even knowing—"

She bit her lip.

He didn't say anything because he wasn't supposed to speak Italian and therefore know that pompous creep had fooled around on her.

But it said so much about how her family saw her.

Maybe how everybody had always seen her. He, himself, had seen her that way once.

Awkward. Geeky.

But then he'd worked on that science project with her.

And found out she was formidably intelligent, but also surprisingly funny, charming and original.

He'd liked her, in the hands-off sort of way that an older guy liked a too young girl. But that moment at prom she had tried to change all the rules.

Jolie had offered herself to him.

That same way, leading with those luscious lips.

And when he hadn't even fully recovered from the shock that the awkward, geeky girl was shockingly sexy, Jolie had announced, a little drunk—from punch he was suddenly ashamed that he had helped spike—that she had decided to lose her virginity that night. And she had chosen him.

He'd hustled her out of there, into his car and home—her home—as fast as he could. He'd dumped her on the doorstep with a stern lecture and watched from the car to make sure she went in the house.

Chivalrous.

He'd done the right thing, even though he knew he'd hurt her by doing it.

And now, here they were. Did you ever really outrun anything in life, or did it always catch up to you?

# CHAPTER SIX

"Do you think you could do me the most enormous favor?" Jolie asked him.

"I thought I just did," Jay returned dryly. And his kindness had been repaid with a reminder he was no prince.

"Could you pretend? That you are? My fiancé? Just until I figure out how to get rid of him?"

He considered that. It seemed a path rife with danger. And excitement. In other words, irresistible.

"Just until he gets it," she said hastily. "And gives up. What do you think?"

He thought it was insane was what he thought. So no one was more shocked than him to hear him answering her, his tone casual.

"Oh, sure. Why not? Nothing like adding an accidental engagement to your résumé."

"It'll help me with the mean girls, too."

"Oh, for Pete's sake. Haven't they grown up at all?"

"Maybe *mean* is too strong."

He doubted it. As a high school boy he hadn't known what to do about that—the constant digs the girls took at her, the put-downs. He felt he should have done more, but the girl world then—and probably now—was baffling to him.

"The problem is probably mine. Dragging along old baggage from high school. I wasn't expecting to be right back *there*. Feeling like I don't quite measure up somehow."

So it was an easy yes to help her out. Like making amends for not coming to her defense sooner. For spiking the punch that night.

"You know why, don't you?" he asked her, softly, even as he warned himself, *Stay out of it. Human relations are a topic you know nothing about.*

"Why what?"

"They treat you like that?"

"I don't actually."

"You know how photocopied pictures look when the printer is running out of ink? Faded and indistinct?"

She nodded uncertainly.

"That's what they were next to you. You were more than them. Prettier. Smarter. Infinitely funnier. And they never wanted you to know. They wanted to keep you down. Like Cinderella and her ugly stepsisters."

"Oh, for heaven's sake. I told you I don't believe in fairy tales."

It was her Dr. Cavaletti tone for sure. Nonetheless, she looked pleased.

"I'll pretend to be your fiancé," he said, "but only on one condition. That you act as if you're worthy of a man who loves you deeply and unconditionally."

There, he told himself. He'd agreed to this crazy plan for one reason and one reason only. Out of pure altruism. To show Jolie Cavaletti who she really was.

But was he going to be able to handle it when she found out?

"I'll make it worth your while," she decided.

He wagged his eyebrows at her wickedly, even as something in him sighed at how thoroughly she didn't get it.

It was okay to let people help you out. You didn't have to pay them back.

"Not like that." There was that smack on his shoulder again. It was a strange thing to like. He liked it.

"Like what, then?"

"I haven't decided. Maybe my firstborn."

"You have a firstborn?"

"Of course not!"

"Oh, but the possibilities," he said. "We could make a firstborn. That could be how you repay. The making. Not the firstborn."

"Maybe a puppy," she said.

"I don't want a puppy," he said. "My worst nightmare."

"How can a puppy be anyone's worst nightmare?"

"Do you have one?"

"No. But I'd like to someday."

"Well, I wouldn't. I've had my fill of looking after things."

He was shocked he had let that slip out.

She regarded him thoughtfully for a minute. He remembered this look, a certain intensity in it, a stripping away of anything that wasn't real.

"Did it all fall on you, after your dad died?"

He nodded, not trusting himself to speak at how quickly and clearly she had seen it.

"And yet, here you are, looking after me," she said softly.

"Temporarily," he reminded her. "You better make sure there's some fun involved."

She looked at him again, as if she saw it all. The late nights, and the two jobs, and trying to keep the house, his siblings and his mother together.

It looked as if Jolie saw the worrying. The constant worrying.

"I will," she promised.

And he wondered, again, just what he was letting himself in for.

"We have a deal," she said, and stuck out her hand, as if she planned to shake on it.

"Oh," he said, "I think we're way beyond that."

And he kissed her with deliberate lightness on her lips.

"Maybe we need to set some, er, perimeters," she said.

"Like setting up a scientific method?" he asked her dryly.

She didn't get that he was being funny. "Exactly."

"Well, he's watching us out the window of the lobby, so what's your method going to be for dealing with that?"

She took his hand. "Will you walk me to my cabin?"

"Of course," he said.

The cabin was nestled back in the trees, with a sign over the door. Jay glanced up at it.

*Lovers' Retreat.*

Good grief. It was his turn to blush. There was an awkward moment when he wasn't sure what to do with his new fiancée in such close proximity to that sign.

She solved it. "Thank you," she said brightly. "Good night."

And then, Jolie Cavaletti, his fiancée, stepped inside her cabin and firmly shut the door in his face.

He traced his steps back to the lodge. The lobby was clear so he stepped in to check in. The receptionist assigned him a room in the main building. From somewhere, he could hear girlish laughter from women he knew were not girls.

He wondered why Jolie wasn't in the main building. Were they that mean-spirited that they would deliberately exclude her?

The laughter suddenly came closer and Jacqui and Gillian—whom he knew Jolie hilariously referred to as Jack and Jill—burst into the lobby.

"Jay!" they shrieked together, as if it had been a long time since he saw them, when in fact they had all been at some kind of prewedding planning session three weeks ago. It had been extraordinarily boring, and he and Troy had entertained themselves by taking turns sending each other emoji faces on their phones as Sabrina rolled out the plans. Wedding music, rolled eyes; bridesmaid dresses, green nausea face; groomsmen attire, laugh-out-loud; cake, licked lips. Terribly juvenile and the only part of the evening he'd enjoyed.

Jack and Jill had taken him hostage and filled him in on Chantelle, the photographer Troy had lined up because she was his mom's best friend's daughter or something. Both of them had done bit modeling, even in high school. Ad campaigns for local shops, some catalog stuff. They had hinted in the past they would be great choices for his sporting goods line, but he had never taken the bait.

Chantelle, they had informed him, beside themselves with excitement and letting him know the opportunity he had missed, was well-known for discovering the next big name in the modeling world. They both seemed to think they were going to be that discovery, though he was not sure how many models were discovered at their age, which was the same as his, twenty-eight.

Jay was never quite sure how his friend, earthy, honest, brilliant, loyal, had ended up with Sabrina. Her inevitable entourage, alone, would have made Jay hesitate.

But Troy loved Sabrina. He'd been a mess when the marriage hadn't worked out the first time—another cautionary tale about love, really. Still, Troy's personality seemed to balance that of his more mercurial wife. And also wife-to-be.

His friend had a kind of affectionate acceptance of the oft quirky Sabrina that was enviable.

Still, the truth was if Jay did not feel as if he owed Troy big-time, he would not even be here.

Jill and Jacqui left in a flurry of giggles and wagging fingers, and Jay slid the key back over the counter. "Have you got another cabin? Something close to…ah… Lovers' Retreat?"

The receptionist consulted her bookings. "How about Heart's Refuge?"

Who came up with these names? A thirteen-year-old reading romance novels? And at the same time, he leaned into it. He wanted to believe there were refuges for bruised hearts.

"Sure," he said.

He found his way to the cabin—next to Jolie's—her lights were on, but he took his heart into the promised refuge without giving in to the temptation to go visit with her for a while. See what she was reading. And if her hair was wrapped in a towel. If she wore pajamas with kittens on them, or silk.

Being engaged to her was going to be way more complicated than he wanted.

If he let it, he decided firmly. He was doing a friend— were they even that?—a favor. Somebody maybe he owed something to, for never standing up for her, for spiking the punch that night.

It would be best, except for when they were "on" to set the perimeters as she had suggested earlier. He would avoid her entirely, except for official wedding activities.

The next morning, his perimeters were challenged almost instantly.

Because he walked into the winery restaurant for breakfast to find The Four, as he liked to call Sabrina and her pals, clustered around a table snickering.

They looked, with their tangled hair and smudged eyes, yoga pants and T-shirts, as if they had survived a late-night pajama party that involved booze. Actually, Sabrina looked clear-eyed. The other three didn't.

When he moved closer, he could clearly see they had a pile of clothing on the table, and on top of it was a bra.

That definitely did not belong to any of them, members of the Gwyneth Paltrow lookalike club.

"Oh, my God," Jill said, "over-the-shoulder-boulder-holder."

He was stunned by his level of fury. This is what these girls had subjected Jolie to all through high school: the constant scorn, the behind-her-back snickering, the snide judgments. He reached in over Gillian's shoulder and took the bra.

"What is wrong with you?" he said to them all, and shoved the bra into his pocket. "Grow up!"

Sabrina widened her eyes at him. "Jay! I didn't know you were here."

He could tell no one had expected to see him, as fingers ran through blond locks and clothing was adjusted.

"You should give that back to me," Sabrina said. "It belongs to Jolie. She left it on the bathroom floor last night."

*Making it sound as if she had been partying along with them, and maybe even been the worst of them.*

They were, of course, unaware he had already seen Jolie last night.

"I know exactly who it belongs to," he said tersely.

There was silence for a moment, and then Beth said, tentatively, "But how would you know that?"

Jolie picked that moment to walk in.

In contrast to them, she looked stunning. Her dark hair was still wet from the shower, wildly curling, but clipped back. She was wearing a lemon-yellow pencil line skirt that showed off the length of her legs and a crisp white blouse that showed off the understated sensuality of her.

She had on just a hint of makeup, a smudge around her eyes that made them look soft and brown, like the doe deer he had startled off the road on the way here. She had so much natural color, unlike the ghostly four, that she did not need blush on her cheeks. She had a touch of gloss on her lips that drew his eye there.

She hesitated when she saw The Four, and Jay watched as she shrank before his eyes, hunching her shoulders ever so slightly, shoving her hands into the pockets of that skirt. She obviously suddenly felt overdressed, as if she had tried too hard. It was all in her face: the insecurity, the fear of being made fun of.

And the jackals gathered around her bra, now in his possession, made her fear justified. It made him feel so protective that Jolie had no idea who she was. And neither did The Four.

"Ew...yellow," Gillian said under her breath.

Jolie glanced down at her skirt, and smoothed a hand over it.

"I like it," he snapped. "I like it a lot."

It was their turn to shrink, eyeing him warily.

But it was exactly as he had told her last night, and that skirt made it apparent. She was full color to their faded sepia. She was a brilliant original and they were copies.

At that moment, he committed.

To showing Jolie who she really was.

Jay strode over to her, put his arms around her and kissed her full on the lips.

It filled him with the oddest yearning that this was real. That he really got to say good morning to a woman like this, in this way.

He broke off the kiss, took her hand and led her back to the circle of women. He had to tug her slightly, she was so reluctant.

He tucked his arm around her waist.

He was quite pleased that he had, from the looks on their faces, managed to completely stun The Four.

Hopefully into silence.

"Jolie and I have been in contact," he said. Just in time, he remembered she had told Anthony they would hold off on a formal announcement until after Sabrina's wedding. As tempting as it was to cut the legs out from under the mean-spirited bride, he didn't.

"We're finding we have quite a lot in common."

He had hoped somehow to build Jolie up with that. Instead, he found he hated it, that the looks on every one of those woman's faces changed, not because of Jolie, but because of his acceptance of her.

His status, no doubt, had gone up steadily in their eyes as his star had risen. He couldn't even say how tired he was of *that*, of people adjusting their opinions about him based on his financial assets.

It was infuriating that they could be so shallow and so smugly unaware of it.

Really? In this day and age, a woman's value could be decided by her choice of a relationship? By a man choosing her?

No wonder she had stayed in Italy all these years. He glanced at her. It occurred to him his rise in the North American business world, while big news with the old high school crowd, was not such big news in Europe and had probably not reached Jolie.

He was pretty sure she had no idea he was a billionaire, and he had a sudden hope of keeping it that way.

Sabrina looked between them, quickly masking how she was appraising her very accomplished sister in a new light because of the billionaire thing.

"Jolie," she said, "I've decided the bridesmaid dress is a disaster. It can't be fixed. You'll have to find another one. There's a city not far from here. Penticton. I'll text you pictures of the other dresses. The essential part is the color. It's important for the photos."

"Color essential," Jolie repeated dutifully.

"Oh, and you left your clothes on the bathroom floor last night. For some reason Jay has taken possession of your bra. Weird. But…" she cast them a sly look "…weirder things have happened."

Queen Bee, buzzing, taking control, Jay thought unkindly. He refrained from saying that a good man like his friend Troy ending up with her would end up very high on his list of those weird, unexplainable things.

A smart, bright, vibrant person like Jolie being Sabrina's sister being another of those things.

He felt more determined than ever to show Jolie—and everyone around her—who she really was.

"Take Jay with you," Sabrina said, her tone dripping acid. "He's cranky this morning and who needs that kind of *energy*."

Completely blind, as those people so often were, to her own toxic energy.

"Yes," he said, "let's grab breakfast in town."

He couldn't wait to get away from them. He took Jolie's elbow and guided her outside. He didn't realize she'd been holding her breath until she started breathing again.

He fished her bra out of his pocket and she snatched it from him and put it in an oversize bag.

"You don't have to come dress shopping," she said.

It was true, it was not how he'd expected to spend the day. He'd thought maybe a bit of waterskiing with Troy when his friend arrived later today.

On the other hand, he hadn't expected to end up accidentally engaged, either.

There was something about the unexpected occurring in his generally well-ordered life that intrigued him, and that he was not going to say no to.

Even if it did mean spending part of a day looking for a

bridesmaid dress, of all things. Though, come to think of it, maybe that was going to be the most fun he'd ever had on a shopping trip.

Because look what he was trying to accomplish and look what he had to work with.

# CHAPTER SEVEN

JAY HELD OPEN the door of his car for Jolie.

"Is this part of your award-winning acting skill?" she asked. It seemed to her Jay was doing a stellar job of pretending he was her romantic interest.

"Afraid not. Small courtesies drummed into me by my dad. Do you mind? It's a new world. I'm never quite sure if someone's going to find it offensive. I did have a lady snap at me once when I opened our office building door for her that she was quite capable of doing it herself."

"Witch," she said.

He grinned. That little dimple popped out in his cheek when he did that. He was wearing a moss green shirt this morning.

The color did wicked things to his eyes.

"That's what I thought, too," Jay said, lightly, "I didn't say it out loud, though."

"But you still open doors, even after that," she said, and something within her sighed with delight at his old-fashioned manners.

"I gauge the recipient," he admitted.

"Well, you gauged this recipient just right," she assured him.

Jolie didn't feel as if she started breathing again until she had settled beside Jay in the passenger seat. How could the very air around her sister and her friends feel so stifling?

She shot him a look.

"What?" he asked her.

"*Are* you cranky this morning?"

"I might have been if you told me you could open your own door," he said, that easy grin deepening his dimple.

This morning's outing—the impossible assignment of finding a dress aside—was as unexpected to her as a prisoner suddenly finding herself escaped from the cell. It seemed as if he was having the same reaction to it.

She sighed with relief. "What a beautiful day. What a beautiful car."

"Thanks, I enjoy it for the few months of the year it's usable in Canada. Top up or down?" he asked her. "We have to choose now. It's not like James Bond. It's not recommended you do it on the fly."

"Down," she said without hesitation.

It was like something out of a dream, whisking along roads that twisted through vineyards and clung to the edge of cliffs that overlooked the sparkling waters of the lake. Jolie was so aware of Jay's complete comfort and confidence behind the wheel. Despite his denial, he could have been James Bond! There was something very sexy about a man who handled a powerful car well, without feeling any need to show off.

After a bit, she took the band out of her hair and let the wind take it. She saw Jay glance over and grin.

"Thatta girl."

"Thank you for suggesting breakfast in town. It minimized the chances of an encounter with Anthony this morning."

"Ha! I can't wait to see the look on The Four's faces when they see two men floundering at your feet."

She hadn't thought of it like that. The wind, as well as being loud, was wreaking havoc on her hair, and with a touch of a button, Jay put the windows up. It helped marginally with the wind, but not at all with the loudness.

"Let's have fun with it," he suggested, and turned on some music. Loud.

"How'd you do that?" she shouted when she recognized music from their high school era.

"Never moved on," he said. "Stuck there. Musically, any-way."

No need to let him know fun did not come naturally to her. She had a sudden sense of being able to be whoever she wanted to be for the next little while.

"And look," he said, "the fun begins right here."

A sign welcomed them to Penticton, the Peach City. They both burst out laughing. She made Jay stop and she deliber-ately waited for him to come open her door. He did so with flourish and then they stood together under the sign. She took a selfie and sent it to Sabrina.

Should have no problem finding the right shade here.

Penticton, located between two lakes, reminded Jolie a bit of Italy with its dry hills, interspersed with vibrant green terraces of vineyards and orchards. It was a smaller city and the quaint downtown was already thronged with early morn-ing tourists trying to beat the heat of the afternoon.

They found a cute little sidewalk café for breakfast, and sat down. Jolie pulled her hair clip from her pocket, but when she tried to scrape her now really wild hair back to retie it, she noticed Jay was looking at her.

"You should leave it," he said softly.

And so she did.

Jolie looked around and marveled at the unexpected turn her life had taken this morning. She watched the couples, young and old, strolling the streets, the families on vacation.

There was a distinctive feeling of summer holiday happiness in the air.

She had heard if you wanted to know who someone really was, to watch how they treated a server in a restaurant.

When the young woman brought coffee, she introduced herself. She apologized for the slow service and confided that one of the waitresses had not come to work.

"Susan, I've been watching you handle things," Jay told her. "You're doing an amazing job."

He said it casually, with just a glance up from the menu, and a quick smile, but to Jolie, as she watched the young woman take on her challenges with new confidence, it told her a great deal about Jay.

A few minutes later they watched Susan rush by with a whipped-cream-and-strawberry-covered waffle that filled the whole plate.

"I wonder if those come in smaller sizes," Jolie said.

"For simplicity's sake, why don't we just share one?"

While they waited for their order to come, Jay read the back of the menu out loud.

"Penticton," he informed her, "was named by the Interior Salish people, and translates to *a place to stay forever.*"

Jolie realized that was exactly what she felt right now, as if she would like to stay in this simple place—coffee and sunshine, people watching and an appealing companion—forever. She liked the feeling of nothing to prove and nothing to accomplish. She liked her hair being wild around her face, and she liked sitting in the sunshine, being perceived as a couple by others, and feeling like a couple, even though they weren't really.

When their waffle came, it hadn't been divided, and the feeling of being part of a couple deepened as Jolie found herself sitting very close to Jay, eating off the same plate. It seemed to her the moment was infused with an intimacy that was not quite like anything she had ever felt before. Considering she had been engaged for nearly a year, that was very telling of her relationship.

Again, she had that sense of just wanting to stay in this moment, forever, to deepen her connection with him.

"I never met your mom and dad, officially," she told him, "but I often watched them stroll through the neighborhood hand in hand."

"Their evening walk," he said. "It was their ritual. Almost sacred to them. It didn't matter if it was thirty below zero and the wind was blowing, off they went. Every day until he was too sick to do it. You mentioned seeing them walk in the card you sent. I appreciated that."

He remembered something she had written in a card years ago. It didn't necessarily mean anything. He had great people skills. She had just seen that with the young waitress.

"I have another memory of them," she said. "There was a little flower bed in front of your house, between the fence and the sidewalk."

"Mom's flower bed. Her pride and joy," he said, remembering.

"I was on the other side of the street, and I saw her out kneeling in front of it, pulling weeds. And your dad came up behind her and tapped her on the shoulder."

She remembered with absolute clarity, the light that had come on in Millie Fletcher's face when she saw who had tapped her on the shoulder. She had gotten to her feet and wiped her hands on her slacks.

"He had something hidden behind his back," Jolie continued, "and he gave it to her. It was a little bedraggled marigold in a plastic pot, the kind you get for ninety-nine cents at the grocery store. I could hear him say he'd rescued it. Your mother took that pot from him and you would have thought he'd given her a diamond.

"They knelt down side by side and put it in the flower bed right away. It didn't go with a single other thing that was in that bed. But every day, I'd walk by it and see it front and center. I don't know that much about flowers, but the next year, it had thrown seeds or volunteered or whatever it is flowers do, and there were more of them."

She realized at some point Jay had dropped his sunglasses over his eyes. He was looking away from her, and didn't say anything when she finished the story. She realized, horrified, that she had hurt him.

"I'm sorry," she said. "I've said something wrong."

"No, not at all," he said. "That's just exactly what they were like."

He lifted the glasses and squeezed the bridge of his nose.

She remembered, then seeing it so clearly last night, after he'd rescued her from Anthony. That it had all fallen on him.

"Jay?" she asked softly. "Why don't you tell me about it?"

He hesitated, taking a sip of his coffee. Then he lifted a shoulder.

"My mom never recovered," he said in a low voice, studying his plate. "She's lost without him. I was nearly grown-up, but I had younger siblings still at home. It didn't matter. Nothing mattered. She's like a shell. That flower bed you mentioned? She hasn't touched it for years now. It's a mess. Like the whole family."

"You held it all together, didn't you?"

He was still looking at their plate. "As much as I was able."

"You're a good man, Jay Fletcher." That came from the bottom of her heart.

He lifted his eyes and looked at her for a moment. She felt the deepest of connections shiver along her spine.

But then he dropped his sunglasses, and smiled.

"I don't want to be a pig," Jay said, eager to change the subject, "but I'd like another one. How about you?"

"I wouldn't normally say yes, but *pig* rhymes with *fig*, so I think it would be fine."

They both laughed, and it seemed they had moved on from the intensity of the moment when he had confided in her about his family, but she was aware of the connection remaining in some subtle, lovely way.

Sharing a second waffle with him proved as impossible to say no to as the prosecco had been last night.

They had just finished the second waffle, when her phone notified her with Sabrina's distinctive ping.

The feeling of intimacy she had been enjoying dissolved as reality intruded.

"Duty calls," she said, wagging her phone at Jay.

He grimaced.

"Ah, yes, dress instructions," she said.

"I was hoping to hold out for the fig leaf."

"Only if they come in peach," she told him sternly.

"Pigs are not peaches," he informed her, just as sternly. "Sorry, I meant figs."

She giggled. She had never really been *that* girl. The one who giggled. She was surprised by how much she liked it.

She glanced at the photos Sabrina had sent of Beth and Jack and Jill in their dresses. Like the bridesmaids them-selves—except for her—the dresses were variations on a theme. The continuity factor was the peach color.

She showed the photo to Jay.

He wrinkled his nose. "Horrible color."

"Probably devilishly difficult to find."

"We could buy some construction paper," he said with a snap of his fingers, "and make it. Peach-colored fig leaves. One for me. Three for you."

She smacked him on the arm, and he pretended he was gravely wounded. She noticed an older woman smiling at them indulgently.

Assuming they were a couple.

Maybe that assumption was part of what made it so easy to reach for his hand as they navigated the busy streets on their quest for peach dresses. Or maybe it was the lingering effect of him trusting her with his broken heart.

They tried shop after shop. She couldn't help but notice how Jay treated people, with a kind of friendly respect that they responded to. Of course, a few of those women in those shops were just responding to his green eyes and dimpled grin!

Still, the search for the dress proved both exhausting and fruitless. There was apparently, not a peach dress to be found in the entire Peach City.

"I'm going to single-handedly ruin my sister's wedding photos," she told Jay.

"I think we should sue Penticton for false advertising."

"But the stay forever part is true," she said, and heard the wistfulness in her own voice.

He looked at her long and hard. "Yes," he finally said, "that part is true."

"Why don't you try a bridal shop?" the clerk in one of the stores suggested. "We have three."

She marked all three of them on a map for Jay and Jolie.

"If this doesn't work out," Jolie said, "I could try online. Sometimes delivery is shockingly fast."

"It's always good to have a backup plan," Jay agreed, as they found the first of the bridal stores.

He stepped in the door first. "Every man's worst nightmare. I think a fairy tale exploded in here. I'm drowning in unrealistic romantic dreams."

She saw the remark in a completely different way since he had shared his family tragedy with her. He was running away from the thing that had brought his family pain—love. And who could blame him?

"It's pretty estrogen rich," Jolie agreed, keeping it light.

She explained her mission to the clerk, who shook her head. No peach dresses. The second and third shops were also strikeouts.

But before they left, Jay squinted at a rack. "I'm no expert on colors, but I could swear that dress over there is the same shade you had on last night."

"Oh, that's not a dress," the clerk said, "It's an underslip."

"It looks like a dress to me," Jay said, moving over to the rack. He pulled out the slip on its hanger and held it out for Jolie's inspection.

"It's not a dress," she told him firmly. "It goes under a dress. Like a petticoat."

"I know what a slip is," he said wryly.

Of course he did! A man like this was likely quite familiar with what women wore under their clothes.

"It looks pretty sheer," Jolie said, doubtfully.

"Oh," he said pleased, "the next best thing to a fig leaf."

In some way, the item he was holding up reminded her of her wedding gown, probably because of its cut and pure simplicity. It was also silk.

"Put it back," she said. She thought she probably shouldn't try that on, but she heard the lack of conviction in her voice. For some reason it was like having more prosecco and another waffle. Irresistible.

"I think you should at least try it. You know, in the interest of having fun. And a backup plan."

Plus, it made her feel as if she would appear to be stiff and uptight if she refused. Oh, who was she kidding? She *was* stiff and up tight. But not today.

Today, she was a carefree woman who had wind-tangled hair and a handsome man at her side, and the whole world felt completely different than it had twenty-four hours ago.

# CHAPTER EIGHT

"FINE," JOLIE CAPITULATED. "I'll try it on and you can see for yourself how inappropriate it would be."

"Oh," Jay said, wagging a wicked eyebrow at her, "I do love me some inappropriate."

She snatched the fabric out of his hands, and marched to the change room. What would it hurt?

She took off her clothes, and slid the silky chemise over her head. Just like last night, her underwear did nothing for it. The fabric was unforgiving of every line. She hesitated then took off her underwear and put the sheath back on.

It floated over her naked skin as sensual as a touch.

She turned and looked at herself in the mirror. She was stunned by the woman who looked back at her: bold and playful and daring. The slip hugged her in places, but it skimmed in others, hinting at what lay beneath.

She had to admit Jay had an eye. The slip was astonishing. Unlike the monstrosity of a dress last night, she looked absolutely gorgeous in it.

Taking a deep breath, encouraging the newer bolder "fun" girl to come out to play, she opened the change room door and stepped out.

Jay went stock-still. The only thing that moved was his Adam's apple, which bobbed in his throat when he swallowed.

"See?" she said, doing a twirl. "It's way too—"

"You," he croaked.

The saleslady came and looked at her. Her eyes widened with appreciation.

"You know, not everyone could pull that off, but you can. Slip dresses look like this one, cut on the bias, with spaghetti straps. They are actually very vogue right now."

"It's almost see-through," Jolie protested.

Jay grinned wickedly. "Fig leafs here we come."

"If I quickly stitched another slip inside of it, it would be absolutely perfect," the sales associate suggested, "but it will still cling a bit, so it depends how comfortable you are going without underwear."

"Commando," Jay filled in helpfully.

"Commando?" Jolie asked.

"That's what it's called. Going without underwear."

"You're a surprising expert on the topic," Jolie teased him, aware of how nice it felt to tease a man.

"Stick with me. I'm full of surprises."

For a woman who had avoided surprises, at all costs, for almost her entire life, she was not sure why that sounded quite so enticing.

"Just take it off," the saleslady suggested, "put on that housecoat behind the door and let me see what I can do with it."

Jolie looked back in the mirror. The chemise was just way too sexy. It was way too bold. Still, it was one hundred and fifty percent better than the other dress.

"Okay," she agreed, part reluctance and part hope. She retreated back to the change room, came out in an oversize fluffy white housecoat and handed the scrap of fabric to the clerk, who whisked it away to another room.

Now she was standing in a bridal shop, in a housecoat with not a stitch on underneath it. She was not sure why that felt even more intimate than standing before Jay in the crazy dress that wasn't really a dress but underwear, but it did.

Jay stared at Jolie. He felt absolutely terrified. It felt as if his mission—to show her who she really was—was going completely off the rails and leading him into dark overgrown forests where it was possible dragons lurked.

It had started when he had encouraged her to leave her hair down.

And then sharing that waffle with her had been strangely erotic.

But the worst thing of all had been telling her about his destroyed family. He'd never unburdened to anyone before.

He was aware that it should have felt like a weakness revealing that kind of information to someone who realistically was a stranger to him.

Except she didn't feel like a stranger.

He *knew* her. He'd known her since she was a kid.

Maybe it had just felt safe to confide in Jolie because their reacquaintance promised to be a short one. She would go back to Italy. He would go back to the blessed distractions of working too much.

The underwear dress she had been wearing was the epitome of what the mission was all about. To show her how bold and sexy she was. To make her not afraid of that.

But maybe he was the one who was going to have to be afraid.

Because all these things felt as if he was uncovering, subtly and slowly, layers that hid the real her.

But this—Jolie standing in front of him in a housecoat—felt as if everything had been stripped away, and what remained was purely her.

How could the housecoat—the white thick terry cloth

kind that you got in upscale hotels—be even more revealing than the underslip had been?

This was the stunning truth: she was beautiful, she was
brilliant and she was kind. He could feel himself leaning
toward the softness he had seen in her eyes when he had
revealed the truth about his family like a sailor looking for
refuge from a storm-tossed sea.

The thing about *her*—with her wild hair and her cheeky
smile, and the way she could rock lingerie as if it was a
dress, but especially her, standing before him in a simple
white housecoat—was that he could picture her in his future.

In his kitchen.

The morning after.

In his life for a lot of morning afters.

Maybe it was because of the backdrop of row after row
of pure white wedding dresses that he could hear the word
*forever* in his mind as if it had been spoken out loud.

Everything was getting all mixed up inside his head. He
was trying to show her who she really was.

But he had known from the beginning that there was a
danger of him not being able to handle that.

Of him finding out who he really was instead.

And it was, terrifyingly, someone who still wanted to believe in what he saw shining in her eyes.

Despite the fact Jay had plenty of evidence to the contrary,
something about Jolie seemed to overshadow that evidence.

That tomorrow would be okay, after all.

He was aware that he had to put the brakes on, right now,
before he drove them both over a cliff.

The clerk returned with the peach-colored scrap of fabric.
She had transformed it into a dress with another slip stitched
expertly to the inside of the original.

When Jolie came out the second time, it felt as if the wind
was knocked from him, like when he played hockey and

suddenly found himself on the ice, staring at the ceiling, unable to breathe, wondering what the heck had happened.

He deliberately kept his features bland, even though he had to fight the guy who wanted to flounder at her feet.

"That's the one," he said, and then glanced at his watch. "Where has the day gone? Wow, it's nearly four thirty. We've got to go. Troy was supposed to arrive this afternoon and I have some business phone calls I have to make."

It would be very late in the Eastern part of Canada to be making calls, but people were used to hearing from him at all hours.

Business, his refuge.

His sister called him a workaholic. As if that was a bad thing!

He was a workaholic for a reason! Because work was predictable, and allowed him to be in control.

Unlike family. That sister, who was so fond of calling him commitment phobic and a workaholic, had been fifteen when their father had died. She had desperately needed a mom to guide her through that time.

Instead, it had been on him. And he'd been clumsy and ill-prepared to be the one who said, *No, you're too young to date*, and *No, you can't wear your makeup like that*, and *No*—actually that one had been *Absolutely no—you can't wear that outfit*.

Begging his mom to weigh in, begging her to come back to them.

But no, it had been Troy who had been his wingman through it all. Being there when Mike had come home drunk, and Jim had gotten in the accident with the motorbike he'd acquired on the sly.

Troy had a way of *seeing* people. It was as if he could see right through their faults and foibles to their souls, Sabrina being a prime example of that.

Watching how Troy dealt with people had helped Jay come to terms with the confusion of feelings around his mom, softened him toward her.

But what had not softened was his fierce decision that he would never put his own heart in a position to be so broken by love.

A resolve he had to firm up right now!

He put the roof of the convertible up for the trip back to Hidden Valley. He was not sure, after having seen Jolie in that dress, that he could stand watching the wind blow in her hair again. It made a man want to comb through those tangles with his hands.

Which made him think of that kiss they had shared last night.

No, things were getting way, way too complicated between him and little Miss Cavaletti.

He steeled himself against her look of disappointment.

"It's too hot," he said. "Bad for the upholstery. Not to mention heatstroke. You would not believe how many people get heatstroke in convertibles, from that sun beating down on their heads."

He should have thought it through more carefully, though, about putting the top up, because now they could hear each other. He didn't want to make any more conversation with her. It felt as if she could pull his secrets from him like a magnet held above steel filings.

He didn't put the nostalgic tunes back on. He chose classical.

And blasted it.

And pretended to be oblivious to the fact his sudden withdrawal was hurting her.

Better to hurt her now than later.

Because his mother and father had shown him what the future held if you loved someone too deeply.

There it was.

Jolie Cavaletti invited a man to love deeply, to want things he had already decided it was best that he didn't have.

And he had to protect both of them from those kinds of desires.

*Desire.* Another complication rearing its ugly head, the element that could guarantee a man could not think straight about anything. Her hair, her lips, the way she had looked in that lingerie? He probably wasn't going to have a sensible thought until after the wedding.

Never mind his mission to show her who she was.

In that little piece of fabric that had somehow been transformed into a dress?

It would be perfectly evident to anyone who wasn't blind exactly who Jolie was.

From the moment Jolie emerged from the changing room, she sensed something was different, that she was back to being on her own. Jay was gone. She took the dress to the front counter.

"You did such a good job, thank you."

"You're welcome." The clerk waved away her credit card. "It's paid for."

Jay was outside, scrolling through his phone.

"You shouldn't have paid for the dress," she told him.

"I wanted to."

"Well, you shouldn't have. It's not the same as holding open a door for someone. You already paid for breakfast. What do I owe you?"

"Your firstborn?"

"I'm not kidding, Jay."

He looked annoyed, but he gave her the amount, and she settled up with him.

After that, Jolie could feel the chill, and it wasn't coming just from the fact that Jay, apparently worried about heat-stroke, had the air conditioner in the car going full blast.

No, he was pulling away from her. It was in the set of his shoulders and jaw, in the line of his lips, in the way he was focused so intently—too intently—on the road, as if he was driving in a Formula 1 event. She tried to think what she might have done to bring on this distressing shift in attitude, but she came up blank. Surely it wasn't about her paying her own way?

Still, there was no mistaking the fact he had gone from warm and charming to remote in the blink of an eye.

It hurt.

But it shouldn't. No! She should be grateful to him. When they had come out of the store and it had been so hot she felt like butter about to melt, she had entertained the notion that they would stop at one of the many beaches they had passed on the way to Penticton and have a swim.

She didn't have a bathing suit with her and he didn't, either, as far as she knew, so what had she been thinking might happen?

A skinny-dip at a secluded beach somewhere?

That was what happened when you just let your hair blow around willy-nilly and were persuaded to try on slips and pass them off as dresses.

That was what happened when you stood before a man with only the thinnest of silky barriers separating your nakedness from him.

Boldness could become a drug, constantly pushing you to go further and further!

She was just getting over one relationship. She certainly did not need to be falling for another guy. Standing before him in skimpy clothing, relishing the look in his eyes, entertaining ideas of skinny-dipping on a hot day.

She slid Jay a look.

Was she falling for him?

How was that even possible? Her logical mind did not like it. Their reunion was not even twenty-four hours old.

That was chemistry, for you. Or maybe it was biology. Or some powerful combination of the two. But, realistically, how much of the present was being influenced by her feelings for Jay from the past?

So, no, she was not. Falling. Falling suggested a certain lack of control, something that *happened* to you, instead of something you chose.

She was too close to her last romantic fiasco to be making the same errors all over again. If she did ever choose another relationship—a big *if*—she decided she would take a scientific approach to it. Emotions could not be trusted.

Jay had done her a favor by keeping the roof up and blasting her with cold air and his own chilliness all the way home. A huge favor.

They arrived back at Hidden Valley, and she got out of the car, not giving him a chance to open the door for her. Who needed that? New independent Jolie did not need old-fashioned shows of chivalry!

She managed, just barely, to refrain from saying, *I can open the door myself.*

"Thanks for a nice day," she said instead, a woman grateful for the huge favor that had been bestowed on her. Why did she sound faintly snippy?

She gathered up her parcel and her purse. She tossed her tangle of hair over her shoulder and *liked* the look on his face, his chilliness momentarily pierced by an ice-melting look of heat.

Or maybe that was actual heat she was feeling. Leaving the car felt as though she was entering a blast furnace. It had probably been very wise of him to leave the top of the car up.

She didn't spare him another glance. She closed the

door—technically, it might have been a slam—and then she moved away from his car and quickly toward the relative sanctuary of her cabin.

With its stupid name that conjured up all kinds of unlikely possibilities.

# CHAPTER NINE

ANTHONY HAD THE exceedingly poor judgment to intercept Jolie as she aimed for the shade that surrounded her cabin. "I've been looking for you all day."

Jolie glanced around for her accidental fiancé and saw that he and Troy had met up and, towels over their shoulders, were walking down toward the lake.

*Getting the swim she had wanted.*

She didn't need a man to rescue her!

"Get out of my way," she snapped in Italian when Anthony looked as if he intended to block her path.

She was aware her annoyance might have had a little more to do with being iced out by Jay than Anthony showing up.

And the heat.

Italians had the good sense to have *riposa* in the midday heat.

Undeterred—maybe not reading her mood, he had never been particularly sensitive to others—Anthony matched his stride to hers.

"You've had a fight," he said with satisfaction.

So, he read more into her than she had given him credit for. Still, how dare he think she was going to confide the personal details of her life to him?

"Go away," she said, still in Italian. "Go home. You're not welcome here."

"That's not what your sister said," he replied smoothly.

She did an about-face. Despite the temptations of the shade and her little cottage nestled in those towering trees, Jolie didn't actually want Anthony trailing her all the way to her cabin. It would be better if he didn't even know which one she was in.

*Lovers' Retreat.* He might see that as some kind of invitation. Who named these places, anyway?

She walked back to the lodge. and stopped at the desk. "Which room is my sister in? Sabrina Cavaletti?"

At least she knew her sister wasn't having a reunion with her husband-to-be, because she had just seen him.

She knew many large hotels would never give out a room number, but there were no such problems at the cozy, smaller lodge, and they gave her Sabrina's room information. Anthony trailed in the door behind her.

"If he asks," she said in a stern undertone, "do not, under any circumstances, tell him which cabin I am in."

She could tell by the guilty look on the clerk's face that it was too late.

She turned and glared at Anthony. "Vamoose," she snapped.

He stopped, gave her a hangdog look, as if somehow he was the victim, then turned and walked away.

Jolie hammered on Sabrina's door. Her sister apparently approved of *riposa* because she was not only in, but in her housecoat.

She had some kind of terrible mud mask on her face. The mud mask looked like something from a horror film, green and dripping, at the same time as being one of those *girl* things that Jolie was excluded from. She glanced over her sister's shoulder. She was alone.

"How could you?" Jolie demanded, without preamble. "You knew I'd broken up with Anthony. Why would you invite him here?"

Sabrina gestured her in, and closed the door behind her. She regarded her for a moment.

"Your hair looks as if you've survived a tornado."

This from a woman with green slime melting off her face! So tempting to say *Jay likes it.* Tempting, childish and off topic.

"How could you?" Jolie repeated.

"He tracked me down online. He told me it was just a spat and that you were being stubborn, which I mean, literally, you *can* be stubborn, Jolie! Mom and I both liked him so much when we met him last year in Italy, and he was being so charming. I thought it was quite romantic how determined he was to be with you. Mom and I think he's perfect for you."

"You and Mom don't have any say in my life."

"Thank you. That's more than obvious since you've chosen to live about a million miles away from us."

Jolie registered that her sister sounded hurt. "Seven thousand kilometers."

Sabrina rolled her eyes. "Anyway, he's a nice guy and very good-looking and he has a job."

"Is that where you set the bar?"

"After I spoke with him, I was convinced it would be right for you to give him another chance."

"No."

"Why not? You were crazy about him. Where did that go?"

"The most correct word in there is *crazy.* I was crazy."

"But what happened?"

"He cheated on me! And that's a pattern from our childhood that I will not repeat. For goodness' sake, Mom named me after a song where a woman is *begging* another woman to quit having an affair with her man."

"That song was called 'Jolene,' and you're Jolie."

"I think we both know what she meant. By changing a

few letters she was trying to, like, have a secret code. It's pathetic. I won't ever be like that."

Her sister looked genuinely stunned. "Jolie, I'm sorry, I had no idea."

"About the song, or Anthony?"

"I hate that song. Every time it's resurrected by another singer, I want to say, *For heaven's sake, take him already.* I just never would have pictured Anthony being that kind of guy."

"Me, either," Jolie said glumly.

"Are you sure?" Sabrina asked.

"Of course, I'm sure. I saw him in the gelato shop making kissy faces over a dish of *spaghettieis.*"

"Is that the ice cream dish that looks like spaghetti and meatballs?"

Jolie nodded.

"But that's your favorite," Sabrina breathed.

"Anthony introduced me to it."

"You didn't have a clue?" Sabrina asked with a tiny bit of insulting skepticism. "You didn't see him making eyes at the servers when you went out for dinner?"

"We hadn't been out much. When I saw him with that other woman, he actually blamed me. He said I focused too much on work."

"Why, that snake!" And then, "Jolie, why didn't you tell me?"

"I just wanted to nurse my bruised dignity in private without you and Mom kicking around my misery like a football with not enough air in it."

"It's very hurtful that you have such a low opinion of Mom and me."

"How is this suddenly about you?"

Her sister sighed. "The same ice cream dish he wooed you with. That is beyond low."

"Yes, *snake* kind of implies that."

"What did you do?"

"I walked away, of course, and sent him a text. That I had seen him and that it was over. Then I blocked him."

"He would have been wearing that ice cream, if it was me. I'll tell him to leave."

"Thank you. I just told him to leave, but I don't think he's going to listen to me."

"I'm really sorry, Jolie. I wish you would have told me sooner."

There was no nice way to say you did not trust your sister with your innermost secrets.

Sabrina unfortunately proved that assessment was probably correct when she seized on the package Jolie was still carrying, and seemed ready to leave the topic of her sister's heartbreak and humiliation behind with barely a pause.

But then Sabrina surprised Jolie by pulling out her phone and scrolling through it. "Here's the messages from him." She tapped in furiously. "There! I've told him to leave. Right now."

"Thank you."

"What's going on between you and Jay?" Sabrina asked, surprising Jolie further by actually showing some interest in her life "That kiss this morning gave us all a bit of a shock."

Interest, then, or judgment? Did they not see her in Jay's league? Well, let them wonder!

"Did it?" she said smoothly.

Sabrina chewed on her lip, struggling between wanting details, and trying to make up for the fact she'd invited her sister's philandering fiancé to her wedding.

"You got a dress!" Sabrina said, wisely putting both Jay's kiss and the debacle with Anthony behind her.

"Yes, I did." She slid it from the package.

"The color! Perfect. The fabric, though. Never mind. Try it on for me," Sabrina insisted, and shoved Jolie toward the washroom.

Jolie put on the remade chemise again. Somehow, she didn't feel it was nearly as much fun as it had been modeling it for Jay.

She stepped out of the hotel room bathroom self-consciously.

Her sister stared at her. Her mouth fell open, and then she closed it. "You can't wear that," she said firmly.

"It's that obvious?" Jolie asked.

"Obvious?"

"That it's an underslip?"

Sabrina frowned, came over and took a closer look. "I would have never guessed that, actually. It looks like the cutest ever little sundress."

"But then—"

"Hey, on Saturday there is one star of the show, and that's me. If you wear that dress, all eyes will be on you. You look stunning. You should dress like that more often. Just not at my wedding."

And then her sister actually smiled at her.

"If I wear the other dress all eyes will be on me, too," Jolie pointed out.

"Sadly, true. Such a disaster. I was trying to find all different dresses with the same color. I ordered them online. I didn't even notice the worms."

"Snakes," Jolie corrected her, and Sabrina snorted back a laugh.

"I think we've discussed snakes quite enough for one day," Sabrina said.

"Maybe you can find something else online. Delivery can be mind-blowingly quick. Thanks for saying I look stunning. You've never said that to me before."

"You know what? One sister is supposed to be the smart one, and one is supposed to be the pretty one, and I'm annoyed—super annoyed, actually—that you're both."

"I always thought you were the pretty one," Jolie said. Sabrina cast herself down on the bed and Jolie joined her.

"That would depend who you asked. You were always Dad's favorite."

"And you were Mom's," she said, feeling the sadness of two sisters in divided camps.

"I was the reason him and Mom had to get married. That came up in every fight. That she *trapped* him."

"I'm sorry."

"It's got nothing to do with you," her sister said, a little too sharply. "Anyway, who knows if that's why you were his favorite. You looked like him. And then, when you were eight or something, you started speaking Italian, just out of the blue, as if it was no big deal."

If Sabrina was a tiny bit mean to her sometimes, wasn't there an explanation for it?

"I'm afraid *vamoose* is about the limit of my Italian," Sabrina confessed.

"It's Spanish, actually, from a Latin root."

"See? That's exactly what I mean! Who knows the Latin root of *vamoose*?"

"From *vadimus.*"

"Or that Italy is seven thousand miles away."

"Kilometers."

"You're such a geek, Jolie. That's why I was literally so happy for you when you found Anthony. He seemed kind of normal. But maybe you should just stick to the geeks."

Which Jay most definitely did not qualify as.

"You don't have to say that as if I'm nothing without a man. It's a little too much like that song. I've decided I won't be doing the romance thing again."

"Huh. Well, that might be one area where I'm smarter than you, sis. Because you don't choose love, it chooses you. If I could choose, do you think I'd choose Troy again? But I love him."

"What happened between you? Please don't tell me he cheated."

"Troy? Never. But we just fought all the time. Then I said I wanted a baby, he said he wasn't ready. No, he said *we* weren't ready. He finally said he'd had enough, and he wasn't bringing any poor, unsuspecting kid into a war zone. It kind of blindsided me because I didn't think it was *that* bad."

"Did you consider the fact that you were comfortable with fighting because that's what you grew up with? Maybe you actually believe that's how things get solved."

"I didn't know your degree was in psychiatry, Doc."

"Our childhoods shape us, whether we like it or not. I wonder how much our childhood had to do with me picking a philanderer."

"Seriously, Jolie, a philanderer?"

Jolie realized, resigned, her sister was commenting on her vocabulary not her choice of men. If you can't beat them, join them, she thought.

Sabrina's phone quacked.

"Mom?" Jolie asked.

"How did you know?"

"I assigned her the same tone."

They laughed together. It actually felt like they might have a sisterly bond.

Sabrina looked at her phone. "She's not arriving now until the day before the wedding."

Jolie thought her sister looked relieved.

"She says Dad's coming with her."

"Together?"

"It sounds like it."

"Reconciliation," both women said together, and not happily.

"You see, if you could choose, who would choose that?" Sabrina asked.

Who indeed? Jolie thought. Her childhood peppered with her dad leaving and her mother begging him to come back.

And she still was? All these years later? Jolie hadn't known it was still going on. She felt faintly guilty about leaving her sister alone with the family drama.

"Do you have an extra one of those? The thing on your face?"

"I do. But go take off the dress first. I don't want it to get wrecked. Just in case."

They actually had a somewhat sisterly moment while Sabrina applied the mask to her face.

"Avocado. It's miraculous."

Jolie refrained from asking to see the pouch it came in so she could study the ingredients. Instead, she allowed herself to enjoy Sabrina's pampering.

"It needs to stay on for one hour," her sister instructed her, in her wheelhouse now, doing exactly the kind of girly things that Jolie had never been able to figure out the appeal of. "If you wash it off right before supper, you'll see. Magic."

Jolie was more interested in the science behind the product than the magic, but it would probably spoil the moment if she said so. Plus, her sister did have enviably fabulous skin, like porcelain.

"Ta-da." Sabrina held up a mirror and Jolie's mouth dropped open.

"I think there was a perfectly terrible movie starring this character."

"It'll be worth it, you'll see."

"You mean I have to walk through the resort looking like this?"

"Maybe Anthony will see you and be dissuaded."

It wasn't actually Anthony seeing her that she was worried about!

# CHAPTER TEN

JOLIE SHARED A laugh with her sister, as if it really was Anthony she was afraid of seeing, and not Jay. She tried, without success, to remember when the last time she had laughed with her sister was.

"Remember, one hour," Sabrina called after her.

Jolie managed to get back to her cabin without anyone noticing her. She was fairly certain she left a trail of melting green globs behind her.

The heat was insufferable.

The cabin, thankfully, was in the trees, cool and dark inside.

She looked at herself in the mirror, horrified. Was she really supposed to wear this for an hour? Her skin already felt weirdly tight. She tapped the goop. Was it hardening at the edges? Would her sister ever know if she washed it off right now?

But somehow that felt like a betrayal of Sabrina's efforts, not to mention that somehow the idea of softly glowing skin, in the face of being spurned by Jay, was too appealing to resist.

*Spurned* was probably too strong a word. She had been imagining a naked swim for two, he had been preoccupied with business. She probably wouldn't have had the nerve, even if the opportunity had presented itself.

Anthony was all the evidence she needed that she was not good at reading the subtle signals men were sending out.

Jolie suddenly felt exhausted. She glanced at her watch. No wonder she was tired. It was the middle of the night in Italy.

She knew the wrong thing to do was to give in to jet lag. You were supposed to tough it out.

She wouldn't have a sleep, she told herself just a little *riposa*, that was all. She'd just close her eyes for a few minutes. She set the alarm on her phone.

She went and took off her skirt, slipped her bra out from under her blouse, and laid down in her bed, on her back, so she wouldn't spoil the sheets with the green goop. Her bedroom window was open and a hot breeze blew over her.

She fell asleep almost instantly.

Jolie woke up feeling disoriented. The scent of avocado was heavy in the air, it was pitch black and she had no idea where she was. It felt as if something was encasing her face. With faint panic, she reached up and encountered a hard surface.

Slowly it came back to her.

Canada.

Her sister's wedding.

Green goop hardened on her face in the interest of glowing beauty.

*Jay.*

The reason for her sudden interest in glowing beauty.

"He can like me the way I am or not at all," she said, glancing at her watch. Of course, if the ride home from Penticton was any indication, he had chosen not at all.

Still, a woman wanted to be at her best when she'd been rejected.

It was past midnight. What had happened to her alarm? She had missed dinner. It had been a terrible mistake to give in to that desire to rest. She would be completely turned around now. She made herself stay in bed. She clenched her eyes firmly shut, and ordered herself to slumber.

Instead, she remembered the day. In detail.

She heard a sound outside her cabin and the hair rose on the back of her neck. First, branches broke, and then there was a groaning sound.

There was a wild animal out there. She was certain it was a bear. Toronto did not have bears, but this part of the world did.

Wasn't there even a warning on the garbage cans?

She'd heard bears had very sensitive noses. She didn't have any food in the cabin, but maybe it was being drawn to the scent of avocado. If she could smell avocado—and she could—surely a bear could, too.

"Don't be so dramatic," she ordered herself. It didn't have to be bear. It could be something smaller. Like a raccoon.

*Or a mountain lion.*

Heart pounding, being so quiet that the night creature, whatever it was, wouldn't be able to determine there was an edible person along with the avocado in her cabin, she slid over to the window and peered out.

Her eyes slowly adjusted to the dark. The moon was out and reflected off the lake. Under different circumstances she might see it as beautiful.

Another branch snapped. And another groan came.

Was she relieved it was Anthony? She was pretty sure she would have preferred any one of the other possibilities. He was placing himself, with a singular lack of grace, on a perch amongst the tangled branches of a large lilac shrub.

She squinted at him. What was that in his hand?

Oh, please, no. It was a guitar. The instrument looked like it may have been a toy. He strummed it thoughtfully. The sound seemed amplified by the pure quiet of the night.

It was worse than a nightmare. Anthony cleared his throat, strummed again and began to sing.

He sang, badly, in Italian. When she first heard her name, she thought it was going to be the song her mother had named her after.

But no, there were, unbelievably, more awful things than that. The song was obviously of his own creation.

It was a ballad about a misunderstood man, and one little mistake. The chorus involved *spaghettieis*, heartbreak—his—and the future children that he hoped would possess Jolie's eyes.

Such was the nature of jet lag that she pictured unruly children carrying between them a bag of eyes.

The caterwauling continued, unabated. Thankfully, her cabin was fairly isolated. There was one next door, but yesterday it had not looked occupied.

Her relief at not disturbing the neighbors—not having witnesses to the serenade—was short-lived. The cabin next door was apparently occupied now, because she saw a light come on.

She took a deep breath, ducked into her bedroom and looked around for the skirt she had abandoned earlier. She was not going out there dressed in only a blouse to shock the new neighbors even further.

Just as she bent to pick it up off the floor, she heard the back door of her cabin open. She froze, realizing she hadn't locked it. Hidden Valley did not seem like the type of place where things had to be locked.

Anthony was inside!

But no, he wasn't, because the singing continued at the front of the cabin.

She peered around the door of her bedroom and discovered it was Jay who stood there.

He glanced her way. Too dark thankfully for him to see

her face, or hopefully to notice she was only in her blouse. Who was she kidding that she would have gone skinny-dipping at the first opportunity?

She was going to duck back behind the door, but what he did next paralyzed her so completely she thought maybe even her breathing had stopped.

Jay's fingers moved to the buttons of his shirt. Her mouth went dry as he dispensed them quickly and peeled off that garment.

She had seen the statue of *David* with her own eyes, and it had nothing on Jay Fletcher. Painted in moonlight, it was obvious he was as beautifully and perfectly made as that marble statue. He was one hundred percent pure man— broad shouldered, deep chested, his stomach a hard hollow.

She couldn't have moved now if she wanted to.

She got what he was doing. Jolie thought Jay's half nudity would be ample to persuade Anthony they were in the cabin together. Lovers.

At *Lovers' Retreat*.

This had to be a dream, but no, when she pinched herself Jay was still there, and it was apparent he didn't do anything by halves.

With a quick bend and a flick of his wrist, he divested himself of his shorts and Jay Fletcher was standing in her cabin, completely unself-conscious, in just his boxer briefs.

He was magnificent, so much so that the serenade outside her cabin faded in her mind.

While her gaze was glued to him, he barely spared her a glance as he strode through her small living area. Just before he threw open the French door to the balcony, he paused and tousled his hair.

Nice touch. Making it look as if he was here. With her. Unclothed. And messy-haired.

A picture *did* paint a thousand words.

Thank goodness he stepped out, because her face turned so hot she could feel the mask softening.

"Hey," he called from the balcony. "What are you doing, man?"

Anthony' voice and the guitar strumming stopped abruptly. Jolie crept to her bedroom window and watched.

"I will win her back," he cried in English. And then added in Italian, "I am the better man."

"You aren't," she called from the window in Italian. "*He* performs like a stallion."

"You're embarrassing yourself," Jay said to Anthony, almost gently.

Anthony looked to the balcony, and then to the window, and then back again. His shoulders slumped in defeat, and he dropped the guitar. It landed with a sad twang as he shuffled away.

Jolie found her skirt, pulled it on, and slipped into the bathroom. Her face looked horrible! She took a washcloth, soaked it, scrubbed.

Everything looked worse! It wasn't coming off!

"Okay in there?" he called.

"Uh, yeah." She rubbed some more. Her face was a mess, green mask slimy-looking now, but still clinging. "Thank you for the rescue. There's no need to hang around. I don't know how you happened to know I was in need, but thanks."

"I'm in the cottage next door. I heard him. I couldn't resist rescuing a damsel in distress."

Suddenly, he was standing in the hallway, looking through the ajar bathroom door at her.

His mouth fell open.

She tried to laugh it off. "You think you're getting a damsel in distress, and you get the Grinch who stole Christmas instead."

It felt as if she had planted her whole face in a newly poured sidewalk. Jay came into the bathroom and regarded her thoughtfully. He was trying not to laugh and, thankfully, he succeeded.

He took her chin in his hands and turned her face.

"What the hell have you done to yourself?"

Oh, geez, sharing her cottage with arguably the world's most attractive man, and she looked like this?

"I'm rehearsing for my part as Fiona," she told him.

He looked blank.

"*Shrek*?" One of her favorite movies, where in the end, Fiona is loved for who she is most comfortable being.

He still looked blank. She realized she'd love to curl up with him, a bowl of popcorn, and that movie.

"Sabrina and I had a little girl time when I got back from Penticton. It's an avocado mask. It's supposed to work magic on my skin."

"Your skin did not need any magic worked on it," he told her gruffly.

She sighed inwardly, and Jay reached out tentatively and touched the edge of the mask around her mouth.

His fingers brushed that vulnerable surface.

*Don't swoon*, she ordered herself. *Friends!*

This could only happen to her. Instead of impressing Jay with her glowing skin, she was looking like the monster from the green lagoon. And this followed being subjected to the worst serenade by a spurned lover in the history of mankind. It was too awkward for words.

Really? Why wasn't he cutting and running?

Because he had decided they could safely be friends?

# CHAPTER ELEVEN

A GREEN CHUNK of her face mask peeled off beneath Jay's fingertips. He studied it as if it was a specimen in those long-ago science classes they had shared.

"Is it edible?" he asked solemnly.

"I didn't have a chance to study the ingredients, but I doubt it."

He put the piece in his mouth and crunched down on it. "Edible," he declared. "Let's face it."

She laughed at his pun and she realized that's what he'd intended. He sensed her awkwardness and was trying to put her at ease.

It was so nice. *Friendly.*

"I might not go as far as edible, it could have hydrogen peroxide in it, and chemicals from fragrances and dyes."

"Will you save me if I topple over?" he asked, seriously.

"I will," she promised, "but at the moment I may be the one needing saving. I've left it on far too long, and it's hurting my face. It was supposed to be an hour. I think it's been closer to seven."

He touched her face with his finger, and then tried to get his fingernail under the mask. He pried gently.

"Ouch."

"I don't think that's supposed to be stuck on like that. I think we better try and get it off."

"I've been trying to get if off."

"I hope we don't need a chisel."

*We?* Oh, geez, wasn't this just the story of her life? She imagined skinny-dipping and instead got green goo turned to cement being chiseled off her face.

"I'll deal with it. You go."

She turned away from him and scraped at her face with the wet cloth. She yelped a little when the mask resisted, stubbornly glued to her skin.

Jay had not taken his cue, merely leaning one deliciously naked shoulder against the doorframe. After watching her for a few seconds, he came up behind her and took the wash-cloth from her hand.

If she had thought eating waffles with him and being with him in nothing more than a housecoat had been oddly intimate, those moments were nothing compared to this, him at such close quarters in such a tiny space.

He dabbed at her face. Scraped. Rubbed. But all with an exquisite effort to be gentle.

Had pain ever felt quite so wonderful? His touch was tempered, and his brow furrowed in concentration, his tongue ever so faintly pushing out between teeth that she noticed were absolutely perfect. As was the naked chest one small fraction of an inch from her breasts.

"Not coming off," he said.

She turned away from him, and back to the mirror. She pried at her face. A paltry little piece came loose.

"I have a sudden vision of myself standing at the altar with my sister, sporting green clumps, Jack and Jill holding back laughter, and Beth and the assembled looking sympathetic."

"We'll get it off."

There was that *we* again, and all it conjured. A life of solving problems, some small and some large, some funny and some serious, with someone you could rely on.

Who would never in a million years embarrass you with a serenade outside your window, no matter how drunk he was.

Despite the spiked punch in high school, Jay had not been a drinker then, and she suspected he still was not.

"Go lie down on the couch," he said. "We'll lay a hot cloth over your face and try it again in a few minutes."

She should protest, of course, but it seemed unnecessarily surly, like women who did not allow doors to be held open for them. Maybe, just for once in her life, she could surrender to being looked after.

So Jolie did as he asked and he busied himself at the sink. A few minutes later, he came and perched on the edge of the couch, gently laid a very hot washcloth over her face. He pressed it down around her eyes and nose and mouth.

She could feel his fingertips on the other side of that hot cloth. It felt like an exotic massage and it was unfairly sensual.

"You don't have to do this," she protested, a little too late, and not too vehemently.

"Ah," he said, "what are fiancés for?"

"I'm sorry. It seems a lot to ask, even of a fiancé, particularly a fake one. It's the middle of the night. Except not in Italy."

"Speaking of Italy," he said, "I have a confession to make."

"You do?"

"I speak Italian."

*With a name like Fletcher? Life was just unfair sometimes.*

"My mom's side."

She could feel the mask melting again. "How well?" she croaked.

"Not well, but better than him." He said it in Italian, and she really thought it was very good. And amazingly sexy.

Twice now, she'd referred to his performance in Italian, thinking he couldn't understand her. "I'm embarrassed."

"Don't be. I should have told you sooner."

"Not just by what I said. But by him. By my choices, I guess."

"It's not your fault he cheated on you." Another thing she hadn't known he knew, because she hadn't known he spoke Italian. "You deserve better."

"My sister and I were just talking about that. Family patterns. My father was not given to faithfulness."

Why would she tell him *that*?

"Don't worry," he said, "I've figured out there's no such thing as the perfect family."

"Yours always seemed like it was," she said a little wistfully.

"Yeah," he said, and his expression hardened, "until it wasn't."

"I'm sorry," she said. "I don't know why I said that. I say the wrong thing sometimes. I wondered if I did it today at some point. You seemed, um, changed on the way home."

"Did I?"

"Was it about me paying for the dress?"

"No, I'm just kind of used to picking up the tab when I'm with a woman."

"If it's a date!"

"We're engaged," he reminded her. "Ask Anthony."

He obviously had not really given the payment of the dress another thought.

"So why were you so different on the way home?"

He didn't answer right away. Then he sighed.

"You make me feel things I don't want to feel," he told her softly. "You saw the perfect family. I grew up feeling it was the perfect family. I never had a doubt. Then my dad died and she fell apart. Love failed spectacularly. She became a zombie. The love of her kids and for her kids wasn't enough to bring her back."

Jolie heard, not bitterness in his voice, but excruciating pain. It made her ache for him.

"Anyway," he said gruffly, "I saw what love did to my mom. I'm not going there. Not ever."

Jolie's heart felt paralyzed again. Jay Fletcher had seen the potential for love between them?

Okay, he'd very sensibly rejected the possibility, but still...

"I'm not going there again, either," she said, firmly. "Look at the mess it brought me last time. I haven't even finished cleaning that up yet. Obviously."

"Really?" Jay said, quietly. "Two people burned by love. We should be the safest two people in the world to be friends."

Jolie's poor face was a mess, Jay thought. The mask had hardened just like the concrete that it resembled and it did not want to let go.

Plan B—the hot cloth—softened it, somewhat, but it still took a long time for Jay to peel it off, trying so hard to be careful and not hurt her. Even with his best efforts, there was the occasional wince and whimper.

He was so aware of her nearness, her scent and her skin beneath his fingers that his whole body was tingling.

Given that they should have been the two safest people in the whole world to be friends, it was funny how this didn't feel safe at all.

Of course, he had known it wasn't safe. That's why he'd been such a jerk on the way home from Penticton, the Peach City, where he had learned to his astonishment that peach was just about his favorite color in the whole world.

Or at least when Jolie modeled it.

He wasn't sure he was ever going to be able to bite into a peach again without thinking about her.

*Danger was not red, after all.*

He was still a little surprised about her vehemence about paying for the dress. This was part of his world now. He had a lot of money and most people knew it. There was an expectation, particularly when he was with a woman, that he would pick up the tab.

He liked it that she didn't know. He liked it very much that she was self-reliant, but not in the way where she wouldn't let a man open the door for her.

Unless she was mad.

At the same time, he would have liked to have purchased that dress for her. After their paths were parted, maybe she would think of him when she wore it.

Would their paths part? Or would they keep in touch? His desire for self-preservation thought a separation of paths would be best.

Still, he'd made one attempt at self-preservation today, and he'd hurt her feelings doing it.

The man he had looked up to most in the entire world— his dad—would not be proud of him.

So, in the interest of being the man his father had always thought he was, Jay decided he could suck it up for a couple of days.

"You missed dinner," he told Jolie as he plucked away at her face. She'd closed her eyes. That should have been better than those brown eyes fastened on his, but with her eyes closed, he noticed the sweep of her lashes.

The curl of her hair.

The fullness of lips that he had tasted.

"Sabrina has some planned activities for tomorrow. Horseback riding."

He thought planned activities were probably very safe. The comfort of the crowd, the perimeters of the activity.

"It's so hot. I can't imagine that would be very much fun for the people or the horses," Jolie said a little dubiously.

"Fun doesn't seem to be the goal. She said it was team building." He kept his tone deliberately neutral.

"Who needs team building for a wedding?"

So glad she had said it.

"She probably organized that before she knew my parents had delayed their arrival. You know, keep everybody occupied, try to keep the friction at a minimum."

So she expected friction between her parents. Well, there was always lots of friction between Troy and Sabrina, too.

Despite the sword hidden in it at the end, had the love of his family been a gift? He hadn't allowed himself to think of it like that, but seeing what Jolie was up against, he wished she could experience what he'd had.

Instead, he thought wryly, he seemed to be experiencing what she had. Friction. As much as he thought team building was a terrible idea for a wedding, he did think a structured environment might help keep those fractious levels of awareness down.

"Are you just about done?" she asked.

He was done. He looked down at her face. It looked awful, with painful red splotches all over it.

"How does it look?"

He didn't want to be the bearer of the truth, so he went to the bathroom, found a hand mirror and held it out to her. Jolie sat up and looked at herself.

"Oh, no," she said.

He saw all her insecurities pass over her face. He remembered how her shoulders had hunched when she'd gone into the breakfast room this morning. He remembered the snide *yellow* comment. He could imagine The Four snickering at her face tomorrow. Or maybe behind her back, since he had chastised them.

He had probably not succeeded at stopping the meanness, just driving it underground.

He knew why they were mean to Jolie, totally threatened by someone who eclipsed them in every single area. With the exception of self-confidence.

He remembered his original mission, before it had gotten waylaid by a peach dress.

*Hold that mirror up to her until she could see who she really was.*

*Be the better man*, he told himself.

Which would mean what exactly?

He was afraid he might say a lot more than *grow up* to those mean girls this time. Because despite all his efforts at distance, this evening after rescuing her from Anthony and the mask, he felt closer to her than ever.

Protective.

Of her. Because he certainly couldn't protect himself and her at the same time. He was leaving himself wide-open in the way he least liked being wide-open.

Vulnerable.

*Suck it up*, he ordered himself again.

"What would you think if we took a miss on team building?"

Her whole damaged face lit up.

See? Vulnerable. A man could live for that look.

"The lodge has some canoes they sign out to guests. I could pack us some breakfast things and come get you first thing in the morning, before the team builders assemble for their outing. I'll send them a text just before we leave saying we've opted out. I bet an hour or two in the fresh air and those marks will completely disappear."

Plus, it wouldn't be anything like sharing the close confines of the car with her, watching the wind tangle with her hair. It wouldn't be anything like sharing a waffle with her.

It wouldn't be anything like watching her try on that little slip of fabric yesterday.

It wouldn't be a hands-on encounter like tonight had unexpectedly turned into.

"Have you ever been in a canoe?" she asked him.

It was a sport his company was not involved in. He was pretty sure it involved about six feet between paddlers. It was definitely a no-contact activity. His view would be of her back for the few hours that they would be on the lake.

"No," he said, making a note to himself to take a quick internet lesson on canoeing after he left here. "But how hard can it be?"

As it turned out, it could be quite hard. Even with Jay having prepared himself with a slew of internet tutorials, he was not sure anything could ready a person for the shocking instability of a canoe.

He was suddenly glad for the life jackets for two reasons: their lifesaving capabilities might come in handy; more importantly, Jolie encased in the puffy orange marshmallow looked nothing like she had in that dress yesterday.

Her hair was sensibly tamed, clipped at her neck. Her poor welted face was in the shadow of a ball cap. Her legs looked long and lean and sun-browned, but once she was seated, he wouldn't have to look at that particular temptation for the rest of the outing.

But even getting seated was not simple.

The canoes were tied along both sides of the dock, and he had been assigned a red one. For a no-contact sport, Jay noticed her hands were pretty tight on his as he stood on the dock and tried to keep her and the canoe steady at the same time as she lowered herself into it.

The boat rocked alarmingly as she found the seat behind her. When it had steadied, Jay handed her the breakfast things to tuck in, and for a moment it seemed all would be lost as the vessel dipped hard toward him as she reached for the items.

She laughed and the morning took on all kinds of dangers that seemed more immediate than a capsized canoe. After she'd gotten the breakfast items organized, he dared to hand her a paddle, and there was more rocking when she reached out to take it.

Finally, he released the vessel—which he already pretty thoroughly hated—from its mooring, and used his paddle to balance on the gunnels to take his place at the back of the canoe, or the stern, as the videos had called it.

He experimentally used his paddle to push off from the dock, then dipped it into the water and pulled it back.

The canoe shockingly obeyed and they moved away from the dock.

"I'll paddle this side, and you paddle that side," he called to her.

Really, once they were moving forward it seemed pretty simple as long as they sat ramrod straight on the extremely uncomfortable seats, and didn't make any sudden movements.

"Talk about team building," he muttered, as they headed out and tried to coordinate their paddles.

"Oh, but this is so romantic."

He grunted disapprovingly.

"I mean," she caught herself, "the *romance* is of the activity, not us. Look how quiet it is, the glide through the water, the morning light on the vineyards. It's wonderful."

It wasn't really. It was hard work to paddle, impossible to steer, and even breathing the wrong way made the vessel sway threateningly to and fro in the water.

He felt overly responsible for Jolie's safety. When a motorboat roared by, they nearly capsized in the wake it left behind it.

But, despite the challenges, they both got the hang of it, and were soon skimming the water and enjoying the novel view of the shoreline. At first there were houses and small businesses, a yacht club and another resort.

The road that serviced those must have ended, because soon they left development—or civilization, depending how you looked at it—behind. The lake was even more beautiful then, with its deep forested shorelines, rocky, steep outcrops, secret coves and sandy isolated beaches.

Jay relaxed. It was a bit of a workout, but it was a great way to see the shoreline. After an hour or so, they stopped in a tiny cove, resting their paddles on the gunnels and enjoying the gentle swaying of the canoe and the silence broken only by the screech of a hawk nearby. A single rustic cabin, cedar shakes grayed from weather, perched on the edge of a steep embankment. It must have only been accessible by water.

Reaching for the breakfast bun she passed him seemed treacherous as it set the temperamental vessel to rocking.

"Chew on both sides of your mouth," he warned her, "or I think we'll tip this thing right over."

"That might feel good right about now," Jolie said, a bit wistfully.

They had worked up quite a bit of a sweat paddling. Added to that, Jay noticed a sudden stifling quality to the air, the life jacket trapping heat against his body.

But he was not about to try either beaching the canoe or trying to swim off of it. He was pretty sure, from the videos he'd watched, getting back in it would be well beyond either of their skill sets.

Besides, he had not come prepared to swim, and he was pretty sure she hadn't, either.

Skinny-dipping was out of the question.

Though once a man had allowed a thought like that into his head, it could be difficult to get rid of it.

# CHAPTER TWELVE

"LET'S HEAD BACK," Jay suggested, after they had finished the buns.

Jolie did not want to go back. Even though her arms and shoulders ached from the unfamiliar exertion of paddling, she was not sure she had ever had an experience as perfect as this one.

Early morning on the lake, stillness, the sharp scent of a man in the air, her and Jay totally in sync with each other.

*Team building.*

"We'll be really ready for a dip when we get back to Hidden Valley," he suggested.

The promise of a different experience made leaving this one a little easier!

They paddled back out to the mouth of the cove. Even before they got entirely back to the main body of the lake, it was obvious something had changed.

While in the cove, protected, they had missed the fact the wind had risen on the main body of water.

Where it had been smooth as glass less than half an hour ago, now the water was moody, and had a distinctive chop on it. In the distance, back the way they had come, toward Hidden Valley, dark clouds boiled up.

"It's unusual to see a thunderstorm this early in the day," Jay said. She heard something in his voice and glanced back at him.

She realized right away that the calm note in his voice was for her benefit. His mouth was set in a straight, determined line. Tentatively, they pushed out into the main body of the lake.

It was quickly apparent that even the most skilled canoeist would be challenged by trying to go into the wind. The water was getting rougher, the chop was pushing back on the canoe. She was soon exhausted, discouraged by their lack of headway and starting to feel scared.

When she glanced back, Jay was a picture of pure resolve. That strength she had glimpsed in his honed body last night made up for his lack of experience. The look on his face was a look a woman could hang on to.

It was the look of a man who rose to what circumstances gave him and dug deep into his reserves of courage and fortitude.

It was the look of a man who did not allow bad things to happen on his watch.

It was the look of a man who would lay down his own life to protect others.

But even Jay's willpower was no match for the mounting storm. The rough water began to form whitecaps. The lake was rolling. A rogue wave broke over the bow, soaking Jolie, but worse, sloshing water into the boat.

"There's a can there," Jay said. "Bail."

Though his tone remained calm, there was no missing the note of urgency.

She rested her paddle on the gunnels and reached back for the can. Unfortunately, in her eagerness to save the canoe from sinking, when Jolie reached for the can—rolling just out of her reach in the center of the wallowing canoe—she overbalanced the vessel. It tipped alarmingly in the stormy waters.

Horrified, she watched her paddle slip off the gunnels

and into the lake. Her every instinct was to make a grab for it, but Jay's voice stopped her.

"Leave it," he commanded, wisely, since grabbing the paddle bobbing tantalizingly just out of reach would further destabilize them.

Trying to be mindful of balance, she made one more desperate effort to get to the bailing can. Her fingertips closed around the lip, and she could have cried with relief.

But there was no time for something as self-indulgent as crying.

"Bail," he yelled over the storm, and she frantically began to empty water out of the canoe. The can did not feel nearly big enough, like trying to empty a bathtub with a teaspoon, but she could see it was making a marginal difference, and redoubled her efforts.

"I'm turning back to the cove."

It was the only reasonable thing to do, particularly now that they were down to one paddle.

There was a precarious moment when the canoe was broadside to the waves.

More water sloshed in, and over her, but she ignored it, working as fast as she could to empty it back out.

Jay turned the canoe around. Obviously the paddling was easier now that they were being driven by the waves instead of against them. Still, with only one person paddling, it seemed as if it took forever to find that mouth again.

Finally, with one last powerful heave from Jay, the canoe nosed into the calmer waters of the cove, though even inside the cove the water now had a chop on it.

But the wind was broken somewhat, and Jolie was able to make some headway on the water inside the boat as no more was sloshing in over the side.

Jay, his chest heaving, his breathing hard, took a much-needed break. She could see him casting a look out onto the lake and at the sky, weighing options.

"We're going to have to wait it out, and maybe not on the water."

"You had me at not on the water," she called back to him. "I can't get onto dry land fast enough."

The first big fat drop of rain fell on them. Jay paddled them toward shore. Though she thought she'd probably had the easier of the two jobs, she was nearly limp with exhaustion.

Despite that, he called encouragement. "Nearly there. Hang in there. Good job on the bailing. Everything's okay."

She needed to look at him. It seemed to be taking a long time to get to shore. It was as if the water, itself, was trying to stop them. Despite her trepidation about doing anything to disturb the balance of the canoe, she twisted in her seat and looked at Jay.

Despite his encouraging tone, she saw the worry in his eyes. Still, he was calling the strength from her, expecting her best, and she found herself digging deep for her reserves.

The water in the cove was getting more storm-tossed by the second. The temperature seemed to be dropping rapidly. The sky had turned a menacing shade of gray.

Another fat raindrop fell. Jolie had heard the expression *the sky opened up* but she was not sure she had ever experienced it as thoroughly as in that moment. The rain poured down. They were already wet from the water sloshing in the canoe, but this was a brand-new kind of drenched.

It soaked through her ball cap and the life jacket. Her hair was wet to her scalp. Her clothes clung to her as if they were suddenly made of cold, slimy mud.

She let out a cry of pure relief when the canoe finally hit shore with a terrible grinding clatter that sounded as if it was tearing the bottom out of the vessel. She scrambled to get out. Even at this last moment, the canoe threatened to capsize. Jay leaned hard the other way to balance it, and she was finally, gratefully and gleefully, free of the canoe.

She was up to her thighs in water. But it didn't matter. Her feet were on solid ground, and it was not possible to get any wetter.

Jay vaulted out, too. He patted his shirt pocket making sure his phone was there. A lifeline. A way to let the others in the wedding party know they were okay.

He came to the front of the canoe, and jerked it from the water, scraping it across the rocky beach. She rushed to help him, but she was shaking so badly she wasn't sure she helped at all.

Finally, panting with exertion and adrenaline, they pulled the canoe well up out of the water, which was now pounding on the shoreline. They overturned it.

She looked out toward the mouth of the cove. It was barely visible through the sheets of rain that fell.

It sank in.

They were safe. Jay had saved them both.

# CHAPTER THIRTEEN

THOUGH JOLIE WAS cold and wet and shaking with exhaustion and shock, she was experiencing something far more powerful than relief.

A beautiful euphoria enveloped her.

She felt so alive. She could feel the beat of her own heart, the blood moving through her veins.

She tilted her head and took in Jay: his hair plastered to his head, the raindrops cascading down the gorgeous lines of his face, his cheekbones, his nose, his jaw.

His lips.

She had seen people, on the news and in movies, kiss the ground in relief when they had gotten off a bad flight, or been snatched from the jaws of danger and finally found themselves on safe ground.

As much as an overreaction as that might have been, she had a wild desire to do that. But watching the rain sluice down his lips made her think, why kiss the ground, when she could kiss the man who had used every ounce of his strength and intelligence, his discipline and his never-quit attitude to get them back to a place where they were safe?

He looked every inch the warrior as he stood there, his gaze fastened on the lake that had nearly taken them.

Suddenly, with clarity she had rarely experienced in her life, Jolie knew exactly what she wanted.

Shockingly, it had not changed much since she was sixteen.

She wanted Jay's lips on her lips and his hands on her body. She wanted their skin together, she wanted to know him completely, for every barrier between them to come down.

She stepped into him.

He thought she wanted only comfort, and he pulled her close—or as close as the puffy life jackets would allow.

And then he kissed the top of her head—as if she was still that innocent sixteen-year-old child—and broke the embrace.

She didn't realize how cold she was until Jay's hand closed around hers, warm, strong, solid.

"Good job," he told her.

He practically had to pull her up a steep embankment to the cottage. The front of it was on stilts, built into the sheer drop off of the cliff. But there was a well-worn path around it, and they followed that to the front entry.

An old sign hung there, so weathered they could barely make out what it said.

Soul's Rest.

"What's with the names?" Jay asked.

But she felt that *exactly*, after the punch of adrenaline fighting the lake had given her, the sturdy little structure whispered of safety and sanctuary.

And something more.

A place for her and Jay to explore every single thing it meant to be a man and a woman. Alone. Together.

Her sense of delicious elation deepened. Maybe it was from escaping the jaws of death, and maybe it was because of the lovely coincidence that they found themselves in a place with a shelter as the storm broke.

But no.

Those elements played into her bliss, certainly.

But the major cause was knowing what she wanted.

And she wanted Jay Fletcher.

A tingling sense of anticipation filled her as he tried the handle. The door wasn't locked. In fact, the latch opened easily and the door sprang open to reveal a small alcove. They finally took off the dripping life jackets.

Again, with Jay's sodden clothes clinging to him, Jolie was taken with the sense of him being pure warrior, all hard edges and honed muscle.

Except for his mouth, the place that looked soft and inviting, the place where she would draw his innate kindness and his warmth to the surface.

Didn't every woman dream of being the one that the warrior laid down his weapons for? That he took off his armor for?

The one that he showed the vulnerabilities of his heart to?

Jay seemed as totally unaware of her as she was totally engrossed in him, taking in the interior of their shelter with the assessing eyes of a warrior/rescuer.

She took it in, too. Despite the fact that it had looked abandoned from the lake, the interior of the cottage looked as if someone enjoyed the space immensely.

It was rudimentary, but cozy. There was a small main room with a faded couch and a patched easy chair, an open-shelved kitchen with a small table in it. A miniature potbellied woodstove with a crooked pipe was in the center of the room. Bookshelves held well-worn paperbacks and jigsaw puzzles and games.

The whole lake-facing wall was windows, now being rattled by the storm, raindrops sliding down the panes.

"Supplies," Jay said, going over and perusing the open shelves. "Hot chocolate. Tea. Some canned stuff."

Here she was admiring the surprising ambience of the

little space—and plotting the conquer of his lips—and he was focusing on banal things.

Survival.

This was why men and women belonged together. They balanced each other.

"We won't be here long I'm sure," Jay said, "but I'll replace anything we use. You look like you need something hot. And to get out of those wet things."

Disrobing felt like the best idea, *ever*, for a woman who had just decided men and women belonged together. Needed each other. Should celebrate their differences.

"Jay," Jolie said softly, "thank you."

He looked up from the hot chocolate supplies, surprised. "For what?"

"Getting us safely off the water."

"Huh. Well, let's not forget it was my idea to be on the water in the first place."

"That's not the point," she said stubbornly. "I lost my paddle. One wrong move and that canoe could have gone over."

"We had life jackets on," he said with a lift of his shoulder. "Instead of looking at all the things that could have happened, I think we should focus on how well we worked as a team to get off the water."

She was so taken with his way of seeing it, not seeing her as weaker than him, in need of his rescue, but rather as part of the team. Equals.

"You are a great person to be with in an emergency."

He gave her a grin. "You, too."

She should have been frozen, but she felt warmed through to her soul by that casual remark.

"You should get out of those wet things now."

Somehow, she had always imagined Jay asking her to get undressed would be slightly different than this.

Had she imagined a request like that?

Only about a hundred times.

Or maybe a thousand.

Or maybe more.

When she'd been a teenager addled by thoughts of romance. She was mature now. She had life experiences.

And it didn't seem to matter.

When it came to Jay, she felt the same weakness of wanting that she had always felt. The storm hadn't caused it.

It had exposed how raw and real that wanting still was in her.

"That looks like a bedroom through that door. Maybe go see what's in there that you could change into temporarily."

Jolie told herself sternly that she had lost command of her senses. Was she seriously plotting the seduction of Jay Fletcher?

Their close call had obviously put her into a bit of shock.

Jay had already busied himself with the business of survival. He was crumpling paper into the woodstove.

It was a good idea to get away from him for a minute, to try and gather her thoughts. She went into the side room and closed the door. It turned out to be a bedroom, the mattress rolled up on top of a double bed.

There was a dresser but when she checked it, the drawers were empty. She went and pulled the string that bound the mattress and it unrolled. The bedding was inside of it.

It was a relief to pull the soggy clothing off. She toweled off with a rough blanket, and squeezed the water from her hair.

She waited for her tumultuous thoughts to calm as feeling returned to her body. But they didn't.

When she was done, she tucked the white sheet around herself, toga style. The fabric felt like a glorious torture on skin that was singing with awareness.

Anticipation.

She opened the door and stepped out into the main room. She felt exquisitely as if she had stepped back in time. A maiden offering herself to her warrior.

Jay was crouched in front of the woodstove. He already had a pot of water on top of it. Focused intently, he fed sticks into it. He had taken off his wet shirt. The reflection of the steadily growing flame gilded his perfect skin in gold.

It only added to the sensation of a steadily growing flame inside of her.

"There's a bit of a cell phone signal," he said, without looking up from what he was doing. "I was able to send a text saying we're okay, that we've got a safe place to ride out the storm."

She said nothing.

Jay turned his head slightly and looked at her.

It was a look every woman would hope to see in the man she had chosen to be her lover. The warrior lowered his shield.

He got up slowly, straightened, took her in.

And she saw clearly in his eyes that he had, as every warrior did, a weakness.

And that it was her.

She saw in his eyes that he acknowledged he was a man, and she was a woman, and that with the slightest nudge he would allow his power to resist to be overtaken by her power to tempt.

The sensation that enveloped her was heady.

*He wanted her. And she knew it. And she loved knowing it.*

She knew she had been waiting for this moment for ten years, ever since he had rejected her.

"You better get out of your wet things, too," she said.

Her voice sounded soft and husky, an obvious invitation. Jay looked at her, *that* look in his eyes—masculine appreciation, surrender.

And then he seemed to catch himself. He cast his gaze wildly about the room, as if an escape route would be revealed to him if he looked hard enough. He actually looked as if he was considering the canoe and the storm!

She frowned.

A little less fight, please!

"Go get out of those wet pants," she said, again.

# CHAPTER FOURTEEN

JAY GOT OUT of that small room with Jolie as fast as he could. He went into the bedroom and shut the door, resisting, just barely, an inclination to lean on it as if some force was trying to push it back open.

The door seemed like a flimsy barrier against that force.

And it was. Because the force—his foe—was not out there. She was not the foe. The enemy was inside himself.

He was in a bad spot now. She obviously had some kind of misguided hero-worship thing going on, believing he had rescued her from certain death.

And she looked astonishing with that sheet wrapped around herself, that wild tangle of wet hair cascading around her, her shoulders naked and slender and perfect. Jolie Cavaletti was like a goddess.

A goddess who had just, more or less, ordered him out of his clothes.

Ten years ago, he had said no to her. He had recognized how vulnerable she was, and that she was not ready for what she had asked him for.

Everything was changed.

They were both adults now. Jolie was a woman who knew her own mind.

And yet somethings remained the same. She was vulnerable. She'd recently lost a relationship. And then today, both of them were coming off a bad shock, a close call.

On the other hand, Jay felt as if he had used up all his strength out there on the lake. He had none left for resistance.

There was a certain euphoric feeling—being alive, having partnered with her to accomplish that—that might make it easy to accept life tempting him with its glory.

*Keep a lid on it*, he ordered himself.

It would be easy for things to get out of hand. He wasn't just fighting her, but the residue of elation from having cheated the lake and the storm.

And despite the fact he had minimized the danger they had just faced, the complete truth was something else. It was not uncommon to see headlines in Canada, this land of rugged extremes, that served as reminders that Mother Nature, while magnificent, also had an unforgiving and cruel side.

*Just like love.*

Jay sucked in a deep, steadying breath, reminding himself he had started today with a mission to be a better man.

This storm—with all its multifaceted dimensions—would pass. Anybody, including someone who had used all his strength, could muster a bit more for a short period of time. He went over to the window and looked out.

Despite the fact it looked as if it intended to rain furiously for a week—please, no—these summer storms tended to come and go very quickly.

He formulated a plan. They would dry off. They would hang their clothes by the fire. They would probably barely have time to finish the hot chocolate and it would be time to leave, to get back in that canoe and make their way down the lake.

One thing was for sure, he was not going out there wrapped in a sheet.

He looked under the bed. To his immense relief there was a trunk, and when he opened it, it had men's clothing in it.

He yanked off his pants and dried himself, deliberately

not allowing himself to focus on how his skin stung, making him feel extraordinary, as if every single cell of his being was singing.

Because he knew if he focused on that, he would know the singing was only partially because of the exhilaration of getting off the lake.

Only partially because of the rough blanket drying his pebbled skin.

Almost entirely because of her. Jolie. The goddess who awaited him in the other room. He pulled on the dry clothes, jeans and a faded T-shirt, and took one more deep breath.

He felt more like a protector than he had felt even when he was trying to get that canoe off the water.

He made the mistake of looking at the floor, and their puddled clothing that needed to be hung up by the fire.

Her sodden underwear was on top.

He picked up his own things, and left hers there. Hopefully, when he strung the clothesline she would get the hint.

A man could only test his strength so far.

"Oh," Jolie said, when he came back into the main room. "You found clothes."

Did she sound disappointed?

She had pulled a kitchen chair close to the fire and was running her fingers through her tangled hair.

*He wanted to run his fingers through her hair.*

She looked as if she knew exactly what she was doing.

"Under the bed," he said with unnecessary terseness. "I think there are things there that would fit you."

"I'm quite comfortable, thank you."

*She would be.* He needed to remember that. Self-defense strategy number one: Jolie was quite comfortable tormenting a man.

He rifled through some kitchen drawers until he found

some twine. He focused intently on getting a clothesline hung close to the stove.

She got up and moved over to the window. Out of the corner of his eye, as he draped his soaked clothes over the line, he noticed her studying the shelves, running her fingers over some of the games there.

"Have you ever played this?" she asked, plucking a slender box from the shelf and showing it to him.

"Probably a million times, growing up. Friday was always game night. My mom loved it so much. You would have thought she was getting ready for the event of the century every week. I think she started planning what treats she was going to serve and which game we were going to play on Monday."

He had not allowed himself these kinds of memories since his dad had died. He didn't want to talk about it anymore. It felt as if he couldn't stop himself.

"Sometimes it was just our family. To be honest, I don't think my dad was a game guy. I think he enjoyed it because she enjoyed it. But lots of times there were tons of people there, my parents' friends, our friends. Even when I got older, and it should have been lame, my friends had to be at our house for game night."

He caught a look on her face. She went from a siren to a faintly wistful little girl in the blink of an eye.

"You haven't played that game?" he asked her.

"We weren't that kind of a family," she said. She slid the box back onto the shelf.

"You didn't play any games? What about at Christmas?"

"Christmas." She made a face. "Always the worst."

*Christmas? The worst?* "In what way?"

Jolie looked pensive, weighing how much to tell him.

"Christmas was party time," she said finally, and he felt the weight of her trust in him. "There was way too much drinking. My father, not that inhibited to begin with, lost any inhibitions he had. He loved attention from the ladies. It seems there was always a Christmas fling. My mom would be furious at first, and they'd have these dish-shattering rows, and he'd leave. But then her fury would die down, and she'd just want him back. It always seemed as if Sabrina and I were being asked to pick a side. I was Team Dad, she was Team Mom."

"That's awful," Jay said. "I can't imagine how you dealt with that."

"I escaped into books. How grateful I was to have different worlds waiting to welcome me. All I had to do was open the cover."

He suddenly remembered how she'd been in high school, the sweet little geek, absent-minded and ethereal. She'd always had a book. He remembered sometimes other kids would say she just carried them to look smart.

*War and Peace.*

*Moby Dick.*

*Les Misérables.*

But even before he'd done that science project with her he'd known somehow when you were smart you didn't have to *look* smart. She probably would have done anything *not* to look so smart.

Even his totally self-centered eighteen-year-old self had known Jolie found refuge in her books and her brains.

Until now, he hadn't known what she needed refuge from.

The memory of Jolie at sixteen—wary, lacking in confidence, trying to fade into the background—diffused some of what he felt when he looked at her wrapped in that sheet.

"Sadly," she said, "sometimes those books made me long for the things I'd never experienced growing up. When Anthony came along, I convinced myself he made me so blissful. In hindsight, I adored his family that he'd found in Italy. It was loud and boisterous and big and everything I had never had. His *nonna* adored me and the feeling was mutual. I realize I did have a few tiny little doubts about him, but I just steam-rollered over them, so invested in my own happy ending."

Jay was reminded, again, of the gifts his family had given him. He could not have been given a more perfect distraction from the intensity that was leaping up between he and Jolie. Despite her admission she was—or had been—a woman in search of a happy ending, he needed to put self-protection aside.

He could be a better man. He went and took the game off the shelf.

"Go get your wet stuff," he suggested, "and hang them up on the line. I'll set up the game and get hot chocolate ready."

For a brief moment, she looked as if she had another plan, but then her gaze went to the game, and he saw that wistful little girl again. She disappeared into the bedroom without a word.

He didn't even watch her put those delicate things on the line next to his as he finished preparing their hot choco-late then set up the game. He scowled down at the board, trying to remember where everything went, and what the rules were.

A good thing to remember: what the rules were.

After she was done hanging her things, she came and set-tled down in a chair, and he took the one facing her.

Her whole demeanor, as he explained the game to her, took him back to her scholarly intensity in high school.

Thank goodness.

The game, called Combustion, was a combination of luck and strategy. Her brilliance was quickly apparent in how fast she caught on to the strategy part of it.

The game was one of those back-and-forth ones, where it looked as if one person was going to win but then, just before that happened, the opposing player could send them back to the beginning to start all over again.

She was intensely competitive, and so was he.

She chortled gleefully when she "killed" him and he had to start over. She cried out with outrage when he did the same to her.

Seeing her childish delight in the game initially did exactly as Jay had hoped and reduced his awareness of the fact she was certainly not sixteen anymore and she was dressed only in a sheet.

But as time went on, he noticed her hair was drying, and as it dried, these crazy corkscrew curls leaped around her.

And she threw herself more enthusiastically into the game, the sheet proved flimsy, indeed. It kept slipping and moving and she was so engrossed in the game she didn't notice.

Either that or she was so diabolically invested in winning she was distracting him on purpose with her malfunctioning wardrobe.

He looked, hopefully, out the window. The rain sluiced down, unabated.

"I win!" Jolie cried.

He saw the pure happiness on her face. Maybe he wasn't so sorry the rain wasn't stopping, after all.

"Want to go again?" she asked.

Jolie won the game three times in a row. She eyed Jay with sudden suspicion.

"Are you letting me win?"

"I'm not that chivalrous."

But she suspected that he was, indeed, that chivalrous. Suddenly, she lost interest in the game. She was with the man she had wanted to be with since she was sixteen years old. There might never be another opportunity like this one in her entire life.

"Jay," she said, "I'm not a kid anymore."

"Thanks," he said dryly, "gleeful winning of games aside, the slipping sheet already let me know that."

She glanced down. She was showing quite a bit more than she thought she was. She was going to adjust the sheet, but then decided against it.

"We were playing for a kiss," she told him.

"No, we weren't!"

"Jay," she said, "I don't know how to be any more direct."

"Look," he said, "you're just breaking up with your fiancé, and our near miss on the water seems to have left you with an exaggerated sense of my heroism."

She actually laughed at that, and he looked annoyed.

"Who told you that you got to make all the rules?" she asked him quietly. "I know you're an old-fashioned guy who likes to hold open doors and all that, but I know what I want. I think I know what you want, too."

"I doubt that," he sputtered.

"Let's find out."

And then, before she lost her nerve, she got up from her place at the table, crossed over to him and wiggled her way onto his lap.

He could have gotten up. He could have pushed her away. But he didn't.

She twined her arms around his neck. The sheet slipped a little more.

He wasn't exactly participating, but he wasn't exactly withdrawing, either.

Experimentally, she touched the puffiest part of his bottom lip with her fingertip.

"If it's not what you want," she whispered, "tell me."

He didn't say a word.

So she leaned in yet closer and touched the place on his lip where her fingertip had been with the faintest flick of her tongue.

She stopped, looked at him. He returned her gaze. He still didn't say a word.

Then Jolie caressed his bottom lip with her top lip, nuzzling, a touch as light as a butterfly wing.

It wasn't like when she had kissed him for Anthony's benefit. It wasn't like that at all. It was more like her heart had waited for this moment all these years, and it sighed in recognition as she deepened the kiss.

Everything about her said, without having to say a single word, *I know you.*

His resistance collapsed when she scraped her lips lightly, back and forth, over his. With a groan of surrender, he caught her to him, bracketed her face with his hands and returned her kiss.

With hunger.

And passion.

With curiosity.

And satisfaction.

And ultimately, with certainty.

His hands moved to her hair, catching in it, stroking it, untangling it. Somehow the sheet slipped between them, and he was balancing her with one arm and tearing off his shirt with the other.

So that they could have this.

Full contact. Full sensation. Full awareness.

Heated skin on heated skin.

His eyes dark with need, his gaze swept her own, looking for permission, for affirmation. He found both, and his head dropped over her breast.

Thunder rolled outside, and the rain slashed the window. Lightning split the sky.

The power of the storm was nothing compared to what was unfolding between them.

# CHAPTER FIFTEEN

WITHOUT MOVING JOLIE from his lap, Jay stood up. She managed to free her legs from the tangle of the sheet and tuck them around the hard strength of his hips.

She marveled at the ease with which he carried her. There was no pause in his lips laying claim to hers. He tasted her neck and ears and her cheeks as he carried her through to the bedroom, the sheet caught between them, and dragging on the floor.

He dropped her gently down onto the bed, pulled the tangle of the sheet completely away from her and paused for a moment, something like reverence darkening his eyes. They looked, suddenly, more black than green.

Then Jay dispensed with his jeans in a flash faster than lightning and came onto the bed. He was poised above her, holding his weight off of her with his elbows, anointing her with kisses and flicks of his tongue.

He was extra gentle with where her face was still splotched from the mask. Still, it felt as if he might be leaving marks of his own, as he trailed fire across her skin.

Jay was an exquisite lover. He was possessive and tender, but there was also no mistaking the leashed masculine strength in every touch of his hands and his lips. He seemed determined to leave no inch of her unexplored, her belly, her breasts, her neck, the bottoms of her feet.

Without saying a single word, his breath on her skin said

hello to each muscle, each limb, each eye, each toe. His lips welcomed her and celebrated this new way of knowing each other.

She could feel need building in her, screaming along her nerve endings, but he would not give in.

He tantalized.

He took her to the edge of desire, until she was nearly sobbing with wanting him, and then inched back, began the dance of knowing her all over again.

Only when both of them were quaking with need, slick with sweat, so desperate that it felt as if death were near, did he combine conquest and surrender.

With an exquisite mix that was part the fury of the storm, and part the tenderness of souls who had retreated from each other for far, far too long, they came together.

Jolie and Jay joined in that exquisite and ancient dance that the very universe felt as if it had been born out of. They came together and then fell apart.

Like a shooting star falls apart, a projectile penetrating a dark sky and then exploding, thousands of sparks of light falling, falling, falling back to Earth.

Winking out, one at a time.

"Jolie," he whispered her name against her throat, and then even softer, "Jolie."

Jay saying her name like that, as if it was a blessing, made her seduction of him feel so right.

Her boldness rewarded.

In those moments after, had Jay shown the slightest awkwardness, had there been even a moment's regret in his eyes, she might have questioned what had just happened between them, and how it had happened.

Her pushing against his reluctance.

But there was none of that.

Instead, he propped pillows up against the headboard,

pulled that sheet up around them, invited her into the circle of his arms.

They talked. They talked about his business, and about her work. They talked about life in Rome and life in Toronto. They talked about their families and shared memories from their childhoods, some funny, some poignant.

There was a sense that they could talk forever, never run out of things to say.

And then, as quickly as the storm had come up, it was gone. The sun came out and streamed across their bodies, made them freshly aware of each other. It felt as if it was her turn, this time, to explore and celebrate every single thing that made up Jay.

After, when she lamented the lack of running water in the cabin, he laughed, and gestured to the window. "Look at our bathtub."

So, wrapped in sheets they made their way down the rocky pathway to the water's edge.

He dropped his sheet first and dove cleanly into the water.

They played. They swam and splashed, and chased each other, until they were exhausted from both laughter and exertion.

Standing up to their waists in the water, Jay pulled her to him and cupped the cold, pure lake water in his hands, and poured it over her hair, worked it through with tender fingertips. And then he did the very same to the rest of her body, until she had never felt quite so clean in her entire life.

It was her turn, and he knelt in the water, so she could easily reach his hair.

But she had hardly begun when he leaped back to his feet. "What?"

"I hear a motor. A boat is coming."

At first she didn't hear what he did, but then there was no mistaking it. Laughing like naughty children, they rewrapped themselves in sheets and scrambled up the trail to the cabin. She was glad they had retreated, because the boat pulled into their cove and cut the engine, drifting in toward where they had been playing naked moments before.

Both of them began pulling on the clothes that hung on the line, still faintly damp, terribly crusty and uncomfortable.

"Hell. It's Troy," Jay said. "He's probably coming to check on us."

He looked around and found his phone. He wagged it at her. "They've been texting for hours. This last one says he's coming in a boat. They'll bring us back."

She realized, stunned, that their moment was over as quickly as the storm.

"I'll go tell him we'll take the canoe back."

"Oh," she said, "I'm not sure I want to. Get back in the canoe."

"I think it's like falling off a horse, Jolie. You get right back on."

"There's only one paddle," she said, desperate to not get back in that tippy little vessel with all its potential for sudden death.

"I saw some under the cabin. We'll make sure we return everything we've borrowed."

"I'm scared," she said.

He laughed. He actually threw back his head and laughed. "No, you're not, Jolie. You're the boldest, bravest woman I've ever met."

It occurred to her you could become the things that someone else believed about you.

Maybe she had done that her whole life, but in the reverse of this. Becoming less than she was, instead of more.

"The thing about fear," Jay said softly, "is that once you've let it take hold, it doesn't want to let go. It takes on a life of its own. It grows and grows."

"Okay," she said, "go tell him we'll canoe back."

After he left, she contemplated the simple courage he was asking of her, that he saw in her, and that he was calling into existence.

This is what love did, then, it made you bigger, stronger, better than you had been before.

It didn't rip you to shreds one little nip at a time.

*Love?*

She wasn't in love with Jay just because she had slept with him. It would be unbelievably naive to think that.

He had made it clear from the beginning that he did not trust love.

Why would she? After seeing her parents? After catching a man she had trusted with her whole heart stepping out on her?

So she would not call it love.

And yet there was no denying the feeling in her heart—even if she left it unnamed—filled her with a deep sense of bliss.

Not quite like anything else she had ever known.

They did canoe back to the lodge. It was not easy getting back in the canoe. In fact, it was terrifying.

And yet, conquering that terror filled her with a sense of her own ability to overcome adversity.

She had Jay to thank for that. The best man pulling the very best from her.

They arrived at the resort to a hero's welcome. The entire bridal party were waiting for them on the shore.

After the stillness and solitude of the cabin, this was a bit of a shock, and not in a good way.

After the intensity of their togetherness, being pulled into the center of a crowd, with everyone asking questions, and doling out hugs and backslaps, Jolie yearned to get back in the canoe, paddle through the stillness of the lake, just *be* with him.

She caught Jay's eye.

He winked at her.

And she saw the bond between them survived.

"Anthony left," her sister told her, with barely a hello.

Jolie felt a certain indifference to whether Anthony had left or not. She and Jay's lovemaking felt as if it had put a shield around her that others—even her ex—could not get through.

Sabrina took her arms and guided her up toward the resort. "And Mom and Dad have arrived."

Jolie hesitated. "How are they?"

"So worried about you!"

"That's not what I meant."

"Oh. How *are* they? Like lovebirds. He's doting on her. I should know better, but I actually wonder if they've worked it out this time."

The names of these cabins. Heart's Refuge and Lovers' Retreat. Maybe this was a magical place.

Where Troy and Sabrina were going to get it right.

Where her mother and father were going to figure it all out, finally.

And where love had touched her.

There was that word again. But why not? It seemed as if it was in the air.

"They were so worried about you, Jolie. I have to take you to them right away. And then a dress arrived that I ordered online. You should try it."

Jolie pulled away from her sister's arm. Once, she might have liked this, being at the center instead of on the outside.

But she had been canoeing since her very sexy rinse in the lake, and there had been no soap or shampoo involved in that.

Plus, she needed to gather herself before a family reunion. "I have to have a shower and change clothes."

"Okay," Sabrina said, "but could you be quick about it? Oh, my gosh, Jolie, we only have one full day left before the wedding. It suddenly feels as if there's way too much to do and not enough time to do it."

Jolie wasn't sure about the way-too-much-to-do part, but it did feel, suddenly, as if there was not enough time.

"A quick shower," she promised her sister.

She went to her cabin, stripped off her clothes and got under the hot steamy jets, lifting her face to them. Her body felt delightfully different, as if she was aware of the sensuality of being alive in ways she had never been before. The steam, the hot water hitting her body, the way the pebbled shower tray felt on her feet all held sensations Jolie had not been aware of before.

Though her eyes were closed, the air changed ever so slightly, a breath of cold air touched her.

It was the shower curtain being pulled back.

She didn't have to open her eyes to know. Her heart recognized that his presence had its own feel to it.

Wordlessly, he got in behind her, nuzzled the silky wetness of her neck, before reaching past her for the soap. She realized, as much as she had been aware of sensation before Jay had gotten into the shower with her, it had not been sensual.

*This* was sensual. His hands, slippery with soap, exploring her entire body, mapping it, marking it, with soap and then with kisses when the soap was rinsed free.

He replaced the soap, and reached by her, this time for the shampoo. He added some to his cupped palm, and then worked it into her hair, his fingertips strong, sure, familiar.

Still, without a word, when the shampoo had rinsed free, and he had wrung her hair out between his hands, and finger-combed the tangles, he lifted her into his arms and put her wet body on the bed.

Wet bodies, it turned out, were twice as erotic as dry bodies.

"Now I have to shower again," she told him, pretending to complain after, gazing up at him, her palm grazing his chin.

He nipped her fingers. "I know," he said. "Isn't that great? It's your turn."

And so she had her turn, soaping him, getting to know every inch of his beautiful body, her hands sliding over hard and soft surfaces, in and out of his ears, the dip at his collarbone, his belly button.

It was shockingly exciting even before the real shock of the water running cold before she was finished. Jay shoved her gently out of the cold spray, finished washing off the soap himself and then came out and they dried each other off.

And that was how the rest of the day, and the hours before the wedding the next day, unfolded.

On the surface, Jolie sailed through her bridesmaid's duties. She met with her parents, and tried on the new dress, which was neither as ugly as the first one, nor as sexy as the second one. It was a nice bland dress that could not dampen down the feeling she carried inside her.

That she had a secret.

The secret was that she was not bland.

The secret was that she was a heated lover.

Jolie and Jay stole kisses behind the arbor they had been assigned to sew flowers onto. He was waiting for her along the pathway to the lodge for the rehearsal dinner, pulled her into the trees with him and covered her with kisses.

And then they sat, one of them on one side of the groom, and one on the other side of the bride, not making eye contact, nursing their secret.

She suspected everyone had assumed their relationship was fake, designed to dissuade Anthony.

Now that nothing about what they were doing together felt fake—it felt, in fact, like the realest thing that had ever happened to her—Jolie had a desire to keep it under wraps.

To not indulge in public shows of affection, to not exchange endearments, to not convince anyone anything was going on.

Ironically, it was the reverse of what she had wanted when she had first asked Jay to pretend he was her fiancé.

Impossibly, that was only a few days ago. The changes between them made it feel as if that arrangement had happened in a separate lifetime.

What was really going on now was so new it felt fragile, like it could be easily broken by a wrong move.

She did not want it scrutinized by her sister's cynical friends.

She did not want them weighing in behind her back on the way she and Jay looked at each other and touched each other and listened to each other.

What had started out as so public now felt intensely private.

You did not put the sacred on display.

# CHAPTER SIXTEEN

JOLIE DID NOT consider herself a wedding person. She had not even really felt as if she was one when she had been planning her own wedding to Anthony.

Despite her enjoyment of the gown she had chosen, planning her own wedding had felt like a duty rather than a joy, something she had to get through in order to get to the next stage of her adult life, which was supposed to have been marriage.

Most of the weddings she had been to just seemed way too much like a stage set, too much about the wedding and not enough about the marriage.

There always seemed to be quite a bit of behind-the-scenes drama with a major wedding event.

Her sister's wedding, with that initial hysteria over the dresses, had held every promise of being the same.

A hysterical bride demanding perfection from an imperfect world.

And yet, as Saturday unfolded, it was so evident her sister's wedding had been pulled back from that bad start.

Jolie gave most of the credit for this to her soon-to-be brother-in-law-for-the-second-time. Troy was just one of those decent, down-to-earth guys. He indulged a certain amount of Sabrina's histrionics, but also wasn't scared to let her know when he'd had enough, or she was going over the top.

Jolie could understand, when she saw Troy and Jay together, why they were such good friends.

They were a type.

Strong.

Reliable.

Hardworking.

And underneath all that—or maybe even because of all that—was a kind of hum of understated sexiness.

But she did have to give some credit to Sabrina as well. The destination wedding had been a good idea. The Hidden Valley setting seemed to invoke calm. The team building exercise with the horses seemed to have succeeded in deepening the relationships of everyone involved.

And though she and Jay had not been part of the team, the canoeing expedition gone so wrong had brought them into the fold and seemed to have strengthened ties within the party.

Everybody seemed aware that it could have been a much different day today if Jolie and Jay had not got off the lake.

Her parents were on their best behavior. She'd had a chance to talk to her father, and he had told her he was a new man because of a twelve-step program he'd found that dealt with sex addiction.

She hadn't really known much about it, and certainly didn't want to know that about her father. Addicted to sex? Yuck!

But, on the other hand, now that she'd had several encounters of the intimate kind with Jay, she could understand why it could be addictive. Maybe she even had to watch out for that particular weakness in herself!

She didn't really want any of the details of her father's transgressions, and he thankfully did not volunteer them.

Instead, for the first time she could ever remember, he

took responsibility for the pain he had brought to the family dynamic.

"I know I caused you all a great deal of suffering. I know I'm the reason you live in Italy," he said contritely, "as far from the chaos as you can get."

"You know, Dad, that might have been my original motivation in going there, but I genuinely love it now. I love my job. I have a sense of purpose and community. Maybe instead of seeing it as you driving me there to get away from you, you could see it as it driving me there to where I was always meant to be. Don't you think life has a way of taking us where we're meant to be?"

Would she have believed that quite so completely before her reunion with Jay?

"Ah, Jolie, always my favorite," he said in Italian.

"Don't tell Sabrina," she whispered.

"That's why I said it in Italian."

They laughed together.

"I like your new beau," he said. "I was never that taken with Anthony."

"You never said anything!"

"I felt I lost my right to comment on such things when I had hardly set an example myself."

"What things?"

"You know. His wandering eye."

"You *knew* that?"

"I only met him once. That time I came to visit you in Rome. I just noticed he always seemed to be searching beyond you."

"Why didn't you say something?"

"I didn't know how. But I like the new beau."

She blushed. "*Beau* might be a little too strong."

"Not the way he's looking at you. Now, there's a man who has eyes for only one woman."

"Don't keep talking about him as if he's a stranger. It's Jay Fletcher, from high school."

Her father looked at her quizzically. "A little more than that, wouldn't you say?"

"You mean his sporting goods company?"

His father gave her another look. "Yes," he said, "that's what I mean."

The day that unfolded just had such a nice feeling. Everyone was relaxed and getting along.

Even Jack and Jill and Beth seemed to have left their hard edges behind them. They actually said really nice things about her hair and makeup and the new dress as they all helped each other, and Sabrina, get ready for the wedding.

It felt to Jolie as if she had finally been accepted—possibly by virtue of the fact they had contemplated losing both her and Jay to that storm.

There was a bit of anxiety when the much-anticipated Chantelle was late, but she finally arrived, breathless, saying she had taken a wrong turn out of Penticton. Jolie was not sure what she had been expecting, but the famous Chantelle was tiny, dwarfed by the multitude of cameras she carried. She was wearing a somewhat dressy form of army fatigues, and peered at them all through huge glasses with colorful frames.

She managed to get a few shots of them getting ready.

"Pretend I'm not here," she said with stern annoyance to Jack and Jill when they started posing for her.

And then it was time.

To the strains of the very traditional "Wedding March" by Felix Mendelssohn, the bridesmaids exited the main lodge, one at a time, slow stepping across the lawns to where the seating and an arbor had been set up by the shores of the lake.

The lake was placid today, mirrorlike, reflecting the vineyards and orchards and the spectacular houses and humble cottages that surrounded it.

The bridesmaids moved down the outdoor aisle, past the guests, the women in their beautiful summer dresses and sandals and hats, the men in light trousers and button-up sports shirts.

The groom and his groomsmen were waiting on a slightly raised dais under the arbor. Jolie only allowed herself to look at Jay briefly.

The groomsmen were beautifully dressed, in gray slacks, crisp white shirts, suspenders and bow ties.

Everything that Jay and Jolie were to each other was reflected in the deep way that he returned her brief look, the upward quirk of that mouth she had tasted over and over again, so intimately.

He gestured subtly to her dress and shook his head, *not you.*

She did the same thing for his bow tie. Even with all these people watching and a wedding about to get under way, she was aware of how the two of them could close out the world.

She reminded herself it was her sister's day, and the looks and wordless communication she and Jay were exchanging felt as if they could steal the very sun out of the sky.

She turned her attention to Sabrina, who was coming down the grassy aisle now, one arm in her mother's and one in her father's.

Jolie realized she needn't have worried about her and Jay stealing the sun. Not today. Her sister was absolutely radiant in a summer gown, constructed of white lace and smoke and magic.

She had eyes for no one but Troy.

When Jolie glanced at Troy, she saw him—that powerful down-to-earth guy—brush a tear from his eye.

And somehow she just knew it was going to be okay this time.

Her mother and father each kissed Sabrina on a cheek and clasped hands, glanced at each other and went to their seats.

It felt as if maybe they were going to be okay, too.

In fact, here at her sister's beautiful summer wedding, with the sun shining and the birds singing, with love sparkling in the air, Jolie felt something she had rarely allowed herself to feel.

As if everything was going to be okay.

The ceremony, and the signing of the register, and the bride and groom's first kiss—extended version—proved her right. Everything went off seamlessly and she felt herself surrendering to the pure fun of the day.

Chantelle was nothing short of amazing. A few days ago, Jolie might have felt awkward posing, especially for some of the more artsy shots, but she just brought that new bolder her to it all. She noticed Jay, too, had given himself over to the day.

Making other people happy, she decided, looking at her glowing sister, was a good way to make yourself happy.

It was something that she didn't think Jack and Jill would ever learn. Instead of making the photo sensation about the bride, they vied shamelessly for Chantelle's attention.

"I think we've got a lot of good photos," Chantelle finally said, clicking through the display screen on her camera.

"If you ever want to do some modeling work," she said, and Jack and Jill nearly fell over themselves to get the card she was holding out. But she ignored them, marched passed them and handed the card to the astonished Jolie.

"Look at this photo," she said, showing it to Jolie.

Jolie looked at the woman in the photo Chantelle was showing her and almost didn't recognize herself. The woman in the photo was laughing, carefree, confident.

Jolie realized it wasn't her, so much that Chantelle had

recognized as the light that was shining from her. A woman who had come into herself, completely and passionately.

She was aware of Jack and Jill also pressed close, both looking at the photo.

"I could get you a job in the industry—" Chantelle snapped her fingers "—like that."

"What industry?" Jolie asked, baffled.

"Ad campaigns, sports magazines, runway work."

"I can't even imagine," Jolie said, diplomatic enough not to finish with, *a life that shallow and dull.*

"Oh, for heaven's sake," Jill said, clearly peeved, "she's a doctor, not a model."

"A doctor," Chantelle breathed. "That explains it. The depth in your eyes. The intelligence in your face. I think the days of the too-thin vapid blonde are done in the industry, and good riddance."

Jack gasped as though she'd been stabbed.

Jolie became aware of Jay standing with them, looking down at the photo that Chantelle was showing. She glanced up at him.

A tiny, knowing smile was tickling the gorgeous line of his lips.

"I saw you first," he murmured in her ear.

It was so true. He had *seen* her first. He had drawn to the surface every single thing that Chantelle had caught with this photo. He had made her alive, and that life force shimmered in her, in a way the camera had captured.

After photos, there was a cocktail hour on the very deck where she had first sat, enveloped in that horrid dress.

She remembered that she had imagined just this: people going in and out the doors, laughter, glasses clinking.

She and Jay finally dared to stand side by side, unnoticed in all the activity.

"As far as weddings go," Jolie told him, and could hear the contentment in her own voice, "this one has been pretty peachy." He handed her a glass of wine.

"To peaches," he said and they tapped glasses. "I actually had this idea about peaches," he said. He lowered his voice to a growl, and spoke the words into her ear only.

She reared back from him, trying not to choke on wine.

He smiled wickedly, and raised an eyebrow at her.

"Jay, I'm leaving tomorrow," she said.

"What? Why didn't you mention that before?"

"I don't know. It just never came up." Their moments had engrossed her so completely that she had not looked toward that thing that never worked out for her, anyway.

The future.

"Aren't you?" she asked him, "Leaving tomorrow?"

"That was my original plan, but I seem to have taken a detour. I could be a little flexible," he said. "Can you?"

"Maybe a teensy bit."

"I'm not ready to let you go." This was growled in her ear, the same way as his naughty suggestion with the peaches had been.

That declaration and the wedding behind them suddenly made it feel okay to be publicly a couple for the first time since Anthony had left.

His hand found hers. He led her to the deck railing, and put his arm around her. She leaned her head on his shoulder as the sun went down.

The wedding feast had been set up in that grand ballroom. Jolie and Jay had not been seated together. Jay was on the groom's side of the table, she was beside Sabrina, but even so, dinner was fabulous, as were the speeches and toasts. She and Jay came together again when the dancing began.

Finally, it felt okay to be them.

It was dark now. The tables were removed from the ballroom and the doors were thrown open between the outdoor space and the indoor one, making a huge dance floor. Thousands of fairy lights illuminated both spaces.

Sabrina danced with Troy. And then they broke away from each other, and she danced with Dad and he danced with their mom.

The formalities of the order of who everyone was supposed to be dancing with seemed to Jolie to go on endlessly.

But finally, Jolie and Jay were together, dancing for the first time since the senior prom night when she had propositioned him.

She realized she was so thankful he'd said no that night. She had not been ready. And it was possible it would have ruined *this*.

Had he said yes it was quite possible what would have happened between them would have overshadowed everything, forever. Because the things he had said to her that night were right.

She had been too young.

She had not been ready.

She had been about to get herself into trouble.

*Yes* might have felt good at the time, but so, so bad later. He'd only been eighteen. How had he known?

Or had he been guided by a force larger than himself? That let him know taking that opportunity that night might remove the opportunity for a future one.

It was partly because of that long-ago no, that when they danced together, his presence invited her to be herself.

That had never been an easy thing for her.

Letting go.

# CHAPTER SEVENTEEN

No, LETTING GO had never come easily to Jolie. And yet right now, dancing with Jay, it felt as if it was the easiest thing in the world.

She was not sure she had felt this good since she was sixteen, drunk on a punch she had been unaware was spiked.

She'd had very little to drink tonight, but she felt intoxicated, nonetheless.

They danced until they were breathless. They danced as if there was no one else on that deck that was canopied with stars. They danced in celebration of all the ways they had come to know each other.

When their feet started to hurt, they kicked off their shoes and danced some more.

He drew from Jolie her confidence.

Her sexiness.

Her certainty in herself as a woman that she had never felt with anyone but him. Even when she was sixteen.

She never wanted this magical evening to end.

But then Jay was called away by Troy for something, he kissed Jolie regretfully and departed. Breathless, she left the deck, and stood there in the darkness drinking in the stars.

"Hey, sis."

"You startled me," Jolie said, seeing Sabrina standing there, with a wineglass in her hand, almost hidden by shrubs. "What are you doing?"

"Oh, just having a moment."

"The stars are gorgeous tonight."

"What is going on between you and Jay?" Sabrina asked. "We could both be brides! You're radiant. Chantelle certainly saw it. Those photos are probably going to be all about you."

It was said without any kind of edge at all. Completely gone was the woman who had told her there was only to be one star of this show.

Jolie lifted a shoulder, not wanting to get into it right now.

The silence was comfortable between them for a few moments, and then Sabrina broke it.

"I'm sorry. About the first night. Making such a fuss over the dress."

"It doesn't matter now. It all worked out. This one is great."

"I've been a bit temperamental lately."

"It's a big event to plan," Jolie said.

"That's not it. Nobody knows this yet, but I'm pregnant."

Jolie felt the shock of that announcement ripple through her. She glanced at the glass in her sister's hand.

"It's sparkling juice," Sabrina said.

So that first night, the juice had been for Sabrina, not her. How often, Jolie wondered, had she been overly sensitive and made it about herself when it wasn't?

"Does Troy know?"

"Of course Troy knows," Sabrina said, insulted.

"It's just that you said nobody—"

"Oh! Do you always have to be so literal?"

Her sister loved to use the expression *literally*. This was the first time in Jolie's memory she'd actually used it correctly.

"Couldn't you just say you're happy for us?" her sister snapped. Apparently, their truce was over, because Sabrina gathered up her dress and lifted her chin. "It's half an hour from midnight. Could you go to the kitchen and check that the midnight snack is on time?"

Then she marched away with her nose in the air.

Jolie realized she still hadn't congratulated her sister. It just seemed there were too many questions, and that it might not be appropriate to ask them under their current circumstances.

For instance, was it an accident? Because Sabrina had told her Troy didn't want to have a baby.

Had her sister planned it? Like a trap? Is that why she was so defensive?

If it was true, if Sabrina had trapped Troy into this second marriage, wasn't it just a variation on the theme from their childhood?

A way of begging someone to love you?

The magic seemed to be draining from the evening as Jolie made her way to the kitchen as her sister had asked.

Her sister was pregnant.

And then another thought followed on the heels of that one.

What if *she* was pregnant? She'd stopped using birth control when she and Anthony had split. Swearing off men had meant her chances of a pregnancy were zero, after all.

She'd been so swept away by Jay that she hadn't even considered that.

No, that wasn't quite true. She'd swept Jay away, not the other way around. It was so unlike her not to think things all the way through. All right, Jay also seemed to have been swept away, not asking any of the usual questions, but ultimately the responsibility felt as if it was hers.

Certainly, protecting oneself from pregnancy would be part of that equation.

Who was she to sit in judgment of her sister?

She looked at her watch. It was, as her sister had pointed

out, nearly midnight. It seemed impossible that time had gone so fast. The evening—the whole day, really—had evaporated.

But she could feel something shifting. Reality poking at the edges of her consciousness.

Wasn't this where the fairy tale ended? Where Cinderella's bubble burst? When she lost her glass slipper, the mice turned into coachmen and the coach turned into a pumpkin? She went back to her old life of being the family scapegoat?

Now, where had that thought come from, like a cloud drifting across a perfect day?

She found the long dark hallway that led to the kitchen. There was a little alcove off of it, and smoke drifted out.

And then a familiar laugh.

Jack and Jill.

Still sneaking cigarettes, as if they were teenagers hiding behind the bus garage at the high school.

Jolie went to move by the alcove when Jill's voice stopped her.

"Omg, what do you think of Jay and Jolie together?"

"Obviously, they were just pretending for Anthony."

"Well, he's gone, and they're still together."

"Are they together, or she can't let go of the pretense, and she's throwing herself at him?"

"I think Chantelle gushing over her gave her a swollen head."

"I bet she asked her to say those things. To play a little prank on us."

"Or maybe Jay did! He's been quite defensive of her from day one. He seems to want to play white knight for her."

Triumphant snickers.

Maybe slightly drunken snickers, which didn't make it any less hurtful.

"No matter what the stupid photographer said, she's punching above her weight, that's for sure."

*What did that mean?*

"I mean she's not the little wallflower she once was, but I don't think being a doctor and living in Italy makes her Jay Fletcher material. I mean even if one photo did give Chantelle pause, Jay is one of the richest men in the world. I heard he has a private jet waiting for him in Kelowna."

"He dated Sophia Binal for a while."

"The singer? He did not!"

"He did. I'll show you on my phone."

"Wow," Jack said a moment later.

Jay was one of the richest men in the world? What? He'd dated one of the most famous and beautiful women in the world?

She remembered her father looking at her oddly when she said Jay had a sporting goods company.

She remembered him paying for that dress as if it was nothing.

Because to him, had it been nothing?

Jolie turned hastily, determined to find a different way to the kitchen to order the evening snack.

But when she passed the bathroom where she had first tried on that peach monstrosity, she couldn't resist ducking in. It was empty, but for further privacy, she found a stall and locked the door.

She did what she had not allowed herself to do in the ten years since she had left Canada. She used her phone and she looked up Jay Fletcher on the internet.

Jay was rich, all right.

He was billionaire rich.

And Sophie Binal wasn't the only spectacularly rich and famous woman he'd had on his arm in the past ten years, either.

While she was there looking things up, she searched what *punching above your weight* meant. It might have been common in Canada, but she didn't recall ever hearing it in Italy. It was a boxing term. It meant you had entered the wrong category and were probably about to get smashed to bits by a superior opponent.

Jack and Jill had obviously meant she didn't have a hope.

Jolie got up, put away her phone and tried to compose herself.

In the kitchen, she asked for the snack, just as Sabrina had requested. When she came back out, the alcove was empty, and she sat down on an upholstered bench, even if it did smell of smoke in there.

Oddly, she did not feel diminished by the remarks she had overheard.

Jack and Jill were simply horrible people. Their opinions meant nothing to her.

She felt as if the few days of being Jay's lover had given her the truest sense of who she really was that she had ever experienced.

And so, while not diminished, Jolie still felt a need to be analytical.

It was time to put emotion—that most unreliable of forces—aside and allow herself to be guided by the facts. Which were: She had been the aggressor. She had seduced Jay.

There was new evidence that sexual addiction ran in the family. Maybe she was in the first stages of that.

She was on the rebound, as Jay had pointed out when he had tried to resist her efforts.

She had been filled with survivor's euphoria when she had made her move.

She had been bonded to the man she perceived as saving her life.

She had not taken proper precautions and there was a remote possibility of pregnancy.

And lastly, though Jay had had many opportunities, he had never revealed the full truth about himself to her.

He was the kind of man women deliberately tried to trap.

Which brought up Sabrina's news.

It all felt like too much. Sabrina's surprise pregnancy, her mother and father's reconciliation, Jolie's awareness of family patterns.

Where did her new love affair fit into all of this?

Jolie suddenly *needed* to be home. Italy was home, and there was a reason for that. It was far away from all this chaos and emotion and family drama.

She needed to ground herself, to be surrounded by her things, her books and her flowers, her cozy tiny apartment, her fulfilling, satisfying work.

She needed to be away from Jay—how could she ever think straight around him?—in order to analyze this situation correctly.

Maybe she was addicted to him, already. Because she knew if she went back out onto that deck and danced with him one more time, she would be completely under the powerful sway of the forces between them.

She would never be able to draw a logical conclusion.

Just as she had that final thought, the clock struck twelve.

It was a confirmation to her that all fairy tales come to an end. It was good to leave fantasies on a high note, before the reality set in.

Part of her insisted on pointing out the clock striking midnight was not the end of the fairy tale. There was still the part about the prince finding the glass slipper, tracking down Cinderella, making his declaration of love.

Jolie sighed.

Wasn't that what she really wanted? To know what had

transpired between her and Jay hadn't been just because she'd seduced him?

Was she hoping, like in the fairy tale, he would come find her?

Of course she was! But that was a terrible, terrible weakness, to want such a thing, to believe in such a thing.

And what if she *was* pregnant? Then what?

Jolie went back to her cabin. She was not sure why she felt like a thief in the night as she quickly changed her clothes, packed up her few things, and bolted for the parking lot and her rented car.

And she was not sure why, if this was such an analytical decision, she kept having to wipe tears out of her eyes to see the dark road in front of her.

# CHAPTER EIGHTEEN

"WHERE'S JOLIE?" Jay asked Sabrina.

"I'm not sure."

Did the bride seem faintly miffed about something?

"I asked her to go organize the midnight snack, but it's here now, and she's not."

Jay frowned and scanned the gathering. The dancing had ended when the clock struck midnight, and the snack had been put out. People were milling around, eating and talking. No one seemed to want to leave. It really had been a perfect day.

And yet, when the clock had struck midnight, he'd had a funny sense shiver along his spine.

The perfect day was over.

On an impulse, he checked his phone. He stared at it, not sure he was believing what he saw.

There was a text there from Jolie. It was not even to him, personally. It was a group text, to her sister and her mom and dad and him. It thanked the bride and groom for the most perfect day ever. It said she'd had an emergency at work, and when she checked flights she'd found one that could get her back to Italy immediately.

I'll catch up with everyone later!

Breezy. Casual.

It didn't even mention him by name.

Jay felt as if he had been punched in the gut, as if the bottom was falling out of his world. Here it was, right on schedule, the sword hidden under the cloak of love.

Not that he loved her.

You didn't love a person because you'd become lovers for two days.

On the other hand, he and Jolie's history stretched back a lot longer than two days. On the other hand, he was not sure he had ever felt quite what he had felt in Jolie's arms.

Or when he was with her, setting aside the lover part.

She had a way of making him feel alive, engaged, challenged. She had a way of making life feel surprising and fun.

It hadn't felt like that for a long time, not since his father had died.

So here was the thing he needed to be grateful for: the potential for love had been there. And its forces were so powerful, so all-consuming, a man could forget the lessons love had already taught him.

Jolie had done him a big favor by pulling back.

Even the abruptness—no goodbye, a text, for God's sake—was a favor. It quashed that very real temptation to go after her, to try and catch her before she boarded that plane.

But no, now Jay could be mad, instead of sad.

Sometimes it felt as if his anger was the only thing that helped him make it through the weeks ahead, as the hot summer gave way to the cooler days of September.

"Jay!" his sister, Kelly, said. "What is wrong with you? You're acting like a bear with a sore bottom."

They had met at her favorite deli, and picked up lunch.

Unfortunately, a guy had been standing outside with a guitar and an open case. His singing—if it could be called that—had reminded Jay of Anthony outside Jolie's cabin that night.

He'd thrown five bucks inside the guitar case, but suggested the troubadour might want to think about a different career path.

Was that acting like a bear with a sore bottom?

"I did the guy a favor," he told his sister. "Like Simon on that show."

"Exactly like him!" Kelly said, triumphantly. "Grumpy old men."

He could protest that he wasn't that old, but he didn't have the energy. In fact, in the last while, since the wedding, he did feel old. Disillusioned. Okay, grumpy.

They were walking together through the old neighborhood, their deli purchases in a paper bag, bringing them to share it with their mom at their old house.

They walked by the high school, and Jay had had a sharp memory of Jolie.

His life seemed to be filled with sharp—and unwanted— memories of her.

He thought, about a thousand times a day, of sending her a quick text. Casual. *How you doing? I'm sorry we didn't have a chance to say goodbye.*

But then all that anger at her leaving like that just resurfaced.

He was pretty sure *bear with a sore bottom* didn't say the half of it. Neither did *grumpy old men.*

"Is that how you treat your clients?" Jay said, determined to deflect his sister, and remove his attention from the high school in a deft two-birds-with-one-stone conversational maneuver. "Is *what is wrong with you* your lead question? I think that's what they're paying you to find out."

"I don't treat family members like clients."

"Well, they can be thankful for that. Would *bear with a*

*sore bottom* be like an official diagnosis? Or *grumpy old men*? From *The Diagnostic and Statistical Manual of Mental Disorders*? I remember the name of the book, because I paid for it."

There. A not-so-subtle reminder that a little gratitude might be more appreciated than *this*.

"I would never diagnose a family member," Kelly said with a sniff.

"It seems to me you've called me both a workaholic and commitment-phobe."

"Those aren't diagnoses! Observations."

Kelly had invited him for lunch with their mom. He'd talked to his mom on the phone a couple of times since the wedding, and taken her out for lunch once, but hadn't been over to their old house.

The house—a museum to how things used to be—was depressing.

"If I didn't know you better, I'd say you're having problems with love."

He snorted derisively. "You know my feelings about love."

"Yes, I do. And that belief system could cause you real difficulties if you found someone you cared about."

*Ha ha, little Miss Know-It-All, as it turns out, I wasn't the problem.*

"You're wrong, you know," Kelly said softly. "About love. Mom wasn't destroyed by the loss of her great love."

"Oh, geez, a lecture from the twenty-four-year-old expert on all things."

"It's because she was so codependent that she can't recover."

He swore under his breath. "I thought you didn't diagnose family members."

"Do you know what codependency is?" his sister asked.

"Vaguely. The more apt question would have been, do I want to know what it is. To which the answer is—"

His sister cut him off, undeterred. "It's putting everyone else's needs ahead of your own all the time. It's knowing what they need, but not what you need. It's knowing what they like, but not what you like."

Jay remembered telling Jolie about his mom planning those game nights. She would start on Monday planning an event for Friday.

As if her whole life revolved around that.

"She just wanted to make us happy," he told his sister.

"Yes, but then Dad died, and we grew up, and she doesn't have a clue how to make herself happy. She used to paint. Did you know that?"

"No." He felt suddenly guilty at how little he knew about the mother who had known absolutely everything about him.

"I've signed her up for some painting lessons. I'm going to tell her over lunch. I want you to back me up."

"Okay," he said, "I will."

"I wish you would remember that when you're convincing yourself about the failure of love," Kelly said softly.

"What?"

"That we had each other's backs. You and me and Mike and Jim. Look at how you stepped up for us, Jay, after Dad died. You took on all kinds of stuff that a young guy probably really wasn't equipped to deal with. But you did deal with it. You made whatever sacrifices you had to make, you did whatever it took to make sure we had education and opportunities, and most importantly, with Mom falling apart, stability. If that isn't love, I don't know what is. You showed us how to step up for each other."

He wondered about his level of self-involvement that he hadn't made note of this before. Yes, initially, he had been the one to shoulder the responsibility when his dad died.

But now his siblings stepped up for him. Consistently. Unquestioningly.

Kelly insisted on coffee or dinner with him at least once a week. His brothers were always coming up with tickets for guy activities. They all texted back and forth. It was now his siblings that arranged family activities that included his mom.

As well as his family, hadn't his friend Troy always been there for him, too? Quietly in the background, saying without ever needing to say the words, *I got your back, bro.*

The faint animosity he'd been feeling toward Kelly evaporated. It didn't have anything to do with her, anyway.

He put his arm around her shoulder and kissed the top of her head.

"You're a good person," he said, and she beamed at him.

They came around the corner, their old family home now in sight, across the street and two doors down. Both of them stopped in their tracks.

There was a landscaping truck out front. The neglected flower bed, the one between the house and the sidewalk that Jolie had remembered, was all torn up.

The weeds were out of it, and it was filled with mounds of fresh, deep dark loam. His mother was outside, in her nightgown. She rarely got dressed anymore. She was walking up and down, shaking her head in disbelief. A landscaper was on his knees, tucking plant after plant into that rich, new soil.

Even though he was no expert on flowers, he knew exactly what they were. Marigolds.

"Did you do this?" he asked Kelly. Had it been part of her plan to bring their mom back to life? Acting out of the love that he had been so certain had failed their family?

But she shook her head. "I was about to ask you the same thing."

Of course she hadn't done it. How would she know about

the marigolds? They crossed the street together. Their mom saw them coming, and gestured them over.

"Did you two do this?"

They both shook their heads.

"It must have been Mike and Jim," she said.

Since Mike and Jim had the combined sensitivity of a rock, Jay doubted that. Very much. Also, there was the question of the marigolds.

"It's a miracle," his mom whispered.

'It's just flowers," he told her gruffly.

"No, no, it isn't. I asked for a sign this morning."

Oh, geez. Signs and portents. Well, if they gave hope did it matter what his mom wanted to believe?

Still, he asked her. "A sign of what?"

"That life could be good again. Even without your father." She looked at him, both guilty for entertaining such a thought, and hopeful.

# CHAPTER NINETEEN

"OF COURSE LIFE is going to be good again," Jay told her. When had he started believing that, particularly in the face of his current misery over Jolie's abandonment?

He put his arm around his mother's thin shoulder and kissed her head, just as he had done with his sister a few minutes ago.

"Years ago, your father brought me a marigold that he'd rescued from somewhere. Sickly thing. I planted it and it seeded itself. This whole front garden ended up having marigolds in it."

"I remember."

"Do you?" she said, surprised.

Actually, he was not sure he had given it a thought until Jolie brought it up.

"That year I had done geraniums," his mother said, softly. "Red, white, red, white, it was all very orderly. I thought of it as my Canadian theme. That marigold did not go at all."

"Why'd you plant it, then?"

"To make him happy," his mother admitted. "The funny thing is, it ended up making me happy, too."

Oh, this complicated, twisted, wonderful thing called family. You couldn't really capture the dynamics of all the different kinds of love—healthy and unhealthy—with labels.

He moved away from his mother and his sister.

"Hey," he said to the landscaper, who set down an armful of the bedding plants and turned to look at him. "What are you doing?"

"Planting," he said, annoyed at being interrupted to state the obvious.

"It's just that this is my mother's house, and she didn't order any flowers. My sister and I didn't, either."

The landscaper became more garrulous. "Wrong time of year, really, and hard to find marigolds that are perennials, but if the price is right miracles can be accomplished."

*Miracles.*

Jay looked over at his mom. "Who ordered the work?" he asked, as if he didn't know.

"Uh, I can't say. It's confidential."

Jay could say, of course, that his mother was the homeowner, and she hadn't ordered the work and had a right to know who did, but that seemed unnecessarily querulous. And might not get him to where he needed to be.

Since the man had already let it be known miracles could be accomplished for the right price, Jay took his wallet out of his pocket and practiced his superpower with two bright red Canadian fifty-dollar bills.

The guy glanced at them, took them without hesitation, and then slid them into his pocket.

"Some doctor in Italy. Weird, eh?" And then he turned back to his work.

Jay stood there, stock-still, for a moment.

Even though he'd known, it hit him hard that Jolie was thinking of him, too.

Not him, precisely, but the thing in his life that was causing him pain, how his family dynamic had changed since the death of his father. Perhaps she, like his sister, saw that as holding him back.

From love.

Did she want him to overcome that obstacle? Is that what this gift of the garden for his mom meant?

Was it a hint?

Not exactly. He saw, suddenly, precisely what it was. It was an invitation. Not just to participate in something that had been dropped in his lap, like their accidental engagement.

But to make a choice for himself.

Choosing it was momentous.

Jolie had to know that.

But what she couldn't have known, was that her gift to his family had arrived on the same day that his mother was pleading for a sign.

That it was okay to go on living.

That life would be good again.

It struck him that he was in the middle of an energetic force that was all intertwined, and that logic could never explain. He was right in the middle of the incredible mystery that was the interconnectedness of life.

What hope did he, a mere mortal, have of fighting such a force? Even if he wanted to?

Which he didn't.

"Hey," he said to the landscaper. "Can I get an address for the doctor in Italy?"

"Oh—" the landscaper looked suddenly shifty "—that's not really my department."

But it turned out, for a price, it could be.


Jolie sat on her terrace and breathed in deeply. She had changed clothes after work, into the slip dress from the wedding. It had turned out it may not have been the perfect bridesmaid dress, but it was the perfect loungewear for hot Italian evenings, particularly now since she had removed the stitched-in second slip.

She loved evenings. Her view and this terrace made up for the tininess of her apartment.

It was breathtaking, looking over the clay-tiled rooves of Rome to the Vatican in the distance. The setting sun was painting the roof of the Basilica of Saint Peter in shades of gold.

She was appreciative of the fact she could once again end her days with a glass of wine, since she was definitely not pregnant.

She took a sip of the wine, and watched a butterfly toy with the edges of the bright begonias that spilled out of her window boxes. She felt, astonishingly, as if she could hear the air under its wings.

She'd had this amazing feeling since returning from Canada.

Not of being diminished by her time with Jay.

But rather, made alive by it, as if his kisses trailing fire down her heated skin had called sleeping senses to life. She saw things differently and deeply, she heard sounds she had never heard before, the scent of a single flower could captivate her whole body.

As she watched the butterfly, a crisp knock came on her door. It was too hot to cook, so she had ordered dinner from her favorite trattoria around the corner. It was already paid for by credit card. The delivery service could leave it, so she didn't miss the setting of the sun.

The knock came again.

Firmer.

At least she was one hundred percent certain it wasn't Anthony. He had contacted her, via new phone number since his old one was blocked, shortly after her return to announce, a trifle smugly, that he'd moved on.

There'd been a picture attached to the text.

Jolie was pretty sure that it was the same woman she'd seen him sharing *their* spaghetti and meatballs ice cream with.

Anthony asked after her engagement, but she hadn't answered, just blocked his new number. There had been no sense of vindication in blocking that number, just a sense of a clean cut, a chapter closed.

The knocking came again, even firmer, and with a resigned sigh she set down her wineglass and pushed back her chair. The woman she'd been a week ago probably would have gone and put a light wrap over her practically transparent dress, but the new her did not care what people thought.

If they thought she was sexy, good. Her time with Jay had taught her that. She *was* sexy. She liked being sexy. It was part of embracing being a woman to acknowledge that about yourself.

She went through her tiny apartment to the door. Her building was three hundred years old, well before peepholes in doors had been a thing.

Not worried it would be Anthony and expecting a question about her credit card, she pulled it open.

Nothing could have prepared her for the shock of Jay standing there.

Her newly attuned senses were flooded. Even though he must have been traveling, he smelled wonderful.

*Of course, private jets would do that, keep the travails of travel to a minimum*, she told herself, trying to keep some semblance of a barrier in place.

He was dressed in a casual suit, which also was not travel rumpled. She'd never seen him in a suit before. It was beautifully cut to skim his sleek masculinity. It hinted at his power, rather than bragging about it.

It was also mouthwateringly sexy.

At least as sexy as the little dress she had on.

But there was also no mistaking, not just in the cut of his

clothes, but in the way he held himself, that the man was a billionaire, just as they were portrayed on the covers of books and magazines.

He had sunglasses on. They shielded his eyes and gave him a celebrity quality. She could see her reflection in them.

She tucked a stray curl behind her ear. She needn't have bothered. It leaped right back to where it had been before.

"Hi," he said, casually.

His hair was longer than when she had first seen him getting out of his car at Hidden Valley all those months ago. But then, as now, the setting sun was adding threads of gold to the light brown strands.

He was also sporting a faintly roguish look, whiskers darkening the perfect, chiseled planes of his cheeks and chin.

"Hi?" she said, trying to hide the hard pounding of her heart. Her attuned senses were flooded with him, and it made it hard to resist the desire to fling herself at him *again.* Had she learned nothing at all from her past flingings?

Jolie folded her arms in front of herself, over the transparency of the dress. It was a small gesture against the swamping of her defenses.

"Hi," she said, "as in you were just in the neighborhood and thought you'd pop by?"

"Something like that. Don't look at me as if I'm a stalker to add to your collection of men you've spurned."

"*Spurned* seems a little strong."

He lifted the sunglasses. Oh, those eyes! A shade of green that should be criminal, since it could be used as a weapon against a weakening heart.

Too easy to remember how the color of those eyes had darkened with passion each time Jay had lowered his head to kiss her.

Actually, it seemed as if maybe they were darkening a shade now, as he took in the dress.

"Does it?" he asked, quietly.

"Does what?" she stammered, getting lost in the look in his eyes, losing the conversational thread completely.

"Does *spurned* seem like too strong an expression for what you did to me?"

"Yes!"

It was sweltering, the day's heat trapped up against her front door. Reluctantly, she stepped back, let Jay in, shut the door behind him.

His presence made her cozy space seem even tinier. She knew, no matter what happened, he would always be here now, his presence leaving an imprint.

"I like this," he said.

The man who could have and buy anything liked her apartment?

*Big deal.*

She wondered if he'd like the bedroom. That was the problem with letting Jay in, particularly since her senses had gone wild.

"I'm trying to understand why you left me the way you did," he said. She wanted to close her eyes and listen. Not to the words. To the tone. The faint rasp.

"Just kind of mid-dance," he continued. "No goodbye."

"Come out to the deck," she said. "We'll catch the last of the sun going down. You can see Saint Peter's from there."

So first she'd invited him in. And now they were going to the deck. And then she'd pour him a glass of wine. In fact, she grabbed a wineglass off an open shelf as they passed through her apartment, the kitchen and the living room all sharing a space.

He was edging into her life, one inch at a time.

And she was allowing it.

If the butterflies in her stomach were any indication, she was *loving* it.

"I sent a text," she said, pouring him a glass of wine. He took off the suit jacket and draped it over the back of his chair, then sat down.

He lifted an eyebrow at her as he lifted the wineglass to his lips. "Right," he said, "a text."

"Okay, maybe I should have done that differently, but you're not exactly without sin, either."

Sin.

She could think of a few she wished they were committing right this second!

# CHAPTER TWENTY

"Sin," Jay said, with a certain amount of wicked relish. "That sounds like something from our Catholic high school."

"You are in Rome. Let he who is without sin…"

"You're keeping me in suspense. What's my sin?"

*His sin? So many of them. Where to begin? Bringing out the passionate side in her, making the entire world with all its rules disappear when she was in his arms, making her believe in something she had sworn off...*

"You forgot to tell me a few things about yourself," Jolie informed him.

"Such as?"

"Oh, you know, the billionaire part."

"Okay, that's a first. A woman saying that as if it's a bad thing."

"It's not the billionaire part, exactly, that's the bad thing. It's you not telling me."

"You left the wedding that night because you thought I was a billionaire?" he said skeptically.

"Aren't you?"

"Having a billion dollars in sales is not the same as being a billionaire."

"Now you're splitting hairs."

"I would have thought success would make me more attractive, not less." He pushed his hair back off his forehead. It flopped back down as if he hadn't touched it at all.

"Jolie, I didn't tell you because I wanted, just for a while, for it to be the same as it was before I achieved success. Like it was in high school, where people just liked me for me."

"You're deluded. They liked you because you were the captain of the football team. And you were good-looking. And had a great ass."

"People are that superficial?" he asked, with mock horror.

"Yes."

"The point I'm trying to make is that when you first achieve success, it's not what you think it's going to be. It's lonely. You can't take people at face value anymore. It's exhausting trying to sort out if someone's interested in you for you, or if their interest is about what you can do for them."

He was actually making her feel sorry for him. That was ridiculous!

"I saw the pictures of you at home with some of the world's most well-known celebrities," Jolie said firmly. "You didn't look exhausted."

"That's what I'm trying to tell you. When it first all hits, it feels like you need a new world. So you gravitate to people who have as much as you.

"Then you find out sometimes those people—like Sophie—have the limelight on them all the time. They're in a cage that they can't get out of. They hate the attention. They love the attention. Often, they need the attention for their careers. Lots of them regard any kind of publicity as good publicity.

"So, yes, I stuck my toes in the waters of that world. I found I couldn't live with that kind of scrutiny. If you stubbed your toe and had a scowl on your face, the day's headline was that you'd had a big fight with your lover.

"The thing is, if you get too deep into that world, you can't get back out. Things are never going to be normal for you again.

"And maybe because that's what I grew up with, that's what I crave. Normal. I had to make choices, and so I've chosen a small inner circle of people I can trust.

"My family, my sister and brothers. Old friends. No one keeps me down-to-earth quite like Troy, saying *Oh, get over yourself, you still suck at a pickup game of basketball.*

"When we first met again, it was so apparent to me that you didn't know about my success, I wanted you to be like that, too. I would have told you sooner or later, but I just wanted to be an average guy for a while. What would have changed if I would have told you?"

Jolie sighed. "Have you ever heard the expression, *punching above your weight*?"

"Sure. Hasn't everybody?"

"It doesn't translate to Italian. I heard Jack and Jill talking. That's what they said about me and you."

"Punching above your weight doesn't have to mean you're in the wrong class. It can mean you have enough confidence in yourself to try anything."

Why did he always, always seem to see her in a different light than the one she saw herself in?

"That's not how they said it," she said tightly.

"And that's why you left? Without even saying goodbye?"

She nodded, tightly.

"I don't believe that's true. Not that they didn't say it, but that anything those two witches said would affect how you felt about me."

"I looked you up online after I overheard them. The plane. Hobnobbing with the rich and famous. It was obvious to me it was true. I was punching way above my weight."

He stared at her, and then he reached across the table and took her hand in his. He squeezed.

"What's really going on, Jolie?" he asked, his voice soft. "Because after that, you planted marigolds for my mom?"

"How did you find out that was me?"

"Oh, you know, that billionaire secret weapon. My superpower."

"What's your superpower?" she asked.

"Throw some money at it."

She looked at his lips. She couldn't stop herself. She said, "That's not your superpower."

He smiled at her. "Now," he said with satisfaction, "we're getting somewhere."

She sighed. What was really going on? With his hand in hers, she felt safe telling him the full truth.

"I was embarrassed, Jay. I set up the fake engagement. And then I seduced you. I was the aggressor. And, all that time, I had no idea how far out of my league you were."

He cocked his head. "There's still something you're not telling me."

It was terrifying to be seen like this.

Terrifying, and as if she had been waiting her whole life for it at the same time.

"Sabrina told me she was pregnant."

His brow lowered. "Holy. Does Troy know?"

"I nearly got slapped for asking that."

"Well, he didn't want to have kids yet."

"So I knew that, and I was considering the super yucky possibility she'd trapped him. Using the same trap my mom used on my dad."

"Oh, Jolie," he said, "I'm sad that's how your parents got together and even sadder that you knew. Kids should not know stuff like that."

"Sabrina got it thrown in her face every time they had an argument."

"That explains a few things about Sabrina," he said.

"I know."

"As gut-wrenching as all this is, what does it all have to do with us?" he asked.

Complete confession time. They were in the Catholic capital of the world, after all.

"In the throes of passion, I didn't think about birth control," she admitted.

He went very still. "That's not totally on you. I must have been carried away myself. I can't believe it never once occurred to me." And then, quietly, "Are you?"

"No."

Did he actually look faintly disappointed?

"No, Jay, I'm not. But if I had been, wouldn't it have looked as if I set a trap for the billionaire?"

"Pretty sure I just saw that title on a book at a kiosk at the airport."

She smacked him on the shoulder. She'd missed doing that. From the look on his face, he might have missed it, too. "I don't think you've been in the public spaces in an airport for quite some time."

"Okay, I saw it at my sister's house, but she'd kill me for outing her for reading *Setting a Trap for the Billionaire*."

"You did not see a book with that title."

"Okay, maybe not *exactly* that title, but I'm still going to summarize that plot, through your point of view, which is romance writer talk."

"How would you know?"

He wagged wicked eyebrows at her. "I know lots of things. So, to summarize, you seduced me, and then thought you might be pregnant. And didn't want it to seem like you were trying to snag yourself a billionaire, so you left without saying goodbye."

"Yes, that sums it up."

"Except for the marigolds."

She was silent for a moment. Then she said, "I just wanted

your mom to know somehow, that when love leaves you, maybe it comes back in a different way."

"I don't think that's all it was, Jolie."

The look on his face made her heart go very still.

"I think it was an invitation," he told her softly.

"For what?" she squeaked

"You were right. You set up the engagement. And then you seduced me." He paused.

"But those marigolds sent me a message. You hadn't left me. You certainly hadn't left me because I was a billionaire.

"You did what a woman with dignity and self-respect—a woman who knows her own worth—would do. You invited me. You said, *You want me? We have a future? It's your turn. You make the move. You be the leader. You prove yourself worthy of me.* And that's why I traveled around the world. To accept your invitation. To make my move."

# CHAPTER TWENTY-ONE

JOLIE LET THAT sink in, stunned.

Jay Fletcher had traveled halfway around the world to make a move on her, to see if they had a future together.

To see if *he* was worthy of *her*.

"So, where should we start?" he asked her.

She knew exactly where to start. She was out of her chair in a flash, on his side of the table, in his lap, twining her arms around his neck.

Kissing him.

"No," Jay said firmly, "not this time."

"I know what I want," she said, nuzzling his lips, feeling like a person dying of thirst who had just found water—

That line had worked so well last time. This time, Jay gently scooted out from under her. She found herself sitting in the chair alone, gazing up at him.

"Jolie," he said firmly. "I'm taking the lead this time."

"What does that mean?" she said, and heard a touch of sulkiness in her voice.

"I knew exactly who you were when you were sixteen," he said softly. "Do you remember what I said to you that night?"

"Almost word for word," she said, and not happily.

"I said," he reminded her softly, "that you weren't a fling kind of girl, that I could see forever in your eyes. You still aren't that kind of girl. Woman. I still see the same thing in your eyes that I always saw. A longing for happily-ever-after. You're the forever kind. We have to find out if I am, too."

"How?" she stammered. Jay was talking about him and her happily-ever-after. *Forever?*

Sometimes you did not allow yourself to admit how badly you wanted something.

And then someone spoke it out loud, and with their word breathed life and hope into your secret dream.

"I'm going to court you, in an old-fashioned way. It means I'm going to treat you with complete honor and respect, just like I did the night of the senior prom."

"Well," she said, and then to hide the fact it felt like she might be going into a good old-fashioned swoon, "that sounds perfectly dull."

"I'm going to woo you and romance you."

"It's getting a little better," she decided. "But we're going to kiss, right?"

He tilted his head, considering. "Occasionally," he decided, and then, dead serious, "Jolie, I'm going to be the man my father raised me to be."

Even though she just wanted to drag him into the bedroom and seduce him all over again, she was also intrigued by the relationship plan he was outlining.

Honored by it.

"So," he said, "if a billionaire dropped by unexpectedly to see you in Rome, where would you suggest going out for dinner?"

"I've ordered dinner. It should be here any minute."

"If you hadn't ordered dinner, where?"

"There's a place I walk by on my way to work at the Colosseum. It's pretty famous for its food and ambience. I've always wanted to go there. It probably takes months to get reservations, though."

"Ah," he said, "billionaire superpower number two. A

personal assistant named Arnold. If he can't do it, it can't be done."

And so it began, with an exquisite candlelight dinner at one of Rome's most exclusive restaurants. She was pretty sure that she caught a glimpse of Al Pacino.

When they got home the dinner she had ordered was waiting on the steps, and they ate that, too!

And that's how it unfolded.

Jay was a perfect gentleman. He spoiled her with surprise weekend drop-ins. He picked her up in his private plane and they explored Paris together. He sent the plane to get her so she could join him when he had business in New York. They explored that city as the leaves began to fall.

They toured museums and sampled wine and had box seats for sporting events and concerts.

As fall turned to winter, they went heli-skiing in the Canadian Rockies, and skating on Ottawa's Rideau Canal.

Jolie loved the glitz and glamour! Of course she did. And yet what she came to love best of all were the unexpected moments that became so special because their very simplicity allowed her to see how Jay shone in the world.

One of her favorite moments was a stop for a hamburger at a little hole-in-the-wall run by a couple who had been married for forty-five years.

Or when they walked through a park and stopping to watch a little boy and his sister making ships out of leaves and sailing them across puddles.

Her favorite things became not five-star restaurants and jaunts to exotic places in the private jet, but pizza, with hand-stretched crust like Nonna had taught her, and a movie at home.

His hand in hers on a chilly day.

The way his eyes lit up every single time he saw her.

The tenderness in his voice when he spoke to her.

The biggest surprise of all was how much she started to love going back to Toronto. In fact, it began to squeeze out their explorations of other places in the world.

When Jolie came home, she and Jay would hang out with Sabrina and Troy, watching her sister's belly grow. It was delightful to witness how excited Troy was about becoming a dad.

For the first time in her life, Jolie enjoyed being around her parents. She wasn't sure if Jay's billionaire status put them on their best behavior, but there seemed to be new rules between them.

If she was not mistaken, her mother was not begging anyone to love her anymore.

Once, when they were together, that song came on.

"My namesake," Jolie said wryly.

Her mother looked puzzled. "What? This song? You were named after my favorite auntie. She died right before you were born."

And so this, too, was a lesson in family.

What you thought about your family was one part truth, and one part myth, and all the other parts were perception.

She loved meeting Jay's mom. She radiated the sweetness of a person who gave their heart completely.

And she gave it completely to Jolie.

She talked Jolie and Jay into taking a painting class with her.

"Do you think the paint is edible?" Jay asked Jolie in an undertone, midclass, obviously getting bored.

"No, it's not edible!" she told him, but giggled, remembering the avocado mask. Was there anything in the world quite as nice as a man who would go to great lengths to make you giggle?

He ate a blob of the paint.

Just as his mother looked their way, too. His mom sighed with a pretense of long-suffering.

"He's always been like that," she told Jolie, and then to Jay's embarrassment regaled the whole art class with stories of things he had done when he was young.

Jay and Jolie spent rowdy nights watching baseball games in sports bars with his brothers. She adored his sister, Kelly, and the silliness of the game events that she held at her small apartment on Friday nights.

She loved being witness to how those people that Jay had chosen for his inner circle loved him.

And respected him.

Through it all, no matter how she tried to tempt him, and oh, she did, Jay would not break.

*Hard no to hanky-panky*, he'd remind her, when she'd plant a kiss on his neck, or sneak one onto his lips.

"I've been thinking about Christmas," he told her one night on the phone. "You said, growing up, it was the worst time for you."

Her heart just filled with tenderness that he always remembered these things.

"So, I thought it's time to make new memories. I want us to have the most spectacular first Christmas together. I've narrowed it down to two places. Rovaniemi, in the Lapland of Finland or Bath, in England. They both would be really unique—"

"Jay, I never thought you would hear these words from me, but I want to spend Christmas at home."

"Home. Rome?"

When had that happened? Rome didn't feel like home so much anymore. She felt like she belonged other places, now, too.

"I just can't imagine not being around your mom at Christmas. Not seeing Kelly and Mike and Jim."

He groaned. "Kelly likes to play *all* those horrible games on Christmas Eve."

"Perfect. And how could we not have Christmas with Sabrina and Troy and my mom and dad? You know, with all its potential for disaster, maybe we could look at getting everyone together."

"One big happy family?" he said skeptically.

"Something like that," she said happily.

Here's what Jay did not like about her plan. He had an engagement ring for Jolie. It had been burning a hole in his pocket for months, while he tried to figure out exactly the right time and the right words.

It had been fun romancing her.

He felt as if he'd gotten to know her and her family, but also himself and his family so much better through the process.

But the no hanky-panky thing was becoming impossible.

A man's honor could only carry him so far.

His was going to carry him and Jolie straight to the altar. After that, he planned to make up for lost time.

Finally, he had decided, Christmas would be the best time to propose even if she had said no to Finland and Bath, both with much higher potential for romance than Toronto.

He wanted it to be Christmas because he remembered her saying it was the worst time of all for her.

And he wanted to start changing that.

With a Christmas proposal.

And then once he'd proposed—once it was official that they were going to be man and wife—if they were in Toronto, he might as well use that. He'd planned prosecco and his king-size bed and a celebration she would never forget. He planned to end their courtship with the complete seduction of Jolie.

An evening with family?

Sheesh.

Could nothing ever go according to plan?

# CHAPTER TWENTY-TWO

"Is EVERYTHING OKAY?" Jolie asked Jay.

"Oh, sure." *Hunky-dory*, he thought to himself. Her plane had been late, they were in the middle of a bloody snowstorm, his sister was having both of their families over for Christmas Eve, and he had to figure out how to get that ring on Jolie's finger.

Tonight.

His mother and Jolie's father were planning the traditional *la vigilia* feast. No turkey for them. The last time he'd spoken to his mother, they were planning seven courses of seafood, since meat was a no-no.

While it was good to see his mom having enthusiasm for life again, where in the seven courses did he fit in his proposal?

Certainly he had to get it in before his sister started her infernal games, and then they were all herded off to midnight mass.

He'd confided in Troy because it seemed to him maybe Troy knew a thing or two about proposals, having done it twice.

It was Troy who had suggested after dinner would be nice. It was rare for the whole family to get together, but they would be on Christmas Eve, so why not do it then?

Troy even suggested they could hide the ring in a Christmas firecracker thing that would be at each place setting.

Now that they were almost at Kelly's house, Jay could feel his feet getting cold. Did he really want to propose publicly? Did he get down on his knee in front of everyone? According to Troy, nothing would say commitment quite like that.

*What if she said no?*

For God's sake, she wasn't saying no. He glanced over at her. She looked back at him. There it was in her eyes. Forever.

He'd prepared his bedroom before he'd gone to the airport. Strawberries dipped in chocolate, prosecco on ice, new, crisp sheets. In the interest of his old-fashioned honor, he'd never let her stay at his place.

She stayed at her parents when she came here. What if she wanted to go there after midnight mass?

She wouldn't want to go there. They'd be newly engaged. It wasn't like she was six and had to be at their house so Santa could find her.

"Are you sure you're okay?" she asked.

"I said I was okay!"

Maybe he should hold off on the proposal? Until they were alone? That would be more romantic. When the heck were they ever going to be alone?

That was it. He wasn't proposing in front of both their families. He slipped into a parking spot in front of his sister's row house.

They were the last ones there. How had his sister's been picked? It was way too small. Oh, he'd gone along with that because he hadn't wanted them all at his place, when he was getting his own private celebration ready.

Troy gave him the secret handshake and a wink when they came in the door. Jolie, his wife-to-be, was swallowed up by both families who hadn't seen her for a while.

Geez, there was her sister. Sabrina looked as big as a house. He had to work at not saying it. Hadn't Troy said she had a month left?

"Sabrina," he said, "you're, ah, glowing."

There was too much noise and too many people, and his soon-to-be father-in-law and his mom were shouting in Italian in the kitchen. The smoke detector started wailing and his sister got under it with a dish towel, and waved with what appeared to be long practice until the smoke detector burped and quit.

This was not going to work.

He saw Troy laying down the firecrackers beside each plate. With the big wink at him as he set down a yellow one beside Jolie's place.

"Jolie," Troy yelled, "you sit here."

Jay scowled at him. Did he have to be so obvious? He felt like he couldn't breathe. He didn't think he could do this.

No, he hadn't thought it through.

A private moment, a nice restaurant, just her and him.

He reached over and slid her firecracker away from her plate and put it in his pocket. Troy raised his eyebrows and mouthed, *Chicken.*

Well, so be it.

Troy good-naturedly took another firecracker from the box and threw it at him. He set it in front of Jolie's plate.

But as it turned out, no one opened those firecrackers.

Because when Troy pulled back the chair for Sabrina, she suddenly clutched her stomach and cried out.

There was a sound like a balloon full of water hitting the floor. And then, as if it hadn't been chaotic enough, all hell really broke loose.

He found himself in the back seat of Troy's car with Sabrina's head on his lap and her terrified eyes glued to his face. Every now and then a whimper of pain would escape her.

Selfishly, he was glad he hadn't proposed. A stupid rhyme went through his head.

*First comes love,*
*Then comes marriage,*
*Then comes Jolie pushing the baby carriage.*

Only it wasn't Jolie, it was Sabrina, but did a man seriously ask this kind of pain of a woman if he loved her?

Troy drove. Jolie rode shotgun.

A whole convoy came behind them.

He said anything that came into his head. "You're doing great. Everything will be okay. Troy's a super driver. Hang in there. Five more minutes. We're almost there."

And then they were at the hospital in the driveway reserved for emergencies. Troy screeched to a halt.

"I can't move," Sabrina whispered.

Jay catapulted out of the car and ran around and over to the other passenger door. He flung it open. If he was not mistaken that was a baby's head. He rammed himself into the back seat.

And then, suddenly, he was holding a very slippery, very bloody baby, trying to protect its fragile body from the snow. For a terrifying moment, he thought the baby, a boy, was dead.

But then it gave an outraged cry, and squirmed in his hands.

And then he was being pushed out of the way, and the baby was taken from him, and there was a stretcher and cops—where had they come from—and nurses and people yelling in Italian.

And then that great wave of noise and chaos moved away from him and it was blessedly quiet.

He sank down on the curb. Alone.

Except that Jolie came and sat on that cold wet curb beside him. And laid her head on his shoulder.

He realized he was crying.

And so was she.

And then she said, "Best Christmas Eve ever."

And he took the crumpled firecracker out of his pocket and gave it to her. There was no way he was going home alone after this.

"I'm sorry," he said. "Under the circumstances it's the best that I can do."

She pulled both ends, and there was a little clicking sound, because of course the firecrackers never worked, but it ripped open nicely and her ring had the decency not to fall out and fall down the gutter.

She took the ring and put it on her finger.

And then laid her head back on his shoulder.

"Yes," she said. "A million times yes."

# EPILOGUE

JAY COULD FEEL his eyes smarting as Jolie walked toward him.

She was wearing the most simple wedding gown he had ever seen. But it did exactly what those dresses should always do, but hardly ever did.

The simplicity of the dress allowed the bride to shine through.

Everything that she had become in the last few months was there: her confidence, her belief in herself, her generosity in love.

But it wasn't any of that that was making his eyes smart.

It was what she carried.

Instead of a bouquet, she had her hands cupped around a single bedraggled marigold in a plastic container.

To Jay, it looked like the most beautiful flower in the entire world. Love was exactly like that flower. If you nursed it, it would come back, stronger and better than it had ever been before. But more than that, when you planted it, it spread. Even when the original died out, as of course it eventually would, it left its mark on the world.

That's what his mother and father's great love had done. It had left its mark on the world. It had nourished him, and his brothers and sister, given them strength, and ultimately the ability to see that love made the world better and it made people better.

It had given him the ability to help heal someone—Jolie—

who had not experienced such love in her life. It had given him the gift of seeing her come to believe.

That love could be strong and true, pure and nourishing.

Eventually the gift his mother and father's great love had given him—that he had lost sight of for a while, that he had turned his back on for a while—would give again. To his children and maybe someday grandchildren and great-grandchildren.

That's what love did.

When everything else had faded away, it remained.

And it went on and on and on.

Forever.

He saw that in Jolie's eyes as she took her place in front of him at the altar. He saw there, what he had seen since she was sixteen.

Forever looked like babies taking first steps and it looked like new puppies on wobbly legs.

It looked like gardens full of marigolds.

It looked like the old ones flying away from this earth, and the sorrow of saying goodbye divided in half by love.

It looked like unexpected challenges and heartbreaking choices and losses that were every bit as much of this amazing dance as the joys were.

Love did not protect you from any of that.

Love, that thing he thought he'd said no to, had not accepted his refusal.

He listened as Jolie said her vows, her voice so strong and so sure, her forever eyes on him.

It was not part of what they had rehearsed.

Not even close.

But when her voice fell away, after she had said "I do," he leaned his forehead on hers, and he said, "Mrs. Fletcher, is that your final answer?"

\* \* \* \* \*

# MODERN

## Glamour. Power. Passion.

## **Available Next Month**

10 brand new stories each month

# MODERN

Glamour. Power. Passion.

## MILLS & BOON

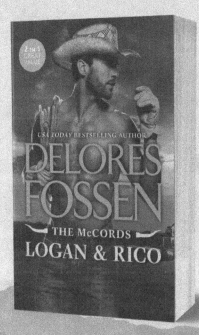

# Subscribe and fall in love with a Mills & Boon series today!

You'll be among the first to read stories delivered to your door monthly and enjoy great savings.

WE SIMPLY LOVE ROMANCE

# MILLS & BOON

## JOIN US

## Sign up to our newsletter to stay up to date with...

- Exclusive member discount codes
- Competitions
- New release book information
- All the latest news on your favourite authors

> ## Plus...
> get $10 off your first order.
> *What's not to love?*

Sign up at **millsandboon.com.au/newsletter**